"*THE ALLEMAGNE DECEPTION turns and weaves its tale of espionage and deception so thoroughly that streets become blind alleys, and even the most trusted of friends must be viewed in shadow.*"

— **JACK LONDON,** Author of '*FRENCH LETTERS*'

"*If any Cold War novel should be turned into a suspense movie production, THE ALLEMAGNE DECEPTION would be first on my list!*"

— **ROBERT R. McMILLAN,** Former Chairman of the United States Panama Canal Commission

"*For those of us who lived through the confusing 1960s, Don Farinacci's THE ALLEMAGNE DECEPTION brings back memories—both somber and frightful—our inheritance from those who lived through the 1940s. This book reminds us that the world was far more complicated than just an unpopular war in Vietnam.*"

— **JOYCE FAULKNER,** President of Military Writers Society of America, and Award-winning author of '*IN THE SHADOW OF SURIBACHI*' and '*FOR SHRIEKING OUT LOUD!*'

"*If you grew up during the Cold War, THE ALLEMAGNE DECEPTION will scare you; and if you did not, it will scare you even more. Destined to be a new standard for cold war novels, thrilling, engrossing and intellectually engaging.*"

— **STEVEN G. BUSTIN,** Author of '*HUMBLE HEROES: HOW THE USS NASHVILLE CL43 FOUGHT WWII*'

"*A powerful blend of action, history, and old fashioned adventure. THE ALLEMAGNE DECEPTION may be one of the hottest novels ever written about the Cold War.*"

— **JEFF EDWARDS,** Award-winning author of '*SEA OF SHADOWS*,' and '*THE SEVENTH ANGEL*'

THE ALLEMAGNE DECEPTION

THE ALLEMAGNE DECEPTION

A NOVEL OF THE COLD WAR

Donald J. Farinacci

NAVIGATOR BOOKS

THE ALLEMAGNE DECEPTION

Copyright © 2011 by Donald J. Farinacci

Photographs © 1967 by Donald J. Farinacci

Navigator Books

www.navigator-books.com

ISBN-13: 978-0-9834168-1-4

Cover design by Navigator Books

Printed in the United States of America

Dedicated to

Patrick J. Finn III
(1941-2010),

whose enduring voice and irrepressible
spirit lives within these pages.

Acknowledgements

I would like to acknowledge the people without whom I would have had great difficulty in completing *The Allemagne Deception* project. First and foremost, was my great friend, Patrick J. Finn III, who read all of my previous books promptly and always provided the honest and constructive insights I found so helpful in formulating this book. His unique contributions will be greatly missed.

My wife, Noreen, deserves special credit for her patience and perspicacity as sounding board and devil's advocate in tempering some of my ideas.

I am grateful to Chris Booth for taking the time to provide valuable information on U.S. Marine deployments during the Cold War and to Laurie Cerroni, Harry Morman, Laurie Morman, and John Farinacci for their ongoing logistical help, encouragement, and belief in my writing projects.

I am also grateful for the unwavering support for all my writing endeavors provided by Charles Weizenecker, Jack London, Bob McMillan, and Carol Christ.

Lastly, I owe a special debt of gratitude to Maria and Jeff Edwards for their belief in this project, and their dedication to excellence in moving it forward. They accept nothing less than the highest quality in their literary efforts and for that, I am most grateful.

Donald J. Farinacci

Author's Note

As the third book of a Cold War series, '*The Allemagne Deception*' evokes a time and place in the mid-20th Century when unheralded American and European heroes engaged in a deadly struggle against the principal menaces of the era — the stridency of the Soviet Union and its acts of aggression.

With the use of its own military might and that of its Eastern European satellites, Soviet Russia's goal was to gain a power-hold over all of Europe, the first step on the path to world domination.

Through the 1950s and 60s, the only thing standing in the way of Soviet aggrandizement was the North Atlantic Treaty Organization (NATO). Yet, NATO could not match the Warsaw Pact's combined forces in sheer numbers of divisions, tanks, and personnel at key strategic locations.

By 1966, when the tale told in this novel of the Cold War begins, the Soviet Union had been seeking for over 15 years to destroy the overall strategic advantage of the United States and its allies in Western Europe, a critical region of the world.

Long before the moderating influences of Gorbachev and Glasnost, NATO was engaged in a deadly shadow war with the Warsaw Pact forces in places like Budapest, the Soviet Missile Sites of Cuba, 'Checkpoint Charlie' at the East Berlin crossing, the streets of Prague, and the back alleys of Vienna. Its weapons were less often tanks and bombs than silencers, stilettos, poison pills, and encoded messages.

'*The Allemagne Deception*' is historical fiction, the medium believed by the author best suited to capture the turmoil and human drama of the era. It tells a tale of a small group of U.S. Army Intelligence operatives stationed in Munich, West Germany in the late 1960s, caught in the cross-winds of Soviet expansion at one end of the spectrum and Eastern Bloc hope and longing for democratization at the other.

The story unfolds under the ever-present penumbra of a potential nuclear holocaust. The principal characters of the piece are ordinary young soldiers swept into military service in the wake of the vast defense mobilization needed by America to fight the Vietnam War. The original inspiration for the voluntary enlistment by many of them was the eloquent Cold War rhetoric of slain U.S. President, John F. Kennedy, who beseeched them to, "support any friend and oppose any foe for their country."

The young protagonists of the story are initially shocked by the sheer brutality of the espionage game, but adapt in time to become effective operatives. Their story is a compelling one, played out in the late 1960s, but one whose pathos and poignancy were at the time drowned out by the more publicized events of the Vietnam War — the Mai Lai massacre, the Tet offensive, the March on the Pentagon, Kent State, draft-card burning, anti-war demonstrations, and the boiling cauldron of protest on America's campuses.

Vietnam and its sequela demanded and received the predominant portion of America's attention. The Cold War, soon to enter its fourth decade, was largely ignored by the press and academia and as a result, became almost a lost history over the ensuing decades. Only recently has interest in the Cold War undergone something of a renaissance.

'The Allemagne Deception' is for the most part about a non-shooting war. It is the author's third in a series of Cold War books, which includes the award-winning non-fiction book 'Truman & MacArthur,' dealing with the Korean War, and the non-fiction book 'Last Full Measure of Devotion,' devoted exclusively to the Vietnam War. As the first novel in the series, 'The Allemagne Deception' is historical fiction rooted in true events. The major historical occurrences, albeit with some embellishments, are reported accurately except for those instances in which the fictitious characters' adventures are interwoven with the real events. There, poetic license, consistent with the theme of the novel and its plot lines, was taken.

The characters in the book are all fictitious. They do, on occasion, however, interact with real-life historical figures, (e.g. Supreme Court Justice Robert H. Jackson, General J. Laughton (Lightning Joe) Collins, Imre Nagy and Alexander Dubcëk). The protagonists of the novel, though fictional, are inspired by real persons. Several of them are composites of two or more such persons. The central facts of the Czech Revolution and 'The Prague Spring' are accurately portrayed.

One of the main intentions of the author was to revisit the under-publicized story of that other war — the 'Cold War' — and hopefully, cast some additional illumination on its historical significance and the invaluable contributions made by both the uniformed and non-uniformed soldiers of that forty-five year epic struggle for freedom against tyranny.

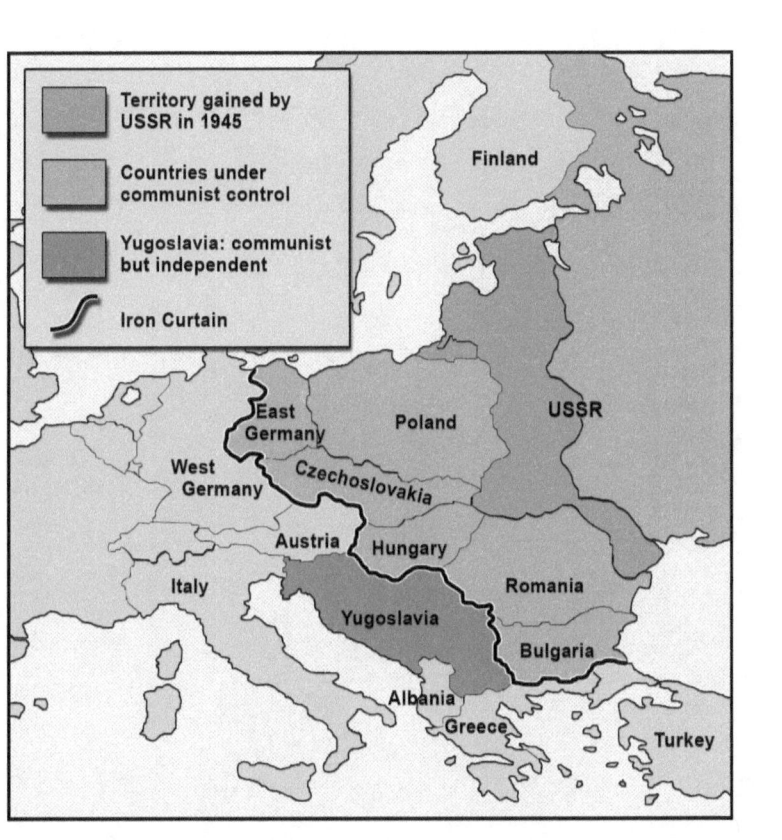

Chapter One

Mr. Kennedy's Boys

Tom Tallifierro (pronounced 'Tolliver')

Tom Tallifierro had always loved history. Even now in June of 1966, having just bagged his second post-graduate degree at age 24 — a Ph.D. in Later European History from Georgetown University — he was bemused by the fact that friends and family actually considered this to be praiseworthy. The way he saw it, his degree was like being honored for naming the most battles in a World War II movie marathon. To Tom, all the pomp and platitudes attendant upon the conferral of his degree and valedictory honors at Georgetown the previous month were laughable. There seemed to be a certain perversity in heaping accolades on someone for having fun doing what comes easy — sort of like making a hero out of Ted Williams for being able to hit a baseball, yet saying almost nothing of the fact that he was a fighter pilot in both World War II and the Korean War.

Tom's college buddies — now ensconced on Wall Street, in corporate law and in academia — spoke non-stop of escaping the pressures of their jobs by getting away to the Jersey shore or Virginia Beach for long summer weekends. How could he explain how different his orientation to life was, short of concluding that his father had propelled him to earth from a doomed planet in a one-person space capsule? While they would all drive for hours to the shore in the Friday afternoon, bumper-to-bumper traffic on the Jersey Turnpike, Tom's only thought of escape was to get back to his leafy sanctuary — the Georgetown campus, where he could read, write and teach history as part of his so-called "duties" as a teaching assistant.

But, June of 1966 brought more serious concerns than Friday afternoon traffic jams. Tom had just received in the mail at his home in Falls Church, Virginia, Uncle Sam's notification that his draft status had been changed from 2-S to 1-A. President Johnson and Secretary of Defense McNamara had found themselves mired in an acre of quicksand in 1965, when it became obvious to anyone who picked up a newspaper or watched Cronkite on television, that the South Vietnamese Army (ARVN), bolstered by thousands of U.S. military advisors, was getting an old-fashioned ass-whipping at the hands of the Viet Cong (VC) and the North Vietnamese regular army (NVA). So, in 1965, the U.S. went to war with the use of its own forces in Vietnam. The Johnson-McNamara build-up of U.S. forces at home and in Vietnam in 1965-66 increased U.S. boots on the ground from a few thousand to over five hundred thousand troops at its peak in 1967-68.

Tom's father, Paul Tallifierro (Tolliver), had left a message with the receptionist at the Georgetown graduate school. In his mail slot in the lobby of the faculty lounge, Tom found a neatly hand-written note saying that his father had called about a matter of "some urgency."

The message came as no surprise. Tom knew what it was about. Draft-age, non-deferred, American men in 1966 were either totally plugged-in to the nuances of their draft status or they were in a coma. Tom briskly walked to the bank of phone booths on the opposite side of the lounge and dropped a quarter into one of the slots.

Paul Tallifierro picked up the phone after only one ring, yet affected an air of detached nonchalance.

"Dad, what's up?"

"Your mother talked me into buying an air-conditioner for the living room. The damn thing is so noisy it drowns out the TV."

"No, I mean what's the matter of 'some urgency' you called about?"

"Well, a letter came from the draft board today, and I thought I'd better open it because it looked important."

"Yes, I agree Dad. What did it say?"

"Okay, it doesn't say you have been drafted."

"Right, Dad, but what <u>does</u> it say?"

"I have to turn this confounded air conditioner down so I can hear you."

"Please do, Dad."

"It says, 'You are hereby informed of a change in your Selective Service classification from 2-S to 1-A.' I'm sure it's nothing to worry about."

After an interlude of pregnant silence, Tom finally spoke, "Thanks for the update Dad. Right now I want to grab some dinner…talk to you later."

Tom might have taken his father's glib pronouncement — that reclassification to 1-A in war time is nothing to worry about — as an insult to his intelligence, but the fact was that his father's choice of words in

"Paul-Speak" meant that he *was* worried about it. Conversely, Tom was not.

It's not that Tom didn't fully appreciate on one level the possible gravity that a draft-notice portended. But it seemed lately that Tom was spending less and less time on the level of stark reality. His almost total immersion in history was plunging him to a dimension not of fantasy, but of disengagement from the here and now, especially when the here and now included himself. His daily journey into the intrigues of Metternich, Rasputin, Garibaldi, the Czars, Disraeli, the Roosevelts, Napoleon III, etc., combined with current events in Saigon, the Mekong Delta and the Central Highlands, had created a peculiar alchemy which transported him to a place where he was a witness, rather than a participant, in history.

This vantage point had become his reality — a reality crafted in part by the soaring rhetoric of John F. Kennedy, now dead only two and a half years — a president who would defend any friend, oppose any foe while asking not what America could do for him but what he could do for America. For Tom and many other passionate young men of his generation, the force of Kennedy's idealism was irresistible.

As many young enlistees in the Armed Services in the early 60s described themselves, they were part of "Mr. Kennedy's Army." Born in the early 40s they were raised in the image and inspiration of towering leaders of Herculean courage — Franklin Roosevelt, Churchill, de Gaulle, Truman, Eisenhower and Kennedy. Unlike the ancient Spartans, they might not have been raised to be warriors but many of them wished to be, nonetheless — cold warriors — soldiers in a war of nerves, will and brains.

The only remaining open question for Tom Tallifierro in early June of 1966 was whether he had the stuff to make the transition from witness to warrior.

Ben Berger

The haunting strains of "Don't Walk Away Renee," sung by the 'West Bank' drifted from out on the Potomac to the shore, and up the gently-graded landscaping of Mt. Vernon. The young man standing on the rear portico of our first president's mansion, now a national museum, ached with envy and longing. He could see the 30 foot cabin cruiser about an eighth of a mile off-shore, with three bikini-clad young women on board, all of whom from this distance looked like Jane Fonda. An equal number of young men in bathing trunks seemed to be plying the girls with what he imagined to be piña coladas. The feminine laughter pierced his already flimsy inner defenses causing in him an overwhelming desire to bolt off the portico, shed his clothing, sprint down the sloped lawn and dive into the Potomac. Then he would use his powerful Australian crawl to reach and join the party at Olympic-record speed.

But forget it. That wasn't going to happen. This was not an Annette Funicello - Frankie Avalon beach movie, and he was no matinee idol. To the contrary, shedding his clothes would require him to cast off a horse-hide vest, coarse britches held up by a length of hemp cinched at the waist, knee-length knickers, black buckled shoes and a three-pointed colonial hat, circa 1775.

Ben Berger was a tour-guide and that garb was his period-piece uniform. And to make things worse, an assortment of tourists were already gathering about fifteen feet away from him in expectation of his next guided-tour of the grounds and mansion, scheduled to begin in ten minutes.

Ben Berger was a twenty-three year old graduate of American University with a degree in communications, and was a classic under-achiever. Born and raised in Washington, D.C. in the ground-floor apartment of a Georgetown brownstone, Ben had eschewed offers of full scholarships from the University of Virginia Law School and George Washington University School of Law. His 149 I.Q. apparently could be put to better use describing George Washington's wooden teeth to legions of school children and senior citizens.

Actually, Ben hated his job as a tour guide. He couldn't help but be struck by the irony that while his best friend since childhood, Tom Tallifierro, was liberated by history, Ben was literally trapped in it — one never-ending time warp in the genteel 18th Century aristocracy of colonial Virginia. At times it was insufferable, but the pay wasn't bad and he had full benefits from the National Park Service. Also, Mt. Vernon was only a short commute from his bachelor apartment in Alexandria. For a young man without any present ambition, the generous time off and vacations the job provided suited Ben just fine.

Ben's dark good looks and irreverent wit assured him of a steady flow of equally vapid, unmotivated and unambitious young women in and out of his apartment, and he rarely wanted for female companionship. Actually, all through college he had had a serious girlfriend, a beautiful and studious co-ed, Melissa Aplan, now gone to the Peace Corps on assignment in Tanzania, at least partly to escape for a time from Ben's stultifying lack of ambition. She seldom wrote.

In truth, there was more to Ben Berger than he was willing to admit. No matter how hung-over he might be in the morning and regardless of whom the company might be in his bed, Ben had an unwavering routine of having his coffee and plain donut before work each morning in a small booth in the corner coffee shop, accompanied only by that morning's Washington Post.

His daily ritual was known to no one except Melissa — not likely to be blabbing his secret all over Tanzania — and his best friend, Tom Tallifierro. An incredibly fast reader, Ben read the Washington Post from front to back every day, particularly focusing on the serious news, both national and international, and the columns and editorials of the Op-Ed page. To maintain his elaborate cover as a vacuous hedonist, Ben always kept an ample supply of *Surfer* and *Playboy* magazines strewn haphazardly throughout his apartment.

The Vietnam War demanded the greatest share of Ben's attention and he was becoming increasingly agitated over the war news. President Johnson and Congress should have their heads examined for jumping into the quagmire with both feet without doing a full analysis of the enemy we faced and the questionable strength of will of the South Vietnamese people to fight and defeat that enemy. And Westmoreland (Commanding General of U.S. Forces in Vietnam), with all his talk of "search and destroy missions," "strategic hamlets" and "overwhelming bombing campaigns to break the back of the Viet Cong in their areas of concentration." Where was this guy coming from? Didn't they teach guerilla warfare anymore at West Point? It seemed to Ben that the bombing was mainly killing innocent civilians and destroying their villages and farms. And who were the Viet Cong anyway?

How could bombing be effective against an amorphous group who always seemed to be on the move, both above ground and through an elaborate system of underground tunnels? Ben resolved on one early June morning to call Tom and get his take on the war from an historical perspective. The two old friends hadn't spoken in over a month anyway and needed to catch up.

"Hey man, you chairman of the history department yet?"

"You mean they actually have phones at Mt. Vernon? I thought the telephone wasn't invented for another 100 years."

"They even have vending machines. George and Martha were both fond of Dr. Pepper."

"So what's going on with you, other than trying to satiate your grossly over-sized libido?"

"I don't know buddy; everything's copasetic I guess. And with you?"

"My love-life's on life-support, my gut is hanging over my belt from too many late-night pizzas and White Castles and, oh yeah, I have been re-classified 1-A."

"Whoa! Run that last part by me again."

"I got my reclassification notice a week ago but have been too busy with this article I'm writing for the *Atlantic Monthly* on the parallels between the ascensions to power of Otto Bismarck and Adolph Hitler. Otherwise, I would have called you."

"So what are you going to do man?"

"Don't know, I have some time. The draft board says my actual draft notice might not come for another six to eight weeks."

"Are you serious? That's not time! You spent ten weeks alone on your monograph on the early-childhood development of John Wilkes Booth. Come on man, this is real life."

"Right. This from a guy who insisted that his one-night stands sign a guest book and list both their home and work phone numbers."

"Okay, that was a bit shallow I admit, but none of my excesses put me in danger of getting my ass shot off."

"Hey, don't worry about me Ben. You know I always figure a way. I'll be alright."

"Listen, you know my dad is a staff sergeant in the D.C. National Guard. His years of currying favor working for the National Monuments Bureau helped him advance in both the Bureau and the Guard. How about I ask him to call in a chit or two and get us both into the National Guard, with only six months of active duty. We'll spend that time at Fort Dix, New Jersey or Fort Jackson, South Carolina drinking 3-2 beer, and then get back to civilian life in one piece. Then all we have to do is go to meetings once a month and to summer camp for a two week jaunt, for six years. That will hardly be a blip in your teaching and writing."

"Sounds great Ben. I'll let you know. Let's both try to stay in touch more often."

"Super. In the meantime, I'll talk to my dad to get the ball rolling."

"Take it easy man, and thanks for the suggestion."

"You too buddy."

Ben gently laid the phone back in the cradle. After hundreds of phone conversations like this one since they were eleven years old, Ben intuitively knew the nuances of Tom's speech patterns and intonations. They communicated more by what they *didn't* say and the rhythms of what they did say than the actual words spoken.

Ben knew with an unshakeable certainty that Tom would not take him up on his offer. Equally disturbing was the fact that he doubted he would even ask his father on his own behalf.

*   *   *

Lonnie Ryan

"Brian, move your college butt, it's not cool to keep the Cardinal waiting."

"Dial it back a notch will you, Lon? With the cathedral packed with a thousand people, he's not likely to notice one Mick sneaking into Mass after the first Reading."

"It's not that, little brother. Dad is one of the organizers of this event and will be sitting up front with the Color Guard of the K of C. You know he will have his eyes peeled for his kids' arrivals."

"Well, you know Mary Katherine will be there on time and so will Kevin and the twins. You go ahead without me Lon, and I'll catch up. A lad in uniform arriving late will stand out a lot more than a college kid in a blue blazer."

As the Newton No. 10 bus carried Lonnie Ryan in his Class-A Army uniform south to Boston proper, past Boston College on the right at Chestnut Hill and through Brookline, the only word in his exchange of fifteen minutes ago with his brother, Brian, that kept repeating itself like a mantra in his fevered brain was "college."

His unease was caused precisely because college was a prized commodity of which he had none. The Army recruiter had glibly assured him that he should have no trouble getting into Intelligence School after basic training even though he lacked the preferred two years of college. But, Lonnie was beset by doubts. The nation was at war, the draft was in full swing and Army Intelligence School at Fort Holabird, Maryland, would be swamped with applications from worthy candidates. Why would Lonnie Ryan, a steamfitter from Southie, even be given consideration?

"Because," said the confident recruiter, "they will not be able to ignore your exceptionally high scores on the armed services entry tests. Besides, you are exactly the type of guy they are looking for as a potential careerist. The Army knows they will lose most of their highly qualified entrants to Fort Holabird after their three-year terms of enlistment expire. For you, a career in the Intelligence Corps would be a step-up from your current career prospects."

Lonnie couldn't agree more. For seven years since he graduated from high school, he had languished in a blue-collar, dead-end job for the Boston Department of Public Works — a job he considered well below his capabilities. He knew he was smart, but where could he go without even one year of college?

The Vietnam War had opened up new possibilities for him and now he could see himself going to Officer Candidate School after graduating from Intelligence School, and beginning a new life as an officer and a gentleman. With such new-found status, maybe he could finally convince Megan to marry him. And then maybe after a five or six year stint as an intelligence officer, it would be off to Washington, D.C. for a career in the CIA or FBI.

Of course, he would have to use his time in the military to get at least a two year college degree. He had already researched the possibilities and knew that the University of Maryland had overseas extension campuses in virtually every foreign city where U.S. troops were stationed. Even a tour in the 'Nam wouldn't be bad. The extra hazardous duty pay would go a long way towards securing a great apartment and nice furniture for himself and Megan after he got out, if he was lucky enough to have her say yes to marriage.

As far as the dangers of service in Vietnam were concerned, just because you went to a combat zone didn't automatically mean you came home in a body bag. The overwhelming majority of those who went to 'Nam came home. This is not to say in what kind of shape they returned.

Anyway, he had only three weeks of "basic" left after five grueling ones already spent at Fort Dix, and it would only be another three before he received his orders and learned if he got his school — the U.S. Army Intelligence School. In the meantime, he would try to enjoy the rest of his 72 hour pass before he was due back at midnight on Monday for K.P. He would catch the 5:30 p.m. bus on Monday and still be back to Dix before the witching hour.

The Knights of Columbus had lobbied hard to get Cardinal Cushing of the Roman Catholic Archdiocese of Boston to celebrate a special mass and blessing for active-duty servicemen of the greater Boston area in this time of war. In getting him to say *yes*, they had pulled off quite a coup. Cardinal Cushing was something of a national celebrity, having presided at the funeral mass of slain United States President John F. Kennedy. His celebrity carried him on special missions and to meetings and conferences throughout the United States and Europe, particularly to the Vatican in Rome, where he was a United States representative to the prestigious Office of the Propagation of the Faith.

Lonnie walked into the cathedral at 9:00 a.m. sharp and as he predicted, his father, Kevin J. Ryan Jr., was turned slightly towards the entrance. His laser-beam-gaze fixed on Lonnie and bore in on him, but with intensity, not anger or annoyance. He was undoubtedly saving that stare for the habitually tardy Brian. Father and son exchanged perfunctory nods and Lonnie looked for his three sisters and brother, Kevin, whom he quickly found seated about mid-way between the front and back of the cavernous cathedral.

His sister, Mary Catherine, 17, was in her last year of high school and currently undergoing spiritual counseling to determine whether she had the vocation to enter the convent and become a nun. His older brother, Kevin, was 28 and a Boston fireman. The twins, Moira and Kelly, were the youngest at age 14. The aforementioned yet-to-arrive Brian was 20 and a junior at the University of Massachusetts. His first choice, Boston College, was well beyond the means of the Ryan family. With partial scholarships, work-study, college loans and grants, U-Mass was manageable for the family. The only one of the Ryan clan who was married was Kevin and he and his wife had recently given birth to an infant son, Kevin J. Ryan, IV.

After exchanging kisses on the cheek with his sisters and a handshake with his older brother, Lonnie took the aisle seat and knelt in silent prayer. Lonnie's faith in God and Jesus Christ as the redeemer of mankind was strong, but his mind was of too independent and curious a bent to simply accept indoctrination. His 8:30 a.m. to 4:30 p.m. job had left him with plenty of time for other pursuits. Outside of an early morning run along the banks of the Charles River, and dates with Megan a few nights a week, Lonnie had spent most of his remaining spare time enjoying his favorite hobby, reading. His tastes were eclectic and he consumed in equal quantity the New Testament, Ian Fleming novels, Marcus Aurelius, F. Scott Fitzgerald, Ayn Rand, Theodore Dreiser, Melville, Dickens, Shakespeare, *Commonweal Magazine*, Saul Bellow, St. John of the Cross, C. S. Lewis, and Thomas Merton; plus atheistic existentialists Sartre, Camus, and Bertrand Russell.

He especially enjoyed the writings of agnostic-turned Roman Catholic, Malcolm Muggeridge. By immersing himself in the works of such a broad and diverse group of thinkers and mystics, Lonnie's faith became deeper and richer — its spiritual and intellectual underpinnings hardened and fortified. His beliefs were now the product of an interior process as much as external revelation.

His faith was there and hopefully always would be, as a bulwark against the trials and tribulations of life. But he rarely spoke of such serious matters, and they weren't really a big part of his daily awareness. Right now he had all the same powerful desires of most young men his age — love, sex, financial advancement, challenging work, seeing more of the world, adventure, and surviving the war in one piece.

*   *   *

The spring Sunday evening bore a promise of gentle enchantment as Lonnie and Megan slowly strolled hand-in-hand through the graceful park overlooking the Charles.   Being apart the last six weeks and the uncertainty of what lay ahead, invested this quiet time together with a special tenderness tinged with sadness.

"I'm sorry I missed the Mass this morning, Lonnie.   All that ceremonious talk of invoking the Lord to keep our soldiers out of harm's way was a little more than I could take right now."

"I understand, Megan. I have to admit my mind was somewhere else through most of it anyway."

"Well, I know you are worried about your orders and so am I, but let's try not to think about it tonight."

"You got it."

"Let's just let this perfect evening push the war and the Army out of our heads for one night."

"No argument here."

"But wait, I almost forgot. What's the Five O Second?"

"The 502nd? Where did you hear about that?"

"When I got back to the office from lunch on Thursday, Reception told me that two men in suits from the 'Five O Second' had been there and asked to see me."

"Megan..!"

"They said they would be back next week and I put it out of my mind…"

"Megan — the Five O Deuce!"

"The *what*?"

"The Five O Deuce, the Five O Deuce — do you know what this means?"

"Lonnie, what are you talking about? You're squeezing my hand too tight. Calm down."

"The Five O Deuce is military talk for the 502nd Counterintelligence Detachment. Its agents are almost all plainclothesmen who investigate security risks."

"Lonnie…what are you saying — that I, Megan from Marketing, am some kind of a national security risk?"

"No, silly. They are mainly going to ask you about me; and you know what that means?" asked the excited Lonnie.

"Haven't got a clue."

"It means, Megan — it means I probably am headed for Army Intelligence School in three weeks. They only check out those who have been accepted into the program. They can't let anarchists and communists learn how the United States intelligence system operates. They also need to know my background in case I need a "top secret" security clearance after graduation. Fantastic!"

"But, Lonnie how do you know all this?"

"Sergeant Stiles, the demon recruiter of Mass Ave., told me. Where is he? I want to plant a kiss on his bald head."

"I'm happy for you Lon — I'm happy for *us*. But I still don't quite get it. Wouldn't they want to talk to people like employers, co-workers, teachers, neighbors — rather than someone like me?"

"Hey, for all we know they already have, or will soon. But under the category of 'friends and close relationships,' you were the only one I listed. I was afraid to list any of my buddies down at the Union Hall or my high school friends. No telling what any of those clowns would say — that is, those who aren't currently doing time. Megan this is *big*! Things are going to be better for us from now on."

A strange sense of foreboding came over Megan and a cloud descended over her face as she replied, "I hope so Lonnie."

Lonnie was already bounding ahead and didn't hear her or notice her expression. "Come on Megan, let's go celebrate."

She quickened her pace, grabbed his hand and they headed for their favorite Back Bay pub.

Chapter Two

The Other War

Tom and Ben, in their U.S. Army Class-A uniforms, each with a single stripe on the right sleeve designating their rank as private first class, settled into adjoining seats on the crowded Boeing 707 preparing to transport them to Frankfurt, West Germany. They carried no luggage of any kind, having deposited their duffel bags and small suitcases at baggage check-in. The flight, which would soon depart from Dulles International Airport, would make a short stop at Shannon International in Ireland before arriving at Frankfurt am Main. There, the flight would be met by some unidentified person who would presumably drive them to their first duty station in Munich, West Germany (München).

The flight was packed to capacity with U.S. uniformed military personnel. The harried, understaffed team of stewardesses were busy trying to get every passenger into his or her correct seat and prepare them for take-off. Later they would have to combine with the male flight stewards to make sure that each of the 229 passengers on board was provided with beverages and served a meal during the eight-hour flight.

It was April 1967, America was clearly on a war-footing and the atmosphere aboard the plane was tense but purposeful. Crew and passengers alike were generally congenial but there was little relaxed banter and few unforced smiles. To many on board, their tours of duty in Europe would be promptly followed by assignments in Vietnam. Most would not see their families again for at least a year.

Tom and Ben had only their parents and siblings but neither had lived at home for some time anyway, so the separation was less painful than for the married men and women — especially those with children — and for those who had left sweethearts and fiancés behind.

After their phone conversation of early June 1966, the two friends never again discussed joining the National Guard or Reserves. One day in early July as they finished their third round of cold beer at a Senators-Yankees game, Tom casually dropped into the conversation that he was going down to see the Army recruiters the next morning and wondered if Ben wanted to tag along.

Ben — who had nothing but time on his hands, after abruptly quitting his tour-guide job the previous week — said, "Sure, what time will you pick me up?"

"Nine a.m. sharp and stay sober tonight. No one should walk into a recruiter's station with his wits dulled by a hangover."

"Does that mean I shouldn't bring the beer for all of us?"

What followed was predictable. Tom had heard about military intelligence and mentioned it to the recruiter, Master Sergeant Dwayne Knepp.

When Knepp found out during the brief exchange which ensued that Tom and Ben were both college graduates, he could hardly contain his enthusiasm. He unleashed a sales pitch of epic proportions — In military intelligence, there would be excitement, drama, foreign travel, intrigue and the chance to meet exotic women.... They would be cold warriors in civilian clothes and the possibilities for jobs later with the CIA, DIA (Defense Intelligence Agency) or the more lucrative world of industrial espionage, were unlimited, and so on.

Tom asked a few perfunctory questions but seemed largely disengaged and unmoved. Ben remained stolid, asking not a single question or making a single comment, as he distractedly fiddled with the silver pendant with the inscription, "Know Thyself," hanging around his neck, a gift from Melissa on their college graduation day.

Within fifteen minutes they both signed the recruitment papers, left the office and immediately searched for a café where they could get a decent breakfast.

Basic training at Fort Jackson, South Carolina was basically easy for the physically-active Ben Berger — more difficult for the sedentary Tom Tallifierro, who passed the PT test with a score of 305, only five points above the minimum passing grade.

The 'Mickey Mouse' psychological harassment was difficult for both of them, but they had each other's company and were able to laugh at the excesses of the DI's[*], in the canteen at night over 3-2 beer and Slim Jims. They both hated the long marches to nowhere.

Army Intelligence School at Fort Holabird, Maryland, was a romp for both of them. Because of its proximity to the D.C. area, they were home practically every weekend. The six month course had a comprehensive

---

[*] Drill Instructors

curriculum which, save for the usual military repetitiveness, was interesting and professionally done. Most of their instructors were Army, Air Force, or Navy Intelligence operatives themselves.

The only really tough day was the day their class's orders were read, shortly after graduation. They all had heard through the rumor mill, by far the Army's most active mode of communication, that a military intelligence regiment slated for Vietnam was forming-up at Fort Bragg, North Carolina and that their entire graduating class would receive orders for Bragg. When none of them did, the rumor mill adjusted quickly and offered the explanation that their orders for Bragg had been rescinded because the Army found it had over-subscribed the regiment when it issued orders to the entire previous Holabird graduating class.

Tom and Ben both received orders for Munich. Others among their class were ordered to Fort Hood, Texas, generally believed to be a staging area for the 'Nam. Some got orders for language school at Monterey, California, to study Vietnamese — no mystery there as to where *they* were headed.

Those, however, whose orders stated they would study Mandarin Chinese at Monterey were a little less certain of their ultimate destination. The rest of the orders were for a smattering of venues, including Seoul, Frankfurt, Bonn and various U.S. installations in Italy and Belgium.

Still somewhat out of touch with the here and now, Tom was vaguely disappointed he would not be a witness to history in Vietnam — an experience that would have had a book in it for him.

Ben didn't seem to care about his orders one way or the other, except that he was happy that he and Tom would not be separated.

Had they known then that several of the members of the preceding graduating class — guys with whom they shared their billets, laughed and drank with — would be killed during the Tet Offensive when their 'safehouse' in the Mekong Delta was hit by a Viet Cong rocket, they might have felt quite fortunate to have been sent to Europe.

The Boeing jet lifted slowly on its upward trajectory out over Chesapeake Bay. Tom and Ben began to relax from the hassles and strains of getting their heavy duffle bags and suitcases checked, their orders examined, their tickets issued, their good-byes said to family and friends; and especially witnessing the palpable sadness all around them as husbands said farewell to wives, fathers tearfully hugged their small children, lovers disengaged from long and ardent kisses and mothers hugged their departing sons.

"I don't know about you good buddy but I need a drink," murmured Ben — his first words since they had boarded the plane.

"You'll have to pay. They don't give away booze or beer."

"No sweat, I'm flush. That big ninety-seven dollars in my pay envelope is burning a hole right through the paper."

"Let me get this one. Old Georgetown U. actually sprang for a separation bonus when I left — part of a PR campaign to show their solidarity with the troops."

Tom signaled the steward and they placed their orders.

"I drink, you pay," proclaimed Ben cheerfully, "just like the old days at the Capital Lounge on Friday afternoons. Why ruin a long-standing and sensible practice?"

"*Former* practice," retorted Tom. "After this flight, our financial situations will be just about identical, and it will be even-Steven all the way."

"Not really professor, because some young fräulein will be picking up *my* bar bills."

"Right, just before she slips you a Mickey and leads you to a dark alley where Klaus & Fritz will be waiting to roll the Ami dumb Kopf."

"Ah jealousy! But seriously Private Ph.D., what do you figure is in store for us in Europe?"

"I don't know Ben. If you believe the returnees to Holabird, Bavaria for them was all Oktoberfest, oompa bands, the beautiful Alps, delicious wurst and rich, cold beer. But, I thought that when they talked that way there was always more than a little bullshit involved. When you pressed some of the instructors about their experiences, they suddenly became diffident and I thought I detected pain or fear, or a combination of both, in their eyes."

Tom lowered his voice. "I've been talking to some of my Langley[*] buddies, and doing a lot of reading. The Cold War... The threat to Western Europe from the Soviet Union and its Warsaw Pact satellite countries, has created an insatiable hunger for good intelligence by Communist and non-Communist countries alike. A whole vast substratum of espionage and counter-espionage has spread to every nation in Europe, threatening to race beyond the control of the so-called governing authorities. Its fuel in the West is the huge sums of money the United States and the prosperous Western European nations have to throw around. In the East, it is driven by desperation. In his greed, Stalin bit off more than he could chew. The Soviets are finding it harder and harder to keep

[*] Langley, Virginia is the location of C.I.A. National headquarters.

their vast network of satellite countries from the Balkans to the Baltics, under their thumb.

"The Soviet Union may have twice the number of troops and tanks under their control in Eastern Europe and East Germany than NATO has in Western Europe, but they lack the sophistication in weaponry and weapons systems of the U.S. and NATO. They can't come close to matching our overall technology and this has created a mass paranoia. They are obsessed with knowing everything they can about every single NATO development and advance in planes, ships, tanks, missiles, rockets, electronics and communications. With the border between the Warsaw Pact nations and NATO allies extending more than a thousand miles, they also are fanatical about knowing every NATO troop movement, deployment, maneuver, build-up and scale-down. They want information on every facility and installation — their relative strengths and weaknesses in personnel and armaments.

"Then, there's Berlin. West Berlin is a thorn in their sides, and East Berlin has always been porous, leaking escapees and secret information to the West. Even the Berlin Wall hasn't stopped it completely.

"The Soviets lack the money to bribe officials and pay legions of spies to the same extent that Western powers do, so they compensate by their sheer ruthlessness and brutality — prying loose information routinely through the use of blackmail, threats, kidnapping, murder and torture. They use these methods ruthlessly to double well-placed Western agents wherever they can and to plant moles under deep cover — sometimes in place for decades. In Europe, spies are everywhere. It's a standing joke in the CIA that if you throw a rock on a Vienna street you are almost sure to hit a spy."

"Okay," Ben said. "So how does this affect *us*?"

"Well, the Army just spent six months training us in intelligence tradecraft. We may be just lowly privates now but we are both pretty bright guys, and once they put us in suits and ties no one is going to know our rank. Look at the map. Western Europe is relatively small and from Munich you can get by car to Austria in a little more than an hour; to the Czech border in a couple of hours and to the East German border a couple of hours after that. Somehow good buddy, I think you and I are going to wind up right in the middle of things."

"Professor, this is one time you and I completely agree. Despite my addiction to watching wrestling matches on TV while checking out the latest *Playboy* centerfold, I'm not just another pretty face. I'm a lot better informed on world events than most people think. There are stirrings in several of the Soviet satellite countries. The dissidents in Prague are slowly moving towards a ballsy confrontation with Moscow. Berlin could blow at any time, and a thousand Russian tanks rumbling across the East German border would definitely tie up traffic on the Autobahn. Based on all the stuff I've been reading in the *Washington Post* the last couple of years, I wouldn't be surprised if the Kremlin — knowing we are getting bogged down in Vietnam — is cooking up some major test for the U.S. in Europe. And if things really get dicey, you can bet that PFC Ph.D. and his sidekick, PFC Jerk-off, will be right in the thick of the shit."

To punctuate his point Ben added one quick and emphatic nod of his head and then drained the remains of his Manhattan.

Ted O'Malley

Chief Warrant Officer Third Class Ted O'Malley spied the two slightly dazed-looking PFCs leaning against a kiosk in the middle of the arrivals terminal of Frankfurt International Airport.

The taller one, Berger, was casually flipping the pages of *Der Spiegel* with one foot resting on his duffel bag and an air of natural self-assurance in his body language — somewhat reminiscent of the insouciance of a young Dean Martin. Come to think of it, he looked something like the famous crooner/comic too.

The other one, Tallifierro, was shorter, stockier and more fair-complected. The first thing which struck O'Malley about him was the intensity in his eyes as he slowly, almost imperceptibly, shifted his gaze in a circular, 180 degree, movement taking in everything around him, like an all-seeing periscope.

The culture of the 409th Special Investigations Detachment located in Munich, Federal Republic of Germany, was one of crisp efficiency and discipline, but conducted with a basically low-key and friendly style, similar to the quiet can-do air affected by fighter jocks and astronauts. The idea was to shape and mold its personnel to create a group of serious but understated professionals who would, because of their inconspicuous and relaxed personas, blend in as well as possible with the native population, and attract no unnecessary attention.

O'Malley approached the two young soldiers to welcome them to the 409th, which barring their curtailment to Vietnam after a year, would be their home for the next two years, plus.

O'Malley was dressed in an American-cut suit which he bought at the main Munich PX for $22.95. He tried to conserve his clothing allowance of $200.00 per year wherever he could.

"Tallifierro, Berger... I'm Ted O'Malley. Welcome to Germany."

The two privates returned the greeting and shook hands with O'Malley, confused about who he was and whether protocol required something more of them.

"Either of you need to hit the latrine before we get going?"

After they both responded in the negative, O'Malley said, "okay, follow me."

Tallifierro was surprised that their greeter had been allowed to park his gray, unmarked Opel Kadet right in front of the terminal doors without any protest from the traffic police officers standing around on the sidewalk.

Tom got into the back seat, Ben the front passenger side.

"Munich is usually about a five hour drive from here on the Autobahn but there are no speed limits so I expect to have you standing before the colonel, reporting in, by 1600 hours. First, we make a little stop at the I.G. Farben Building in Frankfurt, for you to sign in at 44th MI Group Headquarters and to change clothes. You'll get into civilian duds — pants and sport shirts. Say farewell to your nicely pressed uniforms. You won't see them again until the day you leave Germany. Your duffel bags will be delivered to your billets in a couple of days so take what you need till then in your suit cases."

In some ways, the Autobahn didn't look all that different from American super highways of the 1960s. You didn't get to see much scenery and there were any number of chain restaurants along the way. Instead of Howard Johnson's, the West Germans gave you Wienerwald, a chicken eatery.

O'Malley drove south towards Munich — Province of Bavaria — like a madman, all the while keeping up a one-sided, non-stop narrative. He managed to push the medium-power Opel (a subsidiary of Ford Motor Company) up to eighty-five mph and keep it there for hours on end. Along the way he passed BMWs, Saabs, Porsches, Mercedes, Audis and Jaguars.

Tom and Ben learned that Ted O'Malley had grown up in Dayton Ohio, and joined the Army right out of high school. Assigned to the infantry, he had fought under Ridgway in Korea at Chip Yong Ni, received the Bronze Star for his actions in combat in the Central Corridor, then transferred to the Intelligence Corp. After the war he had done tours of duty in Würzburg, Germany; Madrid, Spain; Salerno, Italy; and then Tokyo, Manila, and the Hague. This was his second go-round in Munich. Most of his career had been spent in counter-intelligence, but despite the name of their unit, the 409th Special Investigations Detachment (which suggested a counter-intelligence function), the mission of the 409th was strictly 'area intelligence,' or active operations abroad to acquire intelligence concerning foreign enemies and potential enemies.

It was no accident that the name of the unit suggested a function opposite to its true purpose.

"Always think in terms of opposites, contrasts, and paradoxes in Area Intelligence," said O'Malley. "Things are seldom what they seem to be, that is except when they *are*. The name of the game is 'deception, diversion and distraction' (the three 'Ds'). So be on your toes. Remember that almost everything is intended to deceive, except when it's *not*. But even when things *are* what they're supposed to be, that in itself is sometimes — but not *always* — designed to mislead. To play it safe, *always* expect the unexpected."

Ben turned his head to glance at the expression on Tom's face, to see if he was as bewildered by O'Malley's narrative as Ben.

He was.

'*A very happy un-birthday to you too, Mr. Mad Hatter,*' thought Ben.

Chief Warrant Officer Ted O'Malley was, at age thirty-nine, a seasoned veteran in the field of Intelligence Case Officer development and supervision. He himself, only a slightly above-average field-operative, had discovered his real vocation after he was taken out of the field and assigned to teach and lead young soldiers of the Cold War. With his keen nose for talent and his superb leadership ability, O'Malley would have had no trouble making it in the civilian world. But he had long ago realized that he was a lifer — he loved the Army and would stay as long as they would have him.

His wife, Eva, an Austrian national, had been an Army wife since age 19 and was used to picking up and moving to a new post every couple of years. But she worried that things would be hard for their four year old son, Christopher, once he started school.

Luckily, Ted had not had a hardship, no dependent tour, during their twelve year marriage, but Eva knew that it was only a matter of time. When the time came for her to say her farewells to Ted as he departed for Vietnam or some other hot zone, she would do so stoically and with strength. When she thought about how her mother had suffered during World War II in a forced labor camp and her father had died a few years after the war as a result of his combat wounds, she knew that so-far she had had it easy. She considered herself U.S. Army as much as Ted, and as much a patriot as any girl from Sheboygan or Omaha.

Chapter Three

Misdirection

Peter Toomey

"Good morning, sir," said First Sergeant Pete Toomey, known not so affectionately as 'Sock-it' Toomey.

Toomey was in a good mood even though his favorite target for punishment, the Company Clerk, Specialist Third Class Mario Tonelli, was on sick-call this morning. Giving the needle to the shave-tail second lieutenant seated at his desk in a small cubicle would do just as well. Toomey resented and disliked lower-rank officers on general principles, and especially resented the one he was facing because of the praise the man was getting from higher-up for the firm and skillful hand he had shown in taking control of the Ops-Support Section.

"Good morning, first sergeant. What can I do for you?" replied the lieutenant.

"Well, I just thought you might be interested in what I have to report, sir," said Toomey, with a slight hint of sarcasm in his voice.

"Proceed, sergeant."

"Actually the news is no news. We just opened the courier's pouch and for the 10th straight day there is no communiqué from 14332."

"I see. That is troubling."

"Of course, lieutenant, when Art LeBron headed up Ops-Support we heard from 14332 every 72 hours."

The lieutenant winced slightly from the obvious dig, but chose to ignore it.

"Ted O'Malley thinks the case officer we have tapped to take over 14332, Mal Rhymes, will never work out."

"That may be so, but I intend to head down to Vienna with Sergeant Rhymes to see for myself."

"Begging your pardon, sir, but don't you think Warrant Officer O'Malley should be the one to make that judgment? I mean, with his far, far greater experience."

"Ted O'Malley is not in charge of the Ops-Support Section. He is the Deputy Ops of the whole detachment. This is my responsibility. Will there be anything else, first sergeant?"

"No offense intended, lieutenant," replied Toomey, as he took his leave. "We're all on the same team; right?"

As the lieutenant returned to reading the 201[*] files on the two fledgling case officers due to arrive by 1600 hours from Frankfurt, he shook his head. 'Offense' was *precisely* what Toomey had intended. So be it. Back in the neighborhood, he had dealt with much tougher characters than Toomey.

It was only after they exited the Autobahn that Ben and Tom were treated to a bit of the Bavarian countryside, with its neat and orderly farms, tree-lined roads, and colorful chalets adorned with flowers. But soon they entered Munich, a city that was a blend of the old and the new. Medieval church spires, wooden gates and gothic architecture mingled nicely with modern apartment buildings and department stores.

Built on the banks of the Isar River, there were plenty of steep hills. The in-city transportation consisted of cable cars, automobiles and bicycles, in equal measure. All three modes of transportation seemed to negotiate the hills with ease.

O'Malley zipped through a gate which bore military block-style lettering on the lateral plank over the entrance, announcing that they were entering 'General Maxwell Taylor Complex,' widely referred to as 'The Max.'

In his several hour soliloquy the warrant officer had explained to Berger and Tallifierro that a USAR[*] Complex in Bavarian cities was often a type of large enclosed courtyard built by the Germans before World War II, for military or governmental use.

Vehicles were confined to one service lane on the south side, and the inner area was restricted to use by pedestrians, with the exception of a small parking lot. After occupying Germany in 1945, the U.S. Army had expropriated the complex for its own use, and now it was an American facility in every respect.

The establishments surrounding the central commons consisted of a laundry, a class-six liquor store, a barber shop, a commissary-type supermarket, a movie theater, a snack-shop, a branch of the University of Maryland, and a five-story office building at the west end of the square

---

[*] personnel files
[*] United States Army

bearing no identifying information, either on the exterior of the building or in its miniscule lobby.

On the fourth floor of that building, behind a security gate that opened only from the inside, was the suite of drab offices which housed the 409th Special Investigations Detachment.

The Opel carrying the two new additions to the 409th zoomed down the ramp and into the basement motor-pool. There they were met by a snaggle-toothed corporal with a quasi-demented laugh, who parked the vehicle and stared mirthlessly at the new arrivals.

A lift took them to the third floor and from there they climbed a narrow staircase to an iron gate.

O'Malley pushed a button, announced his arrival and the gate was electronically unlocked, permitting them to enter.

Privates Tallifierro and Berger were first introduced to First Sergeant Toomey at Administration, who eyed them with suspicion, but was otherwise not unpleasant.

Low-rank enlisted men with a 'case officer' (agent handler) M.O.S.[*] received a modicum of Toomey's respect. *Sometimes.*

From the Administrative Section, they walked down a narrow, dimly lit corridor past a small room on the left, which O'Malley informed them was the telex-operator's station.

None of the doors had signs on them.

Further down the corridor was a small reception area where an attractive woman in stylish civilian clothes sat behind a desk.

O'Malley nodded to her. "Gerda, this is Private Tallifierro and Private Berger, the new agent-handlers. Is the old man in?"

The woman greeted them pleasantly, speaking with a faint German accent. She announced their arrival on her telephone intercom.

A few seconds later, they all stood in front of a desk, behind which sat a middle-aged man wearing granny glasses balanced on the tip of his nose. On his desk sat a nameplate announcing that he was Lieutenant-Colonel Frederick Reitenhauser. Introductions were made.

As everyone inside the 409th wore civilian clothes (except for the motor-pool personnel and supply sergeant), there was no standing at attention and no saluting.

The Company Commander quickly sized up the two new arrivals, signaled the three men to take seats and spoke in a friendly manner. "Welcome to the 409th. I have read your 201 files, so no need for me to ask you a lot of questions. I am sure that after your long trip, you are anxious to get settled in your quarters. You will be housed in the

---

[*] Military Occupational Specialty

Bachelor-NCO quarters for tonight, until I decide where to billet you on a more permanent basis.

"I'm sure Chief Warrant Officer O'Malley gave you the usual security briefing on the trip down from Frankfurt, so we will dispense with any further briefings until you meet with Major Barnstable, our unit's Operations Officer, tomorrow at 0900.   That will be all for now. Dismissed."

Frederick Reitenhauser   1945

Waiting for his battlefield commission to be formally processed, Staff Sergeant Fred Reitenhauser was assigned to temporary duty.   With the Seventy Third Military Police Detachment, he was tasked with the job of sifting through the bombed-out craters and ruins of a group of government buildings in Berlin, about a half-mile from Hitler's bunker.

It was late May, 1945, the Third Reich had fallen and Hitler was dead.

The search for Nazi war criminals was running at full tilt and the remains of the Nazi occupied buildings — mostly debris now — were being sifted for clues to their identities, activities, and whereabouts.

Four teams, one from each of the four occupying powers — the United States, England, France, and Russia — set about the task.

"Cooperation and mutual assistance" were the watch-words of the day, but the raw emotions engendered by the recently-ended war turned these words into hollow platitudes. Each of the occupying forces of the victor-nations was on a singular quest to find and capture the miscreants who had perpetrated unspeakable deeds against humanity, and caused such suffering to their individual countries.

Reitenhauser's squad had been teamed up with a Russian squad led by a young officer.

"Sergeant Reitenhauser, allow me to introduce myself to you. I am Field Lieutenant First Class, Uri Putyagin." The Russian spoke perfect English, with an accent that seemed a combination of Russian and British.

"I'm Fred Reitenhauser; pleased to make your acquaintance. Your English is excellent."

"It should be. My father was a mid-level envoy to the Court of St. James before the War and I attended secondary school in London and then three years at Cambridge."

"What did you study at Cambridge?"

"Mostly political philosophy mixed with international studies."

"Well, I hope to get to college too, when all this is over."

"I am sure you will. Do you have any preference as to how we divide the search between our two squads?"

"If it's all the same to you, lieutenant, I would like to hit the area which held the political archives."

"That is perfectly acceptable. My squad will peruse what's left of the so-called 'Reich-Defense Library,' and please call me Uri. The war's over."

"Fine, as long as you call me Fred."

"Agreed."

Mario Tonelli   1967

Tom and Ben were led by a young-looking Specialist Third Class, Mario Tonelli, to an average-size windowless room containing only an old desk, a round table with eight chairs gathered around it, and a map of Europe on the wall.

"Just take seats at the table. The major will be right with you. Can I get you guys some coffee?" Tonelli spoke with a strong South-Philly accent.

"I could use some," said Tom, "But are you sure that's okay?"

"Sure, it's part of the message they try to send around here. In other words, we're friendly and welcoming because we're all part of the same team. We need to have a relaxed atmosphere, so everyone's creative juices can flow freely for the overall good of the unit. We don't stand on rank — that is unless you or someone else fucks-up, in which case you are strictly '*specialist*' or '*private.*' Don't expect any majors, colonels or GS-12s to take the blame for any snafus, when there are low-ranked enlisted men to blame. How do you take your coffee?"

"Black" said Ben.

"Black with one sugar," replied Tom.

"You got it. I'll be back in five minutes, that is unless I run into Sock-it Toomey. Then, you may not see me for the rest of the morning."

Having avoided Toomey's attention, Tonelli returned in less than five minutes with the coffee, including one for himself.

Since there was no sign of Major Barnstable yet, Tonelli lingered at the door for a few minutes sipping his coffee and chatting with the two newcomers.

"After you meet with the major, you should drop by the Administration Section to see me. I'll need to have you sign the usual forms — payroll exemptions, next-of-kin notifications, life insurance beneficiaries — all that good shit. When we have some free time, I'll take you around and introduce you to the other enlisted men. There are only fifteen of us with the unit. Seventeen now, with the two of you. But two just got orders for 'Nam and will be out of here in 15 days. Sock-it keeps threatening me with a transfer to 'Nam, but he knows I know it's bullshit. When the Army decides it's your turn, they *send* you. Not Sock-it or anyone else can do anything to speed it up or stop it. As they say in Saigon, 'sorry about *that* shit!' But now I gotta go see Village and tell him to stop logging in the mileage on the returning vehicles without putting down the name of the guy who took it out. I'm on to him — I know he's sneaking the 'deuce and a half' out after hours to buy beer cheap on the economy. If he conveniently forgets to enter the person's name on the sign-out sheet for the vehicles, he thinks he's covered himself. What a jerk-off."

Tom and Ben looked at each other in confusion.

"Did you say his name is 'Village'? What kind of a name is that?" asked Tom.

"His real name is Yancy Cook. He's the Motor Pool Clerk."

"You mean the corporal with the nasty smile who needs to see an orthodontist?" asked Ben.

"That's him alright."

"So how did he wind up with the handle, 'Village'? What does it mean?"

"Oh, you know 'Village'. It's just short for 'Village Idiot.'"

This news got a rise out of Ben and Tom, who both chuckled with appreciation.

"He's from a mining region of Pennsylvania, strictly the poorest of the poor — played out mines and closed-down mills — the end of the line. They call it *Pennsyltucky*. He's never been to a dentist in his life. But Sock-It has ordered him to see the Battalion dental officer to get his teeth fixed at the Army's expense. So you'll be seeing a bright Colgate smile in a month or so."

"Yeah but I'll wager you it will still be nasty," observed Ben.

"That would be a sucker bet," said Tonelli.

"I'll pass."

The three young men laughed, clearly enjoying the relaxed camaraderie. But soon Tonelli took his leave, after wishing the new men luck.

Edwin Barnstable

"Good morning, privates," intoned the baritone voice of Major Edwin Barnstable.

"Good morning, sir," said Tom and Ben in unison, as they rose a little more quickly and stood a bit more erect than usual.

"Relax men. Sit down," Barnstable decreed, in a firm but friendly manner, as he himself took the seat closest to the door.

Barnstable looked to be the apotheosis of an American security type — grey suit, white starched shirt, blue striped tie, closely cropped crew cut and ram-rod erect bearing.

Eyeing their empty plastic coffee cups, he spoke with a twinkle in his eyes.

"I see Tonelli's been here. How's the 409th's coffee? You don't have to answer that. Tonelli's a good man. Don't let Sergeant Toomey tell you otherwise. As for the first sergeant, there is none better serving in U.S. Army Europe. All our personnel have been hand-picked for their intelligence, integrity and strong work habits."

Ben wondered if that included Corporal Village from Pennsyltucky.

"You have already spent a good deal of time with Chief Warrant Officer O'Malley. I hope you listened carefully to everything he had to tell you yesterday."

Actually, they *had*. They'd been a captive audience.

"Chief O'Malley is a great soldier, and a born teacher. You're privileged to have him as the man in charge of your field training. Ignore nothing that he tells you. Most every earnest word he utters is a pearl of wisdom. O'Malley is the jewel in the crown. He will make you into great case officers, if you just let him. If, however, you fight his instruction, you might as well spend your tours of duty inhaling carbon monoxide with Corporal Cook in the Motor Pool."

Tom and Ben weren't sure if that was a threat, but both guessed that it was.

"Men, you come to us at a time of great peril for America. We are not only besieged by relentless communist aggression in Southeast Asia and Korea, but also all along the broad expanse of the Iron Curtain, and in pivotal regions of the Continent of Africa. Even in our own hemisphere, in Cuba, Central America, and South America. But the most incendiary place of all is Berlin. The Soviet Politburo has chosen Berlin as the place where they will stage the ultimate test of NATO's mettle, and its legitimacy as defender of free Europe.

"We have serious and urgent work to do men, and we expect no small part of it to come from *you*."

With that, Barnstable rose to his full height of about six feet four inches, picked up a pointer from the desk and with Churchillian bearing walked purposefully to the map on the wall.

Tom remarked later that he had half expected the major to demand of them their 'blood, sweat, toil, and tears.'

Barnstable used the tip of the pointer to draw an imaginary line on the map from Munich to the Austrian border at Salzburg. "Austria. One hundred kilometers, a one hour drive," he proclaimed.

He moved the tip of the pointer in a northeast direction to a spot north of the Danube River and brought it to rest with an emphatic tap on the border line between West Germany and Czechoslovakia. "The Czech border. One hundred and fifty kilometers, less than a two hour drive."

Again he moved the pointer upward, stopped it near Dresden and the Elbe River. He paused for effect and with the pointer in place, turned his head and gazed piercingly at Tom and Ben. "East German border. Four hundred kilometers from Munich, roughly a four hour drive."

Barnstable pivoted 180 degrees and faced the two soldiers. "Men, forget all the talk of Gemutlikeit. Forget about Bavarian maidens in short skirts, and ski vacations to the Zugspitze. Don't be fooled by the fact that no one is likely to point a rifle at you. We're still at *war*. And here, in Munich, we are on the front lines."

The major glanced briefly at the map and then turned his eyes back toward the two privates. "We're a short road trip from the Eastern Bloc satellites and Soviet Russia, who just five years ago put offensive nuclear weapons in Cuba, ninety miles off our shores. During the time it takes you to drink two liters of beer, sing one chorus of '*In München Stet ein Hofbrau Haus*,' and practice your best line on Schatsie over by the Isar, the Warsaw Pact forces can drive a company of tanks from the Czech border to Munich."

He gazed intently at the two men seated across the table. "You might be wondering *why* they would do such a thing. I'll tell you why. Because they are our enemy, and we are theirs. The U.S. is the only thing standing in the way of their conquest of all of Western Europe. They covet mineral-rich West Germany for all kinds of reasons — strategic, political, psychological, and economic. If that weren't enough, Russia hasn't forgotten for one second what Germany did to them during World War II. They *hate* the Germans because of it, and they want even more revenge than they have already exacted. It is a source of never-ending bitterness to the Soviets that West Germany under Konrad Adenauer became prosperous, while Russia has never stopped struggling economically.

"Remember, Stalin was a paranoid sociopath. Over a period of nearly three decades, he filled the Communist Party at its highest levels with paranoids just like him. This is one ruthless pack of jackals.

"Stalin tried to grab Berlin in '48, but Truman and Marshall wouldn't stand for it. They airlifted in the supplies that West Berlin needed to stay alive and free from Red control. But I don't think the bunch that's in there now would ever be satisfied with just Berlin. To the Russians, the *real* prize is all of Germany, for openers that is.

"Well that's enough of an overview for now. We don't want to get ahead of ourselves. Chief O'Malley will start your orientation and training tomorrow. But as you progress through it, keep in mind what I have said to you today. For the rest of the day, Specialist Tonelli will introduce you around, give you a cook's tour of the complex and work with you on your paper work. Good day men."

Art LeBron

With that, Barnstable placed the pointer back on the desk and briskly walked out the door. As he headed down the corridor to his office, Art LeBron was coming the other way.

"Grus Gott, Art," said Barnstable, giving LeBron the traditional Bavarian greeting.

"And to you too, Ed."

Having worked closely together for three and a half years, during which time they also formed a personal friendship of sorts, the two men were on a first-name basis. Protocol allowed it because LeBron was not a subordinate officer. He was one of a number of senior United States government civilians employed by the 44th Military Intelligence Group. Trained by the CIA in area intelligence, most of them were certified as 'case officers.' Those who weren't had some other area of specialization vital to Intelligence gathering or Counter-Intelligence.

LeBron was a GS-13, which made him pretty senior in the government pecking order.

"Art, you look like you're carrying the weight of the world on your shoulders."

A chill ran through LeBron at this observation. It wasn't smart to reveal that much about yourself in this business. Especially now.

"No, I'm fine Ed. Just tired. It was my turn to take the two a.m. feeding last night."

"I know the feeling. How are Gina and the baby faring?"

"Great. Oh, did you and Grace get our invitation to the Christening?"

"We did, and we're looking forward to it."

This confirmation was almost superfluous. In the closed society of an intelligence unit, there was little socializing outside the circle of the men and women of the unit and their family members; and very few conflicts over invitations to events.

LeBron found this social cross-fertilization to be stifling, almost a type of inbreeding, minus the biological part.

"Lunch today, Art?"

"Sure."

"Okay, see you at 1300 at the Officer's Club."

"I'll be there."

LeBron continued on in the direction of the telex operator's station, still miffed at himself for having betrayed so much to the Operations Officer. He hadn't realized how much the burden of his worries had imprinted itself on his demeanor. But it was stupid of him to think that his stress wouldn't show. He had never been known for his poker face.

Art LeBron had recently been transferred from the position of Section Chief of Ops-Support when the shave-tail second looie[*] had arrived, to Chief of the all-important Czech desk. In every sense of the word, this was a promotion, from basically a back-office position to the front-lines.

Maintaining a steady flow of reliable intelligence from the Army's covert agents inside Czechoslovakia was a vital part of Group's mission. But he had been able to take no pleasure in his promotion. Even his twin brother's arrival for a visit from San Diego had done nothing to elevate his spirits.

Something was really wrong with the mission, known by the codename 'Kryptonite,' which he had been so instrumental in advancing when he ran Ops-Support. Ops-Support's long-time sleeper agent in Vienna, Number 14332, had become a major cog in the wheel. Over a two-year period he had gone from serving mainly as a passive cut-out for messages coming out of the Balkans, Hungary and Czechoslovakia, to the head of an active covert operation of the 44th, with many of his own sub-agents who had produced invaluable information relevant to Kryptonite.

Agent 14332 was Art's man. LeBron had orchestrated the agent's conversion from a minor passive player to a prized resource of the 409th, and, therefore, of the 44th M.I. Group. In the process, a tight bond had been forged between them.

But now 14332 had gone mute, ten days with no word. What was most troubling was that the agent's silence had started the day before LeBron was transferred to the Czech desk. And now the problem had been allowed by Higher to fall into the hands of a newly-minted lieutenant, not yet dry behind the ears.

What was even more alarming was that — on the day they had informed him of his promotion — both Barnstable and Reitenhauser had told Art that they wanted him to devote his full attention to running the Czech section. He would no longer be 14332's handler. Instead, he was

---

[*] Army slang for lieutenant.

to transfer control to the new second lieutenant. Thus, he had been cut out of the loop of the Unit's biggest operation, and replaced by a novice.

And because LeBron no longer had a *need to know*, he wasn't even sure *who* the lieutenant had designated as 14332's direct contact.

Something was badly wrong. It just made no sense.

Some sort of pernicious psychological virus was sweeping through the Detachment, poisoning the brains and paralyzing the will of its higher command.

If he needed any further confirmation of that fact, he got it that very morning from Winicki, the unit's administrative sergeant, when she whispered to him on the QT that the old man and Barnstable had cleared the baby lieutenant for a troubleshooting trip to Vienna.

That was pure insanity. Kryptonite was a Level One Operation, and the CO and Ops — two men whose judgment Art had always found to be impeccable — were treating it with reckless abandon. LeBron just couldn't get his head around it. Something was *really* out of whack.

He decided to skip his visit to the telex station. It was better if the Telex operator, Bob Scones, wasn't exposed to his anxiety over messages going back and forth with Frankfurt. Besides, Winicki had already told him what he wanted to know.

Detachment command had notified Headquarters about the Vienna conundrum, and reported that it was using its most junior officer and agent-handler to troubleshoot the problem.

LeBron poured a cup of black coffee for himself in the kitchen, walked to his office, entered, shut the door and sat at his desk staring into space.

How could this be? Why would the CO and Senior Ops be so negligent? So wantonly reckless?

The answer to these unspoken questions came to Art at about the same time the effect of the caffeine from the strong hot coffee hit his central nervous system. The answer was embedded in one of O'Malley's corny clichés. *"Things are seldom what they appear to be."*

For all of their hackneyed predictability, the words carried a deep kernel of truth. Things were *often* not what they appeared to be. Art chastised himself for overreacting, and made a mental effort to wipe his mind clean of his own prior assumptions.

Reitenhauser and Barnstable were not impulsive men, and they were *never* careless. Art didn't know what they were up to, but he could be certain that their actions were neither reckless, nor negligent. Therefore, the decision to send the young officer on a perilous mission had not been made casually. It was a carefully calculated move, with specific intent.

The CO had deliberately insulated the entire senior operating group of the Detachment from direct contact with this new activity, *whatever* it was. All of the major players had been cut out of the loop. The CO; Ops officer, Barnstable; Deputy Ops, O'Malley; Czech Deputy Section Chief, Doug Booker; German Section Chief, Mitch Blake and his deputy, Warren Olney; and (of course) LeBron.

This, LeBron realized, was the real reason that he had been transferred out of Ops Support. The CO wanted to keep him well away from Agent 14332.

Suddenly, he realized why the second lieutenant had been selected as his replacement. The young officer was basically expendable. Just like a second looie of a rifle company leads the charge up the hill into the teeth of the enemy's fire, the 409th's new lieutenant had been designated as point man of a dangerous operation.

He seemed like a nice young guy, too — Second Lieutenant Lonnie Ryan from Boston.

Art LeBron hoped that the kid was also smart and tough.

Uri Putyagin   1945

He hadn't been instantly impressed by the American junior officer, Fred Reitenhauser. The American seemed capable enough but like many Yanks Uri had met in England — sons of the vast unknowable region west of the Mississippi but east of the coastal states — Reitenhauser too appeared to have a muted personality. One could not truthfully say however, that the man had an unimposing presence, because there seemed to be a quiet confidence lurking behind the man's bland exterior. It expressed itself in subtle strokes of gesture, tone, and bearing, but something was definitely there.

First impressions aside, during their first couple of days working together it was obvious to both that they had connected on some fundamental level. They held similar ideas on matters of life and death... good and evil... guilt and atonement.

There was no denying that they were both soldiers to the core, but unlike most military men, they seemed to share an abhorrence for war. It revealed itself through even the briefest conversations snatched over cups of instant coffee and K-rations, at various times throughout their long days of searching for clues and evidence.

They seemed to recognize in each other's eyes an unspoken depth of repressed rage mixed with horror over what the Nazis had done to humanity. But it was far more than simply sharing a thirst for justice — although that was certainly true as well.

Their mission dragged on for a full three weeks As they conversed that first day and during the days to come, they seemed to be fellow wayfarers on an intellectual journey. They were co-travelers on a downward trail from optimism and hope to an ultimate destination in a grossly misaligned universe, where malignant forces of thought and action had exposed the fundamental imbalance between good and evil, with the latter holding the clear advantage.

In both men, the journey had led to the loss of any remaining notions of a benign and indifferent universe. It left each of them with a profound ontological doubt as to the purpose of existence. What they discovered in the ruins was that transformative.

On the fifth day of searching through official-looking documents, letters, office files, library books, periodicals, party propaganda, Germanic artifacts, medals, citations for both combat and non-combat achievements, punishment edicts, citizenship revocations and Jewish displacement orders, Fred received a short reprieve from the mind-numbing work when he was called back to headquarters for a brief ceremony during which General J. Laughton ("Lightning Joe") Collins awarded him his battlefield commission as a second lieutenant.

Fred was assigned officially to the Criminal Investigation Division under the immediate command of the Berlin Sector Provost, Colonel Homer "Wink" Welsley.

This development lifted a technical restraint on Uri and Fred's budding acquaintanceship because now Fred too was an officer, they no longer needed to be concerned about non-fraternization rules.

Uri suggested one evening during the joint project that he would like to buy Fred dinner in one of the few surviving decent restaurants in their sector of Berlin, to celebrate Fred's commission. Fred gratefully accepted.

Allemagne[*] was located on a narrow cobblestone street previously named Fuhrerstrasse. Its street sign, however, had been angrily pulled down by the first Russian troops who had entered Berlin from the East in Hitler's final days.

Allemagne was really more of a café than a full-scale restaurant and since it was a particularly pleasant late spring evening, Uri and Fred decided to dine out on the street-side patio. The word dine is used advisedly since before the two soldiers even placed an order for food, they had consumed two full bottles of a nice French Bordeaux and were more than half-way through the third, as they gazed upon the winding, narrow street with no name, and chatted amiably.

---

* The French word for Germany

As the son of a highly-placed Communist Party official, Uri had always had plenty of walking-around money in his pocket and the amount of the eventual bill was no object.

Finally, after repeated throat-clearings from the waiter they each ordered Chateaubriand. Another bottle of the same Bordeaux to go with it, was also ordered.

Their conversation touched upon many different subjects: family back home, girlfriends, school sports, the oddball noncoms from whom each had received his early military training, prostitutes they had encountered as their respective armies had fought and marched across several European countries, their total relief that the war was over, and — finally — the need to bring Nazi war criminals to justice.

"Have you given any thought to your future now that the war's over?" asked Uri.

"My father is an actuary with Mutual of Omaha Life Insurance Company back in Nebraska," Fred said. "There's a job waiting for me if I want. But, I doubt I'll want it. I don't know... This mission has kind of pushed everything else out of my head. I guess I'm sort of in a state of shock over what we have been finding. How about you?"

"Perhaps I am not quite as shocked and surprised as you by Hitler's quest to murder every Jew in Europe. Imagine if the Nazis had won the war... We would live in constant terror that people we love might have Jewish blood in them. But as our armies moved across the Western Russian provinces and into Poland on their final push to Berlin, word came to us through many sources of mass exterminations by the S.S. of the entire Jewish populations of towns and villages in places like the Ukraine, the Balkans, Czechoslovakia, and Poland."

Uri gave a distasteful grimace. "In those regions, the preferred killing method was to march all the Jews out of town, line them up in front of a ditch and shoot them all with rifles or machine guns. However, I had no idea of the enormity of the program. It's just very hard to believe. There has been nothing even approaching the scale of this genocide in the known history of mankind. The death camps were beyond human comprehension."

The young Russian officer smiled ruefully. "But that's not much of an answer to your question. Let me try again... My family is political, but we don't quite have the choices in Moscow that you Americans have. I imagine I am already lined up for some lower-level ministry position in the hinterlands as a start — something like the Latvian Deputy Komisar for Wheat Aphid Control."

Enjoying the absurdity of his surmise, Uri broke out into raucous laughter, made louder and longer by the wine consumed on an empty stomach.

"Well, being from Nebraska I can tell *you* a thing or two about wheat aphids," deadpanned Fred.

"Do not try to inject your corrupt capitalistic methods into something as important as wheat aphids," retorted Uri.

With that, both men laughed heartily, clearly enjoying the irony and absurdity of their exchange.

After a superb meal capped off by a delicious rum-flavored cake and strong German coffee, the two men rose somewhat unsteadily, and headed back to their units on the narrow picturesque street — their acquaintanceship clearly turning into a real friendship.

They continued their relaxed conversation as they walked along the narrow winding street, breaking into laughter from time to time in genuine appreciation of each other's sense of humor.

But something had subtly registered on Fred's antennae. At first he ignored it, but after almost a year of leading combat patrols across France, Belgium and Germany, Fred's instincts for danger were razor sharp. The dinner and coffee had by then blunted the effects of the wine and his senses were almost back to full alert. Right then he had that same nagging feeling he had experienced so often in the hedgerows of Normandy — that they were being followed. He looked back quickly but saw nothing.

Uri noticed Fred's move and asked, "what's wrong?"

Fred never had the chance to answer.

A pistol shot shattered the silence of the evening, and Uri went down face-first on the cobblestone street.

Chapter Four

Dead Drop

1967

"Privates Tallifierro and Berger reporting for duty, sir."

"I've heard some good things about you men," said Second Lieutenant Lonnie Ryan, as he shook hands with the two new arrivals at the Ops-Support Section. Ryan made a casual hand gesture in the direction of the two WW II vintage wooden office chairs in front of his desk, and told them to sit.

"So have you settled in yet? I know the non-com B.O.Q.* is not exactly a Hilton Hotel but it's just temporary. We have three safehouses in the City, which we also use for polygraphs. The CO likes to have them occupied by our personnel to give them the appearance of normalcy. Colonel Reitenhauser told me this morning he intends to move you two into one of them, in a residential neighborhood about a mile from here. You'll share your new quarters with our company clerk, Specialist Tonelli; the detachment's telex operator, Corporal Bob Scones; and Polygraph Operator, Staff Sergeant Glenn Belson, who is with us on temporary assignment from Group. So you'll be in new digs by the end of the week."

Tom and Ben were visibly cheered by this news, their reactions not being lost on Ryan.

Ryan, of course, was an officer and the two young enlisted men sitting in front of him were lowly privates, but he knew that in intelligence operations out in the field, rank usually made little difference. As O'Malley was fond of saying: "In this game, things are rarely what they seem, or what they're called."

Berger and Tallifierro, like Ryan, were from the Eastern Seaboard and — although they had more formal education — Lonnie's prodigious reading habits probably leveled the playing field somewhat. And they were contemporaries of his, who in all likelihood shared some of the same

---

* Bachelor Officer's Quarters

35

tastes in music, entertainment, sports, and women. Technically they were, all three of them, bachelors living four thousand miles from home. Lonnie was still hopeful Megan would accept his proposal of marriage and come join him in beautiful Bavaria. But, that was a pipe dream for another time.

For the present, Ryan was optimistic that the two new additions to Operational Support would be compatible with him and with each other. An infusion of new blood might galvanize the section. God knows, with everything that was going on, he was badly in need of staff members he could rely on.

With their high IQs and with O'Malley as their training officer, Ryan held high hopes that the new men would prove to be quick studies and ready for useful work in the field within a few weeks.

Barnstable had been pushing for sending the two new staffers to the U.S. Army Language School in Oberammergau in the southernmost region of Bavaria, to study German. The CO had vetoed that idea, saying that the unit needed all the personnel it could get right at Munich station.

"Any questions men? If not, welcome, good luck and you now can report to Chief O'Malley to begin your training."

Tom and Ben liked everything they saw about Ryan at this initial, brief meeting. His open manner, directness, and spare, no-nonsense approach, were engaging. They were duly impressed. Of course, they were too green to know that openness in intelligence work could be dangerous.

O'Malley wasted no time in tossing the two men into the thick of things. First he took them to the nearest MP station to fill out the paperwork for international drivers' licenses. They both passed the written test after about a half-hour of studying, and were issued their licenses right on the spot.

Then O'Malley ordered Tom to get behind the steering wheel of one of the unit's ten-year-old Mercedes 4-door sedans and told Ben to ride shotgun.

Fortunately, continental Europe had right hand drive like the U.S., so Tom adjusted to the road conditions of Munich quickly, but he could not say the same about adjusting to O'Malley. With his non-stop staccato delivery, O'Malley, over the next four hours, rattled off the names and stories of every Munich monument, official building, platz or strasse they came anywhere near, with tour-guide-like detail. He then quizzed them on what he had said until it all became part of their storehouse of general knowledge.

After two hours of continuous driving, Ben relieved Tom and drove for the next two hours. They stopped only once for fifteen minutes, to empty their bladders at a 'Pissort' near the Rathaus, at the famous Marienplatz with its intricate medieval architecture, including a built-in cuckoo clock with animated carved figures, synchronized with the music and chimes, which went off every half hour. There they each also downed a quick brochen with wurst and a bottle of warm beer, purchased from a street vendor.

Marienplatz 1960s

The next morning the three men met at the complex's outdoor track at 0700, ran two miles, showered, changed into casual street clothes and had breakfast at 0800 at the NCO Club. Then they checked the same black Mercedes out of the Motor Pool, with Ben driving, Tom in the front passenger seat and O'Malley in the back. For the rest of the morning they toured the areas of Munich they had not visited the previous day, with O'Malley reprising the same chattering drill.

After lunch at the Hof Brau Haus, the world-famous tourist attraction, a lively beer hall, O'Malley began their field training in earnest.

At the unit's pistol range, the two privates practiced for two hours to improve their accuracy with the .38 caliber revolver, the agent handler's designated weapon, which, however, they were not issued except in times of emergency. Ben took to it like a real G-man and qualified within a half-hour. Tom on the other hand would have had trouble hitting the Great Wall of China.

"Having problems, professor? Just pretend that the target is Johnnie Unitas."

Ben's reference was to the star quarterback of the Baltimore Colts, who had sent Tom's beloved Washington Redskins down to so many ignominious defeats. But Ben's continued gibes did little to improve Tom's accuracy.

After a full two hours of practice, peppered with badgering by O'Malley, Tom finally achieved a high enough score to qualify with a .38 caliber revolver.

"Hey, way to go prof," shouted Ben from the adjoining range. "How did you finally do it?"

"Easy. I just pretended the target was *you*."

The chief warrant officer and his two pupils left the pistol range at about 1600 hours and returned to the unit's offices where a notebook was removed by O'Malley from a safe in the office of Major Barnstable while the two PFCs waited in the hall. Only the CO, Colonel Reitenhauser; the Operations Officer, Major Barnstable; and Deputy Operations Officer, O'Malley, knew the combination to the safe, a combination which was changed every two weeks.

O'Malley then directed Ben and Tom back to the room where they had originally met Major Barnstable, handed them the notebook and gave them succinct orders. "You will be locked in this room until 1730 during which time you will study the contents of this notebook and commit as much as you are able to memory. You *will* take no notes and will never discuss what you have read with anyone other than Colonel Reitenhauser, Major Barnstable or myself. You will not even discuss it with each other. Empty your pockets."

Both privates dutifully placed the contents of their pockets on the table, and turned the pockets inside out. Both of them placed a wallet on the table. In addition, Tom placed down a ballpoint pen. The only other item Ben had was a year-old postcard from Melissa, which she had sent him while vacationing in the Ivory Coast. The card was about as succinct as O'Malley's orders:

> Dear Ben,
>
> Don't think just because I am on a week's vacation in Paradise means life is easy. The Peace Corps is a bitch. Back to Tanzania Sunday. Miss you.
>
> Love,
> Melissa

O'Malley scooped up the items from the table and briskly exited the room. "See you men at 1730."

Tom gazed around and noted that there was not a single object in the room save for the furniture, the map on the wall, and the notebook sitting before them on the table.

"These guys are serious," he murmured to himself.

Ben stared silently at the tabletop for several minutes, his mind continents away from the small, monastic room. Surrendering Melissa's postcard to strangers, despite its general lack of expressed intimacies, actually caused him physical pain. He felt as though the jagged edge of a knife had just been thrust into his gut. Instinctively, he grabbed his lower abdomen. The physical pain passed instantaneously but the emotional agony did not so easily subside.

The casual screw-up and playboy side of Ben's nature had never come to terms with his true feelings about Melissa's departure and absence. Now U.S. Army Intelligence, by the act of confiscating one of his only remaining tangible reminders of her, had rudely opened a wound of which he had not been consciously aware.

After a few minutes, his sense of outrage became joined with his emotional pain. In his mind, he shouted indignantly, "What right did they have to take my personal stuff?" After breathing hard for a minute or so, he began to return to some grade of normal and provided the revelatory answer to himself; "…They have every right. I forfeited a personal life the day I enlisted. This is not about me. The world is at war - even though right now they're only shooting at each other in Southeast Asia. This is some serious shit, and I asked them to make me part of it."

Tom read the notebook for fifteen minutes straight and then passed it to Ben. They had agreed to read it by taking turns — turning it back over to each other at fifteen minute intervals until 1730 hours.

After approximately an hour from their entering the room, Ben closed the notebook. It was 1728.

The two men exchanged a wordless communication via the looks of shock registered on both their faces.

It took a good five minutes before Tom was able to form coherent thoughts, much less words. He simply sat and stared at the wall map in shock and confusion.

Then his keen and analytical mind took over. Something was just not kosher here. Why would the powers that be reveal such dangerous and sensitive information to two lowly PFCs, who had completed only their second full day of field training? At Holabird, the instructors had repeatedly emphasized that it was not enough to simply have a Top-Secret security clearance. In order to receive highly sensitive and classified information, one had to have a 'need to know.' But what need to know could he and Ben possibly have for the information contained in that notebook? They were a couple of novices. Neophytes.

Then a dawning awareness arose in Tom's mind. For some reason, someone a lot higher up in the pecking order had made the carefully deliberated decision that the two of them *did* have a need to know; and that need stemmed from some important work for which he and Ben had been inexplicably chosen.

What Tom could not have known was that the decision to fast-track them had been made months earlier, initially at Holabird and then finalized in Washington. Their secret orders had been received by diplomatic courier pouch at Group in the I.G. Farben Building a couple of weeks after that. That's why it had been O'Malley and not some lowly enlisted man who had picked them up at the Airport. They had been singled out for special handling.

Ben gazed distractedly at the notebook. It was now 1745 hours and still they remained locked in the room.

That was probably by design too, thought Ben.

The abrupt unlocking of the door and rapid entry by O'Malley at 1749 allowed Tom to crystallize his thinking. He and Ben had been launched on a journey, probably with others as well, and not everyone was guaranteed a safe return — the grisly photos in the notebook were a reminder of that fact.

He handed O'Malley the notebook, and O'Malley returned their personal belongings.

O'Malley went home to his family for the evening, and the two friends walked to a small beer garden about a quarter mile from the Max, where they each ordered schweinbraten and a stein of dark (dunkel) beer. The brand name was 'Spatenbreu,' brewed with about ten other brands right in Munich.

There was little conversation during dinner, each man lost in his own thoughts. But the beer was cold, rich, and strong. By their second stein, they had relaxed somewhat from the unnerving experience in the locked room.

The next morning they were back on the track at 0700 with O'Malley, followed by a shower and breakfast. They were on the road by 0830, but rather than head directly to downtown Munich, they stopped and picked up another passenger in front of a modern apartment complex, about a five minute drive from the Max.

O'Malley nodded toward the new man. "Art, say hello to PFCs Tallifierro and Berger. Gentlemen, this is Art LeBron and he will be assisting in your training today."

"Glad to meet you. What are your first names?"

Upon their answering his question, LeBron said simply, "Those are the names I'll call you by, and please call me Art. I'm a civilian with no rank in front of my name, so don't call me 'Sir.'"

In downtown Munich, they split up into two teams. O'Malley and Ben were one team with LeBron and Tom the other. Throughout the morning, they practiced case officer-agent meetings. Temporary cover names were assigned to the four of them by O'Malley; and LeBron selected the "bona fides" to be exchanged by case officer and agent, in order for each to satisfy the other of his true identity.

To make things interesting, three separate locations in the old city area were chosen for three successive meets between O'Malley as agent and Ben as case officer. LeBron and Tom were to simulate a hostile surveillance team who would get close enough to the meeting to overhear what was being said without compromising themselves by being 'made' by the participants.

After the three meetings were flawlessly executed, they switched roles with Tom as case officer to LeBron's agent. Ben and O'Malley became the hostile surveillance team.

To really keep Tom and Ben on their toes, for each of the six meetings in which one or the other of the young PFCs simulated the role of case officer, he had a different cover name; and there were also different "bona fides." The designations were all made before they started the exercises.

Upon completion of the six meetings, LeBron just shook his head in wonder and said, "You guys obviously paid attention in class at Holabird."

Neither Tom nor Ben had forgotten or stumbled over their three different cover names, and each had carried out the predetermined and separate bona fides exchanges without a hitch.

The bona fides exchanges had been purposely made intricate. One involved the case officer approaching his agent for their first meeting and saying, "Can you please direct me to the nearest Pissort?" Whereupon the agent would reply, "There is one in Marienplatz but it is closed for repairs. The Hof Brau Haus will let you use theirs but you will have to order something." The case officer's response was to be, "Thank you, I will do that."

At 1200 hours, they broke for lunch. As Tom and Ben still had plenty of the meal money Sgt. Winicki had doled out to them on their first day of training, O'Malley cut them loose to eat on their own, while he and LeBron headed off to have lunch together. O'Malley gave them specific instructions that they were to meet at Koenigsburg Bridge on the Isar River at 1330 hours. This too was part of their training.

The two good friends, Ted O'Malley and Art LeBron, enjoyed a quiet lunch at an open-air café on colorful Sendlinger Tor Platz. Each of them ordered Wiener Schnitzel and they shared a carafe of their favorite Rhine wine.

"So what do you think so far, Art?"

"Well, they certainly lived up to their advance billing. They are amazing. Tallifierro is brilliant, of course, but Berger is smoother and more street smart."

"I agree. I feel a little like the old New York Yankees Scout, Tom Greenwade, when he first saw Mickey Mantle play. He knew a natural when he saw one. Berger was born to be a case officer and he'll go far — that is, unless he self-destructs like so many others you and I have known."

"Or unless he winds up with a shiv in the back," added LeBron.

The two men ate silently for a few minutes, while they pondered that stark imagery.

O'Malley had intentionally chosen a table far away from the desirable seating areas overlooking the Platz. Their table was pushed back against a side wall of the restaurant and too far away from the other diners for them to be overheard.

After they gave the waiter their order for strudel and coffee, O'Malley spoke in a low voice. "Art, I'm going to spend the whole afternoon sending them out to plant and retrieve dead-drop messages. I know they got that stuff up the gazoo at Holabird, but I need to satisfy myself as to just how proficient they are. The first two days I shoved the geography of

Munich down their throats, so I'm going to let them select the dead-drop sites and compose the messages. Since Group forbids us to use invisible ink in training, I'll let them try their hand at composing messages which are cryptic enough so 'Hostile' can't decipher them, but not so cryptic that our translators would be stumped."

"Not to disparage your training old pal, but some of the interpreters we have had lately are from hunger. With agents disappearing left and right — some of them undoubtedly still laying in the morgues of Vienna, Prague, and Budapest — we need instant and accurate readings of the messages. The last two translators, Sergeants Phillips and Feldstein, were living proof that the present generation watches too much TV."

"Art, why do you think they're now headed for Vietnam?"

"Okay, but they were only the most recent of a bad lot."

"Right, but now we have Tallifierro."

Karlsplatz in the 1960s

After lunch at a café near the old gated entrance to Karlsplatz, Tom and Ben waited for the two senior operatives at the Koenigsburg Bridge at 1330. They gazed at the rafts transporting tourists on the clear waters of the Isar to points south of Munich in the foothills of the Bavarian Alps. There, the tourists would run into a bit of rough white water but not enough to pose any problem for the skilled helmsman or danger to the passengers holding their Yashica and Pentax cameras.

Rafting on the Isar

"Okay men, enough lollygagging around. It's time to get back to work. You'll have your chances to float down the Isar and there will be plenty of frauleins who will want to go along. Right now we are going to work on dead-drops."

"We're ready Chief. Good to go;" proclaimed Tom to O'Malley.

In standard espionage trade-craft, a 'dead-drop' is a well-hidden location where one operative has secreted a message intended for another to retrieve at a different time. The reason for the cloak and dagger stuff is simple. First, the message must not be seen or found by anyone else and second, the sender and receiver cannot be seen together. Since a dead-drop is one of several intermediary vehicles allowing communication without personal contact, it falls under the broader category of espionage devices known as 'cut-outs.'

Among other standard cut-outs are the safehouse, and the postal box registered under a number only where permitted, or under the name of a person employing a false identity known as a cover-name.

In a standard M.I. company or detachment, the maintenance and servicing of a unit's dead-drop locations comes under the jurisdiction of its ops support section. Both the Ops and Deputy Ops maintain strict oversight of their support section to make sure they are not getting careless and predictable in both the selection of locations and the quality of the messages. If Higher detects a pattern developing, they will immediately order Ops Support to 'change-up.'

Tom selected a stall of the nearest public lavatory in which to compose his message. He had gone through this drill so many times at Fort Holabird that it was almost second nature. He didn't recall ever buddying-up with Ben on a dead-drop exercise, so at least that part would be new. He wrote his message on the first page of a pocket-size spiral pad given him by O'Malley:

> *Eyes only Control*
> *Tell Ex at 06, Money Penny*
> *To play catch*

Tom read his message to himself with pride. It was sufficiently cryptic that if it fell into the wrong hands, it was highly doubtful that it would mean anything to the receiver. But to an American who happened to be in charge of the operations of the 409th Special Investigations Detachment, it would be easy enough to decipher.

In the current highly popular James Bond books and movies, 'Control' was Agent 007's superior officer. At the 409th the top man was the CO and the writing referred to something that was to be for his "eyes only." "Tell Ex" of course referred to the unit's telex machine. Moneypenny was the name of James Bond's charming and super-efficient assistant. In the 409th that could mean only one person, Sergeant Wanda Winicki, the unit's alternate telex operator and administrative clerk, who was being directed to retrieve a message coming in at 0600 hours (play catch).

Tom tore the page from the pad and wrote the words '*boat basin canoe 5*' on a clean sheet. He then exited the lavatory, walked directly to a vendor in the little park on the banks of the Isar, bought an Italian ice and walked about 100 feet to where Ben was standing, gazing at the young women sunning themselves below at the edge of the water.

Tom handed Ben the Italian ice, together with the second note, which was now wrapped around the paper cup holding the frozen dessert.

They both sat and sunned themselves for a few minutes before Ben got up and walked to the lavatory. Upon exiting the lavatory, he returned to the place where he and Tom had been sitting. Tom was now gone, having departed for the dead-drop site.

Ben sat down and spent the next fifteen or twenty minutes lazily eyeing the bikini-clad girls, and occasionally raising his face towards the sun to catch some of its beneficent rays. Finally he got up slowly, yawned, stretched, and meandered in the direction of the boat basin.

He and Tom had separately reconnoitered the area earlier, and both had noted that there seemed to be no one taking out the canoes, or for that matter, even paying any attention to them.

It was easy enough for Tom in one quick motion to sit on the edge of Canoe number 5 and tape the message against the roof of the canoe's overhang, on the underside, which one could not see short of sticking his head beneath it.

Ben approached the boat basin slowly and casually. There he found an elderly attendant dozing in a booth about fifteen feet from the boats. Ben carried canoe number 5 with its single paddle inside to the booth and handed the attendant four marks for a half hour rental. The old man took the money and promptly dozed off again. Ben who was a practiced canoe and kayak enthusiast enjoyed his half hour out on the water. Once he got out towards the middle of the river he casually stuck his right hand under the overhang at the stern. Not finding the drop, he waited for a few minutes, reached under the bow-overhang, felt the taped item, pulled it free and placed it in his right front pants pocket.

Tom, O'Malley and LeBron were seated at a shaded picnic table in the park chatting when Ben returned. After sitting on the bench beside LeBron, Ben unobtrusively took the retrieved message out of his pocket. He had already discarded the tape.

Tom was smiling broadly in anticipation of the opening and reading of his clever message. His attention suddenly focused on the paper Ben was unfolding. For some reason, all four edges of the unfolded paper were smooth, with no sign of the torn perforations from O'Malley's spiral note pad.

He was dumfounded. Could Ben be playing some kind of prank? No, that wasn't possible. As he raised his eyes from the paper to look at Ben, his confusion turned to alarm.

Ben's face had turned a sickly white and his eyes seemed to register all at once — shock, horror, and anger. He spoke to Tom across the table in a furious whisper. "Is this some kind of a sick joke?"

"Ben, what? I don't know what you're talking about," said Tom.

Ben tried to speak, but he was clearly hyperventilating and only seemed able to wheeze.

LeBron grabbed the note from Ben's hands and read it quickly. He then demanded that Ben take a swig from a hip flask that seemed to magically appear from the pocket of LeBron's windbreaker. The brandy seemed to stabilize Ben enough so that LeBron could turn his attention to the note.

He read it aloud in a soft but clearly audible voice:

We have Melissa Aplan.
She will die tonight unless
you do exactly as you are told.

Your instructions will be
waiting for you at the 409th.

Tom stared at his friend. "Ben, that is *not* the message I wrote. I *swear* it... You know I would never do something like that!"

Ben knew that Tom spoke the truth.

So did O'Malley and LeBron, but unlike Tom and Ben they also knew what had happened. All of them had been shadowed, and kept under surveillance all day by real pros.

Tom had been followed to the boat basin. His message had been removed from the canoe, and the frightening note had been substituted in its place.

Chapter Five

Raptor

1945

When Uri fell face first onto the street with no name, Fred instinctively reached for his side-arm, a Colt .45 revolver which he wore in a shoulder holster under his tunic.

He also fell to the ground and assumed a prone firing position. It was dark, there were few street lamps lit and those that were lit were dim.

Two or three minutes passed without any further shots being fired. Fred decided to risk checking on Uri's condition. Uri lay in the middle of the street about ten feet away.

Without holstering his weapon, Fred covered the distance between them in a low-crawl. When he reached Uri's body, the Russian was moaning softly — probably semi-conscious.

From his prone position, Fred ran his left hand over Uri's clothing until he felt a wet spot on Uri's left side about two inches above his waist. Judging by the considerable amount of moisture, Uri was bleeding profusely.

Fred gathered himself and rapidly sized up the situation. If he didn't move Uri quickly to a safe location where he could administer some emergency first aid — perhaps improvise a tight bandage around his waist, Uri could bleed to death. On the other hand, if he lifted Uri up and draped him over his shoulder, the two of them would make a perfect target.

Of course, he had been in situations like this several times in combat when sniper fire had brought down one of his men. He decided to use both the darkness and his weapon as allies to throw the assailant off stride, if indeed the shooter was still around.

Roughly twenty feet from where Uri lay was what appeared to be the opening of a narrow alley. The closest lit street lamp was more than 15 feet from there. In a smooth motion, Fred fired two shots into the air and in quick succession, rose to his feet, lifted Uri and slung him over his right shoulder.

The Russian was a big man and dead weight, but Fred had been a battalion wrestling champ back at Fort Leonard Wood, Missouri and knew how to leverage a man's weight. As soon as Uri was securely on Fred's shoulder, he fired two more shots into the air and made a dash for the alley entrance. For a fraction of a second he caught a glimpse of a figure, who appeared under a dim street light on the opposite side of the street, fifteen or twenty feet behind the spot where Uri had gone down. The figure wore a cap pulled down over his ears, and an ankle-length coat. Fred was too preoccupied with saving his friend to notice any other details.

He carried Uri into the alley, and placed the wounded Russian on his right side with his back supported by the wall of an adjoining building. Keeping one eye on the entrance to the alley, Fred quickly removed his own tunic, shirt, and undershirt, and then gently did the same with Uri, so that they were both bare from the waist up.

Fred then pulled a small flashlight from his tunic pocket and examined the wound. It looked like it was close enough to Uri's side to possibly have missed any vital organs, but the bleeding was heavy. Using their two uniform shirts and undershirts, Fred fashioned a bandage which would reach all the way around Uri's mid-section with enough left to tie it securely and tightly on the side opposite the wound. After completing his make-shift first aid, Fred pondered his next move.

Uri's breathing was irregular and his pulse was weak. He was probably in shock.

Fred had no way of calling for help and was not about to leave Uri for even a couple of minutes, thereby giving the assailant the chance to finish the job. And if he didn't get Uri to a hospital soon, he would die.

Fred had few options, and he needed to act quickly and decisively. He put Uri's jacket back on him without buttoning it, and put on his own jacket on as well.

Again he hoisted Uri up on his shoulder, moved rapidly out of the alley and fired another shot into the air. He headed north up the cobblestone street in the direction of Kaiserstrasse, a main Berlin thoroughfare.

Fortunately, the gunshots had attracted attention and multiple patrols from the four governing powers were alerted to go to the area from which the noise of the shots seemed to originate.

As Fred hauled his human cargo around the corner onto Kaiserstrasse, a British jeep carrying four men — one M.P. from each of the U.S., Great Britain, France, and Russia — sighted him, sounded its siren and pulled alongside. The 'four men in a jeep' arrangement was a political compromise among the vying occupying nations, who each had been lobbying for exclusive police jurisdiction in various sectors of Berlin. One

M.P. from each country in a patrol jeep was not only a brilliant political compromise but also prevented the participating nations from openly competing against each other in the exercise of police power. The arrangement forced cooperation among them — but made for an often tense situation.

"We need to get this man to a hospital on the double," shouted Fred, as two of the M.P.s helped lift Uri into the back seat. To create enough room for Fred and Uri, the U.S. and French soldiers stood on the vehicle's running boards while the Russian M.P. attended to his countryman and superior officer in the back seat.

The British soldier drove and Fred climbed into the front passenger seat. A second similarly-occupied jeep had pulled up but after a hurried conversation with Fred, headed off in search of the shooter. Its crew, however, had produced an olive-drab blanket and Fred draped it over Uri. The Russian soldier cradled Uri's head in his lap and wore a mournful expression.

Uri's pulse was even weaker and he had lost consciousness completely. On the running board the American M.P. was receiving a steady stream of partly garbled chatter through a walky-talky, but seemed to be getting enough of it to shout directions to the Brit behind the wheel.

"Stay on Kaiserstrasse for twenty blocks. Step on it, hubba hubba," ordered the G.I.

"Keep your knickers on, Yank," replied the Brit.

"Turn right on Hohenzollern and the hospital is the second building from the corner on the right. They say the emergency docs and nurses will be waiting for us."

The jeep roared up Kaiserstrasse. There wasn't much civilian traffic in early post-War Berlin, and the speeding vehicle was making great time.

Fred wondered whether it would be enough to save Putyagin.

1967

The black Mercedes plunged down a hilly street, barreled into the Max and a minute later was in the basement motor pool. With the engine still running, the four men piled out of the car and moved with alacrity to the elevator.

Even Village was alert enough to know something was really wrong — evident from the grim expressions on the men's faces, and the absence of O'Malley's usual jibes.

They rode up the four floors in silence, entered the unit's offices and walked directly to the CO's office.

"Gerda, we need to see the colonel right away."

"Sure Chief," she replied. "He's in with the first sergeant but I think he's just about to leave."

"Gerda-Now!"

"No problem Chief."

She pressed the button of the intercom on her desk. "Colonel, Chief O'Malley and Mr. LeBron are here with the new Ops Support men. I think it's urgent."

The colonel's voice rumbled over the speaker. "I'll be right with them."

Seconds later, the office door opened and the irascible Sergeant Toomey emerged. Giving the four men a hard stare, he was clearly irked, not because they were preempting him but because he wasn't being allowed to stay for whatever was going on.

As it turned out, he would have company walking back down the hall because O'Malley ordered Tom and Ben to return to the Ops Support offices, say nothing about what had happened, and wait there until they were called.

Hoping he could browbeat the two young PFCs into letting him in on the secret, Toomey called them into his office and ordered them to take seats.

"As first sergeant of this detachment, I make it my business to know everything that's going on and I don't take too kindly to anyone who holds back information. Sooner or later I am going to find out anyway; but when its later rather than sooner, that puts me in a very bad mood and I usually don't feel too kindly disposed to anyone who had the opportunity to tell me but failed to do his duty. Do you catch my drift men?" Toomey asked.

"So, what's going on?"

Tom spoke for the both of them. "I'm sorry, sir, we have orders not to say anything."

Toomey registered this news with obvious ire, bringing his fist down hard on the desktop. But he said nothing. Instead, he slowly looked from one of the privates to the other and bored deep into their eyes with a murderous glare. Then he slowly rotated his desk chair until he faced the wall behind his desk. The three men sat in this configuration for several minutes, which to Ben and Tom seemed like hours.

Finally Toomey malevolently hissed his single word command to the wall.

"Dismissed!"

Tom and Ben both responded with a quick, "Yes, first sergeant," and scampered out of the room.

Colonel Fred Reitenhauser listened to O'Malley and LeBron relate the events at the Isar with impassivity, calmly puffing on his pipe filled with a licorice-blend tobacco. As had been his way for his entire life, his surface imperturbability masked the workings of an intricate and intense mind, assimilating and processing the information with the delicacy and efficiency of a fine Swiss watch.

He made no comment until O'Malley and LeBron had completely briefed him on the events and their impressions. Then, he finally spoke. "We don't know for sure that there is a connection between the postcard to Berger from Miss Aplan and what just happened, although a connection is probable.

"Other than the three of us and Berger, the only other individuals who know about the card for sure are Lieutenant Ryan and Major Barnstable. It could possibly have been just a coincidence. I don't think that's likely, but it *is* possible. We'll find out, but right now our immediate priority is Miss Aplan. Let me reach out and see what I can learn. Go and keep Berger and Tallifierro company until you hear from me. Oh, and you better find out whether Toomey has already pumped them for information. Don't talk to *anyone* about this. I'll take care of the major myself."

Reitenhauser then lowered his gaze to the papers on his desk, which was his signal to O'Malley and LeBron that the meeting was over.

O'Malley and LeBron joined Tom and Ben in the Ops Support Offices. Lt. Ryan had not been in when the latter two returned, and the other staffers present apparently had not detected Ben's distress. True to form, Ben was hiding it well. Soon the other staffers, one by one, left for the day.

The four men had nothing to do while they waited for word from the CO, so O'Malley regaled everyone with war stories from his days in Korea — of Pork Chop Hill and Chosin Reservoir.

Whether his stories were based on his own adventures or someone else's was difficult to tell, but it seemed improbable that he could have been at all the places he talked about at the times he claimed to have been there.

It made no difference to Ben anyway because he hardly heard a word the Chief said, lost as he was in a sweet reverie of better times between himself and Melissa.

Finally, after what seemed an eternity, Gerda appeared at the door and announced that the colonel wanted to see all four of them.

Instantly snapping back to reality, Ben felt his muscles constrict and for an instant was immobilized in his chair.

Tom sensed his friend's condition and placed a hand gently under Ben's right elbow, coaxing him to his feet and out into the hallway.

Like a family member in a hospital emergency room waiting for news of a loved one's condition after a crash, Ben was consumed by anxiety as the four men once again entered the CO's outer office.

This time the door to the inner office was open and Gerda immediately ushered them in, closing the door behind herself on her way out.

Reitenhauser was not one to mince words. After twenty-five years of commanding men, he cared about and respected them too much to prolong the agony. He now spoke immediately and without preliminaries.

"Miss Aplan has been reached, and she is safe. The report of her kidnapping was false. She knew absolutely nothing about it, and was shocked by the news."

While the colonel stopped for a second to puff on his pipe, Ben felt waves of relief washing over his entire body.

Tom uttered an emphatic and exclamatory, "All right!"

O'Malley and LeBron were also visibly relieved.

"Group has offered her protection," the colonel said. "She has accepted the offer. She will be in-country by 1800 hours tomorrow, and will contact Private Berger after a debriefing."

Reitenhauser had more to say, but it was on a need to know basis.

"Privates Tallifierro and Berger, you are dismissed, but consider yourselves on alert until further notice. The Duty Officer for tonight is Specialist Tonelli. Please call him every half hour to check in, and do not leave the complex this evening. That will be all."

Ben had many questions but he knew not to linger. His and Tom's dismissal was unequivocal. They had no 'need to know' what the CO was going to discuss with LeBron and O'Malley, and so they were out. As trained case officers, they knew that was the way things worked.

Reitenhauser resumed the briefing once Ben and Tom were gone from his offices, and the door securely closed behind them. The formidable Gerda would make sure that no uninvited persons were admitted to the inner sanctum — and for probably the first time, that even included the Ops, Major Edwin Barnstable.

The CO resumed his narrative. "I have been in touch with Group, and even spoke personally to the new Group Commander, General Stansfield.

He has already dispatched a top-flight C.I.[*] investigations team from Frankfurt. They are driving south on the Autobahn as we speak.

"The general's C.I. Analysis desk is taking this incident very seriously. They are not particularly concerned about Hostile's surveilling and penetrating one of our training exercises. That happens from time to time. We *know* that they are watching us... We're watching them too. There is nothing they can learn from one of those drills that they don't already know. What really has Higher concerned is the Melissa Aplan connection. They are alarmed at the possibility — and so am I — that Hostile learned of her from a source inside our unit. As I said before, it could have been just a coincidence. They could have learned of her connection by penetrating the School at Holabird, or even a leak from the Five O Deuce. But the mere possibility that the info came from a source inside our shop has everyone on red alert.

"You can be sure that a full-scale investigation of the Detachment will begin at 0900 tomorrow. I had hoped to conduct my own in-house investigation before Group's people came storming in here, but now there's no time.

"Both of you should be here at 0800 sharp tomorrow for further briefings. That will be all for now," said the colonel.

He pressed the button on his intercom. "Gerda, tell Sergeant Toomey that I want to see him immediately and to bring the personnel roster with him. By the way Ted, did you ask Tallifierro and Berger if Toomey pumped them for information?"

"He did and according to the boys, they gave him nothing," replied O'Malley.

"Thank you Chief. I don't have to tell you men that — effective immediately — we are on the tightest possible need to know basis."

As the two intelligence pros exited the CO's office, Reitenhauser took some time to review the events of the day in his mind. He would let Toomey cool his heels in the outer offices for a while before summoning him in.

Reitenhauser's long-standing habit when confronted with a problem requiring serious analysis was to place a legal-sized pad in front of him and randomly jot down various words, phrases, or names that had a possible bearing on the problem at hand. Then as he worked through the problem in his mind, he would connect the various items on the page with lines, arrows, and numbers. Once finished, he would place the page in the large ashtray on his desk, and use his pipe lighter to burn it.

---

* Counter-intelligence

The words he wrote on the page now in various locations, using its entire 14 inch length and 8 ½ inch width were:

APLAN   BLAKE

OPS SUPPORT   BELSON

GERMAN SECTION   OLNEY

TALLIFIERRO

CZECH SECTION   TOOMEY

LEBRON

O'MALLEY   14332

URI

BOOKER   RYAN

BARNSTABLE   BERGER

He then spent approximately ten minutes numbering the various words he had written and drawing connecting arrows. The speed with which he accomplished the task was a function of the considerable thought he had already given to the problem over the past several weeks.

The last name he wrote on the page was 'Uri.' As he wrote it, his disciplined mind involuntarily shifted into retro-mode, flashing back to that night at Neuhofer Hospital twenty two years earlier.

1945

"Lieutenant Reitenhauser, I'm Captain Olsen, liaison officer from Allied Command to the Provisional German Authority."

Fred rose from the bench in the emergency room where he had been sitting for the past two hours, and saluted the young officer.

Olsen offered his hand and shook Fred's hand warmly.

"Lieutenant, let me bring you current on what we know at this point. Putyagin has lost a lot of blood, but is on massive transfusions and there is a better than even chance he will survive. His relative youth and excellent physical conditioning are in his favor. He has been assigned to a critical care unit and will be allowed no visitors until he is off the critical list. The German doctors have advised Allied Command that without your prompt and courageous actions, he surely would have died before reaching the hospital."

"Have any security guards been assigned to protect him?"

Captain Olsen nodded. "Yes. Two armed Russian M.P.'s are seated outside the Critical Care Unit, but they may not even be necessary because — with the help of your description — the German police think they already have the assailant in custody. Believe it or not, they caught him lingering just outside the door to the Emergency Room in what they described as an '*agitated state*,' muttering to himself and making erratic motions with both arms. He had no weapon, but there was evidence of powder burns on his right hand. In the squad car he went into a non-stop harangue about how the dirty Russian swines raped his teenage sisters.

"The man is a long-distance truck driver named Otto Kunzman, who hails from a small village on the German side of the German-Polish border. From the reports we have been receiving, his statements — though made in an hysterical state — are credible. There appear to have been massive rapes of German women by invading Russian troops all along the German-Polish border where the Kunzman family lived. For that matter, the rapes seem to have been committed everywhere in those areas of Germany lying in the path of the Russian offensive.

"Kunzman had apparently been stalking Russian officers for a couple of weeks now, and he may have taken shots at some of them before now. As far as we've been able to tell, Lieutenant Putyagin was the first one he managed to hit."

Olsen shrugged. "To all appearances, this was a simple revenge shooting."

Fred nodded. "Obviously, I am relieved they caught the guy, but under the circumstances, I hope the authorities temper justice with mercy."

"That will probably be up to the Russians," Olsen said. "And they haven't shown much mercy towards the German people thus far. I guess vengeance begets more vengeance. It's a cycle. The widespread sex crimes committed by the Russians against German civilian females were largely motivated by revenge for the brutal treatment of the Russian civilian population and its troops at the hands of the Wehrmacht and the S.S. Of course, the Russian war crimes will never be prosecuted, because Russia emerged as the victor. Justice following a war is largely a function of who wins."

The captain sighed heavily. "Anyway, it was a brave thing you did. Don't be surprised if the Russian Command tries to pin a medal on you. Putyagin has found a good friend in you."

1967

Reitenhauser folded the sheet of paper and placed it in the breast pocket of his plain-looking suit coat. "Gerda, show Sergeant Toomey in."

Sgt. Toomey stood in front of the CO's desk until the colonel signaled that he should sit.

"Sergeant, a special investigations team from Group will arrive at 0900 tomorrow. Assemble all personnel for a briefing by me in the large conference room at 0845 hours. After the briefing, which will take no longer than two minutes, accompany the investigation team to the same room and place it at their full disposal for as long as the investigation takes. I expect you and your staff to give the team your full and unconditional cooperation. And have a fresh pot of coffee waiting for them in the conference room."

"May I ask what this is about, sir?"

"You may not. This Detachment is now on a 'classification 1' need to know basis. We are also on full alert. Sergeant Toomey, your attempt earlier to pressure the two enlisted men into giving you information was highly improper and a serious breach of our protocols. You should have known better. If I had wanted you to be privy to that information, I would have brought you into the initial meeting with O'Malley and LeBron. This is not a rifle company, sergeant. We maintain a strict division between our operational and administrative functions. Do not cross that line again or there will be serious consequences. Is that clear?"

"Yes, sir."

"Dismissed."

The chastened first sergeant immediately rose and left the room.

Reitenhauser removed the sheet of paper from his pocket, stared at it and began a silent dialogue with himself:

"Who are we dealing with here? Probably Soviet Intelligence... The East Germans wouldn't have the nerve. Did the leak of the connection between Aplan and Berger come from within our detachment? Almost certainly. The likelihood that it came from anywhere else is simply too remote. It would be too much of a coincidence for there not to be a link between the postcard from Aplan and what happened at the Isar. The first thing I have to do at 0830 is talk to O'Malley about the chain of custody of the postcard. I trust the Chief fully, and I know he had nothing to do with this, but I need that information before the group team begins interrogating everyone. The question is why did Russian Intelligence do what they did? That one seems pretty easy. They wanted to send us a message that they can penetrate, and *have* penetrated our unit, and can so compromise us as to render us useless. But why the 409th? What is so unique about us as to set us apart from the twenty other M.I. Detachments in West Germany — at Würzburg, Stuttgart, Nüremberg, Bonn, Bremerhaven, Frankfurt, Cologne, Heidelberg and all the rest? General Stansfield said there have been no similar incidents anywhere in Group. Why us? We are not even one of the larger units and we have no real current mission with respect to the biggest problem, East Germany."

The answer came to the cerebral commanding officer with a sudden flash of illumination, the thrill of enlightenment tempered by a sobering dread. Slowly he drew a heavy circle around one name on the page of lines and arrows: 'Uri.' Below that, he wrote a single word... 'Raptor.'

Upon O'Malley's arrival at the CO's office the following morning at 0815, Gerda escorted him immediately in to meet privately with the colonel.

"We don't have much time Ted," the colonel said, "so I'll get right to it. Tell me again who you showed the Aplan postcard to besides me?"

"After I showed it to you, sir, I showed it to Berger's section Chief, Lieutenant Ryan, to find out what he knew about Berger's relationship with the woman. He claimed to know absolutely nothing. Then of course, I had to show it to the Operations Officer, Major Barnstable, my supervisor."

"Anyone else?"

"No, sir. But..."

"But *what*, Ted? We don't have a lot of time here..."

"Something did hit me at the time," O'Malley said. "As I was leaving the major's office, I caught a glimpse of him out of the corner of my eye picking up his phone from its cradle. As I walked down the hall I noticed there was only one other office open. It was the Czech section. Doug

Booker was on the phone, listening to whoever was at the other end with a look of total concentration on his face."

Doug Booker was the Deputy Chief of the Czech Section.

"Gerda," the colonel practically shouted into the intercom on his desk. "Get Booker in here at once."

While waiting for Booker to arrive, Reitenhauser ran the last entry he had made on the page the previous night through his mind. *Raptor*... "Is it happening now? Is that why Hostile decided to take a shot at my unit? Can that be why 14332 disappeared? As soon as Ryan is cleared by Group's investigators — assuming that he *does* get cleared — I'm sending him and Rhymes down to Vienna to check things out. They won't know it, but they'll have company. I'll have an armed security team watching their every move in case they run into any trouble."

The buzzer on his desk loudly interrupted his stream of thought. "Sir, Mr. Booker is here."

Doug Booker

Doug Booker, unlike Ryan or Tonelli, had been to the manor born. His full name was Douglas Simpson Booker IV. Scion to the railroad Bookers of Philadelphia's mainline, he was a blue-blood all the way.

The Bookers dated back to well before the Revolutionary War. They had made their original fortune in the slave trade, and then quadrupled their wealth by getting in on the ground floor of the Baltimore and Ohio Railroad.

Doug Booker had been sent to Choate and Harvard where he made "Gentleman's Cs." In the late nineteen-forties, he had been groomed to receive an executive's position in the B&O upon graduation from Harvard in 1950. From there, he was destined for a fast-track to upper management.

But, he had shocked the entire family by enlisting in the army right after the start of the Korean War, on June 25, 1950. After Basic Training, the family had pulled strings and gotten him assigned to a cushy P.R. job at the Pentagon. He had served there for a few months, but then crossed everyone up again by volunteering for the infantry in Korea.

Again the family had used its vast influence and resources to have Booker assigned to Ridgway's Headquarters Company.

This time, because he admired General Ridgway, Booker didn't resist and he advanced quickly to the rank of buck sergeant. At the time, his father's younger brother, T. Whitson Booker, was Truman's Under-Secretary of State for Middle-Eastern affairs. So Ridgway was immediately made aware of young Booker's presence in his headquarters' company. The general ordered his executive officer to "keep an eye on the lad."

Ridgway's staff was so impressed with Booker's intelligence and dedication that Ridgway promoted him to staff sergeant in March of 1951, and transferred him to his G-2.[*]

In late March of that year, during Eighth Army's triumphant final push to re-capture Seoul, Booker was sent into the South Korean capital with an advance reconnaissance platoon to recruit Korean civilians as covert intelligence agents who were to identify suspected Red Chinese counter-insurgents.

After Eighth Army was firmly re-entrenched on the 38th parallel, Doug Booker was offered a direct commission as an Army Intelligence Officer, but turned it down. He served his three year tour as an enlisted man and upon his return to the States, again rejected all offers to enter the family businesses.

Doug Booker was already wealthy because of his income from various family trusts created by his grandfather and great-grandfather. He took the government Civil Service test and accepted an entry-level position with the Defense Department for $3500.00 a year in the Military Plans and Operations Division at the Pentagon.

Again his ability led to rapid promotions, but he also was gradually becoming known as something of a pariah. Booker wrote acerbic articles for various think tanks, complaining that both the military and civilian branches of the U.S. defense establishment were riddled with incompetence. In his opinion, this unhappy state of affairs was the result of the lack of a meritocracy. Too many high level military officers and civilian defense officials held their jobs because of patronage, wealth, and family name, rather than merit.

This, argued Booker, was America's soft underbelly and one of the reasons the Soviet Union was passing the U.S. in defense preparedness. Booker's writings, speeches and ordinary conversations became so strident that he wore out his welcome at the Pentagon.

After being quietly asked to resign, but with strong references to help him to a soft landing, Doug Booker left Washington. Everyone assumed that he would finally claim the place that had always been waiting for him in private industry. Again, he confounded friends and family by accepting a civilian position with U.S. Army Intelligence in Germany.

---

[*] Intelligence Director for an Army Group.

Due to his vast experience as an agent handler during the Korean War, the Intelligence Corps waived his attendance at Intelligence School and made him a case officer in 1960, with a GS-7 civilian classification.

Now in 1967, he was a GS-11, known for his brilliance as an operations planner, but also as an habitual gadfly who constantly tilted against windmills while criticizing Group's policies. But, Reitenhauser didn't want 'yes men' serving in his command, so Booker did well and rose to become Deputy Chief of the Czech section.

Lately however, Reitenhauser had noticed subtle and not so subtle changes in Booker. At some point, the man had crossed the line from healthy criticism to eccentricity. His work was still of a high quality but his personal habits had started to deteriorate. He was getting fewer haircuts at the post barber and as a result, his hair was beginning to overlap the collar of his button-down dress shirts. He cut his fingernails less often and most of his ties seemed to carry permanent food stains, known throughout the unit as 'Booker badges.'

He had lost weight and his suits, rumpled even in the best of times, were beginning to hang on his lanky frame. Some mornings, he forgot to shave or to brush his teeth or to wear a deodorant. But strangest of all, he now seemed to carry the same two, dog-eared books with him wherever he went. One was *'An Uncertain Trumpet'* by General James Gavin — a scathing critique of the failure of the U.S. military to adapt to modern modes of warfare. The other was *'The Confessions of Nat Turner'* by William Styron — a novel about one of the few successful American slave revolts.

Did he carry this book everywhere as a form of atonement for the acts of his slave-trading ancestors? One could not say for sure, because he refused to answer any questions about the ubiquitous books.

As Booker walked into the CO's office, he looked even more smudged and disheveled than usual. Add to that the dark circles under his eyes and it was not a pretty picture.

The first thought that entered Reitenhauser's mind was that maybe he had put too much pressure on Booker, by giving him such a large role in the planning and implementation of "Kryptonite." Well at least he had brought Art LeBron over to the Czech desk as Chief, and Art would share the burden.

The leadership position at Czech desk might have gone to Booker, had he not been such an eccentric. Booker didn't seem to care one way or the other.

Doug Booker sat down with the ever-present books in his lap. "Good morning, colonel."

"Good morning, Doug. How are you today?"

"I was fine until I heard about the inquisition that is about to start."

"Look Doug, we have a serious problem on our hands. Can I count on you to pull with the team?"

"Fred, you shouldn't have to ask that question. No matter what I might have to say about things, my personal loyalty to you has been unwavering."

"Yes it has, Doug. And you have been an exceptional innovator. I want to discuss things with you at greater length later on, but in ten minutes I have to brief the entire unit on what's going on, and right now I have time to ask you only one question. Did you speak on the phone to Ed Barnstable the other evening about a certain postcard of interest to the unit?"

"No. I don't know what you are talking about. The major almost never speaks to me at all, and I don't remember the last time we spoke on the phone. He thinks I'm a loose cannon on the deck and he would love to get rid of me."

"When did all this start, Doug?"

"About six months ago, when I told him his ops plan for Kryptonite was moronic."

"Okay, we'll talk more about this later. I don't understand why I wasn't informed about the rift."

"Colonel, we've kept it between ourselves. Not even Art or Ted knows about it."

"All right. Go ahead to the large conference room for the briefing. I'll be right in."

Confined to the Max after their brief meeting with the CO, Tom and Ben tried to unwind after the day's startling events, over cheeseburgers and vanilla shakes at the snack bar, which bore the name 'The Max Shop.'

"How weird is all of this?" said Tom. "When O'Malley warned us to expect the unexpected, he wasn't just mouthing a cliché. First the notebook of horrors, and now Melissa's getting dragged into things."

"You have no idea how much that pisses me off," replied Ben. "I will find whoever was responsible and he will rue the day he ever even mentioned her name."

Knowing his friend was just overwrought right then, Tom didn't bother pointing out that the odds of his ever coming face-to-face with the perpetrator were infinitesimal. "Well, at least you may be reunited with Melissa."

"Yeah, but I never would have wanted it to be under these circumstances."

"I know what you mean. Hey Ben, we have to call in. It's been more than a half hour."

As he looked around for the nearest pay phone, Tom was reminded of his immediate private reaction when the CO told them Specialist Tonelli was the duty officer. "If I were CO," he now thought to himself, "and my unit was under attack by hostile agencies, would I assign my company clerk, a paper pusher, as my duty officer?"

"Tom, there's a pay phone out front."

They moved quickly to the phone, and called the assigned number."

It was answered on the first ring by a deep-voiced man. "Hello, Mario."

"This is not Mario, who's this?"

"PFC Berger, checking in."

"Oh, yeah I heard about you guys. This is Warrant Officer Olney, the duty officer for tonight."

"Where's Specialist Tonelli?"

"What kind of a question is that to ask, private, over an open phone line? I'll note that you called in at 2230 hours."

Ben then heard the click of the phone as Olney abruptly hung up.

Actually, Olney had no idea where Tonelli was. Both the Ops and Deputy Ops had been looking for him since 2100 hours, but he was nowhere to be found.

Chapter Six

Kryptonite

The entire detachment with the exception of Sergeant Osi Mattatussu, the unit's supply sergeant, and Specialist Tonelli were gathered in the conference room at 0845 hours to receive the CO's briefing. Mattatussu was on leave, but Tonelli's absence was unexplained and Colonel Reitenhauser offered no explanation.

"I'll make this very brief, everyone," began the CO "There has been a possible breach in the security of our unit. A special investigations team will be arriving shortly from Group, and each of you will be interviewed. It is imperative that you give the investigators your utmost cooperation, and that you conduct yourself during the interview and any follow-up interviews with courtesy and professionalism. Do not hold back any information. If you think you know something, no matter how minor or remote it seems, please reveal it. It is far better to err on the side of providing too much information, than to hold something back that may turn out to be important.

"You are to discuss the interviews with no one. That is a direct order and the slightest deviation from it will result in immediate and severe disciplinary action. The investigators will undoubtedly caution you as well.

"I will not be available to anyone during the course of the investigation and until further notice, so don't be pestering Gerda; she has enough to do." Reitenhauser had added this touch of light-heartedness to relieve some of the tension in the room. Judging by the appreciative chuckles he received, it seemed to have had the desired effect.

"Now, I know that you people, as personnel of the 409th, will conduct yourselves in the same manner in which you do your everyday jobs — with thoroughness, competence, and a sense of mission.

"Thank you, ladies and gentlemen. Now return to your posts, and go about your business just as you would on any other day."

With that, Reitenhauser quickly exited from the room, escorted only by Gerda.

*   *   *

Major Barnstable had begun to rise and follow but realized by the colonel's abrupt exit that his presence was not desired.

During the briefing in the large room, the conference table had been temporarily pushed against the back wall, and rows of folding chairs had been set up with an aisle left in the middle.

In keeping with the 409th's protocol, the first row was reserved for the Section Chiefs, Blake, LeBron and Ryan; the Security Officer, Lieutenant Anders Smith; the First Sergeant, Peter Toomey; the Operations Officer, Barnstable; and the Deputy Operations Officer, O'Malley. By tradition, the Operations Officer and first sergeant sat in the two front row, aisle seats.

Everyone else in the unit sat on a first come, first served basis. The assemblage behind the first row was comprised by the personnel from the main sections: the Administrative Office, the Budget and Fiscal Office, the Equipment and Supplies Department, the Motor Pool and the secretaries and file clerks. The officer in charge of procurement and operations of the Administrative Office was First Lieutenant Anders Smith who did double duty as the Security Officer of the unit.

Major Barnstable stared at the colonel's back as the CO quickly and purposefully exited the room. He was barely able to keep his emotions — a combination of shock, anger, and hurt — under control. Never before had the old man turned his back to him after a meeting. As a show of command and unity, they always shook hands and walked out together to the CO's office for a brief post-assembly review.

The rebuff was obvious and stinging. To have intentionally snubbed his second in command was extraordinary, and the CO had left the major crestfallen and humiliated. And worse, after a brief pause, O'Malley and LeBron had followed him out, undoubtedly usurping the Ops Officer's traditional role. In one gesture, the CO had established a new pecking order in the unit, which left no doubt as to who was *in* and who was *out*.

And where was that wop, Tonelli? If something had happened to him or if he had just passed out drunk in some cat house, the CO and first sergeant would have said something to him, or at least shown some signs of stress and concern. No, decided Barnstable, the CO, with the first sergeant's complicity, was using Tonelli to somehow freelance the boss's own side-investigation and was again freezing out his own Operations Officer.

The Operations Officer's take on what had just happened was composed mainly of misimpressions, mistaken judgments, and wildly exaggerated over-reactions. Ironically, these elements had characterized most of his thinking lately, and had formed the basis for why the colonel had just treated him in the manner he had.

Contrary to what Barnstable assumed, O'Malley and LeBron did not follow the CO to his office. They returned to their own sections to try to be a comforting presence when their staff members were called in by the Group investigators for questioning.

Reitenhauser had returned to his office alone, closed the door, lit his pipe and for company had only his own thoughts.

It is true that he was angry with Barnstable, but more importantly, he was disturbed by the major's recent behavior. Reitenhauser had known for several hours that the Group investigative team was totally unnecessary, because the identity of Melissa Aplan and her connection to a case officer of the 409th had leaked out of the unit through a basically innocent set of circumstances.

It had happened because of the incredibly poor judgment exercised by Barnstable in ordering a security check through Group on Aplan almost immediately after O'Malley had shown him the postcard. What had possessed the major to think that this young Peace Corps volunteer serving in Tanzania was any kind of a threat to pierce the security veil of the unit through her boyfriend? It was simply unfathomable. He wouldn't put it past Barnstable, judging by his recent paranoid behavior, to believe that the Peace Corps was a hot bed of disloyal leftist kooks and Fifth Columnists, just laying in wait to spy for our enemies. Unbelievable!

Well, at least they now knew that Group's Internal Security Division had been penetrated and compromised by Hostile. But, back to the major. First, Barnstable had maneuvered and manipulated to have LeBron transferred out of Ops Support for the ludicrous reason that — because Art was so close to 14332 — he might inadvertently reveal sensitive details about Kryptonite to the Austrian agent.

Reitenhauser had gone along with the move only because he felt LeBron's talents were needed in the Czech section anyway, as a stabilizing influence over the brilliant but erratic Booker. In addition, the CO knew what no one else in the unit knew, which was that the neophyte Lieutenant Ryan was not being just cast adrift in spy-saturated Vienna without a life preserver. Ryan and Rhymes would be under close observation and protection at all times.

Next, knowing that Booker was eccentric in the extreme, the major had allowed Booker's careless criticism of his ops plan to devolve into a prolonged personal grudge. Not only was this a clear error in judgment, it was plainly contrary to the interests of the 409th and its operations.

Finally, knowing how vital his deputy ops had become to the Detachment, out of pure jealousy, Barnstable had for many months been seeking to undermine O'Malley's access and influence at every turn — withholding the assistance of personnel from him, denying his requests for innovative surveillance equipment, and attempting to keep him in the dark about Kryptonite.

Well, Barnstable had left him no choice.

He could not let the Group investigative team go forward on a fool's errand. As soon as the team arrived, he would bring them into his office, call the major in as well, and confront him in front of the investigators. As to whether Barnstable could still be an effective Operations Officer, he would decide that after the investigators were dispatched back to Frankfurt, where they could be more useful investigating Group's own internal leak.

But, first he had an unpleasant phone call to make to General Stansfield, to explain what had happened.

1945

Suffering the effect of shock and blood loss, Uri wandered in and out of consciousness for the first 48 hours after his arrival at the hospital. Hooked up to an IV, oxygen tubes, and a catheter, he wasn't able to move around much, even when he did start to regain consciousness for longer intervals.

The doctors had found it necessary to operate the first night because of internal bleeding and a perforated kidney. So when Fred broke away from the Berlin excavation site on the late afternoon of the first day to visit Uri, he found the young Russian officer drugged from the anesthesia and pain medication, and mostly incoherent. His condition was still listed as critical.

Fred returned each evening after going off duty to visit Uri in the hospital, and usually stayed for at least an hour. Some of Uri's fellow officers and soldiers under his command would also show up to visit him from time to time, bringing books or magazines. But Fred was struck by the fact that none of them appeared to be particularly close to Uri, and few of them stayed any longer than a quarter of an hour. Their visits appeared more obligatory and pro forma than motivated by genuine concern and caring.

After a week in the hospital when Uri was finally able to engage in a half-way lucid conversation, Fred asked him if any of the officers and men who had been visiting were friends of his.

"No, not in the slightest," replied Uri. "When you are the son of a government and party official, it is very difficult to make friends, except with other officials' sons. It is an unfortunate fact of life that when one lives in a country where the state holds absolute power over its citizens, the average person seeks to avoid people like me for fear that if they get on my wrong side, I will turn them in to the Party's watch dogs. Now that I am out of combat, I am able to write to my family in Moscow more often and have learned that the average individual's fears are not misplaced. Every day, Russians are disappearing in alarming numbers, from their homes, their jobs, and right off the streets. And very few of them ever come back. Many are simply never heard from again. Others suffer a different fate.

"Rumors persist of landscapes surrounding major cities, in rural areas and of course on the frozen expanses of Siberia, dotted by hundreds of forced labor camps. The overwhelming majority of the denizens of the camps are there for political reasons — for alleged crimes against the State. Some of the so-called traitors wind up being summarily shot by firing squads. Many thousands more die in the camps. The very small percentage who — somehow — eventually make it home, are never the same. The camps extinguish any light of humanity a person may have had before his incarceration. I am afraid that Mother Russia has become a fearsome and forbidding place," Uri observed, while looking around to make sure no one else was within listening range before finishing his sentence — "under Stalin and his murderous cabal."

In the weeks that followed, as Uri made progress in his recovery but also developed frequent infections along the way, Fred visited him whenever his duties permitted. He kept Uri informed of the evidence the U.S. and Soviet Search teams were amassing of the vast Third Reich program of genocide, and other Nazi war crimes.

Uri's higher command replaced the German doctors with a team of Russian physicians, and imposed severe restrictions on who *was* and *was not* permitted to visit him. Uri demanded that Fred be allowed to visit him at all times, and — given Uri's standing in the Party — no one was willing to refuse him.

On one particular sunny afternoon after Fred had wheeled Uri out to the Solarium and they were about to begin a game of chess, Uri looked his friend in the eye and with a fervency in his voice stated simply, "Fred, you saved my life at the risk of your own. Then, you stayed at my side while my own comrades abandoned me. I will be indebted to you for the rest of my life."

Then, without further comment, he returned to setting up his chess pieces.

1967

The fallout from the security leak incident was now over, and things were basically back to normal at the 409th. Although General Stansfield thought Major Barnstable a bit of a fool, he did not find sufficient grounds for taking disciplinary action. After all, how much can you fault a man for erring on the side of an excess of caution, by ordering a security check?

Stansfield's real problem was in his own Internal Security Division, and he had wasted no time in ordering a sub-rosa investigation of the entire division.

Major Barnstable kept his job as Operations Officer, but the chasm that had opened in the relationship between him and the colonel was irreparable. It was only a matter of time before big changes were made.

On the night of the Aplan incident, the colonel had simply advised the first sergeant when Specialist Tonelli went missing that the latter was on 'special assignment.' No one other than the CO and Tonelli knew what that meant, and neither of them were talking.

Sergeant Mattatussu had returned from leave and almost immediately heard about the incident through the unit's well-lubricated gossip engine. The unofficial headquarters for the unit's lead gossipers was the Max Shop, the hangout for the single men and women of the unit. There, the proprietor usually looked the other way when its patrons opened bottles of their own beer at the end of the workday.

Mattatussu acted with indifference to the news. None of it made any difference to his dull and monotonous job as supply sergeant.

Ben received one phone call from Melissa, and they made plans to meet between Frankfurt and Munich at a popular resort village in the Black Forest, as soon as he could wrangle a weekend pass. They wouldn't have much privacy since Melissa would be accompanied by a body guard. She would be returning to Tanzania soon to her Peace Corps job, so Ben was hoping to get a pass for the coming weekend.

Tom had started meeting with Kate Drummond, a twenty-six year old Russian-Czech linguist from Edinburgh, for coffee one or two evenings a week after work. Kate was a U.S. Government contract-employee, hired as a translator by Group and assigned to the 409th. Although she had been raised in Scotland from the age of five, she was a United States Citizen. Her father was a career investment analyst for Barclay's Bank and the Drummond family had moved to Scotland from Cleveland, Ohio right after the Second World War, when her father accepted a position with Barclays' Edinburgh office. Kate had returned to the U.S. for college, taking her Bachelor's and Master's degrees in Eastern European languages at George Washington University.

Both Ben and Tom were assigned to the Operational Support section of the 409th. Tom and Kate struck up an acquaintanceship based in the beginning on comparing notes about various student haunts in Georgetown, which both had frequented during their undergraduate days. But this had merely been a way of breaking the ice for two people who were clearly attracted to each other.

Kate was mesmerized by Tom's penetrating intelligence and supreme self-confidence. He may not have been as handsome as his heartthrob friend, Ben Berger, but his presence was overpowering to her nonetheless.

Tom was equally smitten with Kate — with her looks, brains and sense of who she was — an academic totally devoid of pretense with an abiding compassion towards all of humankind and an unfailing decency and kindness towards those she encountered in her daily life. Tom had not asked her out on a real date yet but that could come as early as this evening when they met at the Max Shop.

LeBron and Booker were working well together on Kryptonite, but there was still no word on the fate of Agent 14332. Lieutenant Ryan and Sergeant Rhymes would tomorrow embark on a two-day trip to Vienna via the Orient Express. Maybe they would return with some news.

Mitchell Blake and his deputy, Warrant Officer Warren Olney, at the German desk, were clearly envious of the extent to which Kryptonite was a Czech Section operation, but not so much that it affected their performance. At least not on the surface.

The German section was in many ways the preeminent department of the Unit, with a proud tradition dating back to the Berlin Air Lift of 1948. General George C. Marshall himself had awarded the 409th a special Certificate of Merit for the vital intelligence it had acquired both before and after the Air Lift, the operation which had saved West Berlin from falling to the Soviets.

Since 14332 had gone silent, there had been a dramatic spike in the telex traffic between Frankfurt and Munich. Scones and Winicki were now working overtime to keep up.

*   *   *

Second Lieutenant Lonnie Ryan and Buck Sergeant Malcolm Rhymes reported to Colonel Reitenhauser at 0800 hours on that June day in 1967. One seldom has an inkling when he wakes up in the morning that he is about to start one of the memorable days of his life, and this morning was no exception.

The two young soldiers were filled with excitement over the upcoming trip. The Orient Express would depart from the Munich Bahnhof at 0928, and two tall Americans in inexpensive European-cut suits would be on board. They would be recognized by most of their fellow passengers as Americans almost immediately — by their mannerisms, haircuts, bearing, posture, shoes, and other telltale signs almost impossible to hide. Their American passports would identify them as Edward Daughtry and Forrest Simms, the respective cover names for Ryan and Rhymes. Each would carry a small Samsonite suitcase and little else. They would carry no weapons.

Gerda escorted Ryan and Rhymes into the CO's office immediately upon their arrival that morning.

The colonel wasted no time with preliminaries. They had already been over the mission many times and there was little left to say.

"Remember, you are on a fact-finding mission only. Don't depart from your itinerary for anything less than a threat to your lives. And do not under any circumstances place yourselves in a position where you can be taken. You are case officers, not agents, so don't try to be spies, and don't take unnecessary risks. Remember your escape and evasion training at all times. And do not contact us here in Munich for any reason. If you get in trouble, you have the address and phone number of our Vienna safehouse. Good luck with your mission and I will see you again when you report back to me in 48 hours. Any questions?"

Both men indicated they had none, so the meeting was over.

Reitenhauser had taken over this mission completely, excluding Barnstable.

LeBron had, after considerable soul-searching, confessed his fears to the CO that Lieutenant Ryan was being set up by Barnstable as the fall-guy for whatever was going wrong in Vienna. That may have been true, but to the CO it didn't matter. Ryan was his choice anyway. And again, LeBron didn't know that Ryan and Rhymes would not be alone.

Both the Czech section chief and the CO did know one thing for sure about LeBron. He was far too valuable an asset and knew too much to be exposed to being taken captive by Hostile.

*   *   *

The Orient Express reached the Vienna Bahnhof without incident. Ryan and Rhymes exited the train station, and immediately began looking for a cab.

The plan called for the two case officers to go directly from the station to the residence of Agent 14332. The more they wandered around Vienna, the greater the risk of being tailed.

Intent upon finding a taxi, and perhaps struck by the charm and grandeur of the city, the two Americans had not noticed the ordinary-looking, stout man wearing a fedora and a baggy suit, who had followed them off the train. They didn't notice when he trailed them out of the station.

On the street, the stout man leaned casually against a wall, and began reading an Italian newspaper.

The two Americans had no trouble hailing a cab. As it pulled away from the curb, the man with the fedora signaled to a black Peugeot, to pull over. He jumped into the front passenger seat and the Peugeot headed out onto the Vienna street, on the tail of the taxi cab.

A third occupant sat in the back seat of the Peugeot. All three men carried Berettas in shoulder holsters under their suit coats.

Mario Tonelli had tried to keep a low profile in the Detachment since the night of the Aplan incident. He was in at 0900 each morning, worked hard and quietly all day, and tried to be out of the office by 1700 hours. His last official act of the day was assisting Lieutenant Anders (Andy) Smith in collecting and disposing of the 'classified waste' from each office. With Smith wearing a side arm and Tonelli behind the wheel of the Deuce-And-A-Half, they would transport the classified waste to an equally classified location. Once the truck was back in the Motor Pool garage, Tonelli was free to go off duty without returning to the fourth floor.

Unlike the evenings before his 'special assignment' for the CO, Tonelli returned directly to his quarters without stopping at the Max Shop to kibitz with his co-workers. In the evenings, he pretty much remained at his quarters reading, except for the occasional outing with Mattatussu to the NCO Club for a couple of beers.

Old Sock-it Toomey had stopped riding Tonelli, and their relationship had become serious and professional. He didn't really have to worry about unwelcome questions from Major Barnstable either, because the latter had stopped communicating with him entirely, except indirectly through Andy Smith or Pete Toomey.

Discovery of the source of the Aplan leak had been easy. Only three people had been told about the postcard — the CO, the Ops Officer and the section chief of Ops Support. Obviously, the CO was not the source of the leak. He was the one who had requested the investigation by Group, as well as Tonelli's special investigation. Lieutenant Ryan was too new and too much of a straight-arrow to be a likely source of the leak. So that left the major.

Tonelli decided to check outgoing communications by telex first, because they were the easiest to discover. The colonel had given him the combination to the door of the telex room on Tonelli's first day with the 409th. His five years with the Clandestine Services Division of BOSS and another two with the Office of Security had given Tonelli the skills to handle this challenge almost routinely.

It had been relatively easy to trace every message sent from the Unit's machine on the day Barnstable had seen the postcard. While it was true that the machine encrypted a message before it reached its destination, it was not encrypted when fed into the machine by the telex operator.

By observing how the often sloppy Bob Scones operated the telex, Tonelli learned that — after receiving the typed hard copy of an outgoing message — Scones often violated protocol by not immediately disposing of the hard copy after the transmission was completed. Too lazy to march the hard copy down to Lieutenant Smith's classified waste bin, Scones would often accumulate a week's worth of messages before disposing of them. In this instance, he ran true to form.

In a stack of hard copy messages in the bottom right hand drawer of Scones's locked desk which Tonelli had opened with a simple hair pin, was a standard 'RSC,' or 'Request for Security Check.' This particular request had as its subject, one 'Melissa Aplan, Peace Corps Volunteer, Tanzania.'

In the blank next to 'Reason for Request,' Barnstable had printed, "Personal Relationship with an 'M.O.S.-120' of Requester Unit."

There it was — enough information for disloyal personnel of Group's Internal Security Division to provide Hostile with the wherewithal for a bogus blackmail threat.

It was 0100 hours when Tonelli made his discovery. The only unit personnel left in the 409th's offices were the duty officer, Warren Olney, who had been substituted for Tonelli when the CO decided he had more important plans for him; and the colonel himself. Tonelli folded the form, stuck it in his back pants pocket, re-locked the desk, turned off the lights and softly closed the combination door behind him.

Two minutes later, he was handing the paper to the colonel, who quickly examined it.

"Good job, Mario."

"Thank you, colonel."

"I would like you to disappear for a day, Mario. You know where to go. If either of us really needs to reach the other, we'll use a courier."

Looking at his watch, the colonel added, "I'll see you back here in 32 hours. Get some sleep. You may need it."

Tonelli had little else to do than eat and think during his day and a half retreat in the safehouse. It was kind of amazing, mused Tonelli over a liverwurst sandwich. The colonel had been able to pluck him and another top-flight operative right out of the most elite unit of one of the greatest intelligence agencies in the world, and plant them in innocuous cover jobs within his own unit.

He had to chuckle over how everyone in NATO went to such pains to refer to his real employer as BOSS, an acronym for Bureau of Standardized Systems. Who were they kidding? Everyone — friendlies, enemy intelligence services, virtually all personnel of Group and their dependents, even the putzfraus (German cleaning women) who cleaned BOSS's offices, knew that BOSS was only a cover name for CIA.

He had enjoyed his cover as a happy-go-lucky company clerk. It had served its purpose, but Tonelli knew that it would end soon and he would be placed back under deep cover. It was a shame in a way. He had liked most of the people at the 409th, even 'Sock-it.' But, a year was more than enough, and new challenges loomed ahead.

Of course, his real name was *not* Mario Tonelli. What should he choose as his next cover name? He would ponder that question over a cold bottle of Augustinerbrau.

His mind then shifted back to a much more intriguing question. Where did the CO of the relatively small Munich Military Intelligence Detachment get the clout to run his own covert spook team, and man it with super-elite operatives from the CIA? He had his doubts that even General Stansfield would be able to pull that one off.

The rumor having the most currency over at BOSS was that Reitenhauser had for years run a 'Mole' planted deep within the Soviet defense network, who was totally non-transferable to any other case officer under NATO's umbrella. The Mole was off limits to anyone else in Group; to CIA, to Britain's MI-5, to French Intelligence, and so on. Well, that was the rumor anyway. Who could know anything for sure in this crazy business?

The only thing the soon to be, formerly-known-as Mario Tonelli, knew was that he genuinely enjoyed working with a man of Fred Reitenhauser's caliber. He hoped it would continue.

Upon returning from leave, Supply Sergeant Osi Mattatussu, was more unpleasant with his co-workers than ever. On the counter of the lower portion of the narrow Dutch door to the Supply Room, Mattatussu would rest his elbows and glare at the many petitioners seeking typewriter ribbons, boxes of cheap ballpoint pens, packages of white bond paper, steno pads, supplies for the copy machine, etc. Rarely would he exchange even a greeting with the secretaries, clerks and junior enlisted men sent by their section chiefs. He would simply point to the next receipt signature line and wait sullenly for the required signature.

Mattatussu's size and build alone were intimidating. His six foot three inches carried 220 pounds of pure muscle, evenly and tautly distributed over a sculpted physique. An American Samoan, he had built his body in amateur swim competition and weight-lifting.

Mattatussu's greatest expressed disdain was for young Americans from the mainland, who he purported to view as spoiled, pampered and shallow. He never referred to any of them by their real names, if he referred to them at all. He had nicknames for some of them based on superficial physical, geographical or ethnic characteristics. Fair skinned enlisted men were usually addressed as either 'Archie' or 'Jughead.' If a soldier happened to have blonde hair, he was 'Beach Boy.' If it was a blonde young woman, she was just 'Hey Blondie.' Tonelli was 'Dago;' Tom was 'Egg Head;' Ben was 'Movie Star' and Scones was exclusively and somewhat fittingly referred to as 'Dufus.' Mattatussu reserved the title 'Gomer' for Motor Pool Clerk, Cpl. Yancy Cook. Mattatussu knew that everyone else in the unit referred to the Motor Pool Clerk as 'Village.' He didn't care what everyone else did. As far as he was concerned, the idiot's name was Gomer.

Each nickname was pronounced in a mocking tone. If the soldier's hair was longer than average, he was 'Hippie.' If it was exceptionally long, he was 'Draft-Card Burner' until he broke down and got a haircut, at which time he became merely 'Hippie' again.

As was to be expected, Sergeant Mattatussu had no friends in the Detachment, with the exception of Specialist Tonelli, who it was said could get along with anybody.

It was no surprise to anyone that the first suspect for the Aplan leak in the minds of Lieutenant Smith, First Sergeant Toomey, and Warrant Officer O'Malley was the disgruntled Osi Mattatussu. He was just the kind of sullen malcontent who couldn't really be trusted not to jump over to the other side.

Toomey decided that it was long past the time when they should start keeping a special eye on Mattatussu, and now this would be his own pet project.

The night before Lieutenant Ryan's trip to Vienna, German Section Chief, Mitch Blake, and his deputy, Warren Olney, sat in a dimly lit booth in 'Oscars,' a German pub which catered to Americans. Their moods matched the lighting conditions.

Blake slowly stirred the ice in his Scotch rocks with his pinky while gazing into its opaque murkiness, as if expecting it to yield-up answers to the questions weighing on his mind.

"I'll be damned. Why in hell would the old man send a peach-fuzzed lieutenant out to Vienna at this critical time? If what he was worried about was protecting his protégé, LeBron, he could have gone to you or me. Art has got to be basking in glory. Kryptonite is *his* now. He is being fast-tracked by the CO, and I won't be surprised if he is the first ever here to get his GS-15. Meantime, you and I, supposedly heading-up the flagship section of the Unit, will be eating his dust. What a load of horse shit!"

Across the table from Blake, Olney sat shrouded in an inscrutable and silent stillness.

At the Max that night, the CO had summoned polygraph operator, Glenn Belson, who now stood before him.

"Sergeant Belson, in case we bring someone in out of the cold over the next few days, be available at your quarters in the evenings and be ready to put him on the box."

"Yes, sir."

Mal Rhymes stared out the window of the taxi at the State Opera, the Burgtheater, and the other majestic buildings set back along the Ringstrasse, Vienna's main boulevard. The imposing structures were set behind broad and deep expanses of landscaped lawns, interspersed with stately gardens. On the opposite side of the Ringstrasse was one charming sidewalk café after another, doing a robust business in their specialties — Viennese pastries and rich coffee.

Something of a history buff, Rhymes knew most of the major historical facts of Vienna — its origins, dating back as far as 500 B.C. and its epic struggles over the centuries to survive against invading hordes of barbarians, and the armies of the Ottoman Empire. Its close proximity to

Czechoslovakia and Hungary made it a gateway to the East; and it had first been a bastion for the defense of the eastern edges of the Roman Empire. It had later become capital of the Holy Roman Empire of Charlemagne and his descendants.

In the 1400s, under the influence of the Hapsburg Dynasties, the city had evolved into a cultural center for the arts, sciences, and music.

Vienna had been largely rebuilt and restored to its former grandeur after the Russian Army had destroyed sizeable portions of the city in wresting it away from the Nazis in 1945. Since then, mostly under the governance of the Social Democratic Party, it had survived as Austria's capital — its largest and by far most important city.

Lonnie Ryan was too preoccupied to take much notice of the sights. He thought he had caught sight of a black sedan pulling out behind their taxi when they had left the train station. He had glimpsed a black sedan pulling up alongside them at a traffic light, though he could not be certain that it was the same car.

He gave the cab driver the address of 14332's residence, which he understood was in one of the forty some-odd villages incorporated within the city limits during the mid-nineteen hundreds.

The colonel had given him only the sketchy outlines of Operation Kryptonite, consistent with his need to know. Although the colonel didn't say so specifically, Lonnie gathered that Kryptonite was big; that it was part of a multi-nation project, and that Army Intelligence was only one of several agencies involved.

Since taking over Ops Support, Lonnie had gathered from reading his section's case officer reports, before they went to Ops, that Prague, Czechoslovakia played prominently in Kryptonite.

Each report was totally compartmentalized, and it was difficult to discern a common thread running through them. But if there *was* a common thread, it seemed to be that agents controlled by the 409th in Vienna and other areas of Austria were part of a network of operatives with each one, identified by a number only, having a counterpart in Prague. The reports contained no clue to the objective of Kryptonite, or how that objective was being pursued.

His and Rhymes' mission was simple — go to 14332's house and re-establish a line of communication with him (if possible), with Rhymes as the agent's case officer. If 14332 did not answer the door, make a surreptitious entry through the back door, gather whatever evidence might exist as to his whereabouts or what had become of him, and then quickly leave.

What Lonnie did *not* know was how vital a role 14332 played in Kryptonite, or that Rhymes would be his case officer only until he could be turned over to a more senior man.

The taxi pulled up in front of a charming cottage in an out of the way neighborhood on the very fringes of the city limits. They exited quickly as Lonnie paid the driver in Austrian schillings, adding a generous tip. This prompted a friendly "danke" and "guten nacht" from the taxi driver.

Lonnie then paid him an additional gratuity and asked him to return in one hour. He calculated that the promise of even more schillings would ensure the driver's return.

Lonnie and Mal approached the front door. There was still plenty of daylight but it would begin to give way to darkness soon. Outwardly neither of them displayed any signs of nervousness, but each could sense the other's tension. There were a few cars parked on the short block but no traffic. It was fitting that a spy should have found such a quiet neighborhood for himself.

There was no car in the driveway and no garage, but this was not a surprise. The CO had briefed them on how 14332 eschewed automobiles, and had never owned one. The public busses suited all his needs.

There was no doorbell, only a bronze doorknocker molded in the shape of a bearded man in a pointed Tyrolean hat.

Lonnie knocked on the door, giving it three emphatic raps. No answer and no signs of any activity inside. After a minute or so, he rapped again — this time with greater force. Still no response.

After a third series of even louder raps yielded no better result, Lonnie looked at Mal: "He may just be out, but we have our orders. Let's go."

The rudimentary lock-picking tools provided to Rhymes by Mattatussu over the supply room counter were more than equal to the task of picking the simple tumbler lock of the back door. There were no bolts, chains or combination locks. 14332 had always figured that if Hostile ever showed up at his door, no locks would keep them out. He didn't own a gun either. Ultimately, a gun would provide him with no protection against professional assassins.

For two decades 14332 had effectively protected himself while conducting intricate espionage operations, building a formidable network of spies under his control. To accomplish this, he had employed two weapons: anonymity and ordinariness. He was so ordinary in every aspect, so unprepossessing, that when he took the bus to downtown Vienna, most of his fellow passengers never even noticed him getting on or off. He had no wife, children, girlfriends, or social friends. His only friends were his agents, and one former case officer who he knew only as

Mr. Winters. At the 409th, this friend was called by his real name, Arthur LeBron.

It would, however, appear that 14332's protective weapons had finally been overcome. As Sergeant Rhymes pushed open the back door, he and Ryan were instantly assaulted by the unmistakable stench of decaying flesh. Each of them immediately took a handkerchief from his pocket and held it over his mouth.

The master spy's decomposing body was sitting straight up on the kitchen floor with his back leaning against the refrigerator, supported and kept from falling over sideways by the overhang from the kitchen stove.

From the advanced stage of decomposition, it looked as if the agent had been dead for several weeks.

Ryan turned on the overhead kitchen light and quickly walked to the corpse, almost choking from the overwhelming smell. He and Rhymes had been prepared for just this eventuality. The extent of decomposition would have made facial identification all but impossible; but even if he had been dead for only a couple of minutes, it wouldn't have mattered.

Agent 14332 never allowed himself to be photographed, so no known picture of him existed. Only two people with the 409th had ever seen him face to face, Reitenhauser and LeBron, but any description they might have provided to Ryan and Rhymes would have been useless. Agent 14332 was always in disguise when either of them met him, and he never wore the same disguise twice.

Anonymous in life, he was now even more anonymous in death. Identification had always been established between 14332 and his agent handler by a pre-determined exchange of bona fides. Such an exchange would have occurred in this instance between the agent and Rhymes, if they had found the man alive. But the colonel had instructed them on how they could identify 14332 if they found him dead.

One evening in 1956 in Budapest, Reitenhauser and 14332 had drowned their sorrows over the brutal suppression of the Hungarian revolt by the Soviets, with a quart of Vodka. During their drunken conversation, 14332 had revealed one fact about himself to Reitenhauser — a lapse which had never occurred before, and would never happen again. During the 1943 siege of Stalingrad, 14332, then a young Wehrmacht corporal, had taken a piece of shrapnel from Russian artillery in the left ankle, which had left an elongated, though jagged scar. His defenses loosened by drinks, the agent had proudly displayed the scar to Reitenhauser. The next day, he hadn't remembered the display. Reitenhauser had never forgotten it.

Before getting down to work, Lonnie and Mal opened all the windows. Then lifting 14332's left pant leg and gently pulling down his sock, Ryan inspected the left ankle. There had been some breakdown of tissue, but not enough to obliterate the four inch scar still clearly visible on the ankle.

Ryan quickly withdrew a Minox camera from his jacket pocket and snapped two pictures of the scar, and two more of the entire corpse.

While Ryan knelt next to the corpse and searched through its pockets, Rhymes searched the house for any files, documents, or other materials that might be relevant to the agent's work. He found nothing.

As Ryan expected, 14332's pockets were empty and he wore no watch or jewelry. Placing the tiny camera back in his pocket, he joined Rhymes in searching the house.

Agent 14332 had lived with the extravagance of a Trappist Monk. His furniture consisted of a cheap kitchen table with four chairs, a living room couch with a standing lamp next to it, two cushioned chairs facing the couch, and a coffee table of rough wood.

In the adjoining bedroom, there was a single bed, a dresser, and a night stand with reading lamp,.

The one luxury the agent had allowed himself was a finished maple-wood book case in the living room, containing perhaps 150 volumes — mostly the classics.

The house had no basement and though there was probably an attic, there was no staircase or any other access to it. Agent 14332 appeared to have lived entirely on one floor consisting of three small rooms and a bathroom. There was no television, radio, or phone. There were, however, stacks of newspapers and news magazines everywhere.

Ryan perused the cottage a second time but also came up empty. Maybe Hostile had already found whatever might have been important, but Lonnie thought not. Agent 14332 had been murdered by a single bullet to the back of the head and his body had been placed in the sitting position in which Rhymes and Ryan had found him — probably a sign of professional respect to a worthy adversary.

Not a single thing in the house appeared to have been disturbed. The killing had all the earmarks of a professional hit by assassins dispatched to terminate 14332 quickly and efficiently; and then leave.

Lonnie silently gazed about the rooms several times. "The books are the key," he said. "If 14332 left anything for us, intentionally or inadvertently, it's in one of those books. Looks like we're going to have to go through every one of them. You take the top three shelves and I'll take the bottom two. Don't bother looking for things written on the pages themselves. We don't have that kind of time. Just search for loose papers or objects inserted between the pages. Okay lets hit it."

Both men had fashioned their handkerchiefs into bandannas, wet them down at the bathroom sink and tied them around their heads with the widest portions covering their mouths. The stench was still overpowering but the bandannas provided some relief.

Ryan sat on the living room floor with a pile of books next to him and began leafing through the pages. After twenty minutes, neither of them had found a thing. Then an illumination flashed across the surface of his mind. "Hold it! Mal, help me out here. What was LeBron's private nickname for 14332?"

Mal Rhymes was famous at the 409th for his incredible powers of recall, and Lonnie could see by the distant expression on his face that Rhymes' mind had shifted into memory mode. No more than a couple of seconds later, the hard-drive of his brain spit out the answer: "Queequeg."

"Attaboy Rhymes!"

Ryan jumped up and pulled a thick volume from the shelves, 'Moby Dick.' According to LeBron and Reitenhauser, it had been Agent 14332's favorite book. And Queequeg had been the agent's favorite character.

Holding the book by its spine, Ryan gently shook it. A single sheet of lined 8 ½ by 11 paper folded once in the middle floated to the hard wood floor. Ryan pulled a pair of rubber gloves from his jacket pocket and put them on before picking up and opening the paper.

Rhymes did the same, and they took turns examining it. The paper appeared to be blank but both men knew from their training that 14332 had written on it with invisible ink.

Rhymes then produced a folded soft plastic report cover from his breast pocket and carefully placed the piece of paper within it. Ryan took the plastic cover from him and placed it inside a copy of '*Der Spiegel*' which he had quickly bought at the Bahnhof.

"Great Job, lieutenant. I'm glad we have at least *one* well-read man with the unit."

"I'm glad we have one with a photographic memory," responded Ryan.

The two men had little left to do. Keeping the rubber gloves on, they laid out 14332's decomposing body on the kitchen floor and placed over it a large plastic garbage bag they found under the kitchen sink.

Next, they removed their gloves and put them on top of the plastic bag. They put the books back on the shelves, and straightened up whatever had been disturbed during the house search.

When they got back to the Bahnhof, Lonnie would find a pay phone and call the number of the safehouse, which he had committed to memory.

The only words he would speak were "Daughtry here. The package needs to be picked up."

A team would immediately be dispatched from the safehouse in a refrigerated truck bearing Austrian plates, to Agent 14332's residence. They too would enter the house from the rear, remove the body, re-lock the door and transport the corpse back to the safehouse where it would be stored in a meat locker until it could be moved to a nearby BOSS laboratory for autopsy and further testing. Two nights later, a very brief, private and secret ceremony would be held at the 409th, in memoriam for a fallen comrade.

Ryan and Rhymes washed their hands thoroughly at the bathroom sink and with Ryan carrying the copy of *Der Spiegel* only, they walked as quietly as possible out the back door and re-locked it. As they walked around the right back corner of the house, they saw that the taxi was parked on the street in front with the engine running and the lights on. It was fifty three minutes since the driver had dropped them off.

"I told you he'd be back" whispered Lonnie.

"With the extravagant tip you gave him, who wouldn't?" replied Rhymes.

Both of them were upbeat and definitely feeling a buzz from the combination of adrenaline and natural excitement. It was true that discovering 14332's body was an unpleasant shock. But it wasn't as if they knew him, and after all, they had found the promising sheet of paper. Now, even the compliant cabbie was waiting for them with the engine running. The mission was literally going off like clock work.

Mal opened the curb-side back door of the cab and got in while Lonnie walked around the front to the driver's side. The cabbie had his cap pulled down over his eyes and at first glance through the closed window, appeared to have dozed off. But something was not quite right. Lonnie had no opportunity to ponder this further because his next sensation was one of sharp pain as he crumbled and fell to the ground from a blow to the back of his head.

Seeing Lonnie go down Mal quickly slid over to the street side of the cab and opened the door. He was met there at face level by the front end of a silencer attached to a Beretta.

"Do not move," was the command hissed by a shadowy figure with some sort of an Eastern European accent.

He heard the other back door being opened but simultaneously caught sight from the corner of his eye of a figure darting in front of the cab towards the driver's side. Lonnie was silent, and Mal from his seated position with a gun in his face, had no move he could make.

For a few seconds, everything was blanketed by a discordant silence, which only added to Mal's sense of dread and the horror he felt at seeing his colleague go down. Then the suffocating silence was pierced by a muffled but clearly audible report of a silencer, followed immediately by two more muffled gun shots in quick succession. Then, more paralyzing silence. Mal's dread was now mixed with grief over the shooting of Lonnie Ryan.

Mal uttered a quick and silent prayer as he awaited a similar fate. But the silence continued and the Beretta was no longer pointed in his face. He felt a new emotion almost imperceptibly begin to mix with his horror, dread and shock... A sense of incipient hope.

The silence continued for several more seconds, which to Mal Rhymes were widened into an eternity. Then, another darkly-clad figure appeared where only seconds before had stood the menacing stranger with his weapon in Mal's face.

The new figure quickly dragged an obstruction away from the street in front of the open car door and helped Mal out of the cab. To his right was another individual kneeling over Lonnie's prostrate form. Lonnie seemed to be moaning softly on the ground and Mal was instantly filled with relief that he was still alive. Mal, still in a shock-filled daze, looked about and saw that the obstruction dragged away from in front of the rear car door was a body laying totally still about five feet away from the door. A second lifeless form was on the ground a few feet away from Lonnie. The two men still standing wore black ski masks.

As soon as Rhymes recovered enough to speak, he blurted out a few rapid fire words, as he pointed to the opposite side of the vehicle, "There's another one!"

The masked figure who had helped him out of the cab, replied in a soft but somewhat familiar voice, "No, he's been taken care of."

Mal dashed around the back of the car and found a third motionless figure lying face down on the sidewalk. When he returned, his apparent rescuer had joined the other man, they had lifted Lonnie back on his feet and were helping him take a few tentative steps. The man who had attended to Lonnie now looked at Mal and spoke softly but urgently, "Let's go! We have to get out of here. I'll lead the way...you two help this guy walk."

But before doing anything Mal picked up the *Der Spiegel* magazine and quickly checked to be sure the covered sheet of paper was still inside. It was.

Mal grabbed Lonnie under one of his arms, with the larger of the two masked men supporting him under the other. The other rescuer took the point with weapon drawn as they walked towards another vehicle parked a good fifty yards behind the cab. As they slowly walked away, Mal eyed the man on the ground.

"Don't worry," said the point man, "They're all dead. Raptor can cross off three more names from their roster. The cabby's dead too."

Despite the point man's bravado, none of them felt out of danger yet.

In the smaller of the 409th's two conference rooms, the colonel sat at the head of the table with a telephone in front of him. Also seated at the table were O'Malley, LeBron, Booker, Blake, Olney, Smith, and Toomey. It was 2330 hours, and there was still no word from Vienna.

Tension permeated the atmosphere of the room. The CO had decided to include Blake and Olney in the meeting because he had sensed their alienation and wanted to bring them back into the loop. He needed all personnel fully integrated and engaged by the unit's huge challenges with both Kryptonite and Raptor. Toomey was included because those were his boys out there, possibly in harm's way, and he had a right to be on the scene.

The phone finally rang at 2345 hours. Reitenhauser picked up the receiver and listened for about three minutes, poker-faced and betraying no emotions. He finally said "Thank you" to the caller, and hung up.

The others stared at him in tense anticipation.

"Agent 14332 is dead. Our boys are all right. Hostile has taken casualties. Our case officers will be returning with a package. Lieutenant Smith, I want you to meet our boys at the Munich Bahnhof with two armed security guards, escort them back here and take custody of the package under controlled conditions. Agent 14332's body has been retrieved, and will go to BOSS for processing tomorrow. There has been one civilian fatality and we have that body also."

Relief was etched on the faces of the men in the room. LeBron felt sad about 14332, but this was war and the agent was a soldier who knew the risks and was not afraid to die. The important thing was that the 409th's men were okay and, hopefully, what they were bringing back would be of value.

"Now, I have a brief announcement," said the colonel. "Changes have been made. Major Barnstable has been transferred to Fort Holabird, where he will hold the position of Assistant Dean of the Army Intelligence School and senior instructor. He is already back in CONUS[*] and will

---

[*] Continental United States

report to Holabird tomorrow. Chief Warrant Officer Ted O'Malley has been issued a direct Commission by General Stansfield as a captain, and — effective today — is the unit's new Operations Officer. Lieutenant Anders Smith is our new Deputy Operations Officer. Congratulations men."

"That will be all... Dismissed."

The men rose, extended their congratulations to O'Malley and Smith, and filed out of the room.

During one memorable session, the soldiers and civilians seated at the conference table had shared anxiety; learned that their colleagues in Vienna were safe but that a great man and valuable resource was dead; and were informed that a colleague was gone from their presence but that two others had been elevated to key positions. Yet none of them outwardly displayed any of the emotions that most of them were feeling.

The intelligence field did not leave much room for emotion. It was not because its operatives grew calloused from the job. It had to do more with what the job demanded they carry within themselves — endless secrets they could never reveal to anyone, coupled with a unique awareness which those outside of the game did not possess, that of the daily, minute by minute, life and death struggle of global dimensions between the power-crazed and ruthless of the world — the Hitlers, Stalins, Tojos, Himmlers, Mussolinis — and everyone else on the planet. The burdens and singular challenges of espionage and counter-espionage usually left no time or room for the display of emotions.

Chapter Seven

Into the Breach

With the slow-moving Lonnie in tow, it took Mal and his two masked rescuers a good five minutes to reach the vehicle. The self-designated point-man's eyes darted in all directions, and Mal noticed that the other rescuer had his weapon drawn and at the ready. The two protectors were dressed identically in black jeans and t-shirts. They wore black sneakers as well.

By the time they reached the car, Lonnie was somewhat improved and able to walk on his own, albeit unsteadily. His jumbled thoughts were beginning to clear, and he remembered the basic facts of what had just happened. The sharp, throbbing pain in the back of his head helped clear away the haze from his mind and curb the powerful urge to fall asleep.

The four men reached the car and Lonnie leaned against it to steady himself while one of the rescuers unlocked the driver's side door.

After slapping himself hard in the face, Lonnie spoke to the other man. "Who are you guys?"

"We'll tell you in the car."

"Not good enough," Lonnie said. "You tell me *now*."

"Look, we have no time for that now."

Lonnie stood his ground: "Either you tell us now, or we don't get in the car." The tone of crisp command in his voice left no room for debate.

The taller of the two rescuers removed his mask first and Lonnie and Mal had just enough moonlight to recognize his face. Their surprise was total.

"Good evening sir," said Supply Sergeant Osi Mattatussu.

Ryan and Rhymes were speechless as they watched the second man remove his mask.

"Specialist Tonelli at your service, sir."

Still in a state of semi-shock, Lieutenant Ryan spoke one word only as he signaled Rhymes to get into the back seat. "Incredible."

He lingered for a few seconds, staring at each man's face, and then wordlessly climbed into the front passenger seat.

*   *   *

The drive back to the Bahnhof was uneventful and before Lonnie and Mal climbed back on the Orient Express for the return trip to Munich, Lonnie made his phone call to the safehouse.

Mattatussu and Tonelli, now dressed in slacks and collared sport shirts, stayed close to Ryan and Rhymes until the latter two climbed aboard the train. They then seemingly evaporated into the pungent train station air as quickly and silently as they had materialized in front of 14332's house.

Neither Lonnie nor Mal believed that either of their protectors would ever be seen at the 409th offices again. That was true. At the 409th, their covers were now blown. None of the four men could possibly have predicted how intertwined their fates would be in the future.

Once Ryan and Rhymes had settled in their seats and had their passports ready for inspection — declaring that they were 'Daughtry and Simms' — Lonnie gazed out the window. He almost expected to catch a glimpse of the two fleeting apparitions who had just saved them from at least capture, and possibly torture and death.

He spoke mainly to himself, admiringly, and too softly to be heard, "Now I know why they call guys like them 'spooks.'"

1945

By late August of 1945, Uri had mostly recovered from his wounds and was back to work. He and Fred continued to make dramatic discoveries of Nazi atrocities and genocide. They even recovered an 8mm film showing the mass hanging of so-called Jewish trouble-makers at the Bergen-Belson concentration camp.

On September 9, 1945, they both received official orders from their respective commands that they were to be part of an elite joint-command investigative team charged with organizing, evaluating, and categorizing the evidence which would be presented against the surviving top Nazi leaders at the international war crimes trial scheduled for late November, 1945. By then, Hitler, Himmler and Goebels were dead; Bormann was believed dead; and Eichmann and other top Nazis had escaped to South America. But, there was still Goring, Hess, Speer, Von Ribbentrop and a host of lesser lights to put on trial.

Fred and Uri began putting in sixteen hour days almost as soon as they arrived at Nuremberg on September 10th, and began work at the Palace of Justice, the site of the International Military Tribunal.

Although Uri never complained, Fred could see that he had not recovered his strength enough to fully handle the grueling work schedule.

And there was no end in sight. The trials, especially the first one of the top 22 Nazis, were expected to last for months.

Uri's father had just been named Deputy Komisar for the Caucasus, and now was in charge of the Soviet Union's richest oil region. A rising star in the Party, he could easily have arranged an easier assignment for his son; but Uri was totally committed to his present work and wouldn't hear of it. Both he and Fred were acutely aware of the rare opportunity they had been given to be both witnesses to history, and contributors to the effort to right the horrific imbalance of justice imposed upon the world by the Nazis and their cohorts.

Fred would occasionally find Uri dozing over a long table piled high with eye-witness affidavits, official reports, handwriting analyses, photographs, finger print and hair samples, hand-written letters, film canisters, typed correspondence on the letterhead of the Third Reich, and many other varieties of documentary and physical evidence.

Uri would often awaken to find that a particular tedious task he had been working on had been completed by Fred. He would return to his work without comment, but with unspoken gratitude. A bond of friendship, fortified by a common cause, had formed between these two men from radically different backgrounds. It was a bond which would never be broken.

1967

Ben was prepared to take a train to meet Melissa in the Black Forest but when he pulled weekend duty as the armed guard of the unit's yet-to-be installed new crypto machine, he had to bow out. But all was not lost; Tom who had daytime duty, traded with Ben who had nights, and Melissa grabbed a flight from Frankfurt to Munich. Ben's Ops Support section chief, Lieutenant Ryan, allowed him to sign out the unit's Opel Kadet to pick up Melissa at the airport.

At 1100 hours on a Saturday in mid-July, Ben waited nervously at the domestic arrivals gate. He had not seen Melissa in two and a half years and that thought, together with the shaky state of their relationship when they had parted, filled him with anxiety. He now knew that he had never stopped loving her, but was not sure she felt the same way about him.

How would he greet her? With a kiss, just a hug, or *what*? What were they to each other now? Lovers, ex-lovers or simply old friends?

Mercifully, he didn't have to torture himself much longer because passengers began streaming through the exit gate. Ben caught sight of Melissa when she was still about a hundred feet away. She carried no suitcases, just a knapsack strapped on her back.

In the fashion of the late 1960s, she wore blue jeans, moccasins, and a buckskin jacket. Her jet black hair was long and straight, falling well below her shoulders. She had what appeared to be some sort of colorful tribal beads around her neck and wore an understated pink lipstick, but no other make-up. She looked spectacular.

Ben did not have to agonize any longer about how he should greet her because as soon as they came together, Melissa wordlessly threw her arms around Ben's neck and delivered a long and ardent kiss on the lips. Ben was instantly swept away. All the loneliness, regret, and self-disdain of the last two and a half years seemed to dissolve in that one lingering and passionate kiss.

When their lips finally parted, Melissa, seeing how moved and temporarily disordered Ben was from the intensity of their greeting, spoke first. "I see you're still wearing the 'know thyself' pendant."

Ben simply nodded once. "You look great."

"You look pretty great yourself. I didn't realize how much I missed you until I saw you standing there waiting with that silly Washington Redskins cap on your head."

"Melissa, I am really sorry about what you had to go through with that note incident. Are you okay?"

"I'm fine. I needed a break anyway from babies with distended bellies, children dying from cholera, and adults massacring each other over stupid tribal rivalries."

"But still, you shouldn't have had to go through that. I feel responsible and a little guilty about it."

"Ben, forget it. I made you feel guilty enough in the old days for one lifetime."

"Well, I had that coming."

"That's not true. I had no right to judge you. Anyway, how are you?"

"A lot better now that you're here. But I'm okay. I guess I'm kinda finding a niche for myself here in Army Intelligence. I've learned that the war over here and in many other places didn't really end when the shooting stopped. All that really happened is a new cast of characters put on the black hats."

"And what color hat do you wear Ben?"

"White... most *definitely*."

"I think so too," said Melissa as she put her arm inside Ben's and they walked happily toward the parking lot.

Because Tom switched duty assignments with Ben, *he* — not Ben — would be sleeping on a hard cot Saturday and Sunday nights at the

Detachment in a windowless room with only a telex machine and a .38 revolver for company.

Such was the strength of Tom and Ben's friendship that Tom broke his date with the lovely Kate Drummond for Saturday night just to help out his friend. And Ben had not even asked him for the favor. It was strictly Tom's idea, and he never once wavered in keeping his promise.

Kate understood once Tom explained some of the background of the long but uneven relationship between Ben and Melissa. She already knew about Melissa's bogus abduction through the unit's grapevine. As a strong and secure young woman, Kate did not feel at all threatened by the situation and she and Tom postponed their date until Wednesday night.

The U.S. Army's intelligence operation in West Germany was reeling from the twin shocks of the death of the highly valued Agent 14332, and the revelation by means of the Aplan incident that hostile agencies had penetrated Group's internal security division. What was even worse was that after a six week intensive investigation, Group was no closer to discovering the source of the leak. Although Group had several suspects, it lacked real proof of complicity by any of them.

As a result, General Stansfield was forced to order the entire security division to stand-down until the mystery was solved. U.S. Army Europe and Seventh Army simultaneously created a temporary internal security section composed of investigators from its Criminal Investigations Division (CID). A crash program was instituted. Agents from the Five-O-Deuce in Washington, D.C. worked around the clock doing background checks on the candidates selected, so that they could be issued provisional top secret clearances.

Simultaneously, the candidates were required to attend a three week, twenty-one day, total immersion counter-intelligence course at the I.G. Farben Complex. The legendary instructor, Captain Ted O'Malley, was selected as one of the teachers, and had to fly to Frankfurt every Friday afternoon and return Sunday night after conducting classes on Saturdays and Sundays.

This new demand on O'Malley's time could not be allowed to interfere with his duties at Munich station as Operations Officer, given the fact that the 409th was on the cutting edge of Operation Kryptonite. Both Reitenhauser and Higher were very firm on that point.

The stoic and stalwart Eva O'Malley took the news in stride. To European women of her generation, who had suffered so much during World War II and the post-war years, this was only a minor inconvenience. Anyway, it was only for three weeks.

The irrepressible Ted O'Malley was having the time of his life. He wouldn't even celebrate his 40th birthday until December, and now he was playing a vital role in two exercises of critical importance — the re-tooling of Group's internal security operation, and Operation Kryptonite.

Upon O'Malley's elevation to Operations Officer of the 409th, Art LeBron took over the training of the highly-touted Tallifierro and Berger, both of whom had been promoted to the rank of corporal.

The difficult challenges faced by both Group and the 409th were only heightened by the BOSS-prepared transcript of the 14332 document retrieved by Lieutenant Ryan and Sergeant Rhymes.

It seemed that the cover for 14332 and his network of over twenty agents had been the Vienna branch of the Philatelists Society, the largest organization of stamp collectors in the world. The paper, written entirely in 14332's hand, in invisible ink was a list of the names and addresses of each of the twenty two members of the so-called 'Vienna Chapter' of the Society. If the listed agent was dead, vanished or no longer operational for any reason, 14332 had simply written next to his name, "membership inactive." The names were all cover-names of course, but the addresses were accurate.

The restored handwriting of 14332 had been verified from other handwriting exemplars in Group's possession. The document was unquestionably authentic, and the news it delivered was shocking. Of the twenty-four agents listed, including the 'Chapter President,' Agent 14332 himself — known to the Chapter by the cover name, Horst Berkenfeld — only five were listed as still active. The rest had apparently been either liquidated, kidnapped, compromised; had defected, died, or been deactivated for some other reason.

Agent 14332's network had formed the core group of Kryptonite. The inescapable conclusion to be drawn from the document was that the program had been gutted, and was no longer viable. Recent Kryptonite reports emanating from top agents in Budapest, Bratislava, Dresden, Krakow, Bucharest, Sarajevo and other cities, were now suspect. The entire United States and NATO intelligence effort in Eastern Europe had been dealt a devastating blow. Added to this was the serious security breach in Frankfurt.

Still, it might not be too late to restore and revitalize the Kryptonite program. Clearly, however, it was time to regroup.

On August 27, 1967, a special top secret meeting of all military intelligence station chiefs in West Germany was held, presided over by General Stansfield. Even the two Navy Intelligence station chiefs from

Bremerhaven and Hamburg were in attendance, as was NATO's G-2 from the Hague, Lieutenant General Parsons Wells.

Fred Reitenhauser, who had just been promoted to full-bird colonel, caught an 0800 flight out of Munich Airport on the 17th, with Gerda in tow. He wanted to make sure that a full account of each session of the conference could be dictated immediately to Gerda upon its completion, in one of the many small conference rooms available to the attendees.

The conference was shrouded in secrecy. To avoid as much press attention as possible, it was held not in Frankfurt, but in the historic city of Heidelberg. It was scheduled to last twelve hours, broken down into three four-hour sessions, beginning at 1000 hours and ending at 2200 hours.

The day-long conference was interrupted by one meal served at 1530 hours. Coffee and pastry were available throughout the day. By the time the press got wind of the conference, it was over and the participants were on their way back to their respective home bases.

Much to his surprise, Colonel Reitenhauser was directed upon his arrival at the conference to report immediately to General Stansfield. Unlike the other station chiefs, he spent the entire twelve hours in executive session with Generals Stansfield, Wells and their staffs, further underscoring the vital role Munich Station was to play in the planned restoration of the crippled Operation Kryptonite.

Gerda could hardly contain her excitement. A career woman who had hitched her star to Fred's skyrocketing career, Heidelberg had been a major step up for both the colonel and herself. First there was her personal admiration for and dedication to the colonel. After six years as his executive assistant, she knew well what a remarkable man he was. Then there was her burning hatred for the Soviets and their henchmen in East Germany. As residents of East Berlin, Gerda's two closest cousins were trapped on the other side of the Berlin wall. She hadn't seen them since they were all in their early 20s.

Both Fred and Gerda were single, and that had led to the usual office rumors of a relationship between them that was more than just professional. Admittedly, Gerda had always been a little bit in love with the colonel, and suspected he might have feelings for her also. But anyone who knew them both well — a short list, involving no more than two or three intimates — also knew that they were both far too driven and much too professional to allow a personal relationship to intrude upon their shared vision-quest: the defeat of the Soviet bloc.

*　　　*　　　*

Several events were coalescing for the 409th, at roughly the same time. O'Malley's dual role as instructor and Operations Officer ended just before Labor Day Weekend, and the colonel gave him the three days off to recover from the grueling twenty-one day stint.

Although he would always be something of an odd-ball, Booker had shed some of his more eccentric tendencies. Fred suspected that the positive influence of Art LeBron was the cause of Booker's improvement.

The field training of Tallifierro and Berger was complete and, although the CO would have liked to see them do a stint in the minors, he didn't have that luxury. No, they would be thrown head-first into the major leagues — the big show.

Based at least in part on their impressive performance in Vienna, Lonnie Ryan received his first lieutenant's bars and Mal Rhymes was promoted to the rank of staff sergeant.

Sergeant Wanda Winicki became the Chief Telex Operator with Bob Scones as her assistant. The jobs of Company Clerk and Supply Sergeant were combined into one new position, that of 'Administrative and Supply Clerk.' The position was now jointly held by PFC Tyrone Davis, formerly the Assistant Motor Pool Clerk, and Corporal Bob Scones. Davis was promoted to corporal so that they would be co-equal in both rank and responsibilities.

Corporal Yancy 'Village' Cook was left in the motor pool. It wasn't that the CO believed Cook was anywhere near as dumb as he looked and acted. Reitenhauser simply did not trust the man, and figured he could do the least harm in the Motor Pool.

Despite wild speculation, mostly heard at the Max Shop, no one knew what had become of Mattatussu and Tonelli — that is, except Colonel Reitenhauser, and he wasn't telling anyone. Even General Stansfield, after satisfying himself from the colonel directly at Heidelberg that both agents were alive and well, asked no further questions. They were Reitenhauser's responsibility as far as the general was concerned. He didn't want to know where they had gone, or what they were up to. That way he could invoke 'plausible denial' in the event that the shadowy duo were caught committing some particularly outrageous deed.

Colonel Reitenhauser pressed the button of his desk intercom. "Gerda, get me O'Malley, Smith, LeBron, Booker, Blake, Olney, and Ryan. If they have anything else scheduled for this morning, tell them to cancel it."

Soon the summoned chiefs and their deputies were seated around the table in the large conference room, the use of which alone signaled big doings at hand.

It was 0905 hours on the Tuesday morning after Labor Day. A coffee maker sat on a side table, emitting the rhythmic and soft rumble of percolation and the wonderful aroma that went along with it.

The sense of excited anticipation in the room was palpable. Everyone present knew that an important meeting had taken place at Heidelberg and that O'Malley had now resumed his full-time duties at the 409th.

Of course, it was difficult to tell from the placid demeanor and poker-face of the colonel that anything new was at hand. He quietly sat at the head of the table, his glasses perched near the tip of his nose, peering at the lead column of the Army Times which had just arrived at the unit. The colonel's placid exterior however, did nothing to tamp down the enthusiasm of the men assembled. They knew the colonel's ways, and sensed that they would comprise the leadership team for an exciting new initiative.

"Good morning gentlemen," said the CO, looking up from his newspaper. We have a lot to cover so I won't waste any time with chit chat. (Translation: "You may have had a party-filled and long weekend, but I have no interest in any of that, so forget about it and let's get to work.")

"Ted, have you identified Ed Barnstable's files and verified that we have them all?"

"Yes, sir. But one of the files looks a bit suspicious to me. It has a label that appears to have been added recently. The file number is in sequence, but the label itself is too new to match the age of the file."

"What about that, Andy?"

"I don't know sir, I'll have to look into it," replied Lieutenant Anders Smith. Though Smith was now Deputy Ops, he had also retained his position as the unit's security officer.

"If you don't find the answer within twenty four hours, I want you to telex Major Barnstable at Holabird — eyes only — and ask him about it."

"Yes, sir."

The colonel then addressed all those present. "I have met with each of you privately and briefed you on a need to know basis as to recent developments in Austria, in Frankfurt at Group, in Heidelberg, and here at the 409th.

"Gentlemen, we find ourselves at a cross roads and the decisions we make and the way we implement those decisions could very well affect the outcome of the Cold War. The road we have chosen to travel — to reverse the recent setbacks suffered by United States Army Europe's intelligence initiative, and to advance Operation Kryptonite to a newer and higher level of performance — will be filled with every kind of obstacle we can possibly imagine. But we *must* succeed. The idea of defeat is unthinkable. If we fail, the international apparatus so carefully put in place over the past twenty years to ensure the security and viability of Western Europe will be severely compromised.

"So listen carefully to what I am about to tell you. This room was swept yesterday and is secure. You are to discuss what is said in this room with no one other than the eight of us. You will make no notes, either during or after this meeting. Should you violate this order, you will be prosecuted to the full extent of the law."

He paused for a second, looking at each face around the table. "Some of you know a few of the details about Kryptonite. Others know most of the details. None of you know all of the details. My briefing is geared to those who know little or nothing about the operation."

The CO continued. "Approximately a year ago, we received word through Agent 14332 that non-communist insurgents in Prague were making inroads in winning over government officials and industrialists to the cause of seeking to topple the Soviet-controlled regime in Czechoslovakia. The intent would be to replace Soviet rule with a non-aligned socialist regime, officially neutral but secretly sympathetic to NATO. This information was passed up the line, all the way to the Pentagon and the CIA at Langley. I am informed that it was authenticated, and deemed to be of high credibility. America's response to the news came, I am told, directly from the White House.

"The 409th was chosen for reasons I cannot disclose, to join with BOSS's Bavarian field station in a cooperative effort to conduct a multi-faceted program of espionage, subversion, insurrection, sabotage, blackmail, character assassination and, coup dé tát — if feasible — against the hard-line Communist government of Czechoslovakia. All of this to be worked in conjunction with the indigenous insurgency already in place.

"Several trips were made by case officers from the 409th — it is not necessary for you to know their identities — to meet with Agent 14332. He was already controlled by us, and engaged in highly important intelligence gathering missions, with a network of about a half-dozen sub-agents whom he had personally recruited.

"Agent 14332 enthusiastically embraced the program, Code-named Kryptonite, but his network was too small to handle it. So with one of our people acting as his control, we began an ambitious program to expand 14332's network. The plan was to run operatives across the Austrian-Czech border, to train, advise, and actively work with the Czech underground in order to subvert the present regime. Within a few months, 14332 had built his network up to almost 25 agents, all of whom he controlled under the umbrella of a cover organization, the Vienna Chapter of the Philatelists Society. A steady stream of his agents crossed the border and helped the Czech underground compromise the regime's internal security system. They bought many of its officials with U.S. dollars and British pounds, and blackmailed a number of its hard-line Communists — after supplying them with women and drugs — into betraying state secrets, resigning, or becoming operatives of the insurgency. They planted false stories, and true ones about other officials in the Prague Newspapers; revealing all sorts of unsavory information about them — pedophilia, homosexual dalliances, serial adultery, patronizing prostitutes, lying about their backgrounds, engaging in graft, and being closet capitalists." The list was unending.

"In the meantime, 14332's agents supplied the money and know-how to the local insurgents to plant favorable stories in the press and on television about anti-Soviet politicians seeking office. They also channeled funds to those politicians. One of them was an up-and-comer named Alexander Dubcĕk; and if all goes well, you will hear much more about him in the future.

"Things were falling into place for us, to an extent that we couldn't have imagined. The Czech government had become extremely shaky from the combination of scandal and internal subversion. Our success can be attributed to a few principal factors: the brilliance of 14332, the proximity of Vienna to the Czech border, the unique relationship between 14332 and his handler, together with certain other resources, which this unit alone possesses.

The CO paused again, and his voice took on a note of quiet gravity. "But then something went wrong. We don't know exactly *what*, but we believe we were betrayed at a high level. The Soviet Union initiated a counter-insurgency operation, code named 'Raptor.' Suddenly, 14332's agents started disappearing, and we began receiving photographs of them at our postal dead-drops, depicting the agents undergoing gruesome torture, including amputation of limbs and other body parts; beheadings, evisceration, and many other horrors.

The men around the table exchanged glances.

"A few months ago," the CO said, "14332 himself fell off the radar screen. Thanks to the productive mission of Lieutenant Ryan and Sergeant Rhymes we now know that he was assassinated and that his network of nearly 25 agents has now been reduced to no more than five.

The colonel's voice grew hard. "But we have been striking back aggressively since Lieutenant Ryan's June sojourn to Vienna. Our valuable resources under deep cover on the other side have revealed much to us about Raptor, and we are attacking it at many levels. Fortunately, that includes using some muscle over which Group has given us exclusive control. However, gentlemen, it is now imperative that we resurrect Kryptonite. And now I will tell you how we plan to go about it.

"Our moles have identified most of Raptor's top agents. They are broken down pretty much evenly among three cities: Vienna, Budapest, and Warsaw. Group is already busy taking out many of the agents in Warsaw, and has promised me that we will receive additional muscle to go after Raptor in Vienna and Budapest, which fall within our geographical sphere. Some of those Group people will have to be diverted from Raptor to provide security for our case officers, which leads me back to Kryptonite.

"Gentlemen, we are going to push forward, full bore, beginning today to rebuild 14332's network."

The CO looked at Ted O'Malley. "Ted, you will direct the in-house effort to review every single case officer report we have on 14332's meetings, to identify candidates to fill the vacant agent positions."

He shifted his gaze to Lonnie Ryan. "Lonnie, you have a massive index card file at Ops Support, listing hundreds of potential agents gathered by all our case officers. Your staff will have to go through the entire index and identify all possibles who live in Bavaria or Austria. Your people will then prepare a typed profile on each possible, while Ted's staff does the same for each of those potential agents listed in the case officer reports of 14332's meetings. The profiles will next be circulated through our Czech and German sections, to be enhanced or devalued by the addition of any information each of those sections has on the profiled candidates."

The CO's eyes moved to Booker. "The completed profiles will then go to Doug Booker. Doug, your job will be to evaluate all the profiles, cull out those you believe to be unsuitable, and prepare a typed dossier on each suitable candidate. Then you will deliver a copy of each dossier to me for final selection. Knowing your skills as an analyst, I am not likely to veto many of your choices."

Each of the three men nodded in turn.

"While this vetting process is in progress, we will dispatch a case officer team to Vienna to attempt to make contact with each of the five remaining active agents on 14332's list. The team will reconfirm the status of each agent, gather new leads, and assign one of our team members as the agent's new case officer. Each new or reconfirmed agent will receive six months wages in advance, as a sign of our good faith.

"The case officer team will consist of six men, working in two-man units. The first unit will be Rhymes and Berger. The second unit will be Olney and Tallifierro. A third unit will also go to Vienna, but will be held in reserve, waiting at the hotel until needed. That unit will consist of Ryan and Blaulicht."

Buck Sergeant Kurt Blaulicht was a case officer with the German section. Born in Germany and a naturalized United States citizen, he was completely fluent in German.

"Unit 3 will have a dual function. Lieutenant Ryan will be the officer in charge on location. Sergeant Blaulicht will be available in the event a German linguist is required.

"The officer in overall charge of the operation will be Ted O'Malley. His deputy will be Mitch Blake."

The colonel paused again. "Now some of you may not like this, but Messrs. LeBron, Blake and Booker were all U.S. Army Reserve Officers. I received word last night that — due to the emergency in which Group finds itself at the current time, and in order to avoid any command conflicts which might impede our critical mission — the Secretary of the Army has called all three of you to active duty. Effective immediately, you are all three back in the Army, with the rank of captain."

All three of the new active-duty captains were surprised, but not displeased about their new positions. Each felt a tinge of pride in his own way.

Doug Booker, who had resisted all efforts to make him an officer in Korea, had eventually been promoted to the rank of second lieutenant in the U.S. Army Reserves. Now suddenly he was an active duty captain. This afternoon he would make a visit to the post barber.

Finishing up, the CO moved his eyes from one side to the other, making direct eye contact with all present. "My final decision is that effective immediately, my new executive officer is Captain Art LeBron."

"Gentlemen, you are all on alert, until further notice. First Sergeant Toomey will deliver your orders to you this afternoon. Dismissed."

Sergeant Wanda Winicki had worked a long day in front of the telex machine. Her back hurt and she looked forward to a slow gin fizz back in her apartment with her feet up.

The traffic on the telex between Munich and Frankfurt today was especially heavy. She was thinking about asking Pete Toomey to get Scones to relieve her, but she knew that he too was busy with an imposing number of administrative tasks.

In fact, the entire unit buzzed with activity. Big things were happening. She just wished she knew what they were. Maybe she would stop for a sandwich at the Max Shop, to see if she could pick up some of the skinny on what was going on.

The telex began noisily typing away again. Wanda hoped it wouldn't be another three pager. She sat in a stupor as the machine typed out the usual heading of Group Headquarters, Frankfurt, West Germany. But as the noisy machine began printing out the reference line, she was instantly yanked from her stupor and gave her full attention to the communiqué: "Re: Major Edwin Barnstable, USAR."

Great! It was news about Ed Barnstable. She had been saddened by his sudden removal from the 409th. Their brief affair had not been one of the great romances of the 20th Century, but she still had some feelings for the guy.

Wanda suddenly felt herself being slammed against the back of her chair and held there motionless by some unseen force. Rendered immobile, she retained the capacity only to stare at the message before her.

```
------------------------------

Re: Major Edwin Barnstable, USAR

In    reply    to    your    attempts    to
communicate with subject, Be advised
Edwin Barnstable, Major USAR, expired
31  August  1967.    Cause  of  death
unknown.

Remains interred September 3, 1967.

------------------------------
```

Chapter Eight

Winds of Liberation

1946

By mid-December of 1945, with the trial of the top twenty-two Nazi leaders in full swing, Uri had regained most of the strength he had lost as a result of the shooting. But he knew that the only reason he was almost all the way back was because Fred had repeatedly covered for him, and taken up the slack when he was simply too weary to read another incriminating letter from the Fuhrer to Göring, or from Goebbels to von Ribbentrop.

None of this escaped the attention of the United States Chief Prosecutor, Robert H. Jackson. Jackson was well aware of the fact that Uri was not pulling his full load, but was perceptive enough to realize that the team of Putyagin and Reitenhauser was still the best investigation/ evidence prep team he had. The reason was simple: team work. The chemistry between the two men was exceptional. So what difference did it make that one of the team members worked harder than the other, so long as the job got done?

The other thing that Jackson noticed when the entire trial and investigations team would meet for a skull session in his office, at the end of the work day over sandwiches and beer, was that even in the midst of the most heated discussions over politics among members of the diverse national groups, Uri never argued against the Brits or the Americans. Of course, he never had anything negative to say about the Soviet government and spoke about the existing regime respectfully, but he was a lukewarm Marxist at best, and a Stalinist not at all. If anything, he was an internationalist with a global view of economics, world security and humanitarianism.

Jackson was certain that if it weren't for his powerful father, Uri Putyagin, the intellectual and idealist, would never make it in the Communist Party. In fact, without his father's influence, he might now be in Siberia or some place even worse. Nevertheless, he was a tough young soldier as was Reitenhauser, and Jackson needed both of them if he were going to bring home the major convictions and death sentences he was gunning for.

The trial dragged on through the winter and spring of 1946. For the most part things were going well, but not on a consistently upward trajectory. When the supremely self-confident Herman Göring took the stand and testified for more than a week, it was Göring and not Jackson who was the star of the proceedings. By constantly playing to the gallery with sly smiles and wisecracks, Göring virtually took over the courtroom. His co-defendants were delighted with Göring's performance, and their morale was at its high point. Göring was the unquestioned leader of the 'Nuremberg Twenty Two.'

From the balcony of the courtroom, Uri and Fred looked on. It was difficult to tell what the inscrutable Fred was thinking but there was no doubt about how Uri felt. He was seething with anger. Uri hated evil more than anything else in the world, and now here was evil incarnate, in the pudgy body of Herman Göring, seemingly carrying the day.

Jackson's cross-examination of Göring was largely ineffective, and the nasty snickering and sarcastic asides of the German Luftwaffe Commander and Reichsmarschall were getting more and more brazen, earning him appreciative laughter and applause from the other defendants.

Göring's day in the sun however, was only a temporary setback for the prosecution team. A regime having as its main premise the imperialistic conquest of the world and the murder of an entire race (along with anyone else who happened to get in the way), cannot hide its criminal deeds for long. The evidence was overwhelming and well-presented by prosecuting lawyers from the United Kingdom, the United States, the Soviet Union, and France.

After more than ten months, the trial of the twenty two finally ended on October 1, 1946. Jackson got his convictions. All but one of the twenty two were found guilty, and thirteen of them were sentenced to death by hanging. Those destined for the noose included Göring, Bormann, Jodl, Kaltenbrunner, and von Ribbentrop. Hess received a sentence of life imprisonment and Speer got twenty years. Göring cheated the hangman by poisoning himself in his cell the night before he was to be hanged.

Naturally, there was much celebrating over the convictions, and Fred and Uri did their share.

Soon transferred back to their permanent duty stations in West Berlin, they decided upon a quieter and more reflective dinner celebration back at the place where their friendship had first taken hold, the superb Allemagne.

Fred had noticed a brooding pensiveness in Uri since the war crimes tribunal had disbanded, and decided to ask him about it over their second liter stein of Lowenbrau. It was mid-October, 1946, but still warm enough to have their pre-dinner drinks on the patio.

"So what's troubling you, Comrade?"

Not one given to diffidence, Uri replied immediately, "Is it that obvious?"

"Probably not to everyone, but I've gotten to know your moods pretty well."

"All right my good friend, I will tell you. I am deeply troubled by the direction in which my homeland is headed. Stalin and his bunch of gangsters, after a great victory over the evils of Nazism, have learned nothing! Instead of working towards international peace and freedom, they have become just as imperialistic and tyrannical as the Nazis. Through military force they have subjugated the Baltic states, Poland, Czechoslovakia, Hungary, Albania, Yugoslavia, Bulgaria, Rumania and East Germany. I have it on good authority that they will lay siege to all of Berlin when the time is right, and they have serious designs on Greece, Turkey, and Iran. And this is only the beginning. Like Nazi Germany, the hard liners in the Kremlin have designs on the entire world. They would have grabbed Japan if you Americans had not gotten there first. At this very moment, they are working diligently to ensconce Soviet puppets in Korea and Indochina."

Fred nodded toward his friend, a gesture of understanding, as well as an invitation to continue.

Uri lifted his stein to his lips, but lowered it without drinking. "Things are equally bad at home. Stalin is incredibly paranoid. He is not only murdering his political rivals, but also anyone he suspects of being a rival. Now, he's going after anyone who *might* become a rival in the future."

The Russian officer shook his head sadly. "It's a blood bath. The KGB has extended its tentacles into every corner of life in Russia. They have managed to turn brothers against brothers, sons against fathers, and wives against husbands. Much of the population — at least that part not in deep denial — live in constant fear. The people are utterly oppressed. They lack even the most basic freedoms. It is an insidious tyranny — growing worse all the time."

Uri stared into the depths of his beer. "And Marx's famous *dictatorship of the proletariat*? What a joke that turned out to be! Modern Russia is a dictatorship of one man. One maniac, who is as crazy and vicious as Hitler ever was. And even his death won't end it. When Stalin goes, he will be replaced by another dictatorship. A few corrupt bastards sitting at the top of the pyramid — the small cabal who dominate the Communist party and the Politburo."

Fred was surprised neither by the depth of his friend's anger, nor the vehemence and passion with which the Russian expressed it.

"Well Uri..." he said softly. "Have you ever considered coming over to *our* side?"

Uri looked at him. "Of *course* I have considered it. I think about it all the time... But it is impossible. They would retaliate against my family. My father would be a dead man. I don't know what those monsters would do to the rest of my family, but I know they would suffer in ways that I can't begin to imagine."

The young Russian sighed heavily. "No, I cannot defect. The cost is simply too great. I will go back to Moscow in a couple of months, retire from the military, and take a position that my father is holding for me in the Department for Defense of the Soviet Republics."

Uri smiled weakly, and made a feeble attempt to change the subject. "How about you, Frederick? Do you have any plans?"

Fred nodded. "Remember the last time we were here together? I told you that I had no desire to go back to Nebraska. I still don't. I have pretty much made up my mind that I want to make the Army my career, and serve abroad. I'll go home soon for thirty days leave to visit my folks, my brothers and sisters and my friends. After that, I have orders for Army Intelligence School."

Uri pondered this news for a few seconds, taking several swallows of beer before responding. Finally, he nodded. "Frederick, we must never fall out of touch. But it might be wise if we conduct our future communications through an intermediary. Except for dire emergencies, of course."

Fred considered this, and nodded. "I agree."

Uri smiled. "Well, my friend, do you have any thoughts as to *who* might fill that role?"

Fred ruminated over the question while Uri ordered another round of beers. Their table inside was now ready and the beer would be served to them there.

Now Fred was the pensive one as they walked to their table; but not so distracted that he didn't first look around the room at the other patrons. Uri picked up the signal and slipped the maitre'd a ten mark note as he pointed to a distant corner table.

After placing their orders for dinner, Fred remained silent.

Uri, by far the more voluble of the two, began talking about his intended, the lovely and socially-connected Katrina Ivanovich

Borashevsky. They would marry and live on an estate outside of Moscow, where they hoped to have at least three children whom they would teach to ride at a very young age and…

"How about Horst?" interrupted Fred.

"Horst?" Horst *who*? What are you talking about?"

"As an intermediary."

"Horst. You can't be talking about that Austrian we played chess with in Nuremberg?"

"Yes I am."

A slight frown creased Uri's forehead. "All the man ever talked about was collecting stamps."

"Precisely my point," Fred replied. "Isn't stamp collecting one of your hobbies?"

"Yes," Uri said. "But Horst? What do you even know about the man?"

"A lot. Uri, do you really believe that my only function for the past year has been to search for evidence of Nazi war crimes? In the early days at Nuremberg when you would collapse on your bed from fatigue and I would go out, did you honestly think I was out partying? You know me better than that. Horst has already been cleared by OSS[*] and is on the payroll."

"Go no further," Uri said. "Your point is taken."

"Good. I will fill you in on the details before you leave for Moscow."

1967

Lonnie called Tom and Ben into his office right after the CO's briefing, and gave them their team assignments for Vienna. Then after their departure, he brought Staff Sergeant Rhymes in to brief him privately.

Tom grabbed Ben by the elbow as they walked out into the corridor. "Man, we've made the big time, Kimosabe," said Tom. He kept his voice down, so as not to betray his excitement to the whole unit.

"Right you are professor! Come on, I'll buy you a ptomaine burger at the Max Shop to celebrate."

"You're on, big spender."

During their rigorous training, first under the watchful eye of O'Malley and then LeBron, lunch had been a catch-as-catch-can proposition — often just an oversized soft pretzel and some radishes at the beer garden closest to wherever they happened to be when hunger struck. But now that they had something to celebrate, the two newest operatives gorged themselves

---

[*] Office of Strategic Services, the forerunner of the CIA.

on an unhealthy American meal of bacon-cheeseburgers, fried onion rings, French fries, and double thick vanilla malts. Maintaining strict discipline, however, they stuck to non-business topics during lunch.

Tom swallowed a bite of cheeseburger. "Heard from Melissa lately?"

"Yeah," Ben said. "We write each other about once a week."

"How are things going with you two?"

Ben gave a thumbs-up gesture. "A-okay, Houston, all systems are good to go." He smiled. "I guess she finally realized I'm not just another loser... That I've got some drive and purpose after all. If we can both get leave at the same time, we intend to fly to Rome for a long romantic weekend."

Tom grinned. "Careful there, Valentino. I don't want any Ben Juniors getting in the way of our assignments — not just when we're finally headed for the big show."

Ben shook his head. "That's not going to happen. Anyway, I could say the same thing about you and that Scottish lassie."

"You could, and I admit she is incredible," Tom said. "But we're nowhere near that kind of relationship. We're taking it slow."

"Good, I'll have enough to do on missions, watching out for your academic ass. The last thing I'll need is to have you distracted by love."

"Ben, I'll tell you what — we are two motivated hombres and when the bell rings, we'll be ready."

"Roger that professor."

News of Barnstable's death swept through the unit's offices like a prairie fire. Momentarily paralyzed by the shocking news, Winicki had quickly regained her composure and double-timed the typed message down to the CO's office.

"Gerda, this is code red — I need to get in there."

Without comment, the ever cool and professional Gerda rose from her chair quickly, walked to the colonel's door and gave it one loud rap, their prearranged signal for an emergency.

"Come in." Gerda and Winicki hurried through the door.

"Have a seat, Sergeant Winicki. Captain Blake and Warrant Officer Olney were just leaving."

Taking their cue from the CO, the two men followed Gerda out the door and closed it behind them.

Winicki rose and handed the colonel the telex message.

Even before reading it, Reitenhauser knew it was bad news, from the shock and grief registered on Winicki's expressive face.

The CO read the message quickly and then placed it on the desk in front of him. In an even voice he spoke to the obviously shaken Winicki.

"Wanda, thank you for your immediate action in bringing me this terrible news. I know you have lost a friend and for that please accept my condolences. Because we are not a combat unit, people sometimes forget that every now and then we too suffer terrible casualties."

The CO was clearly signaling that by no means did he consider Barnstable's death to be the result of either natural causes, accident, or suicide. He had learned to trust his instincts, which had never let him down and had enabled him to survive both a shooting war and the Cold War for twenty six years. His instincts now told him Barnstable had been murdered.

"Sergeant, please prepare the appropriate memo to the entire unit notifying them of Major Barnstable's passing. Gerda will contact the Protestant Chaplain and arrange for a non-sectarian memorial service to be held later today in the chapel here in the building. Her memo will advise all personnel as to the time but, subject to the Chaplain's availability, we'll do it at 1700. I am going to ask Art to give the eulogy."

Then, he dropped the formality from his voice and looking directly at Winicki, spoke to her softly. "Ed was one of us, and we owe him no less than that."

After sending Winicki on her way, Reitenhauser asked Gerda to come in, whereupon he told her the tragic news. Barnstable had been neither her favorite nor his, but neither one of them doubted the man's dedication and loyalty for even an instant.

But already a host of questions were insistently accosting Fred's mind, demanding answers. What had spooked Ed Barnstable so much that he had moved Heaven and Earth to get LeBron away from 14332? Why had he formed a vendetta against Doug Booker? How could he have panicked so much as to run a top secret security check on a Peace Corps volunteer in a tenuous relationship with a rookie case officer? And the biggest question; why was a substitute file jacket for 'Baker 55447,' left in the Ops filing cabinet with a brand new label, giving evidence of a recent substitution for some other file — the real 'B55447.'

"Gerda, please have Captains O'Malley and LeBron and Lieutenant Smith come in, ASAP."

Mitchell Blake and Warren Olney

Although lacking the eccentric brilliance of a Doug Booker and the all around talent of an Art LeBron, the team of Blake and Olney had competently run the German desk for six years. They may not have moved anyone with their inventiveness, but had done some fine intelligence work nonetheless. They had learned from their agents in Leipzig of Krushchev's plan to block open access between East and West Berlin more than a month before it had actually happened. This had enabled BOSS to extract over fifty of its agents from East Berlin, and as a result, preserve their viability as operatives and prevent their capture. The inevitable extraction of sensitive Western bloc secrets under torture would have followed had the agents fallen into Hostile's hands. Then the survivors of that process would have been given the choice of either becoming double agents, or standing before a firing squad.

The gregarious Blake and the taciturn Olney could not have been any more different in personality and background. Blake was 'old boy' network all the way. His parents, both successful physicians in Bethesda, Maryland, had set him on the path they had preordained for him — Exeter, Princeton, Cornell Medical School, and then a direct commission as a Navy physician. The problem was that Blake was unable to withstand the intellectual rigors of med school. He had dropped out just ahead of an invitation to leave, and was drafted just as the Korean War broke out. Through family connections, he had stayed out of the infantry, received a direct commission as a second lieutenant, and was assigned to serve under Willoughby, MacArthur's G-2, at the *Dai Ichi* Building, General MacArthur's headquarters in Tokyo.

Although Colonel Willoughby wasn't much of a role model, Blake applied himself and learned his trade well. After the war, he was transferred to Germany and worked effectively in area intelligence at Stuttgart and Mannheim. He left the Army as a captain in 1958 but immediately applied for a position as a civilian area intelligence specialist with Army Intelligence. He had been hired at the grade of GS-9.

Blake didn't make a lot of money, but didn't care. He loved intelligence work, and loved living in West Germany. He had found his true vocation.

Nevertheless, Blake's life was no utopia. He remained burdened by the social status pressure which was the legacy of his upbringing. With his Exeter-Princeton background, he really only felt comfortable socializing with the upper crust. This was the 1950s and there weren't too many social renegades. At a formal ball at the U.S. Embassy in Bonn, Blake met his future wife, the daughter of the CIA Station Chief at the Embassy, whose cover title was Chief Cultural Affairs Attaché. In the 1950s the CIA was rife with old money scions of Eastern bankers and industrialists — many from Yale and Harvard. Blake's new father-in-law was a prominent member of the 'old-boy' fraternity and his only daughter was used to having nothing but the best. Blake did have some of his own money and his wife had her trust fund; but it still was a constant financial struggle for them to keep up with their peers.

Blake and Olney had one common background link. They both were natives of the State of Maryland. It ended there. The son of a dock worker, Olney had grown up on the mean streets of Baltimore. He had quit school at seventeen to join the Army in 1953, shortly after the Armistice was signed at Panmunjom in Korea.

Opting for becoming an Airborne Ranger, he was stationed near the 38th Parallel where he began making top-secret reconnaissance jumps into North Korea. He soon caught the eye of 'black intelligence' operatives, and was assigned on a full-time basis to Special Ops. In 1958 he was transferred to Saigon as a special undercover operative charged with recruiting and leading anti-communist agents on missions of sabotage, kidnapping, and assassination against the communist Viet Minh, the forerunner of the Viet Cong.

Always a man who spoke his mind, Olney wore out his welcome in Saigon through his constant criticism of the corrupt Diem regime in South Vietnam, and the softness of its Army's intelligence service.

As a result in 1959 he found himself on a plane to West Germany. There, faced with constant conflict and crisis at the border with East Germany and at the line of demarcation between East and West Berlin, the U.S. Army needed men with his skills and audacity. By then Olney had attained the rank of Warrant Officer Third Class. USAR Europe officially transferred him to Army Intelligence and assigned him to its Munich station. In 1961 he was named by Colonel Reitenhauser as Deputy Chief of the German section. His promotion roughly coincided with the erection of the Berlin wall.

Given to dark moods and long brooding silences, Olney was the perfect counterpoint to Blake's sometimes overly sunny enthusiasm. Each was the antidote for the excesses of the other's personality, and a fine working balance developed between them. This not only worked well operationally, but was the foundation for a bond which grew between the two men. Though the quintessential odd couple, they became fast friends.

Nevertheless, whether because of his hardscrabble life, heredity or some recondite character flaw, Olney was most times irascible and antisocial. He was deeply resentful of how O'Malley, Booker, and LeBron had gained such favor with the old man.

"I'd like to see one of those pantywaists climb the Berlin wall at 2:00 a.m. to pull an agent free from the barbed wire," Olney would often bitterly complain to Blake over his fourth scotch and water at Oscars.

"Hey, Oln, take it easy.   Those men are all good intelligence professionals.   We have to work together as a team," was a typical rejoinder from Blake, whose usually upbeat manner had a calming effect on Olney.

A bachelor with few financial obligations, Olney would almost always grab the bar bill off the table, pay it and over-tip the waitress. He knew Blake's financial vulnerabilities and saw it as part of his job to help protect him from the constant demands of his elaborate lifestyle.

After the dignified memorial service for Barnstable, Fred Reitenhauser found himself in a reflective mood as he sat alone in his office with the door closed and his feet propped up on his desk. The preliminary medical examiner's report was that Barnstable had died from a broken neck. Certainly not inconsistent with a professional hit, especially since there was no sign of an accident. His body had been found on the ground floor of an abandoned factory building in the manufacturing section of Dundalk, a working-class area near Fort Holabird.

What weakness did Ed Barnstable have that brought him to that place? Fred wondered. Almost all men have an Achilles heel, which can be their undoing under the right circumstances. This thought then led Fred to think about the Achilles heel of each of his other key people. With Booker, it was his extreme eccentricity. LeBron's Achilles heel was empathy, and an over-identification with his agents. Blake's was money, and O'Malley's was ambition. Olney's was jealousy, and Uri's was idealism.

Most men were held hostage by one or more of the seven deadly sins, to a greater or lesser extent. But, unlike in most walks of life, in the espionage game, your unchecked character flaws could get you killed.

This didn't seem to apply to Horst, Agent 14332. He had suffered from no obvious character flaws, but he was dead anyway. But Horst was a different case. He was a soldier killed in battle through no fault of his own.

Fred's thoughts returned to the men and women of the 409th. What about himself? An argument could be made that his frequent and varied trysts with various sophisticated German ladies and single American women at the U.S. Consulate signified that his deadly sin was *lust*. He had always been extremely discrete and secretive about these liaisons but with what was going on now, maybe it was time he settled down with one woman. An image of Gerda suddenly flashed across his imagination, but he just as quickly dispelled it and concentrated on the foibles and weaknesses of his key personnel.

Both Anders Smith and Lonnie Ryan had clear potential, and their grooming for major operational roles needed to be accelerated. Professional intelligence men had a way of burning out, and good back-ups were always needed.

Kryptonite Redux

On 21 September 1967, the three case officer teams were dispatched to Vienna at staggered departure times.

The two operational teams, each composed of a rookie and a veteran, did not stop to check in at the hotel in Vienna but took taxis directly to their destinations. Each team member had committed to memory the name and address of 14332's surviving sub-agent to which that team was assigned.

When the CO had briefed his assembled key men a few weeks earlier, he had told them everything they needed to know at that time — but not everything *he* knew about the plans of the Munich Station for what he had named "Kryptonite Redux."

At about the same time the first team was arriving in Vienna, Art LeBron was at Hof in West Germany near the tip of the Czech salient, which jutted into German territory. Hof was — for reasons of geography — a well-known point of embarkation for both Western agents penetrating the Czech border and Warsaw-Pact agents who had crossed the Czech-German border on missions into West Germany.

Accompanying LeBron was Czech-born Kázimir (Káz) Penchak, whose parents had fled the Sudetenland for America shortly after Chamberlain had sold Czechoslovakia down the river to Hitler at Munich in 1938. The 32 year old Penchak was a tough special ops officer who had been with the Czech section for five years. Unlike most of the men dispatched to Vienna, Penchak was no stranger to Kryptonite. His imminent incursion across the border into Czechoslovakia was just one more mission on a long list over the past few years.

The souped-up Volkswagen sped towards the tip of the Czech salient at 0300 hours on 22 September. Behind the wheel was Art LeBron; in the passenger seat was Káz Penchak, quietly loading rounds into his Walther PPK.

In exactly one-half hour Penchak would crawl under barbed wire into Czechoslovakia, about three miles from the nearest check point. He would wear the standard rough coveralls of a Czech farmer. In his battered rucksack was a pair of generic Czech-made slacks and plain brown shirt. He would walk across mostly farmland for about five miles to the predesignated contact point, where he would be met by members of the Czech Underground. There he would shed his farmer's garb in favor of the simple Czech-made slacks and shirt, and would be transported to Prague by pickup truck.

While Penchak loaded his weapon, LeBron shifted his vision back and forth between the road ahead and the pair of headlights in his rear-view mirror, about seventy five meters behind them, which had been a constant presence since they left Hof. The road had become bumpy and soon the surface was nothing but packed-down dirt and stones. LeBron now kept the vehicle to his rear in almost constant view as he made a quick right turn onto a path and into a copse of trees. The path was just barely wide enough for one vehicle.

Káz stuck his weapon into an ankle holster under his right pants leg. Art slowed the VW almost to a stop and turned off its headlights. The trailing vehicle, a black Audi, had also turned onto the path and now was not more than fifteen feet behind them. It too killed its lights after stopping about ten feet to the rear of Art and Káz's VW. A full moon above provided the only light.

The front doors to the Audi opened and two men got out. They walked slowly but without hesitation towards the VW. Art and Káz also stepped out of their vehicle onto the bumpy path and turned to face the approaching duo. No one spoke. Then suddenly when the approaching men were no more than two feet away, there was movement.

Art LeBron extended his right arm and shook hands with Mario Tonelli. Káz Penchak did the same with Osi Mattatussu. Without anyone uttering a word, Osi, Mario, and Káz fanned out and entered the woods to the east of the vehicles, with Káz in the middle, Osi to his left and Mario to his right.

The footfalls of the three special ops pros on the brush, foliage and branches beneath their light moccasins could barely be heard as they disappeared into the woods at 15 foot intervals. Once clear of the border, Káz would dispose of the moccasins in favor of a pair of light, Czech-made rubber-sole shoes from his rucksack, which he would have noiselessly dragged under the barbed wire.

LeBron stayed behind and checked his watch as soon as the other three were out of sight. Its luminescent face reported that it was 0330 sharp. LeBron nodded once in satisfaction. So far the operation was running right on time. He would remain motionless, leaning against the side of VW for sixty minutes. At 0430, Mattatussu and Tonelli would return and, hopefully, report that Penchak had crossed and gotten safely clear of the border without incident.

LeBron stood silently and gently tapped his black windbreaker under his left shoulder to feel the comforting presence of his Luger in its holster. By long habit, he also carried a second pistol, a .38 caliber revolver, in an ankle holster. His mind did a simulated exercise consisting of all three of his men crossing the border — Osi and Mario first, to do some quick reconnaissance, and if feasible, silently liquidate any hostile personnel they might encounter.

When his real-time check of his watch indicated that it was the pre-appointed time for Mario and Osi to cross back over the border after an uneventful crossing, LeBron felt himself relaxing, just ever so slightly. No matter how many scores of times he had dispatched agents into denied areas, it never got old. He would remain leaning against his car in coiled tension until Káz's two guardians emerged from the woods.

At 0430 hours two black-clad, ghostly — almost other worldly phantoms — silently emerged from the woods. Tonelli gave LeBron a thumbs-up, signaling mission accomplished. The three men immediately climbed into their respective cars and drove away — LeBron back to Munich; Tonelli and Mattatussu to wherever.

The taxi cab carrying Berger and Rhymes down the Vienna street in a middle class urban neighborhood, moved slowly so that they could see the number of the apartment building where Lugash Magyaar, one of the survivors on 14332's list, supposedly lived.

"No offense Ben," said Rhymes, "but if we find this guy I'll do the talking."

"None taken."

"Okay, there's the building."

After Rhymes paid the fare, the two case officers climbed the front steps to the entrance of number 3988 Ludwigstrasse. There were no names listed on the outside of the building and no door bell or buzzer.

Rhymes, not wanting to attract attention, decided not to knock but instead gently turned the doorknob. The door gave way and they entered a small but clean and well-lit vestibule. An elevator to their right revealed that there were six floors, but again no directory of occupants.

"All right," said Mal. "We'll have to hit every apartment till we find the right one."

As if on cue, the elevator door opened. A pleasant looking, well-dressed, middle aged woman exited.

Without any overt sign of nervousness she offered a friendly smile to the two presentable young men. "Guten tag."

"Guten tag," replied Rhymes. "Ist hier, Herr Lugash Magyaar?"

"Ya, ya, funf und fierzig," she answered breezily, as she ambled past them and out the door, displaying no sign of trepidation.

This must be a pretty quiet and safe neighborhood, thought Ben, given the woman's openness with two strangers.

When the elevator door opened on the fourth floor, directly across the corridor from the entrance was a freshly painted blue door bearing the number '45,' printed in clean white paint.

Rhymes pushed the buzzer three times before the door slowly opened, after the occupant had eyed them through the peephole. Rhymes had decided to dispense with all pretense. He would get right to the point as to why they were there.

Standing before them was a man who appeared to be in his thirties, about six feet tall, lean and with a muscular build. He was dressed in Levis and a white t-shirt which amply revealed his muscles. He wore no belt, shoes or socks and his longish blonde hair was clean but unkempt, as if he had just gotten out of bed. Stuck prominently in the waste band of his jeans was a .45 caliber Smith and Wesson revolver.

"Mr. Magyaar?"

"Yes."

"We're friends of Horst," said Rhymes.

"What took you so long?" Magyaar replied.

"Can we come in?"

"Suit yourselves."

Magyaar made way for them to enter and, flopping into a comfortable armchair, signaled casually for them to sit on the couch.

"Coffee?"

"No thanks," said Mal, "we had ours."

"You won't mind then if I have mine?" The man spoke perfect English with a Hungarian accent.

"Of course not."

Magyaar rose effortlessly and walked into the kitchen, his athletic grace on display, gun still protruding from his waistband.

Mal and Ben could smell a pot of coffee brewing and soon Magyaar returned carrying a large and aromatic mug of what smelled like a fine Columbian blend.

The inscription on the mug was in a foreign language which Ben guessed to be Hungarian. There were Roman numerals after the writing and underneath was a fading picture of a pole-vaulter in mid-air.

Magyaar smoothly re-positioned himself in the armchair, took a gulp of coffee, and smiled with pleasure. "So, what can I do for you gentlemen?"

Looking directly towards Magyaar, Ben noticed for the first time a pair of top of the line white Keds tennis shoes sitting next to the armchair.

Rhymes, encouraged by the fact that they had gotten into Magyaar's apartment without any problem, didn't beat around the bush.

"Mr. Magyaar, we would like you to resume the type of work you were doing for Horst."

Magyaar raised an eyebrow. "You mean the kind of work that got him killed?"

"Of course, we can't offer guarantees," Rhymes said. "But the program has been greatly expanded and strengthened. We will be able to offer you significantly greater security."

This pronouncement caused Magyaar to break out into laughter, laughing so hard that he spilled coffee on the uncarpeted floor. "I'll be sure to pass that on to the widows of a dozen other members of the Philatelists Society, which by the way hasn't held many meetings lately."

Magyaar laughed even harder, amused by his own joke. "All right Mr. Whoever; what are you calling yourself today? Never mind. Look, if I were even slightly interested in going back to work, which I'm not, I would beg you to please keep your security. Your security has a way of making people dead. In fact, the only reason I'm still alive is because I provide my own security."

Without breaking the pace of his peroration, Magyaar off-handedly touched the handle of his Smith and Wesson and for a quick second lifted his right pant leg slightly to display a stiletto in its holder strapped around his upper ankle. He continued on in a similar vein for several more minutes, totally disdainful of Rhymes' appeal to him and particularly dismissive of the latter's occasional protests that Magyaar would be very well compensated.

"Compensated? I already have more money than I can spend in a lifetime — especially since it would be a very *short* life time if I went back to work for you people." Again a burst of laughter punctuated his oration.

"But you must have found persuasive reasons for working with Horst," Rhymes offered lamely.

"You are not Horst!" said Magyaar with finality.

An awkward silence enveloped the three men. Ben had not said a single word since they knocked on the apartment door. He had obeyed Rhymes' instruction to let him do the talking. But, things were going badly. Maybe Rhymes had made a mistake in plunging into the approach too quickly, without preliminaries. It was a judgment call which had fallen flat. Whatever the reason, if somebody didn't do something immediately, the mission would crash and burn.

A different approach was needed and Ben knew instinctively that Mal could not deliver it. They had to somehow unlock the key to whatever made this man tick.

Ben had noticed several things that he believed formed a pattern. The man sitting across from them had something special about him. The Columbian coffee, the expensive tennis shoes, the American-made Levis, his almost perfect English — all suggested someone who had traveled widely. He was no provincial. His athletic build and graceful movements, combined with his self-confident, almost cocky, manner spoke of someone with a unique background.

Ben decided to take a stab at it. It was now or never and they had nothing to lose. "Which Olympics were you in?"

"Excuse me?"

"I couldn't help but notice your coffee mug," Ben said. "Is that from the Olympiad?"

Magyaar nodded. "Yes, that's right."

"I take it you were a pole-vaulter?"

"That's correct, each member of the team received one."

"By the *team* do you mean the Hungarian National Track and Field Team?"

"No just the pole-vaulting team at the Olympics."

"Did you medal?"

"Almost," Magyaar said. "But not quite. Fourth place finish."

"It looks like the Roman numerals on your mug say that it was the 1952 Olympics."

"Correct again. You are observant. In 1956, I was involved in a different kind of competition."

"How so?"

"Instead of vaulting over poles, I was vaulting over burning cars to escape from Soviet tanks on the streets of Budapest."

"Then, you're a freedom fighter." Ben's use of the present tense was not an accident.

"A *retired* freedom fighter," Magyaar said.

Ben did not have to affect admiration when he next spoke, because he truly felt it. Softly and sincerely he stated simply, "In America, you were our heroes."

"We were just defending our homeland," protested the Hungarian. "Anyone would have done the same in those circumstances."

"That's not true," observed Ben calmly. "If *anyone* would have done the same, then there wouldn't have been so few of you. You few Hungarians fought Russian tanks with rocks and homemade Molotov cocktails, while the rest of the free world just stood by — to their everlasting shame — and let you fight for them, and die for them. If you and your fellow freedom fighters are not heroes, then *no one* is."

"Well that's all behind me," Magyaar said. "I am retired from athletic competition and everything else. I mostly spend my time now just trying to stay alive."

"If you don't mind my asking, why do you stay here? Wouldn't you be safer in England or the United States."

"You are naïve. If the KGB wants you dead, they can reach you anywhere. Besides, this is my home. I like it here."

"I can understand that," said Ben. "Well, we have to get going. Thank you for sharing a little of your background with us. It was truly inspiring. Things are really heating up for us in Eastern Europe and in a few months or even less, it may be Hungary — 1956 all over again. It's a shame that you are going to sit this one out."

With that Ben rose and Mal followed suit. Magyaar stood also, and handshakes were exchanged. Mal and Ben turned towards the door and started to leave.

Just as they were about to walk out, Magyaar spoke. "Wait a minute gentlemen. What are your first names?"

Mal and Ben told him their cover first names, Forrest and Bart, respectively.

The Hungarian sighed. "Okay, I will work for you on one condition. I get to choose my own three-man team. Both of the other two are from the small group of survivors who worked for Horst."

"I am sure that can be arranged," replied Mal.

"Good," said Magyaar. "Then I will hear from you again shortly."

"You will," replied Mal and the men shook hands again to seal the deal.

"Oh by the way, although my first name is Lugash, my friends call me 'Lou'."

"Then we will too," said Mal.

As Mal and Ben walked down Ludwigstrasse to find a pay phone to call a taxi, Mal turned towards Ben and with something approaching awe in his voice said, "Ben, that was masterful."

Ben nodded. "Thank you."

The team of Olney/Tallifierro also managed to get one of 14332's agents to re-up but only after a second meeting at which Blaulicht was present to bridge the language gap.

Rhymes/Berger was on a roll and Lonnie Ryan with his impeccably good judgment decided to continue playing the hot hand. After the team had effortlessly pulled another 14332 survivor back into the fold, he decided to ride the momentum as far as it would take him. He would not let Rhymes/Berger return to Munich until they had suffered two consecutive refusals. He sent Tallifierro back to Munich to explain his decision personally to the CO.

Ben and Mal were now working off the new list compiled by the section chiefs and Booker. Occasionally, they would have to send for Blaulicht but not too often because most of their subjects spoke English. Unlike most American school children, whose education in foreign languages is weak, European children received intensive schooling in at least English and French.

Mal Rhymes adapted his style to Ben's and in subject-interviews, they played off one another. All told, the team stayed in Vienna for three consecutive weeks, changing-up by moving into a new hotel every three days.

Lonnie Ryan was ordered back to Munich after a week to work with Tallifierro on evaluating and coordinating the data now pouring in on the new recruits. The back-up team in Vienna became Olney and Blaulicht, and Olney was named as Officer in Charge of the on-scene operations.

Rhymes and Berger were now handling three recruitment sessions a day. They also met with Magyaar two more times, including one meeting at which his two other team members were present.

The entire Munich station had been galvanized by the astounding success of the Vienna operation, plus the Prague operation, in which Penchak had taken a firm hand in consolidating the subversive activities of the Czech Underground against the hard-line regime. In January of 1968 the progressive Alexander Dubček replaced Antonin Novotný as the new Communist leader of Czechoslovakia.

Group had sent a half-dozen additional special ops agents to augment the team of Tonelli/Mattatussu, which roamed back and forth across the Austrian-Czech border, capturing or immobilizing Hostile's agents, depending on what the situation called for.

This added security allowed Reitenhauser to form a two-man operations unit composed of LeBron and O'Malley to temporarily interact with Magyaar in Vienna and launch him and his team on new operations at or near the Czech border.

Ryan and Tallifierro picked up the slack left by LeBron and O'Malley by taking firm control of the organizational and planning efforts in Munich, with invaluable help from the creative genius of Doug Booker.

With two days remaining on the 409th's current assignment in Vienna, the previously moribund Operation Kryptonite had been fully revitalized.

When Berger and Rhymes got on the train to return to Munich after twenty one consecutive days in the field, their totals were astounding — four renewals of 14332's surviving agents and twenty eight new agents recruited. There would have been even more but six recruits failed to pass Ryan and Tallifierro's rigorous vetting process.

The colonel placed a moniker on his new star team, consisting of a contraction of their names. Henceforth in Munich, at Group, and in military intelligence folklore, they would be known as "Rhymesberger."

On Hof Road Rides

Securely taped half way back under the wide side-altar of the Frauenkirche, in old Munich, was a single folded piece of 5 x 7 stationary. The only writing on it was in black print, in English, and above the fold:

ON HOF ROAD RIDES THE
NEW WORLD PROPHET TO
THE CAPPODOCCIANS

Frauenkirche in the 1960s

In making his normal daily check of Munich station's pre-designated dead-drops, a new case officer with Ops Support retrieved it. Ryan's careful review back at the 409th revealed, by reason of its off-center fold, that it was a coded message from Hostile.

Its encrypted content was then, immediately upon the CO's approval, sent by telex to Group for evaluation. The original message itself arrived at Frankfurt six hours later in a courier's pouch.

It was because of that evaluation that Captain Michael Iannucci from Group now sat with the CO, LeBron, and O'Malley in the colonel's office.

"Group's top analysts believe the Hof Road intercept to be of enormous intelligence value and profound implications," said the Harvard-educated Iannucci, who had been building up to a dramatic finish.

Somewhat impatiently, Reitenhauser spoke. "What do they say it *means?*"

"I am afraid, colonel, that I can only reveal that information to you alone."

"Captain, anything you have to say to me can be heard by LeBron and O'Malley as well. Now, what do they say it means?"

Iannucci squirmed in his chair and furtively gazed around the room.

"Don't worry, captain," the CO said. "This room is totally secure."

"Yes, sir. They have concluded that it means Warsaw Pact forces will invade Turkey upon the pretext of protecting its many Soviet bloc citizens from repression by the pro-Western government in Ankara. The word 'Hof' refers to 'Hof bei Salzburg in Austria near the Bavarian border, which is known to be a major center in Austria for Soviet covert operations."

Iannucci lowered his voice. "The analysts at Group believe that Warsaw Pact agents will be dispatched by automobile together with a Soviet general in civilian clothes from Hof bei Salzburg, through Austria, across the border into Hungary, carrying the operational plans; and from there through Rumania and Bulgaria to the Bulgaria-Turkey border. That general is believed to be the 'prophet,' as Paul of Tarsus was the Christian prophet to the Cappodoccians. It is believed that Warsaw Pact forces will make an amphibious landing from the Black Sea into north-central Turkey, in or near what was the ancient province of Cappodoccio — hence the reference to the Cappodoccians. They will likely also launch a land attack across the Bulgarian-Turkish border. Considerable troop movements in Warsaw Pact countries indicate that the invasion will happen soon."

"How soon?"

"Perhaps sir, within the next three weeks," Iannucci said.

The CO leaned back in his chair. "You got all *that* out of an eleven word message?"

Iannucci shook his head. "Oh no, sir. Many corroborating bits of intelligence were combined by the analysts with the Hof road intercept to form the complete mosaic. Also, sir, I've been instructed to notify you that General Stansfield has summoned you to Frankfurt for a personal meeting the day after tomorrow."

"Fine," the CO said. "But please inform the general that Captain LeBron will accompany me."

"Yes, sir," Iannucci said. "I will relay your message, but General Stansfield made it clear that he wants to meet only with you."

"That's an order, captain," the CO said. "Will there be anything else? If not, you are dismissed."

Iannucci stood and left.

The colonel spoke to his secretary. "Gerda, please find Doug Booker and tell him to come in."

Without pausing for acknowledgement, the CO turned to LeBron. "Art, I want you and Doug to put your heads together over this photocopy of the intercept. Let me know what you make of it as soon as possible."

*   *   *

LeBron and Booker spent the rest of the day dissecting the intercepted message. They poured through texts provided by BOSS on decoding cryptic messages, checked as far back as the original trade craft manuals of the OSS, and read through hundreds of previous encoded communiqués intercepted by Army Intelligence. At the end of the day, they traded information and then walked down the hall to the CO's office.

"We haven't got a clue as to what this message means," said LeBron. "I guess we have to assume for the present that Group got it right. In any event, Doug and I both believe that an historian, preferably a scriptural historian, is needed to at least analyze the biblical allusions."

A light bulb instantly went on in the colonel's head. "Gerda, find Tallifierro ASAP."

Tom was simultaneously flattered and nervous about the important assignment given to him of trying to decode the block-lettered, eleven word message. He was impressed by the fact that O'Malley had even given him a briefing on the Unit's covert operations to serve as context for his interpretive efforts. That he had also been given unlimited access to the unit's library and archives to aid him in solving the puzzle would have made him feel special, were it not for the fear that he might blow the assignment.

Tom sat totally alone at a long oak table in the musty library, under dim, low-hung, florescent lights — staring intensely at the eleven words on the paper before him. He hadn't moved a muscle in fifteen minutes, still stunned by the monumental significance of Group's interpretation of the message, which O'Malley had not told him until right before he left Tom alone in the library.

Had Group's analysts correctly deciphered the message? He prayed for the sake of the world that they had, so that NATO could move quickly to thwart the Soviet Union's plan. The absurd logic of that thought did not occur to him, lost as he was in the daunting challenge at hand.

Next to the piece of paper he had placed a World Atlas map of continental Europe. His synapses began to connect: Hof, Turkey, Paul to the Galatians, Rome's persecution of Christians, Prague, Káz Penchak, Warsaw Pact, invasion within three weeks, troop movements, message taken by Tonelli from Czech agent.

"Wait," he spoke softly to himself. "Why would a Czech agent crossing the German border from Western Czechoslovakia into a remote region of Bavaria be carrying such an important message? Who were the parties of interest near the crossing point, to whom this message of imminent war would be vital? Most high-level Communist bloc operatives in non-communist Europe were in West Berlin, Bonn, and Vienna. Munich and Frankfurt were both swarming with United States counter-intelligence people, so it was probably too risky to deliver such an apparently sensitive message to Hostile's people there.

Tallifierro's deep analytical mind began offering him hypotheses but he couldn't close the deal on any of them. Something was eluding him — something in the detailed background briefing O'Malley had just provided. He reviewed the briefing in his head with almost 100% recall, stopping to conjure up straw man inferences from the information, and then quickly discounting them as flawed.

After repeating the process several times, Tom did reach one conclusion. There was nothing significant in the big picture outlined in the briefing. If what he was looking for was there, it was in some solitary fact, just as the meaningful study of history usually required concentration on a few oft-overlooked facts.

Often seemingly random occurrences were the clue to finding the common thread — the trend, or the pattern. So, Tom switched gears and began running the specific people, places, and dates mentioned in the briefing through the filter of his mind... Rhymesberger, Ryan, Olney, Blaulicht, Booker, LeBron, O'Malley, Magyaar, Penchak, Blake, Belson, Vienna, Cappodoccio, Prague, Munich, Budapest, Bucharest, Ankara, Hof, October 27.

What other dates had O'Malley mentioned? None that Tom could recall. October 27th? That was tomorrow... O'Malley had talked about something that was supposed to happen on October 27. What had it been?

Revelation suddenly struck like lightning. Then, within five minutes every piece of the puzzle fell into place.

Leaving the Atlas on the table, Tom snatched up the piece of paper, left the library, and practically ran down the hall to O'Malley's office.

Ten minutes later O'Malley and Tallifierro stormed into the colonel's outer office. LeBron, summoned by Gerda, followed them in.

Reitenhauser was standing in the outer room waiting for them. "We'll meet in the small conference room. It was just swept for bugs this morning."

After situating themselves at the conference table, the CO paused for half a minute to let everyone catch their breaths. Just from the fifteen second heads-up O'Malley had given him in the corridor, the CO knew the potential magnitude of the report he was about to hear.

He nodded towards Tom. "All right, Corporal Tallifierro, let's have it." The colonel's voice was even, betraying no tension or emotion.

Tom cleared his throat. "Sir, I believe that Higher has misread the intercepted message. They seem to have overlooked the symbolism and hidden meanings of some of the words."

"First of all," Tom said. "*Hof* is not meant to be 'Hof bei Salzburg' in Austria. It is Hof, Bavaria, near the Czech salient. The 'Hof Road' is meant to designate the road that runs from the tip of the salient to the town of Hof. Also, 'Cappodocians' is not a reference to an area in what is now central Turkey."

"Why not?" asked the colonel.

"Because, sir, that reference is not to be taken literally. It's symbolic."

The CO nodded. "What's your basis for that conclusion?"

"The Group analysts have ignored early Christian history," Tom said. "Emperor Tiberius and his successors in first century Rome engaged in a reign of terror against all Christians throughout the Empire. This included the Cappodocians. Cappodoccio had one of the highest percentages of Christians anywhere in the Mediterranean. St. Paul the Apostle himself had converted many of them. They revered Paul, and greatly feared the Romans. They had heard the stories claiming that Paul was executed in Rome for his beliefs. So what did the Cappodocians *do* to avoid falling into the hands of the Roman persecutors?"

"They went underground," said Tom, answering his own question. "I mean *literally* underground. They burrowed deep beneath the ground and created one of the most sophisticated subterranean civilizations in the history of mankind. Much of that underground city is still intact today. So when the composers of the coded message used the word Cappodocians, I think they were speaking figuratively and symbolically. They meant it to be a symbol for the 'underground.'"

O'Malley nodded. "And the primary active underground in existence in Europe today is the Czech Underground," he said. "And its Western advisor is Penchak."

"That's right sir," continued Tom. "And the 'New World' is a reference to the Americas. The 'New World prophet' to the Czech Underground is an American."

"Of course!" said LeBron with excitement in his voice. "Káz! We should have realized that."

"It sounds like an interesting theory, so far," the CO said. "But that's a long way from evidence. What makes you so sure that your interpretation is correct?"

"The date sealed it for me, sir," Tom said. "Part of the briefing I received from Captain O'Malley. He mentioned October 27th."

"What about October 27th?"

LeBron answered the CO's question. "The message was intercepted three days ago, a couple of miles from where Penchak crossed the border into Czechoslovakia. Tomorrow, 27 October, at 0530 he will cross back over the border into Germany, very near the spot where he was first injected into Czech territory. He will be met by two escape and evasion experts from Group, who are supposed to drive him on the Hof Road to the town. Except he will never get there. The vehicle will be intercepted on the Hof Road, the escorts will be killed, and Penchak will be taken back to Czechoslovakia — or someplace worse — for interrogation, torture, and eventual execution. That is, unless they are able to double him, which they *won't* be. The coded message was an alert to Hostile in and near Hof as to where he will surface. 'On Hof Road rides the new world prophet to the Cappodoccians.'"

LeBron nodded towards Tom. "It's the proximity of time and place, colonel, that confirms Tallifierro's interpretation of the symbolic meaning of the words. Timing and location take them out of the realm of speculation, and into the realm of near-certainty."

"But the message was intercepted" said Reitenhauser. "How do we know Hostile's muscle on the German side even got the word?"

"When it's an important message," said O'Malley, "Hostile always sends out three separate couriers with the identical message. We only caught *one* of them."

The CO pondered this for a minute before he spoke again. When he did, what he said was crisp and decisive. "It's now 2100 hours. In eight and a half hours our boy comes across the border. I don't trust Higher to come to our aid. For all I know, the interpretation of the message they gave us was intentionally bogus. The mole in Internal Security may still be operating.

"Here's the team: LeBron, Smith, Rhymes, and Olney. LeBron is in charge. Olney is second in command. He has more experience in this kind of mission than any of us. Draw weapons, haul ass up to Hof immediately and bring our boy back. And each one of you is ordered to wear a vest. Clear?"

"Yes, sir."

"All right. We meet in the motor pool for final briefing in 15 minutes. Art, assemble the team. Ted, go with him. Good job Tallifierro."

*   *   *

"Oln, where do you think Hostile will try to intercept Káz?" asked LeBron to Olney, as the black Mercedes hummed quietly on its northward trip to Hof.

"At his first destination on this side that they're able to predict," replied Olney quickly.

"That would be where the road from Hof to the border ends," said LeBron. "There's a path there into the woods."

"Then that's where they will set up their stakeout." Olney had not the slightest doubt.

"Okay, listen up guys," said the team leader. "They know when Káz is scheduled to reach that point, but what they *don't* know is that we're going to be there too."

"So will Group's two escorts," said Anders Smith from the back seat, where he was busy cleaning the barrel of a sawed-off shotgun.

"No," said LeBron. "The old man was somehow able to call them off. This is going to be our show only."

"Just like in the Nam," said Smith, who had been part of a Special Forces recon team fighting alongside the Montagnards in the Central Highlands of Vietnam.

"So what's the plan?" asked Rhymes. "I would just as soon not walk into a trap the way Ryan and I did in Vienna."

Kázimir Penchak tried to keep his slain grandfather and uncles firmly in mind whenever he felt imperiled in a denied area. As he trudged through the darkness over mile upon mile of furrowed farmland, they were an abiding presence — invisible sentries, ever-vigilant protectors, warning him where danger lurked, and guiding him on secure paths to safety.

That his spiritual body guards had died nineteen years earlier at the hands of the evil Stalin and his despicable henchmen, Molotov and Beria, mattered not to Káz. He knew that his invisible guardians were with him, just as they had been during his solo covert incursions into East Germany, Poland, and Rumania.

The greater his sense of danger, the stronger was their presence; and right now their aura was powerful. Without his murdered kin and the untold number of other Eastern European heroes who had risked torture and death for freedom, Penchak would have never received the inspiration and courage he needed to do the work he did. To save the women and children of their Czech village from violent death in 1948, his close family members had sacrificed their own lives — thereby becoming for him anonymous saints upon whose intercession he relied.

Soon the flat farm region began to give way to abutments, hills and brush; and then to trees and rivulets of water. The border was fast-approaching. Upon the urgent entreaties of his spiritual guardians, Penchak now ran full speed toward the barbed wire border.

But, suddenly Káz was visited by an intimation of doom. Something beyond the barbed wire was amiss. The free land of Bavaria which should soon have been his deliverance, had somehow morphed into a portent of death. His senses were electric with this chilling premonition. And then intuition graduated to fact.

On the other side of the fence, beyond the copse of trees, the night suddenly became a deadly 4th of July fireworks celebration — with deafening explosions throwing off shards of piercing light, the blast of a shotgun, screams of agony, men shouting everywhere in several languages, the acrid smell of gunpowder, the moans of dying men, the steady staccato of a sub-machine gun. The trees between the border and the road had suddenly been ignited and were ablaze, the fire's light and heat moving towards the barbed wire.

The angel of death would soon leap the wire and claim Káz as its prize... its force inexorable, its finality inevitable.

"But I will not succumb without a fight, Grandfather," said Káz into the night air as he released the safety on his handgun while simultaneously feeling for his reserve clip of ammunition.

"I owe you that much."

Chapter Nine

Linked Destinies

The bedlam stopped as abruptly as it had begun. The cacophony of shouts, explosions, gunshots, and screams of pain ceased instantly, leaving a strangely ringing silence that was broken only by the crackle and hiss of the burning brush and trees.

The heat from the flames stung Káz's face and hands, but he remained motionless in a prone position, elbows propped on a slight elevation in the contours of the ground, with both hands gripping his new .44 Magnum revolver. He kept the barrel pointed in the direction of the barbed wire, and waited.

Hostile would soon be coming for him in strength of numbers, aided by the illumination thrown off by the flames. They would try to flank his position, but he would be able to see them clearly and pick them off as they moved forward to his left and right. His big problem was ammunition. He had only twelve rounds all together. But Káz had no real thoughts of death. His quickly formulated plan was to fell one of the attackers for each of his loved ones who had suffered at the hands of the Communists — his aunt who had been beaten and raped by the secret police after being seized at an anti-Stalin rally in Prague; his uncle who for the rest of his life was immobilized by guilt-induced depression over the incident; his murdered grandfather, uncles, cousins and so on. Now they all implored him to mete out justice, not to exact vengeance. They formed a jury of peers rather than an unruly mob; and he would fulfill their mandate swiftly and decisively.

He would try to make each round count and once he was out of ammo, Hostile would take him, but hopefully not until he had delivered justice to one or two more with his now-unsheathed knife. This would be for Káz his end of days — the personal Armageddon he had envisioned for himself since childhood.

Already he could see the blurry silhouettes of several darting figures moving into position on the other side of the barbed wire. He could hear the clear sounds of sharp metal against metal made by wire cutters. Káz's long-held vision had preempted the here and now. The apocalyptic agents of evil would soon make their charge. They would be surprised by the righteous mayhem which would suddenly be inflicted upon them from the barrel of Káz's weapon, his instrument for justice. He would smite his enemy in the name of the Penchak family.

The barbed wire had been breached and pulled aside to create a ten foot wide opening. Several of Káz's foes were on the move, 100 feet away, and then 75. Káz would not shoot until they came within 30 feet of his position.

"Baker to Omega. Extraction is a go. Copy. Repeat. Baker to Omega. Extraction is a go. Copy."

Káz heard the words but in the distant regions of consciousness that he now occupied, he could not be sure from where they came. Had he imagined them? No, he thought not. They were too much a part of the urgency of the *now*, which he felt closing in on him. That sense of heightened immediacy caused him to select the first of the attackers he would shoot, and he aimed for the chest.

"Baker to Omega. Copy." He knew the words. They were as familiar to him as his serial number. They were a prearranged signal. He hesitated in squeezing the trigger.

How had Hostile gotten that Signal? Káz felt his finger tighten on the trigger. But, the voice which spoke the words also seemed familiar. It was that familiarity which wrenched from Káz seven words he was not fully aware of speaking... "Roger that, Baker. Omega ready for extraction."

Káz had spoken the pre-set reply signal and in doing so, had purged his sense of danger. He stood to his full height. The approaching figures were now on top of him, slapping him on the back and shaking his hand, and just as quickly leading him back through the opening in the barbed wire, through the trees, onto the path and then out into the road.

"Hey, good to have you back Káz" said LeBron as he gently pushed Káz into the back seat of the Mercedes and then sat next to him.

Olney was already turning the key in the ignition as Lieutenant Smith leaned partly out the front passenger window with shotgun at the ready.

On the other side of Káz, Rhymes sat gazing intently out the window with his Smith and Wesson .44 Magnum Special, held vertically in a two-handed firing grip. LeBron sat in a similar posture with Luger in hand. The Mercedes lurched forward past the dead bodies lying in and around the road and headed back towards Hof and safety.

*　　　*　　　*

The team sat around the table in the small conference room. It was 27 October 1967, at 1600 hours. They all wore their usual civilian clothing. Rhymes' hair, always a bit on the long side, had been singed along the front hairline and his forehead had been burned, superficially. Both of Smith's hands were bandaged from burns, and Band-Aids covered cuts on his chin and forehead. LeBron had various contusions on his face and superficial cuts on his hands. Olney walked with a decided limp and his face looked like he had just gone fifteen rounds with Smokin' Joe Frazier.

As usual, the CO sat at the head of the table. "Captain LeBron has already given me a written after-action report and I first want to congratulate you on the success of your mission. Although all of you are banged up, I am grateful that none of you sustained serious injuries."

"If I may, sir," spoke Anders Smith. "We would not be sitting here right now were it not for the element of surprise. Hostile had a larger team, but they walked right into a trap. This may sound callous, but after that it was like shooting fish in a barrel. And I won't even ask how our resourceful supply sergeant came up with those hand grenades. They really did the trick. But, most important, Sergeant Penchak is free and alive today because of Corporal Tallifierro's brilliant work. His breaking of Hostile's code was an invaluable service to the 409th and to Group."

The CO was somewhat put out by Lieutenant Smith's interruption, which bordered on over-stepping his place, but he decided to let it go under the circumstances.

"Well, lieutenant, tomorrow I will send a request to Group for the promotion of both Corporals Tallifierro and Berger to the rank of sergeant on an expedited basis, based on their extraordinary accomplishments. And I am recommending that each of the four of you be awarded the Silver Star. Of course, if my request is granted, your medals will be presented here in a strictly confidential ceremony.

"Warrant Officer Penchak is being treated at a secret location for stress, exhaustion, and post-traumatic psychological injuries. His debriefing by Group is being deferred for several days to give him a chance to recover. Right now he is heavily medicated and catching up on some long-overdo sleep. His mission in Prague has contributed vastly to our objectives there, and I am putting him in — confidentially, of course — for the Medal of Honor.

The CO let his eyes travel over each face in the room. "Men, I would like you all to get treatment for your injuries, as needed. Lieutenant, the doctor tells me you need treatment for those burns so you are off-duty until 29 October at 0900. The rest of you should return to duty tomorrow if your injuries permit it. Dismissed."

As the men stood to leave, the CO added, "Art, please hang back. Ted will be joining us shortly."

O'Malley smiled upon entering. "What can I say, Art? Outstanding work!"

"Thanks Ted. I really appreciate that. But as far as I'm concerned, it was a unit accomplishment."

"Well, maybe so, but you guys pulled it off and frankly, I am a little envious."

"Look men," said Reitenhauser, "we are all professionals here. It was an emotional situation but today is like the Monday morning after the big game-day win. It's time to assess our injuries and plan for the next big game. So let's move forward."

"Our biggest problem is Penchak," said the CO. "The preliminary psychological evaluation indicates that he is something of a burned-out case. One too many operations in hostile territory. As tough as it may be to admit, his days as a covert operative may be over. This presents us with a critical situation. Káz brought the Prague Underground to its highest level of effectiveness thus far. The Novotný Regime is reeling, but without a real leader and organizer, the underground could quickly back-slide. The general is concerned about that, and so am I. The Dubček people are ready to make their play, but they can't move unless they know that they'll have major support in the press, inside the government, and — most importantly — with the public. After a rest, Káz was slated to go back in to help organize mass demonstrations in late November. But all that is by the boards now."

The CO rubbed his hands together. "So, gentlemen, what the three of us have to do now is put our heads together and come up with a replacement for Penchak. The general wants our recommendation within five days. Any ideas?"

"Colonel, I think my deputy should be in on this. He is the one who is up to all hours of the night reading and studying agent profiles."

Reitenhauser, without hesitating, pushed Booker's extension number on his console. "Doug, its Reitenhauser; please come down to my office."

A couple of minutes later, a pale and drawn-looking Doug Booker was escorted in by Gerda. Booker was preoccupied of late by the resurgence of Kryptonite and the Hof Road intercept.

The CO did a double-take when he took note of Booker's gaunt look. His less than hearty appearance was impossible not to notice, as was the fact that he walked slightly stooped over, as if carrying the weight of the world on his 155 pound frame.

"Welcome Doug, lost a little weight, have you?"

"I hadn't really noticed, colonel. I've had a lot on my mind lately."

"Oh, is that so? Anything you'd care to share with us?"

The colonel saw a fleeting expression pass almost imperceptibly across Booker's face — a look of indecision mixed with trepidation, as if he wanted to speak but the region of his brain which counseled caution forbade him from doing so.

An awkward silence followed. Reitenhauser decided not to press the issue. He would wait until he was alone with Booker before pursuing the matter.

"Doug, I'll share with you what I just mentioned to Ted and Art. Káz Penchak needs some extended R & R right now, and we need someone to substitute for him on business trips. Anyone you can recommend?"

Again the same look of indecision mixed with fear passed over Booker's face. "Yes colonel, there is one obvious candidate." Then Booker fell silent.

"Doug? Are you all right?"

Booker appeared startled by the question, which seemed, however, to yank him back into the moment.

"Yes, yes, I'm fine, sir. If the colonel doesn't mind, I would prefer not to use names."

"Absolutely, Doug. Go ahead."

"The individual I had in mind is Agent 17760. He's gutsy, tough, smart and experienced. Since he's now on his second go-round with us, we can be reasonably sure of his loyalty, but I think we should put him on the box before making a final decision on him."

The CO nodded. "Good. And how would you rate his leadership abilities?"

"Top notch. He is already running his own team like a well-oiled machine. From what Berger and Rhymes tell me, he's a charismatic chap. And we know how strong and resourceful he is. He survived Hostile's largely successful attempt to liquidate 14332's entire group, without any help from anyone. We have it on pretty good authority that every assassin Hostile sent to take him out, wound up floating face down in the Danube. I doubt that he can be turned, but as I say, we need to put him on the box. But, in the final analysis, we can never be 100% sure of any operative — even inside our own unit."

This last gratuitous observation by Booker, almost a throw-away line, appeared to startle his three colleagues in the room.

LeBron in particular seemed stunned. "Just what do you mean by that, Doug?"

Booker shrugged. "Nothing in particular. Just a general, but self-evident, statement."

The CO spoke next with a tone of urgency. "Captain Booker, if you have any information or even suspicion of a security problem within this unit, I want you to tell us right now."

But Booker's eyes told them he had already wandered away to that metaphysical oasis where talk is not an imperative.

The CO and his two top deputies sat with their eyes fixed on Booker, each in his own way trying to get a handle on what was going on with their brilliant but strange colleague.

Finally, after three or four minutes of total silence, Booker spoke in a manner and tone suggesting there had been no lengthy pause at all. "Someone here sold out 14332 and his whole team. It seems likely that whoever it was also betrayed Penchak."

In the manner of a trial judge, Reitenhauser gave Booker one of his renowned penetrating stares. "What is your evidence of that?"

"Ockham's Razor."

The colonel frowned. "*Whose* razor?"

"Ockham's Razor," Booker said. "Ockham was a 14th Century theologian and logician. His theory held that the simplest, most obvious answer or explanation to a puzzle or a mystery is almost always the right one. Let's apply that standard to the facts we have at hand... Agent 14332 was this unit's top external agent. Káz Penchak is this unit's top internal operative. They were both betrayed within a few months of each other. The two men had never met and as far as we know, neither knew of the other's existence. One man worked and lived in Austria. The other lived in Germany and worked mostly in Communist bloc countries. 14332 did not personally operate on the other side of the Iron Curtain, whereas Penchak rarely worked anywhere *but* on the other side. The only common link between them was the 409th Special Investigations Detachment. Ergo, they were betrayed by someone within the Detachment."

"Hold it," said LeBron. "Aren't you making a big assumption, Doug?"

"What assumption is that?" Booker asked calmly.

"That either or both of these men were betrayed at all," LeBron said. "It's equally possible that Hostile learned of their activities by some other means. Both of them conducted large, ambitious operations which directly or indirectly touched many individuals and groups. The methods they used were not bullet-proof. Too many people were involved. Discovery was always a risk."

"Au contraire," was Booker's nonplussed response. "Ockham would argue that the best explanation is the one which draws the least number of new assumptions. By your thesis, Art, several new assumptions would have to be drawn. For openers, that Hostile had some facility for compromising both men's channels of communications, other than by betrayal. Secondly, that the fact that both men were employed by this unit was merely a coincidence. Thirdly, that random discovery of an agent is more likely than intentional disclosure from a human source."

Booker shook his head. "No. Ockham's Razor dictates that disclosure by a human source is the simplest explanation, and that betrayal is the most likely type of disclosure. As both men worked for the same unit, the likely source of that betrayal is obvious."

"Is that the sole basis for your conclusion, Captain Booker?" asked Reitenhauser. "Your entire foundation is the theory of a 14th century logician?"

"Yes, sir," Booker said. "But the theory is eminently sound. The only remaining mystery, as far as I'm concerned, is the identity of the traitor. But it is only a matter of time before I find him."

"All right, that's enough for now," the CO said. "Ted, get with Berger and arrange to have Rhymesberger pitch 17760 on the expansion of his job description. If he agrees, send Belson down to Vienna to do a polygraph exam on him. You and Art are dismissed. Doug, I would like you to stay."

"You want me to *what*? Join the Czech Underground? I am a Hungarian. What would I have in common with them?"

"Lou, for one thing you speak Czech," Ben said. "Secondly, you're a man of the world. Thirdly, you're all freedom fighters. And most important, they are waiting anxiously for you and cannot continue their work without you. Nor can we."

Magyaar sat quietly for a couple of minutes mulling over what Ben had just told him, a look of bemused skepticism on his face which gradually changed to one of total concentration.

"All right," he said finally. "I'll do it on one condition. Étan goes with me. I can't foment an insurrection and worry about security at the same time. I want some muscle with me for protection."

Ben had not seen this one coming, and he was clearly thrown by Magyaar's demand. An uncomfortable silence filled the air.

"We accept your condition," said Mal Rhymes. "You and Étan, however, will have to take a polygraph exam. It's just routine, and the place where it will be given is no more than ten minutes from here."

"No sweat, as you Americans say. Étan and I have both been through it many times."

Ben was duly impressed by the decisiveness with which Rhymes had acted. In the eight months Ben had been with 409th, Rhymes had gone from being an almost invisible lower-rung agent handler to a scarred veteran of two physical confrontations with Hostile. Together with Smith, LeBron and Olney, he had been awarded the Bronze Star for the team's actions on the Hof Road and had been promoted to the rank of master sergeant.

It took guts for Rhymes to make the call he had just made on his own authority. But that's what it took to be an effective soldier in any war — not excluding the Cold War.

1952

Uri and Fred, who had not seen each other in five years, were spending some time over coffee and Viennese pastry on the Ringstrasse, just catching up. Uri was in Vienna for a short three day holiday with his wife. Fred had taken the Orient Express from Munich to meet with him after Uri had called from his hotel in Vienna the previous evening.

Uri was now the Director of Defense Preparedness for the Western Soviet Republics. Fred had recently returned to Europe after completing a tour in the Far East with U.S. Army Intelligence, serving first under Eighth Army Commander Walton W. Walker in Korea, then briefly at MacArthur's headquarters in Tokyo and finally under General Matthew B. Ridgway, Commander of all U.N. Forces in Korea.

Fred was now a major assigned to the 409th Special Investigations Detachment in Munich. He was also matriculating at the University of Maryland extension campus there, taking a full load of evening classes in pursuit of a bachelor's degree in international relations.

"I understand that congratulations are in order," Fred said. "You now have twin boys."

His Russian friend nodded. "Yes, my wife and I are quite happy. They are a joy to us, a ray of sunshine in the dark times in which we live. I hate the idea of raising children in a country so politically repressed, but we must live our lives as best we can. And I still have hopes that things will change."

Fred took the way Uri stared directly into his eyes when he spoke the words "things will change" as a signal.

"Well, old friend," Fred said. "You and I made quite a bit of a difference back in '45 and '46."

"That we did."

"The question now is whether changes in our circumstances will allow us to work together again."

Uri sat back in his chair and took a sip of coffee, while formulating a response.

"Sometimes," said Uri, "one needs to transcend his circumstances for the greater good. And the very circumstances which may seem to shackle us can, if viewed properly, present great opportunities."

There it was — a clear opening presented by Uri. Fred felt the excitement building within him, and hoped he would not betray his emotions too soon. He had to respond in a measured way in order to give the conversation the breathing room it needed to gather the momentum to carry it forward.

"I agree," replied Fred. "Time and events that may seem to widen the gulf between opportunity and action, sometimes actually create new possibilities."

"How true that is," said Uri. "While we may think that an ever-widening separation in time and distance is closing doors, in fact things such as access and power may be opening those doors wider than ever."

"Well that's quite a coincidence, because just this past week my friend Horst — you remember Horst from Nuremberg — said almost the exact same thing."

"Ah, I never realized that the stamp collector was so intelligent," said Uri with a laugh.

"Oh, he definitely is. In fact, the two of you have much in common. I had hoped that we all could get together for coffee — perhaps tomorrow — for old time's sake. I am sure Horst would want to explain his views in detail."

Fred had just cast out his line. All that remained was for Uri to jump onto the hook. Uri knew that the three of them could not be seen together, and Fred *knew* that Uri knew.

"Good," said Uri. "I know of an even better pastry shop further north on the boulevard, right across from the opera, called 'Amadeus.' Shall we meet at the same time tomorrow?"

"Excellent Uri. It's done. Now, I have to take my leave," said Fred, as he rose and shook Uri's hand. "Till tomorrow then, at 10:00 a.m."

"Till tomorrow," said the Russian. And by that prosaic exchange, an alliance of historic moment was cemented.

The next morning only Horst and Uri would meet at Amadeus, and there they would work out the details, which would make a high Soviet defense official into a clandestine agent of the United States of America.

This was an extraordinary conversion, as remarkable as the defection by continental Army General, Benedict Arnold, to the cause of the British during the Revolutionary War. Only the mystically linked destinies of Uri Putyagin and Fred Reitenhauser could have forged such an unlikely union.

1967

Étan Gaborski was wired into the polygraph equipment while Glenn Belson asked him some preliminary test questions. The exchange was in English:

"What is your name?"

"Étan Gaborski."

"Where do you live?"

"Right now, I am staying with a friend."

"What is your friend's name?"

"Lugash Magyaar."

"What is your date of birth?"

"June 9, 1938."

"Where were you born?"

"Budapest, Hungary."

"Are you an operative of a Warsaw Pact Intelligence Agency?"

"No."

"Have you ever been?"

"No."

"What is your citizenship?"

"Hungarian."

The questions continued in that vein until Belson gradually moved the exam into more substantive areas, including Gaborski's current and previous covert activities. After twenty minutes or so, there had been no indications of deception. Étan was hitting Belson's questions out of the park.

The picture which clearly emerged after about forty five minutes of interrogation was that of an honest, highly motivated, anti-communist zealot. The man seemed almost too good to be true — childlike in his innocence. Guileless.

Belson would for some odd reason never forget the exact time of the question... the question that clearly separated everything in his life up to that moment from the events which happened afterwards. It was 1655 hours, 38 seconds on 12 December 1967.

Question: "Do you know the names of any Warsaw Pact officials who are operatives of Western intelligence agencies?"

The examination had been in progress for close to an hour and Belson was about to wrap it up. He was glad it was coming to an end because he was beginning to feel sluggish. It was his second examination of the afternoon, the first being that of Lugash Magyaar, which lasted an hour and a half.

In his eight years as a polygraph operator, Belson had never received anything other than a "no" to the question, and none of those answers had ever caused the machine to react in a manner indicative of a lie.

He slouched in his chair waiting for the inevitable "no" to emit forth from his subject, already tasting the first shot of Schnapps he would enjoy later at his favorite Vienna restaurant. But, the expected answer still was unspoken. Thirty seconds had passed and there had been no reply from Gaborski.

Belson began to feel uneasy and no longer slouched. He always considered this standard question to be useless and stupid, but it was one of Group's mandatory questions, so he had to ask it. But why wasn't the subject answering? Belson asked the question a second time — still no answer. Almost a full minute went by with no words passing from Gaborski's lips.

"Sir, please answer the question," said Belson, now feeling impatience tempered by confusion. "Damn," thought Belson to himself; "this should have been a wrap by now. What the hell is going on?"

Then suddenly — "*Yes.*"

Belson bolted straight up in his seat. He was no longer sluggish. Shock had banished his malaise.

"Is that your answer?"

"Yes."

To be certain that the subject had not misunderstood the question, Belson asked it for a third time.

"Yes." The machine registered no deception. Gaborski had answered truthfully, or at least he *thought* he had.

Belson framed the next question carefully, and asked it in a deliberate manner. "Do you know the name of a Warsaw Pact official who is an operative of Western intelligence?"

"Yes." That answer was also truthful.

"What is his name?"

"Uri Putyagin."

"Do you know the names of any others?"

"No."

*   *   *

Glenn Belson

Belson's gaze had been locked on to the panoramic beauty of the Austrian countryside from his window-side seat for the past half hour. His compartment on the westbound Orient Express seated no less than four passengers, but Belson had purchased the tickets for the entire compartment and sat in tortured solitude. The idyllic scenery provided no balm for either his fevered brain or tormented conscience.

He had asked many follow-up questions to Gaborski designed to both impeach his credibility and undercut the factual basis of his astounding declaration that Colonel Uri Putyagin, Director of Defense Preparedness for the Western Soviet Republics, was a western spy. But Étan had fielded the questions effortlessly, and revealed no signs of prevarication.

Putyagin was "stationed in East Berlin but traveled widely throughout all the Warsaw Pact nations," declared a calm and confident Gaborski. He had been planted as a mole by one of the NATO nations' intelligence services almost fifteen years earlier. He was the first to report to his Western handlers that Khrushchev was planning to build the Berlin wall. What was the source of Étan's information? He had refused to answer. From whom had he first heard about Putyagin? He would not say.

Belson agonized over what to do, if anything, with the explosive information imparted to him. No recording had been made of his polygraph interview. The questions weren't even written down. He had asked the same questions so many times, they were committed to memory. Should he report what had been said to Ops? To the CO? What if the room in which he conducted the exam had been bugged? Highly unlikely, contrary to Army Intelligence S.O.P., and the Army usually played things by the book.

But Gaborski seemed such an honest, guileless individual. There was no telling how many people he had made the same claim to. Still, the great probability was that he, Glenn Belson, was the only person in the world who had the information actually corroborated by the results of a lie-detector test.

Hostile might be willing to pay six figures for the juicy piece of info he carried in his over-heated brain. For this thought, Belson immediately chastised himself. He had always been a patriotic and loyal American. He was a soldier who did his duty. He was no shirker. But then, look where it had all landed him. At age 36, he had no wife, no children, a balance in his bank account of $78.00, and gambling debts stretching from Las Vegas, to Reno, to Cannes and Monte Carlo.

He had already had the fingers of his left hand broken once, and had blamed the injury on a skiing accident. And the Army had never given him his just due.

After volunteering for and serving a year in the 'Nam, they turned down his application for OCS. After fifteen years as an enlisted man, a Purple Heart and an Army Commendation Medal, he was no better off financially than he had been as a twenty-one year old buck private. For Chrissake, they wouldn't even let him be an officer!

Self-pity began to well up inside of him. "And that dirty commie, Putyagin, has probably been paid millions," Belson said to the train window with teeth clenched.

In fact, Uri had accepted no compensation at all. But Belson was no dummy, about either other people or himself. He was aware of the seductive powers of rationalization and self-pity, although he might not have chosen those specific words.

He knew from long experience when other people were lying; and when he was lying to himself. On those not infrequent occasions when he became morose about both his present and future — like now — he would find himself blaming everything on the Army. But truth be told, the Army had always been pretty square with him. It wasn't the Army's fault that he had no college, or that he had scored poorly on the OCS entrance exam. He would have turned himself down.

He thought about Clarissa, whose parents had so frowned upon their relationship because he was just a poor G.I. Suppose he was suddenly free of his gambling debts and returned home to Phoenix with enough money to buy a house? Would they look at him differently? Would Clarissa?

Guilt and Fear. They had always been the twin stanchions to which Belson's mind was tethered. They were the first principles of his actions, and drove his every impulse and major decision, including the decision to enlist in the Army, to re-enlist four times, to frantically seek a big score at the roulette tables, and to use back-stabbing to wrest prime assignments as a polygraph man away from his competitors.

That he acted from fear so often did not make him a coward. He did not lack physical courage. But moral courage was another issue entirely. Belson could not honestly credit himself with that quality — at least not so far.

His guilt was a habit of mind, nurtured in him from earliest childhood by unbending and judgmental parents. When he had turned twenty-one and they no longer held such power over him, was it any wonder that he had joined the military, one of the greatest guilt-manufacturing machines known to man?

Though his compartment on the Orient Express held no other passengers, Belson was not alone. Guilt and Fear were his constant traveling companions. He liked to tell himself that his Lord and Savior, Jesus Christ, was his one true companion; but lately Guilt and Fear had muscled Jesus out of his front-row-center seat. Belson worried that if he betrayed his country, God would punish him with hellfire and damnation. He wasn't thinking about what Jesus might do, or about what was the good and loving thing to do. The god of guilt and fear had replaced the one of goodness, peace, and redemption.

With the help of God's grace, could he put himself back on the road to salvation? That thought ignited a silent but fervent prayer which flipped a switch releasing a surge of power, causing waves of depression to recede. The agonizing throes of indecision loosened their grip. Fear and Guilt retreated to a place not far. The grimy train windows became pristine windows to the soul.

"I can do the right thing. I *will* do the right thing. Tomorrow, I'll seek out O'Malley. By then I'll feel stronger — just like during that poker game when I called Morgan on a $10,000.00 pot when all I was holding was a pair of sixes."

But now a new surge coursed through Belson's veins, the all-too-familiar thrill of the play. He had held many strong hands at the poker tables and each time he drew one, that indescribable thrill came together with the cards. But he had *never* held a hand like the one he had now.

Now God's earthly monuments — the magnificent range of the Bavarian Alps within his sight line — threw down their challenge.

Belson was emboldened. "Maybe I need to think twice before revealing what I know to O'Malley. Glenn Belson never shows his cards too soon. And what a hand I'm holding. I need to build the pot. The risks of playing out this hand to the end are high, but I've been there before — the place where the captivating force of the gamble takes hold and pushes out all other thoughts and emotions — banishes fear, guilt, depression, compassion, and even love."

"Before I do anything, I need to talk to Morgan. He's the only one who will be able to show me with perfect clarity, how what I have can be parlayed into something really big... The biggest thing I have ever known."

As the train pulled into the Munich station, what had begun as prayer had morphed seamlessly into unmitigated greed.

Since the changing of the guard several months earlier, when Barnstable had been replaced by O'Malley and the rest of the lineup had undergone some shuffling, the Chiefs and Deputies had adopted the practice of meeting once a week for dinner at Oscars. The food was mediocre, but Oscar had made a backroom available to his friends from the 409th, where they could meet and confer with absolute privacy. Oscar even cooperated with the internal security boys who did a sweep of the room fifteen minutes before each gathering.

The CO approved of the weekly dinner meetings but did not attend. O'Malley presided, but brought no agenda. The idea was to keep the proceedings loose, so as to encourage and stimulate creative thinking on both operational and administrative matters.

The permanent attendees were O'Malley and Smith from Operations, Ryan and Rhymes from Ops Support; LeBron and Booker from Czech Desk, Blake and Olney from German desk.

No hard liquor was allowed at these events, but each man was permitted either two glasses of beer or two glasses of wine with his meal — fairly modest fare consisting of one main dish per week, alternating weekly from veal to chicken to beef and then starting the same rotation all over again. A salad, potato, and vegetable also accompanied the main dish with either strudel or a pudding for dessert.

One dinner meeting a month was devoted entirely to administrative, staffing, supply and logistical matters. For that meeting, First Sergeant Toomey was also in attendance. It was invariably the least relaxed and most unpleasant of the gatherings. Sergeant Toomey and Captain Booker clearly disliked each other, and the mutual enmity in the room was palpable. In addition, Toomey resented the special access both O'Malley and LeBron had to the old man, and went out of his way to make negative comments about any idea or initiative that either of them offered.

Even when Toomey was not present, there was less than meaningful participation by some members of the group. Ryan had relatively little to say, probably because he was still pretty new to the business. Olney also said little, because he was taciturn and anti-social by nature.

One participant, Lieutenant Anders Smith, spoke far more than his limited experience in intelligence operations warranted. Lonnie Ryan sensed that — as to Smith — he had better watch his back.

Doug Booker approached the door of his apartment after one particularly acrimonious dinner meeting. He had only water with his meal, and merely picked at his food. Yet an attack of vertigo caused him to stagger through the doorway and fall onto the couch. The room was spinning as if he had just consumed five extra-dry martinis. Waves of nausea passed over him like the infantry crossing Utah Beach on D Day.

He knew that soon his condition would force him to bolt for the bathroom, but right now his legs felt anchored to the couch while his temples withstood the kind of pounding he imagined would be inflicted by a billy club.

After gaining some relief by finally hurling his dinner, Booker collapsed onto his bed fully clothed. These attacks were occurring more and more often now, but he would not let them disable him. He was too close to having all the evidence he needed to expose the traitor in their midst.

Caught up in the euphoria of Gaborski's revelation, the one factor Belson had not given much thought to on the train trip back from Vienna, was the danger to himself of possessing the information. Gaborski may very well have told Magyaar what he had revealed during the lie-detector test. Now, Belson was on the brink of telling Morgan.

Fear gripped him, just like it always did when he reached a pivotal moment in his life. It was clingy, like an irritating former-buddy whose company he no longer enjoyed, or a girlfriend he had lost interest in. Fear never let him alone. It had engulfed him when he had enlisted in the Army for the first time, when he had volunteered for Nam, and right before he had doubled down on a lucky number at a Monte Carlo roulette table and lost $20,000.00 on the next spin of the wheel.

He knew that Barnstable had known too much, because he himself had provided the major with much of the information. Now Barnstable was dead. Were things different in this case?

He considered Morgan a friend and a mentor. He was enthralled by what Morgan could teach him, and enjoyed his company enormously. But could he really trust him? Of course not! Morgan was a traitor. He had already betrayed his country and if push came to shove, he would think nothing of betraying someone as insignificant as Belson — or of putting a bullet in his brain.

On the other hand, only Morgan had the potential to arrange a big payday for Belson. Providing highly dangerous information to Morgan without getting caught, collecting a six figure payoff, and then walking away for good... scot-free. It was a long shot. But for his entire adult life, Belson had always bet the long shot, had always thrown caution to the wind.

Would he pull the trigger here? He did not want to wind up in prison or before a firing squad. He did not want to betray his country. He did not wish to wind up floating in the Isar with a bullet in his head. Most of all, he did not want to lose his immortal soul.

But some men create patterns of living which are self-destructive and destructive of others. For some deeply embedded reason, such men rarely deviate from their patterns of chaos.

Belson picked up the phone and dialed Morgan's number.

Chapter Ten

Betrayal

1968

Doug Booker always held the highest regard for Colonel Reitenhauser. But regardless of how adamant the colonel was about the necessity of Booker's divulging what he knew about the treachery within, Booker had so far been unable to do it. Information was the intelligence game's equivalent of a hand grenade and Booker knew from long experience that like a hand grenade, if you released the lever too soon it would explode in your face.

He had wanted indisputable proof before he disclosed what he knew to his commanding officer. Once he handed off the full evidence to the CO, his life expectancy might be extended, since he would no longer constitute as great a threat to the traitors. His own personal safety, however, was not his top priority.

Doug looked gloomily at himself in the mirror as he washed away the remaining patches of shaving cream from his gaunt face. The hollows in his cheeks seemed more pronounced than the last time he bothered to look at himself. Now a man of sallow complexion with bloodshot eyes stared back at him.

On his face was a querulous expression which seemed to ask, "Who are you looking at and why do you bother?" For just a fraction of a second a look of sadness mixed with fear flickered across his face and then was gone. Perhaps an ever-so-brief reminder that he was human and mortal.

But Doug was not like most men. Lacking in self-awareness, he simply took the fleeting expression as a reminder that time was running short. Doug Booker had little patience with introspection. He was nothing if not outer-directed. And now that direction was towards the final showdown with the malignant force inhabiting the 409th Special Investigation Detachment.

At their one-on-one meeting in less than a half hour, the colonel would be sure to remind him that last week's ascendancy by Dubcëk to First

144

Secretary of the Communist Party of Czechoslovakia, after the forces of liberation had deposed the hard-liner, Antonin Novotný, was only the first step towards the sweeping revolutionary changes scheduled for the spring. He would almost certainly add — as he had before — that unless they now moved fast to radically remove the cancer from the body of the unit, it would metastasize and kill not only the 409th Special Investigations Detachment, but possibly the entire liberation movement in Eastern Europe. Doug had come to agree with the CO, and knew that it was time to make his move.

Tom Tallifierro did not mind at all having to spend Saturday morning working at the unit. The grayness of the cold January morning did nothing to dampen his enthusiasm. The warm afterglow of his date with Kate Drummond the previous night rendered him impervious to the unusually cold temperature.

There was an added quickness and jauntiness to his step as he walked across the Max towards the unit's offices. He was in love, and he believed that Kate was too. Having reached their mid-twenties, both of them had had several relationships of varying intensity, but none of them had come anywhere close to matching the maturity and fullness of this one.

They were truly soul-mates. Even the rumor that he and Berger could be curtailed and sent to Vietnam did not dampen his spirits. After nine months, both he and Ben had carved out important niches for themselves with the unit, and he believed Colonel Reitenhauser would pull out all the stops to keep them both in place.

He was not so sure that the same could be said for guys like Sergeant Larson Knowles in the German section or Company Clerk, Tyrone Davis. And whenever he thought of the German section, it brought to mind the brooding Warren Olney and that, in turn, would open the closet in his mind where strange and unusual occurrences were stored.

Why had Olney after at least nine months of indifference, now seemed to have befriended former head telex operator, Bob Scones? This struck Tom as odd. Whenever he ran into the two of them at the Max Shop, they would appear to be locked in intense conversation in a booth by themselves. What was that all about?

Equally unfathomable was why First Sergeant Toomey had decoupled the positions of Company Clerk and Supply Clerk and moved the perennial screw-up, Corporal Yancy 'Village' Cook out of the Motor Pool and into the Supply Room as the new Supply Clerk.

Having failed with Tom and Ben, and harboring racial prejudice against Davis, might old Sock-It have planted Village in the center of the detachment's offices just to give himself another set of eyes and ears? And why had the CO approved it?

Anyway, Tom would make a greater effort to keep his own eyes and ears open. As O'Malley always said, in the intelligence game, things seldom are what they appear to be.

Tom spied Captain Booker who was also headed for the front entrance of the building, but with hardly the same purposeful strut. Booker seemed to shuffle lately rather than walk, kind of like a zombie in one of those living-dead movies.

Tom held the door for Booker as they entered the building together. Booker seemed to have aged ten years in the last six months. Had he shown-up for sick call instead of at the 409th, the Army doctors probably would have admitted him to the hospital for tests.

Tom greeted Booker with a "good morning, sir," but the captain offered no reply. Instead, he stared at Tom with a far-off expression on his face, which yielded no sign of recognition.

Neither man spoke on the lift or as they walked down the long corridor toward their respective offices. But then just as Tom was about to peel off to enter the Ops Support Offices, Booker without turning to look in Tom's direction, spoke with a distracted air about him, "Good work Tallifierro on that Hof Road business."

A stunned Tom Tallifierro managed to croak out a "Thank you, sir," though Booker didn't appear to hear it.

Fred Reitenhauser found himself on this cold Saturday morning to be more concerned about the discordant notes sounding in his command than ever before. He had reluctantly let Toomey move Cook upstairs, mainly because it would be easier for him to keep an eye on both of them. Also on his mind was Belson. It might have been a mistake asking General Stansfield to assign the man to the 409th on a permanent basis. Belson seemed to him to be at loose ends, hardly the kind of stoic, nonplussed individual that one looked for in a polygraph operator. Then there was Scones. The CO had decided that in this time of crisis, he did not want someone as lazy and barely competent as Scones in his unit. He had put in a request to Group to transfer Scones out ASAP, and had informed Scones of the decision.

And what was up with the apparent newly-formed friendship between Olney and Scones? He would also need to keep an eye on that. Olney reminded him of some of the super spooks he had known in Berlin during the early days of the CIA: silent, brooding and indecipherable. There was something truly menacing about Olney, which was fine so long as he was only a menace to the enemy.

Reitenhauser needed to have that long overdue talk with Mitch Blake about Olney. The CO and Blake would be meeting for their monthly extended lunch at the Officer's Club on Tuesday, and that would be as good a time as any to bring up the subject.

Overriding all of his other concerns, however, was the problem of Doug Booker and the secrets he was carrying around inside of him. Reitenhauser strongly suspected that the unbearable burden of those secrets was the main reason for Booker's obvious physical decline. Booker needed to unburden himself for his own wellbeing but more importantly, as far as the CO was concerned, for the good of the unit.

Booker was due for an appointment with the CO in ten minutes, and he would receive an ultimatum. Either he disclosed what he knew this morning, or he would be relieved of his duties.

After grabbing a cup of the 409th's strong coffee, Booker ambled towards the colonel's office. His first order of business would be to finally tell the colonel everything he knew about the treason extant at the 409th Special Investigations Detachment.

Only his long-time companions, guilt and fear, had thus far prevented Belson from approaching Morgan to arrange a deal. He would provide the name of the mole if Morgan could secure payment to him from Hostile.

His price was $100,000.00, and it was non-negotiable. If Hostile believed the information to be credible, it would not dicker over the price. They would either pay it in full or pay him nothing, and torture the information out of him. He would have to trust Morgan to refuse to reveal Belson's identity until the deal had been made. Hostile would not renege once it had committed itself because if that got out, too many of its sources of information might dry up.

Belson knew the danger he would be in as soon as he told even one other person what he had learned from Gaborski. But, actually, he had been in danger since the second Gaborski had spoken the name, "Uri Putyagin." True, the risk to life and limb would be dramatically increased once Morgan knew; but as long as he was already exposed, Belson reasoned, he might as well try to make some real money out of it. The whole deal was risky as hell, but the potential pay off made it well worth his while. He liked the odds. But then again, when *didn't* he?

*   *   *

Morgan

What Belson had just told him was incredible. Fool though he was, Belson had come up with the goods this time. He would, of course, downplay the polygraph man's role and inflate his own to Hostile, but that was par for the course in this business, and everyone would expect it.

The $100,000.00 payoff should be no problem. He had negotiated more money for less information in the past. Of course, he would have liked more than his standard 10% commission, but he might go along with the $10,000.00 for himself. It should be a fast and easy ten grand and, in any event, this was about more than just money.

He would like nothing better than to take those bastards, Reitenhauser and Stansfield, down a peg. After Putyagin was blown as an agent, it would cost them their commands at the very least, assuming they weren't both forced into retirement.

But now the man known as 'Morgan' to the army of lowlifes and bottom-feeders who owed their pathetic existences to his largesse, gently reprimanded himself. "You're thinking small again. Don't look at this thing like a third-rate wheeler-dealer. This information is dynamite. Hostile is going to need my help in utilizing it to maximum effect. And they don't know enough about the inner workings of NATO's intelligence network to pull it off. I do. And for that reason, they *need* me. This is going to make me a major international player and, in the process, it's likely to change the face of the map of Europe. I want, and will get, more than a measly ten grand."

Káz Penchak reported for duty to Colonel Reitenhauser after his extensive period of R&R on the southern coast of Italy. He now stood before the CO, looking tanned and fit.

"Welcome back Kázimer. Please take a seat."

"Yes, sir."

"Would you like a cup of coffee?"

"No thank you, sir."

"Káz, first let me congratulate you on what my sources tell me was a highly successful operation in Prague, one which contributed to the regime change in Czechoslovakia."

"Thank you sir, but I don't think I did that much."

"Yes you did, and the Army has seen fit to award you the Silver Star. A private ceremony will be held here in the large conference room on 10 February, at 1130 hours."

"I am overwhelmed sir," said a clearly touched and surprised Penchak.

"You deserve it," the CO said. "Now let me move to the business at hand. You know that you can no longer be operational outside of West Germany. But there is no reason why we can't alter your appearance a bit, give you a new cover, and have you work on some special assignments directly for me."

"That would be a great honor, sir."

"The assignment I am about to give you is one of the utmost sensitivity. You are to discuss it with *no one* but me. If you need to contact me, make an appointment through Gerda."

Káz nodded. "I understand, sir."

"Good," the CO said. "Now, let's talk details. I need you to conduct an internal investigation."

East Berlin

Uri had paid keen attention to unfolding events in Prague, and was not surprised that Dubcëk had moved quickly to lift restrictions on the press and allow open political gatherings and meetings without fear of reprisal from the government. He had heard from reliable sources that this was a harbinger of many more reforms to come during the spring of 1968. Uri was, however, a bit mystified as to why the regional commandment of the KGB wished to see him, to discuss matters of mutual interest concerning the Soviet Socialist Republic of Czechoslovakia.

Seated in his 5th floor office in East Berlin overlooking Leninplatz, Uri gazed fondly at the framed photograph on his desk of his wife and four teenage children. The two oldest, the twins, were now away at university in Stalingrad. The two younger children, a boy and a girl, were carefree secondary school students.

For fifteen years, Uri had lived with the threat of arrest and possible execution if caught, every waking minute and sometimes while he slept, when his worst nightmares came to visit.

Uri had no regrets for himself. This was the way he had chosen to live his life and — given the same choice a second time, he would make the exact same decision. He was a man of both ideas and action. Had the Bolsheviks created a just and fair society, he would undoubtedly have been a dedicated soldier for the regime, willing to lay down his life for the cause at any time.

Uri did, however, regret marrying and having children. His family never ceased to touch the softest part of his heart with an ineluctable tenderness which had given him his only refuge from the arctic coldness and mindless cruelty of the totalitarian state. Still, it had been terribly selfish on his part to subject them to ruin if he ever got caught. Only the single life was appropriate for a man with his vocation, for an enlistee in a war with no foreseeable end.

The East Berlin branch of the KGB occupied the entire basement of the same building in which Uri had his offices. There the Soviet Union's main clandestine security agency and secret police was housed in a warren of grey windowless and cube-shaped offices with sheet rock walls, barren of decoration of any kind. Each individual room had been carefully sound-proofed.

The offices ran along both sides of four linear corridors, each two hundred feet in length, running parallel to one another, with a solid steel door at the far end of each corridor. One could only speculate as to the nature of the activities conducted on the other side of the steel doors.

After clearing several rigorous security checks, Uri was admitted to the Commandant's office. Perhaps as a concession to rank and position, the floor was covered with some kind of generic government-gray carpet.

The Commandant sat behind a decent oak desk, adorned only by a couple of family photos in cheap frames. Two drab guest chairs were arranged in front of the desk, with a third against the wall. The room contained no other furniture.

The Commandant rose to greet Uri and the two men shook hands. "Comrade Putyagin, I have been wanting to make your acquaintance for some time. It is a pleasure to finally meet you."

Though Uri didn't believe him, he doubted that he was being called to headquarters to be arrested. The KGB didn't work that way. If they were going to arrest him, they would drag him from his bed in the middle of the night.

"The pleasure is mine Commandant. I have heard many good things about you."

"From a man of your prominence to a simple civil servant such as myself, that is very flattering Comrade Putyagin."

'Simple' was not the word that Uri would have chosen to describe the Commandant.

"Comrade Putyagin, I have called you here this morning on a matter of the greatest importance to the State. I assure you that I sought and obtained the approval of the Politburo to speak to you. A person of your standing is entitled to at least that courtesy." Another lie.

"I shall get right to the point. Your services are required for a secret mission, vital to the interests of the Soviet republics."

*   *   *

Munich

Art LeBron was deeply worried about his friend, Doug Booker. The man's physical deterioration over the last couple of months had been dramatic. Art had been nagging him to see a doctor for a complete check-up but his pleas had fallen on deaf ears.

Yet, Booker showed up for work every morning and was carrying his full load. LeBron had to marvel at the man's stubborn, yet gallant, persistence. However, he knew Booker well enough to perceive that it was more than his legendary stoicism which was driving his relentless forward motion. LeBron sensed that Doug Booker was engaged in his own private war, and was determined to see it through to the end with every ounce of strength left in his body. It was now pure will that fired his internal pistons.

LeBron also wondered if the frequent presence of Olney, Toomey, Blaulicht and Smith seated in the old man's reception area, was akin to the overhead circling of the buzzards.

If that group had formed some sort of a cabal within the unit, LeBron could easily counter it with a coalition of his own composed of O'Malley, Ryan, Rhymes, Winicki, Berger, and Tallifierro. After all, as executive officer with greater access to the CO than anyone else, he could easily command a following. But it was mainly because he was XO that such a prospect was anathema to him. Cabals were corrosive of a company's strength and unity. He would rather pluck out the bad apples than adopt their tactics. In his heart, he knew that the private war of Douglas Booker was about just that.

Elsewhere it was carnival time in Munich, and the sights and sounds of young revelers in costumes ranging from the beautifully exotic to the grotesquely macabre filled the February night time streets of the club district.

The festival, known as *Fasching*, was a magnet for young men and women of all stripes from across Western Europe — everyday office workers, laborers, artists, college students, expatriots, tourists, vagabonds, hippies, hustlers, grifters, pimps, prostitutes, entertainers, Euro-trash, servicemen, playboys, mimes, jugglers, and street musicians — all thrown together into a festive smorgasbord of excited laughter, music, reunion, gaiety, and romance.

The spectacular costumes provided the commonality which granted anonymity and bridged the vast differences among the thousands of participants.

Among those revelers were Tom Tallifierro, Kate Drummond, Ben Berger, and Melissa Aplan.

Melissa had used a week of her annual two weeks leave to fly in from Africa to spend time with Ben and to enjoy the festival.

The two young couples sat at a window table in a small café slightly off the beaten track, but still within the area of the Fasching celebration. Their costumes were less bizarre than many, but imaginative nonetheless. Tom was George Harrison, and Ben was John Lennon, from the cover of the Beatles album, 'Sergeant Pepper's Lonely Hearts Club Band.' Melissa was Morticia from the Adams Family TV series, and Kate was a pretty convincing 'Some Like it Hot' version of Marilyn Monroe.

They had decided to beat the crush of the biggest crowds by having an early dinner ahead of the main celebrations, which didn't peak until around 10:00 p.m. It was only 6:30 as they sipped cocktails and gazed upon the Munich street, where isolated costumed groups of threes and fours traipsed about. The conversation was light-hearted, a combination of gentle ribbing and catching up on what was going on in each other's lives.

Of course, Ben, Tom, and Kate could not talk about their work and were pretty much relegated to safe topics like hobbies, movies, skiing, and current events. Kate was just remarking on her surprise that the widowed Jackie Kennedy had just married the much older Greek shipping magnate, Aristotle Onassis, when Tom caught something out of the corner of his eye. A spanking new, top of the line, BMW moved slowly past the window of the café. Behind the wheel was a familiar figure.

Tom did a double-take, and then spoke excitedly. "That's Belson driving that BMW."

"You've got to be kidding!" said Ben. He craned his neck to get a closer look at the car. "No, you're right. That's definitely Belson. How does he afford a new BMW on a non-com's pay? Anyway, he's always talking about how broke he is."

Several days after the Belson sighting during Fasching, Morgan took advantage of his brief three-day holiday in Zurich to deposit his $100,000.00 in cash from the Belson/Putyagin deal into one of his several numbered Swiss bank accounts. His commission from Belson was only $10,000.00 but unbeknownst to the polygraph man, Morgan had negotiated another $90,000.00 with the KGB as a finder's fee.

Morgan sighed with satisfaction over the quick hundred grand windfall he had just garnered. He then took ten seconds or so to do a self-appraisal. Would it have been honorable to tell Belson about the finder's fee?

"Forget what's honorable," he thought; "Why would I have any honor? I'm a criminal."

Anyway, Belson would have no use for the extra money. He had been found dead two days before, during the Fasching festival, lying face down in an alley of the Munich red light district — a shiv protruding from his back.

The corpse had revealed no evidence of torture. Morgan was mildly annoyed by this fact, because it told him that the KGB had probably recovered whatever part of the $100,000.00 Belson had not yet spent. Had Belson refused to tell them where the money was, or declined to cooperate in its recovery, he would have been beaten and tortured until he had a change of heart.

The bodies were starting to pile up around the 409th Special Investigations Detachment.

Temporarily consumed by smug satisfaction, it hadn't yet occurred to Morgan that maybe Magyaar had gotten to Belson before the KGB.

Chapter Eleven

The Prague Spring

"You say you want a revolution
Well, you know
We all want to change the world...
You say you got a real solution
Well, you know
We'd all love to see the plan."

— John Lennon

Prague

The early days of a revolution witness the most intense passion, intellectual vigor, and emotional power. So it was on the streets of Boston in 1775 when inspired patriots dumped British tea into the harbor; in 1917 when young disciples of Karl Marx exuberantly harangued passers-by on Moscow's streets with Marxist-Leninist dogma; and in 1956 when Imre Nagy and his strident young freedom fighters — including Lugash Magyaar — threw down the gauntlet to Russia's army of occupation during the Hungarian anti-Soviet revolution.

The days of radical change, optimism, and exhilaration for Czechoslovakia really began on January 5, 1968, with the inception of the brief reign of Alexander Dubček as leader of that previously beleaguered nation.

Much of the sweet euphoria, magnificent bravery, innocent self-delusion and madly intoxicating ideas, upon which so many young revolutionaries binged in the squares and parks in those glorious days of the Prague spring, were captured by Franco-Czech writer, Milan Kundera, in his profound 1984 novel, '*The Unbearable Lightness of Being.*' One, however, might take issue with Kundera's philosophical thesis in this trenchant work, that because one's decisions and actions together with fortuitous events, occur but once and then are gone — never to return or

154

recur, life is invested with a certain lightness of being. A weightlessness that renders it unbearably empty of meaning.

But this is philosophy in the abstract and the march of history is one way to demonstrate to the philosopher that his theories do not truly meet the test of real events. Nietsche went to the other extreme in positing that life's experiences recur over and over again for all eternity and, therefore, are of great weight.

But somehow, war and revolution, don't lend themselves well to profound philosophical thought. They are too much a part of the painful here and now — too much an aggregation of unique and intensely individual decisions and acts — to fit neatly into existential theories. It would seem that just like in all of life, random, fortuitous events heavily influence the outcomes of wars and revolutions. This is not to say that individual acts of inspired idealism, morality, and courage are somehow stripped of their meaning. In the long Cold War, they meant *everything*.

Prominent among such individual feats were the democratic reforms instituted in Czechoslovakia by the new First Secretary of the Communist Party, Alexander Dubcëk, with full participation by Ludvik Svoboda, who replaced Antonin Novotný as President on March 22, 1968.

In February, Dubcëk spoke eloquently of his desire "to build an advanced socialist society...that corresponds to the historical democratic traditions of Czechoslovakia, in accordance with the experience of other communist parties..." It quickly became clear, however, that Dubcëk's vision would radically depart from the Soviet paradigm of a communist state. His 'Action Program' launched in April of 1968 was replete with liberal reforms designed to increase freedom of press, freedom of speech, and freedom of travel. His goal was clearly to limit the power of the secret police, to enhance the quality and accessibility of consumer goods, and to maintain good relations with Western nations.

His was an enlightened socialism, crafted to provide for "a fuller life of the personality than any bourgeois democracy." Dubcëk's plan called for a ten-year program of gradual democratic elections with an ultimate new form of democratic socialism replacing the status quo.

Munich

At the 409th a sickly Doug Booker assiduously studied the Dubcëk speeches and other proclamations. Astounded by their breathtaking audacity, he knew that Secretary Brezhnev and the other members of the Soviet Politburo would not take this lying down. There would be trouble for certain, just like in Hungary in '56, and once the repression started, there was no telling what its scope might be and where it would lead.

Booker was more determined than ever to ready the 409th to play its part in the battles to come, by identifying and exposing the traitor within the unit. Not for a single instant did he believe that it had been the now-deceased, Glenn Belson, alone. He had already disclosed to the CO whom he thought the real traitor was, but he needed solid proof.

Booker scoured hundreds of case officer post-meeting reports with renewed dedication. Blessed with a powerful memory, he was able to retain fact patterns built on repetition better than most people. Failure to change-up comfortable routines had been the downfall of many agents and agent handlers. Meeting too often at the same location, staying repeatedly at the same hotel, using the same dead-drop or cover for too long a period of time, were all traps resulting from laziness and carelessness.

Now Booker had begun to discern something he had not picked up on during his first read-through of the reports. Agents were not always paid in U.S. dollars. Some preferred payment in other European currencies and most intelligence agencies accommodated them. In the 409th's geographical areas, U.S. dollars, German marks, and Austrian schillings were the most commonly used currencies, but payment was also made occasionally in French francs, Swiss francs, or British pounds. Oddly, one particular case officer of the 409th paid his agents with Swiss francs approximately 75% of the time. No other case officer of the unit had ever utilized Swiss francs to pay his agents more than 10% of the time.

Booker could see no particular reason why the agents of this case officer would have a preference for Swiss currency. Like the rest of the unit's case officers, the man's agents were predominantly German and Austrian, with a few Czechs, Hungarians, and Yugoslavians thrown in. Maybe the preference was that of the case officer, rather than the agents. Why would that be? Perhaps the motive was the one that most often drove patterns and habits of human behavior, simple convenience. And why would Swiss francs be the most convenient? Because they were the easiest to get. But why would that be? Perhaps because the case officer spent a good deal of time in Swiss banks, where dollars, pounds, or marks were readily exchangeable for Swiss francs.

But unit records had never shown this particular case officer as seeking reimbursement for a trip to Switzerland. And it was unlikely that his reports would ever make reference to Switzerland. So now, Booker would go through the hundreds of reports of other case officers, to see if a circumstantial link to Switzerland could be established.

"Wait a second," Booker said to himself. "Maybe I already have it."

Contained within the thousands of pages were the half dozen or so incidents reported by the unit's agents, of a gentleman who claimed to be from Zurich, and who had attempted to recruit them to spy for East Germany. What was the name the man used? Ah yes... *Morgan*.

Kázimir Penchak's secret investigation for Colonel Reitenhauser had skirted the edges of the body of evidence. He had uncovered circumstantial evidence of the target's possible duplicity, in his travel records, his personal friends and associates, his spending patterns, his past activities and associations, etc.

But now the CO had asked him to tail the target for an entire week — to go wherever he went — so long as the destination was not in a hostile country or denied area. His target was now about a hundred feet ahead of him as they both boarded the express train from Munich to Berne, Zurich, and Geneva.

Lonnie Ryan's mood was glum. After a full year as head of the Ops Support Section, he felt he had accomplished much in that position. His department had grown from six to eleven people since he'd assumed his duties; and he had received some real kudos from Higher for the work he had done with Rhymes in Vienna the previous summer.

His temporary capture by Hostile had not been perceived negatively. His fellow officers with the unit seemed to view the incident as Lonnie earning his spurs. After Vienna and the 14332 adventure, he was no longer perceived as a combat virgin. And he had also gained some favorable mention for efficiently managing the hottest case officer team, not only in the 409th, but in all of the 44th M.I. Group — the amazing Rhymes and Berger, or 'Rhymesberger.'

Then there was the spectacular deciphering of the Hof Road intercept by his man, Tallifierro, which was also something of a feather in the cap of the Ops Support Section. Lonnie hoped that with all of this on the plus side of the ledger in his 201 file, a promotion to captain would be coming soon. Once that happened, he would be ready to make his big move to convince Megan to marry him and join him in Munich, where they would take up residence in one of the commodious officer's apartments not too far from the Max.

With all of this good stuff going for him, he had been surprised and somewhat taken aback when Colonel Reitenhauser had called him in after lunch the previous day and unceremoniously announced that he was taking away one of Ryan's two best men. Tom Tallifierro was to report to Captain Booker by 0800 the next day, to assume his new duties as Deputy Chief Analyst for the 409th. Along with his new title went a promotion to buck sergeant.

Booker was to assume the newly-created position of Chief Analyst of the unit. It was contemplated that others would be added to the fledgling analysts' team in the near future.

Of course, Ryan had no way of knowing that this move did not reflect poorly on him. He had no need to know yet, so he had not been brought into the loop concerning the CO's suspicions about Belson or the frantic efforts by the CO and Booker to discover hard evidence of treachery by a certain member of the 409th.

This was the nature of an intelligence unit. Compartmentalization was the name of the game. No one except the colonel, O'Malley, and LeBron even knew that Káz Penchak was operational again. The Max Shop rumor mill had him in a rubber room somewhere at one of Group's funny farms. The CO would, however, tell Booker of Penchak's reactivation.

Munich in springtime was a wondrous place. Brightly colored flowers — reds, violets, and yellows were everywhere. The temperatures were consistently ideal, mid-sixties to mid-seventies. The aromas of the rich, dark Mai-bach beer were omnipresent. Chalet-style homes adorned with tulips of dazzling hue and in full bloom, gently set back from the tree-lined country roads just outside of the city, lent a Hansel and Gretel feel to the entire region.

In stark juxtaposition with the fantasy-like ambiance of Munich and its environs was the village of Dachau right outside of the City. The former Nazi death camp had been restored as a Holocaust memorial and museum.

As Tom Tallifierro sat alone in the unit's windowless room adorned only by a wall-map of Western Europe, the mind-blowing dichotomy between the incomprehensible horror and malignant evil of the former death camp and the glorious springtime Bavaria presented an insistent razor-edge paradox, which Tom's mind simply could not process and assimilate on this particular magnificent spring morning. How could such a vile obscenity co-exist with the marvelously beneficent gemutlikeit of Munich?

Suddenly for Tom, Bavaria's mythical charm and beauty dissolved into a cruel joke. Gone for him was the sense of mystical wellbeing Munich usually evoked. Now he hated Munich, and Bavaria, and Germany, and Germany's Germans. Despite his transcendent joy of being in love with Kate, the defilement of everything human and sacred and beautiful by the remembered barbarism of the Nazis, so starkly symbolized by Dachau, had turned his insides into a toxic, bilious well.

But Tom did not dwell for long on his inner turmoil. The historian in him permitted a withdrawal to a plateau of detachment faster than most.

He would use the disgust which had overtaken him as motivation in the present war against the evil living in the time and place to which he had been thrust by fate — a time of dead young freedom fighters lying in the streets of Budapest and East German citizens who had tried to escape to freedom, riddled with bullets, their bodies trapped in the barbed wire atop the Berlin Wall.

The table was strewn with case officer reports, maps, surveys, polygraph readings, transcripts of phone taps and bugs, and other arcana of the trade. Where to start? Probably with Group's six-inch thick geographical analysis of Hostile's 'Resource Recruitment Demographics.' Booker was especially anxious that Tom give that report top priority.

Tom's initial perusal of the massive report was unproductive. The dry statistics as to the incidence of reported Hostile activity on a percentage basis, city by city and province by province throughout West Germany and Austria, was about as interesting as watching toenails grow.

But Tom was persistent and methodical. He fought off lethargy and sleep in equal measures for the first three quarters of an hour, until something caught his attention just as he languidly flipped another typed page. It was the percentage summary of Hostile recruitment efforts for the year 1967. At the top of the list were three cities: Munich with 17%, Regensburg with 16%, and Salzburg with 15%. From highest percentage down the page to lowest percentage, thirty German and Austrian cities were listed.

Next came Vienna at 10%, but of the remaining twenty six cities on the list, no single city had a higher percentage than 2%; and some had percentages of less than one.

Two facts tugged at Tom's thoughts and competed with each other for his attention. One concerned the troika of Munich, Regensburg, and Salzburg. Only three cities out of thirty hosted forty-eight percent of the activity. The second was that those three cities formed a connection in his mind to some other important fact. What was it?

He taxed his brain, but could not remember. He decided to mentally review the main permanent assignment he had handled thus far with the 409th, the vetting of potential new resources for project Kryptonite. To jog his memory, he used a piece of tracing paper as an overlay and laid it on the map of Germany and Austria on the table. He then connected the three cities, using a ruler, by drawing three lines so that a triangle of sorts appeared on the page.

Referring to the map's scale, he estimated that he would be able, without speeding, to drive from Munich to Salzburg to Regensburg and then back to Munich easily in about four hours. The high concentration of

Hostile's activities within that small triangle was what had caught his attention once before.

Then he remembered. In vetting the potential new agents (mostly recruited by Rhymesberger) in that tri-city region, he had been especially diligent, because his research had revealed that Group reported six fully functional chapters of the Magisterium of Red Guard Army Networks within that tri-city area. Tom had been struck at the time by the fact that there had been only three chapters within the triangular area in 1966, and only two in 1965.

Putting the high volume of Hostile recruitment within that area together with the obvious growth of the Red Guards, a particularly deadly Marxist group, told Tom that something big was coming. Moreover, the expansion of the Red Guards in the triangular hotbed running to and across the Austrian border and within fifty miles of the Czech border was roughly contemporaneous in time with the growth of the liberalization movement in Czechoslovakia. The temperature of the Cold War was clearly rising.

Tom's mind drifted back to that day when he and Ben had sat in this same room during their training. Then the only thing on the table had been the book provided by O'Malley, containing photos of shocking atrocities against Western espionage agents — eviscerations, castrations, burn marks from head to foot, eyes gouged out, stumps where once had been hands, decapitations, and every other imaginable desecration of the human body. All of that had been the handiwork of the Red Guards.

In the months and years after World War II, the clandestine efforts of the Red Guards had been instrumental in the Soviet bloodbath of democrats in Bulgaria, the brutal communist repression of Yugoslavia, as well as the 1948 coup d'état in Czechoslovakia, which had saddled the Czechs with a Soviet-controlled dictatorship.

The Red Guards had even been active in Italy in 1946 and 1947, attempting to foment a Communist putsch to overthrow the pro-Western government. They were also suspected of having tortured government workers into giving false testimony against thirteen Polish officials accused of treason by the Soviets in one of Stalin's first post-war show trials.

Tom shook his head in unpleasant recollection. There was no doubt about it. This was one nasty bunch. He was tempted to call it a day and simply report his findings to Booker. But there was too much meaningful data before him, calling for more analysis; and begging for inferences to be drawn. If he didn't do it, Booker would take it all on his own shoulders. From the look of the man, one of these days, Doug Booker was liable to collapse from the weight.

Tom took a break, walked down the hall to Admin and asked the brand new assistant Clerk, PFC Joseph Cherniewski, to please pick him up a tuna fish sandwich and a coke from the Max Shop. He didn't dare stick his head in the Ops Support offices to see Kate, lest he break both his concentration and willpower to remain sequestered in his monastic cell of a room for several more hours.

The sandwich was good, piled high with tuna salad, lettuce, and tomatoes, with sweet pickles on the side.

The mid-afternoon lunch plus the caffeine in the coke restored Tom's energies. "Let's hit it," he said to himself. "The Red Guards are not likely to be taking any afternoons off."

Tom's reading picked up where he had left off, with the data on resource recruitment by Hostile. When the colonel and Booker had given him his intelligence briefing for the new position, they hadn't held much back. He had the need to know most, but not all, of what they knew in order to properly do his job as an intelligence analyst. He now knew about Belson and their suspicions that one of their own people was a traitor, who used the cover name *Morgan*.

They had not identified the person they suspected. That kind of information could get you killed. For that matter, if there was a traitor in their midst, Tom was in danger just by virtue of his present job description. A chill ran down his spine, which he quickly dismissed.

He needed to home in on the specific current predicament of the 409th. Tom's deep study of history had taught him that there were few pure coincidences of any real importance. His gut told him Group's security breach, Barnstable's death and Belson's murder were all closely connected. His brain confirmed it. He also knew that — regardless of Booker's suspicions — without hard evidence, Morgan would remain a shadowy and opaque figure, just beyond their grasp.

Tom was also convinced that Morgan could not be trapped by tailing him, tapping his phones, bugging his apartment, or opening his mail. The reported contacts with the so-called 'Morgan' by local national agents of the 409th, now numbering more than a dozen, went as far back as 1961 and the Berlin Wall Crisis. Anyone who could operate as a fully active resource — not a dormant sleeper agent — for so long without leaving any semblance of a trail, had to be one wily and elusive operator.

Tom did not suffer from hubris. He knew that after only one year as an intelligence operative, he still lacked the seasoning and experience to make him boldly confident of his ideas. But on the other hand, the CO, LeBron, Booker, and O'Malley had all seen something special in him, and had entrusted him with a big job. They were expecting him to produce dramatic results. There was no time for humility. He had to trust his own judgment as much as they did. If he was wrong, so be it.

One of Tom's convictions was that in order to catch Morgan one had to dig from the inside out — from the center to the outer layers — and not from the outside in. Morgan was elusive primarily because they knew almost nothing about him. They needed to find out who this traitor was at his core, what he was like as a man. What were his likes and dislikes? His habits and patterns of behavior? His world view? His normal traits and his deviant ones? His philosophy? His sexual orientation? His friends and associates?

They needed to send their field agents out to interview as many as possible of the agents who had encountered the man, who had interacted with him. Those agents had to be pumped for every little detail they could recall about him. Then all of that data had to be synthesized into a personality profile, a dossier on the mysterious Morgan.

Tom next charted and graphed the agents who Morgan had contacted, No help there. There was no obvious pattern geographically. What about 14332's list? Not one of the agents involved were mentioned there. A connection by any of them to Magyaar? To Penchak? Or to Belson? As to the first two, Tom found nothing. When Tom came to Belson, he realized that he might have discovered a lead.

Nine of the twelve agents Morgan had approached had first been polygraphed by Belson. But Belson was dead, and for the time being that fact led nowhere. But what was interesting was that all of those polygraph tests had taken place before Belson came to the 409th. When he had put those agents on the box, he had been assigned to Group's Internal Security Division (I.S.D.) a very promising link to that compromised unit. He drew another triangle on a separate sheet of paper:

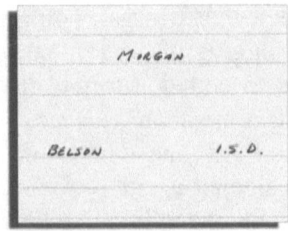

Who else could he link in? Two others were dead, 14332 and Barnstable. Agent 14332 and his sub-agents appeared to be an autonomous group firmly handled by Art LeBron. Tom had never seen a shred of evidence connecting them to any of the others under his scrutiny — not to Belson, Barnstable, Penchak, the Morgan from Switzerland, or the suspected '409th' Morgan, who might (or might not) be one and the same. It was almost a little too neat and convenient. But wait, that was not entirely true. Hadn't Belson's last polygraph exam subject been Gaborski, Magyaar's right-hand man? Yes... Another interesting fact that required follow-up.

Next, Tom read through Barnstable's 201 file, in a search for possible linkage. He found the usual summary of promotions, duty stations, citations, medals, and comments by commanding officers. It was all pretty prosaic stuff. The comments were bland and boring. Barnstable was "conscientious," "competent," "a good soldier," "loyal," "a leader of men," and so on.

By its nature, the 201 file of an area intelligence officer was almost always sanitized. Nothing of importance related to the performance of his duties was going to be put in his official records, which traveled with him to every new duty station, and would be read by many individuals lacking both the necessary security clearance and the need to know.

Barnstable's previous duty station prior to Munich station was I.S.D. in Frankfurt. That was certainly interesting. Tom rubbed his eyes. His vision was getting blurry from six straight hours of reading. He was on the last page of Barnstable's file when suddenly another nugget was yielded up to him from the page.

In Colonel Reitenhauser's handwriting was the following entry:

'4 April 1966 — Probable inappropriate personal relationship with female non-com of the unit.'

There was no further elaboration. Tom quickly grabbed Winicki's 201 file from the wheeled cart next to his chair, containing the files for all personnel of the unit. The materials now had his full attention. Before beginning his reading of Sergeant Winicki's file, Tom got up to make sure the door was locked.

He read through the same type of window dressing and eyewash in the thick file as had appeared in Barnstable's folder. There were also the usual dry facts, including all of her duty assignments.

It was her duty station immediately preceding Munich that caused in Tom an instant elevation in adrenaline:

'44th Military Intelligence Group, Regensburg station, 1 October 1962 to 30 September 1965. M.O.S. 120, Case Officer.'

"Case officer? You've got to be shitting me. I thought she was just a fucking telex operator. What the hell is going on here?" Tom heard himself speaking and swearing aloud. He immediately reprimanded himself into silence.

He probed his memory to call up what his prior research had told him about Regensburg. He remembered instantly the line in the Group overview report he read at that time:

'Regensburg, Land of Bavaria, close proximity to Austrian and Czech borders, believed to be the location of the largest single Red Guards unit in Western Europe.'

Tom yanked a fresh sheet of paper from his pad and drew a new configuration:

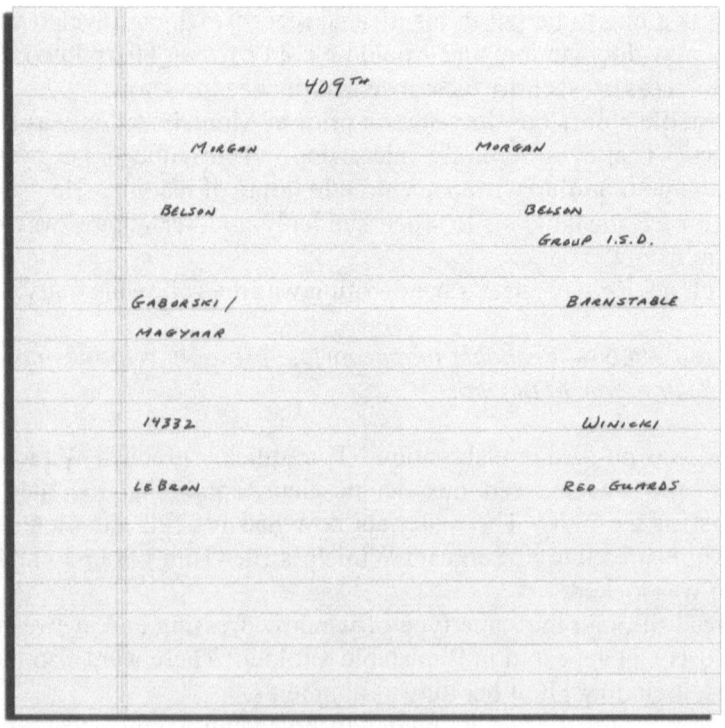

Tom then looked at the ponderous and self-important full name of the Red Guards — *'Magisterium of Red Guard Army Networks'* — too long.

He printed just the first initial of each word in the title under "Red Guards" on his chart:

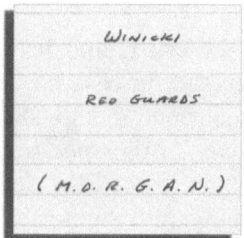

He stared in disbelief at what he had just printed on the page. "Holy Shit! How did I not notice that before?"

He sat in silence for several minutes, assimilating the information on the paper in front of him, assessing its implications. Some of the connections on the page were tenuous at best and proved little at the present time. But, if each of the links in the chain from Red Guards up to Winicki, to Barnstable, to I.S.D., to Belson and Morgan, and then to the 409th, proved to signify what Tom *thought* they did... Then the highly dangerous and insidious Red Guards (MORGAN) had penetrated the 44th Military Intelligence Group's flagship station — the 409th Special Investigations Detachment.

Tom just sat and tried to process what had been revealed. Was Morgan just an acronym, not a person? Or was it one man? Or several different men? Or was it a woman?

He was amazed to see that it was 2100 hours, and he had been sitting at the table of the locked, windowless room for eleven hours. There was probably no one left in the building except the duty officer.

Tom needed to talk to the CO, but not here. He didn't even want to be seen going into the colonel's office.

He was afraid to talk to Booker before he had a chance to brief the CO on what he had discovered. Booker had an air of doom about him which, Tom was afraid might be contagious.

He wanted out of this room, out of the 409th offices and away from the Max, right *now*. He needed to see and talk to Ben about all this; but he could not. He was sworn to secrecy. Loneliness crept up on him, making his fear even worse. Two colleagues from the unit were dead. One of its top agents was also dead. As he sat in the bleak room, he could not be sure others weren't dead as well.

He couldn't really be sure who he could trust either. But, he had to trust *somebody*. But first a claustrophobic urge to run from that dismal room overwhelmed him. He would leave everything on the table. The reinforced steel door locked from the outside automatically and the colonel had shown him how to activate the second lock — a combination lock — from the outside.

First, he had to destroy the charts and lists he had drawn. It was too risky to have them on his person, in case he were killed or taken captive. He quickly looked around the room and spied a large ashtray in the corner on the floor — probably there for the specific purpose Tom had in mind. He put the ashtray on the table, placed the several pieces of paper in the ashtray and lit them with his cigarette lighter.

Because he had torn the pages out of the pad, ahead of time, no indentations from his writing had been left on the pad.

Tom passed the duty officer, Sergeant Kurt Blaulicht, on his way out of the unit's door and they exchanged a brief but not unfriendly greeting.

He ran down the short flight of stairs and then hopped aboard the lift which descended towards the main floor. The agonizing slowness of the ancient contraption heightened his anxiety incrementally as he approached each floor, half-expecting the bad guys to stop the lift, get on and murder him.

When Tom had started his new job, O'Malley had insisted to the CO that Tom be armed. He now carried a thirty-eight revolver in an ankle holster. O'Malley had also been so alarmed by his lack of proficiency with the weapon that they had spent a couple of hours practicing at the pistol range at the end of every work day. After five days of O'Malley's careful coaching, Tom's accuracy had improved significantly. He was now grateful for O'Malley's concern as he gripped the revolver in his right hand.

When the lift reached the dimly lit lobby on the ground floor, Tom slowly looked out both sides of the lift before bolting out of the gate and then the building with great dispatch.

Tom literally sprinted to his VW Beetle in the Max parking area, looked around quickly to make sure he had not been followed, unlocked the door and within less than a minute was speeding towards downtown Munich.

He would not go home, not just yet. How could he reach the colonel? Then he remembered that the colonel had made him commit a Munich telephone number to memory, in case of an emergency. Right now, a galloping case of paranoia would have to pass for a genuine emergency. He pulled over to the first public phone he saw, dialed the number and waited through three rings, his eyes darting in every direction. The call was answered in English on the fourth ring by a man with a very slight Eastern European accent.

"Hello."

"This is Tallifierro calling." He hoped his voice had not betrayed his nervousness.

"Good evening Tom, This is Káz."

"Káz! I can't believe it. Am I glad to hear your voice. I didn't know what had happened to you."

"What's up, Tom?"

"I have to speak to the old man right away."

"Where are you now?"

"I just parked on the main road into town. I'm at a pay phone."

"Okay," Káz said. "Listen carefully. Drive to Sendlinger Tor Platz. Park on the street. Sit on one of the benches in the Plaza under a street lamp. I'll meet you there in a little while. Just in case, what kind of a car are you driving?"

"1966 VW Beetle, white, with USA plates."

"I will see you in a little while. Tom, if I am delayed, do not leave. Just wait for me; okay?"

"Roger that."

Ten minutes later Tom pulled into the first parking space on the plaza he could find. To his right beyond the curb was a six foot spiked iron fence surrounding a statue of one of Munich's heroes — Crown Prince Ludwig of Bavaria (affectionately known as "Mad Ludwig"). To his left, on the opposite side of the circular road, was the central plaza, blanketed with flowers and dotted with several park benches.

Tom turned off his lights and ignition, tapped his ankle holster for the reassuring presence of his .38, and unlocked his driver side door. Before he could open it, however, a Munich police car with its traditional revolving blue light on the roof pulled along side of him. The revolving light cast undulating beams over the entire plaza as an unmistakable signal that serious business was at hand.

But, Tom knew he had done nothing wrong and was not worried. He casually rolled down his window, prepared to practice his beginner's German.

The grey-uniformed police officer seated on the passenger side also rolled his window down. There was no room between the vehicles for Tom to open his door, so he just said, "Guten Abend," and waited for instructions.

The police officer did not return his greeting, but simply continued to look down, occupied with something.

"He's writing me out a ticket," Tom said to himself. "I don't remember doing anything wrong, unless maybe I made an illegal left turn into the plaza."

But something was not quite right. The driver of the patrol car kept looking out his window from front to back, paying no attention to Tom or to his partner. Also, his partner didn't seem to be writing. When his hands came up from his lap he was not holding his summons book. Instead, he had an elongated dark object in his right hand as he turned toward Tom. It was a silencer and it was pointed at Tom's head.

"Oh shit," said Tom, as he instinctively dove to his right, his abdomen hitting the console between the two bucket seats. Even as he moved, he felt the air from something whizzing over his head and shattering the passenger side window.

Then a second muffled shot zinged overhead, this one crashing into the door below the window. Tom's face was pushed into the passenger seat. Shock and surprise blocked any awareness of the reality that he was about to die. The only thought Tom had was whether he could somehow reach back and draw his weapon. It was very risky because it meant elevating his body enough to give the shooter a better target. But, it was the only chance he had. On the next shot, his assailant would probably have adjusted the angle of his arm so that the flight of the bullet would hit Tom squarely in the head or upper back.

Tom made his move, reaching back with his left hand extended towards his ankle holster. As he reached back, another shot was fired but it too seemed to miss its mark. The sound of the third shot, however, was different. It was an explosion — not a muffled noise. And then there were no more shots, only the sound of tires squealing and the roar of an engine.

Tom lay still, draped across the seats. The only noise coming from the outside now was the sound of excited voices. They were all speaking German and he was only able to catch a word here and there.

"Tom, its Káz; are you hit?"

"No, I don't think so."

"Come on. We have to get out of here fast!"

The sounds of multiple police sirens could be heard in the distance. Káz opened the door, quickly pulled Tom up into a sitting position and helped him out of the car. The keys were still in the ignition. Using one hand to brace himself against the car, Tom walked around to the passenger side and got in.

Káz got behind the wheel of the VW and they sped off, leaving behind them a puddle of blood in the street. Káz's Smith and Wesson .45 had put a hole in the middle of the phony cop's forehead — the source of the puddle of blood.

The next night, Blake and Olney sat in Oscar's at the furthest booth from the door. The dim lighting would have made it difficult to recognize them from more than fifteen feet away, but Olney kept one eye on the entrance anyway and one hand on the .45 revolver protruding from his belt.

This night, they didn't even bother with mixed drinks. They were on their third round of bourbon shots with beer chasers.

Blake, as usual, was talking while Olney listened. "Can you believe this? They came at us right in our own backyard. I doubt it was KGB. Those guys are too professional. This to me looked like the work of amateurs. But why go at someone like Tallifierro — a kid? Why not Reitenhauser or LeBron?"

Olney stared at his face and spoke. "Did LeBron or Reitenhauser break the code that saved our ass on the Hof Road? Are either one of them a top analyst? No. And forget Booker. Right now, the kid is our biggest threat to them."

As Security Officer for the 409th, Anders Smith was the first to get the word the previous night as to what had happened at Sendlinger Tor Platz. He received a call at his bachelor apartment at 2300 hours from the CO, ordering him to report immediately to the unit. No explanation was offered and Smith said nothing other than a calm, "Yes, sir," which revealed no sign of surprise.

Reitenhauser found that somewhat odd. "Smith," said the CO, "come armed."

Again a quiet, even, "Yes, sir" from the lieutenant, with no questions asked.

Colonel Reitenhauser then tried to reach First Sergeant Toomey but had no luck. Toomey didn't answer the phone at his quarters, and had left no word with the duty officer as to where he could be reached. A sense of foreboding began to circle around the CO, though not yet moving in to clutch him in its grasp. The many crises of his life had taught him not to succumb to anxiety.

Anxiety clouded one's thinking and weakened the will — fatal defects in a commanding officer. Reitenhauser was a facts-first man. Assess the situation, and then take action appropriate to the facts.

The situation now was relatively stable for the time being. Penchak had been ordered to take Tallifierro to one of the safehouses and keep him there until further notice. The location of the safehouse had been known only to himself and LeBron.

The colonel now called Lieutenant Ryan, told him in one brief sentence what had happened, and ordered him to immediately relieve Sergeant Blaulicht as duty officer. Ryan was also ordered to carry his side arm.

Next, Reitenhauser called LeBron and told the XO to place the unit on full alert. Non-military employees were to be told not to show up for work in the morning, but to stay by their telephones. Military personnel were to follow their usual routines, and report at 0900.

Sergeants Rhymes and Berger, two of the unit's most clever and resourceful operatives, were given the assignment to go out and locate Toomey, without delay, and bring him back to the unit. They wouldn't have to be told to carry their weapons — they would just know to do so.

As for himself, Reitenhauser called O'Malley and told him to grab his AK-47 and pick him up immediately. The CO still felt uneasy about Smith's demeanor during their conversation of ten minutes earlier, but he would judge for himself whether there was a problem about 15 minutes from now, when they all met in his office.

Finally, Ryan was ordered to reach out to the rest of the section chiefs and deputies and get them into the unit's offices.

The CO then sat back in his chair and withdrew his own Colt .45 from his shoulder holster, cleaned it quickly, and began loading it from the box of bullets he had placed on the telephone table.

Seated across from Reitenhauser on the Danish modern sofa was Doug Booker, who had been working with the colonel on the 'Prague Spring' phase of Kryptonite when the call had come in from Káz Penchak about the assault on Tallifierro.

"Doug, I need you to get over to the safehouse and debrief Tallifierro on whatever it was that spooked him, and made him reach out via the emergency number. As far as I am concerned, it's time to shift to wartime mode. I will alert the others at the unit that we are in lock-down mode under Code Alpha. The only communications in and out of the unit will be via telex. Winicki and Scones will be on duty together in the telex room at all times, and both will sign off on every outgoing and incoming transmission.

"You will go to and from the safehouse under armed guard, and report only to me when you return."

With that, the CO picked up the phone, dialed a number and waited. The phone was answered on the second ring. Without formalities, the colonel gave his succinct order. "Code Alpha is in effect. Meet me in the motor pool in ten minutes."

The colonel hung up, placed his Colt .45 in his shoulder holster, and put on his suit coat. He buttoned his collar, tightened his tie, and said to Booker, "Let's go. Ted will pick us up downstairs in about two minutes. Are you carrying?"

Doug nodded and tapped his ankle holster.

The two men headed down the staircase to the back parking lot. O'Malley would pull right up to the rear entrance so that his BMW would serve as a shield against shots aimed in the direction of the entrance.

The pick-up and short ride to the 409th turned out to be uneventful.

O'Malley pressed the garage door opener to activate the electric eye and the BMW carrying the three men drove down the ramp and into the motor pool garage.

The garage was unoccupied with the exception of Tonelli and Mattatussu who stood near the lift, each dressed in black jeans and jackets. A large dark canvas bag sat at the feet of each man-carrying a deadly array of single shot and semi-automatic weapons.

O'Malley was out of the BMW first with the AK-47 strapped over his shoulder. The CO and Booker followed.

Perfunctory handshakes were exchanged all around. The CO gave a few brief instructions and Mattatussu, Tonelli and Booker took off in Tonelli's black Audi. The CO and O'Malley then took the lift up to the unit's offices.

Reitenhauser was relatively satisfied that with LeBron, O'Malley, Ryan, and Smith, he had plenty of fire power at the unit. Unless of course, Smith had wandered off the reservation… But he should know that soon enough. And with Tonelli, Mattatussu, and Penchak, he had plenty of guns and savvy at the safehouse. But where the hell was Toomey?

Toomey sat at the end of the bar — as far away as he could get from the loud-mouths and show-offs who usually gathered near the center, where Oscar often held court and was most likely to award buy-backs. Even though it was a weeknight, the place was as packed as always. The patrons were mostly Americans; but other than that were a pretty homogenous group — GI's; tourists; male and female civilian employees at the Max, American Express and the University of Maryland extension campus; encyclopedia and life insurance salesmen and various other door to door peddlers who fed off the marrieds in the U.S. government apartment complex.

As a young enlistee in the late 40s at Fort Hood, Texas, Toomey had spent a good bit of his off-duty time at the local country music bars, where he developed a taste for tequila, which he sipped as he listened to Hank Williams and Eddie Albert on the juke box. Toomey had been a basically happy kid back then, twenty-one years old, with no inkling whatsoever of what combat was really like. Then a warm mellowness from the combination of the tequila and the country love songs would creep slowly through his body, until he reached that euphoric state where all seemed right, where everything fit.

But all that was before Korea and Chosin Reservoir, before a reckless glory-seeking General Ned Almond had refused to acknowledge that Seventh Division would soon be outnumbered eight to one by tens of thousands of Chinese infantrymen. Before the idiotic general had compounded his own mistake by refusing to order a retreat until the Division had been almost completely wiped out.

Toomey and about 500 other stragglers had somehow stumbled and staggered through the arctic-like cold for thirty miles to Hagaru-ri, only to be routed there by another wave of Chinese attackers and forced into a forty mile retreat to Hungnam on the coast. From there, the fleeing soldiers had finally been evacuated by the skin of their teeth, just before the pursuing Chinese had arrived. And instead of the court martial he deserved, that same callous and reckless general had remained in command of Seventh Division for the next round of battles in the Central Corridor.

Now, when Toomey's memories took him back to Korea and 'Frozen Chosin,' he felt nothing but bitterness and anger — anger over the small stumps on his right foot where he had lost two toes to frostbite, and the bullet fragments still embedded in his back, too close to his spine to remove.

But beyond simple anger was his fury over the needless slaughter of his buddies at Chosin, the best friends he had ever known — guys he drank tequila with, sang with, played cards with, and listened to attentively when they talked about their girls back home.

Now when Toomey drank, he didn't get mellow. He just got drunk. And when he got drunk, he got bitter, and ornery, and spiteful.

And this night at Oscar's, he had his full package on. He no longer sipped the tequila; he just downed one angry shot after another. As he hammered down the drinks, he got more and more pissed-off. To think that after what he had gone through in Korea and the VA hospitals, he now had to take orders from (and be humiliated by) a know-it-all egg-head commanding officer. Almost as bad, he had to play nursemaid to a bunch of phony candy-asses in civilian clothes, several of whom now outranked him. It was more than a man should have to bear.

Through the fog of his inebriation and the thick tobacco smoke, he recognized two of those pseudo-soldiers walking towards him — Rhymes and Berger, the big-deal agent handlers.

Good. This would be a chance to take them down off their high horses. He fixed them with a hard stare as they approached.

"Sergeant Toomey," said Rhymes.

"That's first sergeant to you, Sonny," Toomey responded.

"Excuse me, first sergeant. Colonel Reitenhauser needs you to go immediately to the unit."

Toomey reacted with a nasty laugh and then addressed Rhymes and Berger with contempt dripping from his mouth: "And what, he sent you two piss-ants to escort me back? Since when did you two jokers become the fucking M.P.s of the unit?"

For a moment, Ben and Mal just stood there in an embarrassed silence. Finally Ben spoke, "Begging your pardon, first sergeant, there has been an attempt by Hostile on Sergeant Tallifierro's life. One of our people took defensive action, and Hostile has sustained an apparent fatality. You are needed back at the unit."

Toomey absorbed this news in silence and without expression on his face. He stood up, took his remaining cash from the bar, leaving a generous tip, and wordlessly followed the two men out of the bar.

The chilly late-April night air cleared his senses somewhat. When they reached Rhymes' car, Rhymes reached into the back seat, removed a thermos, opened it and poured Toomey a cup of black coffee. The first sergeant stood next to the car and drank it without comment.

The small conference room had become a makeshift war room. Gathered around the table were Reitenhauser, LeBron, O'Malley, Blake, and Toomey.

Smith stood guard outside the door and Ryan did the same at the unit's main entrance.

Before they gathered, the CO had met privately with Anders Smith. Smith claimed that the reason he asked no questions was that he was not alone. He had answered the phone in his bedroom, and had not wanted to say anything in front of his female companion.

The CO judged that the man was telling the truth, and dismissed Smith after first explaining his current duties to him.

Reitenhauser knew as soon as Toomey reported to him, that the sergeant had been drinking heavily. But whatever he thought of the life

Toomey led, the first sergeant had been off-duty when he was tracked down, with no reason to expect that he would be called in at close to midnight.

Right now, it was all hands on deck and the CO could see that Toomey was doing his best to hold it together.

The meeting with the chiefs would be quick, and Olney would then be given the assignment of driving Toomey to his quarters and making sure he got to bed. The CO needed everybody to be at the top of their game from now on.

After reviewing the facts briefly to those assembled in the small conference room, the CO directed that all unit personnel were to report for duty at 0900 sharp. LeBron was placed temporarily in charge of the unit's headquarters. Lieutenants Smith and Ryan were assigned the security of the offices until further notice. They would take turns guarding the front entrance and the classified areas of the premises, including the now locked room where Tallifierro had been working.

As for himself, as soon as he dismissed the others, he would head to the safehouse, with O'Malley and his AK-47 riding shotgun. Over the next twenty-four hours or so the safehouse would become the nerve center of the unit. With Tonelli and Mattatussu there, it would be as safe as any place could be. After having a cup of coffee, the CO would join Booker in fully debriefing Tallifierro. Then with O'Malley and the two analysts as his brain trust, he would formulate their next course of action.

Reitenhauser would not report the shooting incident to Group. Until he decided it was safe, there would be no outgoing communications from the unit, unless approved by him personally.

It was regrettable, but the CO did not trust Group Headquarters enough to bring them into the loop. There was little doubt that the 409th was in a battle for survival. Technically it may have been just an outpost, but circumstances over the years — the recruitment of Uri Putyagin, the work of Agent 14332 and his successor, Lugash Magyaar; the intellectual brilliance of Doug Booker and operational mastery of O'Malley and LeBron, had converted the 409th Special Investigations Detachment into a vital organ of Western intelligence — the repository of some of the most sensitive and critical secrets of the Cold War. The enemy desperately needed to both capture those secrets and totally disable and derail the 409th's operational capacity.

As he drove through the Munich night, Fred Reitenhauser was confident he had within the unit the brain power, talent, and muscle to thwart the enemy's assaults.   Yet, a nagging worry, as relentless and merciless as an abscessed tooth, preyed on his mind from morning till night — that they would ward off the external threat, only to be subverted and destroyed from within.

Chapter Twelve

Shattered Dreams

July 1968 - Munich

Art LeBron's pace quickened to a near sprint as the automatic doors to the Emergency Room of the U.S. Military Hospital, Munich, gave way for him. Flanking him on either side were Tonelli and Mattatussu. The single M.P. on duty at reception knew the moment the three men came through the doors that theirs was no ordinary visit. The dark suits and authoritative manner signaled urgent government business — FBI, CIA, or military intelligence kind of business.

The duty nurse behind the long counter had seen them coming too, and was already on sensory alert.

The three men flashed CID[*] credentials to the M.P. as LeBron spoke to the nurse with the quiet self-assurance that often accompanied those with official status. "May I see your admission records for this morning, please?"

The young nurse looked at the M.P., who signaled that it was okay, with a quick nod.

It took LeBron all of five seconds to find who he was looking for, and next to the name were printed the initials 'CCU.'

The three quickly departed. Alerted by the emergency room nurse, a doctor, Major Paul Dunleavy, met the three men in front of the entrance to the Critical Care Unit. Dunleavy quickly engaged LeBron and the others in earnest conversation.

LeBron blanched noticeably on hearing the grim news. Captain Douglas Booker lay near death in a deep coma in the Critical Care Unit.

There he was connected to three separate IV drips containing antibiotics and other medications to combat organ failure and cardiac arrest. He was also hooked up to an oxygen tank and a cardiac monitor. The doctor somberly reported that Booker was suffering from multiple

---

[*] Criminal Investigation Division of the U.S. Army.

infections and his heart rhythm was highly irregular. It was too early to know the full extent of organ damage and central nervous system dysfunction, but signs of both were evident. In short, Doug Booker was gravely ill.

"Do you know what caused this, major?" queried LeBron.

"Well, we have to run a few more tests and I'm not ready to fire-off a diagnosis just yet," stated Dunleavy with a southern drawl. "But if y'all would like to drop by a little later today, I may know more."

"Major Dunleavy, this is a matter of urgent national security! I am the XO of the 409th Special Investigations Detachment. The CO is Colonel Frederick Reitenhauser. You may have heard of him."

"I guess most everybody around here has heard of Colonel Reitenhauser," drawled the physician.

"Well, then you know that neither he nor his top people would exaggerate something of this seriousness. So tell us *now*. What do you think caused this?"

The physician guided LeBron and his two escorts into an office situated a little further back along the corridor and shut the door. He then spoke directly and without hesitation: "Preliminary blood and urine tests indicate an acute exposure to arsenic poisoning. Captain Booker has high levels of arsenic in his body. We just received the results of tests I ordered on his hair and fingernails. The chemists in the lab are still evaluating those test results, but their preliminary findings point to the presence of arsenic in his system over the past six to twelve months, in all likelihood ingested by Captain Booker in his beverages."

LeBron grimaced. "In his beverages? How could arsenic get into his beverages over a six to twelve month period, unless somebody put it there on purpose?"

"In my opinion," said Dunleavy, "it couldn't. There are only three possibilities for the long-term poisoning of the fluids Booker consumed: accident, self-administration and the intentional acts of others. Rule out accident right off the bat. This could only have been done intentionally. Could Booker have systematically self-administered arsenic over half a year or more? Possible but so unlikely as to not warrant serious consideration. In my opinion, he would have to have been psychotic to do such a thing. And we know that Doug Booker was a bit eccentric, but definitely not psychotic. He has been my patient for six years, and I have found him to be one of the sanest men I know. No, this appears to have been a case of attempted murder."

LeBron did not trust the phones and the detachment was only five minutes from the hospital, so he hurried back with Tonelli driving to give his report to the colonel in person. Mattatussu remained at the CCU to guard Booker.

Ten minutes later, LeBron was seated across the desk from the CO, telling him everything he knew.

All that Reitenhauser had known up to that point had come from the duty officer, Sergeant Knowles, who had taken a 3:30 a.m. call from Booker's neighbor. The neighbor's apartment was one floor below Booker's, and he was awakened by a loud crash from above. Fortuitously, the neighbor was a Company Commander in the local M.P. battalion. He knew the sound of a body crashing to the floor when he heard it, and delayed only long enough to throw on his uniform trousers. He then dashed up the one flight of stairs carrying his pistol belt over his shoulder.

One of Booker's many idiosyncrasies was to fall asleep on the living room couch with his door unlocked. The neighbor entered the apartment unimpeded with weapon drawn. Booker lay unconscious on the living room floor, barefoot and wearing only an old pair of patched khakis and an olive drab undershirt.

The M.P. gave Booker emergency mouth to mouth resuscitation and then quickly called the hospital. An ambulance was there to pick Booker up in less than ten minutes. He remained unconscious continuously from the time he was found, and now was in a coma.

Characteristically, the colonel sat in totally absorbed silence as LeBron described Booker's condition and what the physician had reported. As he listened, another part of his brain was integrating this new information into the long and detailed report provided by Tallifierro. The connections the young analyst had made and conclusions he had drawn were all sound and stood up under the harsh light of the CO's and Booker's independent analyses. Even so, Winicki's role was most likely innocent.

She had interacted with both Morgan and Barnstable, and the information she gave to the now-deceased Ops in the course of their intimate relationship, had probably been offered without knowledge of its vast importance.

But both the CO and Booker believed that Barnstable had put it all together, had confronted Morgan with his suspicions, and that was probably what had gotten him killed. And Booker's vigilant quest to find the enemy within and expose him may be the reason he now lay in extremely critical condition.

Unwitting though she may have been, the CO felt it was too great a risk to both Winicki and the unit to allow her to stay on. She had been rotated back to the States, to an unknown location under secret orders. Rumor had it that she was working as a company clerk somewhere in the Pacific Northwest.

Finally, Reitenhauser spoke. "Tell Tonelli to meet me in the Motor Pool. I want to see Doug and speak to the doctor myself. When I come back, you, Ted and I will meet. We have had enough. Now we move on Morgan."

August 1968

Had Doug Booker not lain comatose in a Munich military hospital, he would have been thrilled by the upbeat tempo of the aggressive activities of his colleagues.

In Munich, Colonel Reitenhauser had been given the use of three M.P.s to add to the team he had assembled in order to move in on Morgan and take him into custody. The traitor would be arrested at a location away from his residence, while simultaneously a second team would enter his home with a search warrant issued by the Judge Advocate General, for the seizure of his books and papers.

The arrest team was composed of O'Malley, Penchak, and Tonelli plus the three uniforms. The search and seizure team was comprised of Smith, Ryan, Rhymes, and Berger.

The CO would not directly participate in either raid, but would be in a radio car with Mattatussu as his driver and body guard not too far from either location, and would direct both operations from there. LeBron would remain at the unit with a couple of tough CID types in plain clothes, and would direct operations there in Reitenhauser's temporary absence.

A contingent of nine M.P.s with high security clearances now provided around the clock protection for Booker at the hospital. They worked in three-man shifts, rotating every eight hours.

Each of the personnel of the 409th on the two raid teams, despite the official name of the detachment, had an area intelligence M.O.S. only. They had no law enforcement credentials and, therefore, had to be deputized by the Provost Marshal in order to legally participate. General Stansfield personally cut the order, bowing to Reitenhauser's determined wish that Morgan's apprehension be kept a 409th-controlled operation.

With the exception of O'Malley, none of the members of either team would be informed of Morgan's true identity until one hour before the coordinated operation was to kick off.

Meanwhile in Prague, Czechoslovakia, things had reached a fevered pitch. Building on the firm foundation laid by Káz Penchak, Magyaar was leading the underground to become more and more vocal each day. And it was all resonating with a restive public, which was now demanding immediate and widespread reforms. Censorship had been formally abolished on June 26, 1968, and anti-Soviet polemics appeared frequently in the press. Political commentary flooded the mainstream media. Magyaar's Czech counterpart in the underground was the zealous patriot, Jan Palach.

The Soviet reaction, which had been tempered in the early days of Dubcëk's reforms, had grown increasingly hostile. The Soviet leadership first tried to halt the pace of the changes through a series of negotiations in which the entire 'Warsaw Five' (U.S.S.R., Hungary, Poland, Bulgaria, and East Germany) weighed in.

On August 3, 1968, the 'Five' plus Czechoslovakia signed the *Bratislava Declaration*, which affirmed their fidelity to Marxism-Leninism in an implacable struggle against 'bourgeois' ideology and all 'anti-socialist' forces.

At the 409th, at Group in Frankfurt, and in the elegant study of Uri Putyagin's country estate, alarms went off over the serious threat contained within the Declaration. The Soviet Union would intervene in a signatory nation if a 'bourgeois' system — a pluralist system of several political parties representing different factions of the capitalist class — was introduced.

The unsubtle threat was aimed at the very heart of Czechoslovakia's democratic reforms. Fred Reitenhauser considered it to be another reason to expunge Morgan from Hostile's forces as soon as possible.

Central to the Bratislava Declaration was the Soviet Union's reaffirmation of its firm policy that satellite states of the U.S.S.R. must subordinate their national interests to those of the Eastern Bloc, lest they be subjected to military force. This became known as the 'Brezhnev Doctrine.'

But, the die had been cast. Jan Palach led a vocal rally in Prague, vowing to fight to the death for the Dubcëk reforms. Having been given a taste of freedom, the citizenry's appetite had merely been whetted for a lot more. Anti-Soviet rallies, demonstrations, and journalistic commentary only intensified in the wake of the Bratislava Declaration.

As is often the propensity of those who champion revolutionary change, the leaders of the Czech movement were tone-deaf when it came to power politics at the international level. Anyone with any sense of the diplomatic history of Europe since 1945 would have known that — once the First Secretary of the Communist Party in Russia, Leonid Brezhnev, had elevated the Bratislava Declaration to the lofty peak of a doctrine with his name attached — there would be blood in the streets if such doctrine were overtly challenged.   Prestige being the wide shadow cast by diplomacy, when such prestige is endangered, diplomacy usually fails.

Astute observers of the jockeying for position and power within the Eastern Bloc, such as Fred Reitenhauser and Uri Putyagin, could feel the political tectonic plates beneath the ground of Eastern Europe shifting dramatically, a portent of a cataclysmic upheaval soon to come.

On the night of August 20, 1968, as three dark grey sedans pulled out of the 409th's motor pool in pursuit of Morgan and the documentary proof of his treachery, Eastern Bloc armies from four Warsaw Pact nations — the Soviet Union, Bulgaria, Poland, and Hungary — were invading across the borders into Czechoslovakia.

Lugash Magyaar and Étan Gaborski were also on the move, but in the opposite direction, in the back of a truck speeding away from Prague and toward the Austrian border.   The underground's superb communications network had given them early warning of the Warsaw Pact's drive into Czechoslovakia.

"I feel like a cowardly rat deserting my friends," said a despondent Gaborski.

"Don't be stupid," scolded Magyaar. "Our most important job is to not get caught. We have to get to Vienna, and I have to send a message to our control. Don't think for even a second that all that's happening here is an invasion to quiet a bunch of protesters. If for some reason I don't make it across the border and you do, you have to reach the Coach (Magyaar's name for Berger), and tell him that 'Carlton needs to speak to the G.M. tonight.' It can't wait. But use the telex machine at the safehouse. Don't call Munich unless there is no other way for you to make contact...   but *make* contact you must."

But it wouldn't be Gaborski who carried out the mission — not this one, or any other, ever again.

A round from an Uzi submachine, one of many which penetrated the canvas cover over the back of the truck, hit Étan directly between the eyes, a split second after Magyaar had finished his exhortation.

Étan did not move from the bench, lodged against the side of the truck's canopy. His erect sitting position might have led one to believe that he was still listening attentively to Magyaar, were it not for his dead eyes and the circular red hole in his head.

*   *   *

Munich

Reitenhauser sat calmly in the passenger seat, with Mattatussu behind the wheel of the gray Citroen. The CO pressed the button on the hand-held transmitter and spoke. "Gray Beard to Units, do you copy?"

"Alpha copies."

"Beta copies."

"Move in."

"Roger that. Alpha moving in."

"Beta moving in."

The six Alpha team members quickly exited the roomy four-door Mercedes sedan and seconds later, four of them entered Oscar's. Two of their number went around to the back to cover the rear door. It was 2200 hours.

At roughly the same time, half-way between the Czech-Russian border and Prague, the lead Soviet tank in a long column was moving at a snail's pace. It seemed that Czech partisans, having heard the Soviets were on their way had painted over the road direction signs with black paint.

The lead tank commander, Major Ivan Petrovich, shook his head — having trouble masking his exasperation. "I knew this wasn't going to be as easy as everyone said. Nothing is with these damnable Czechs."

Elsewhere, less than a minute after the firing began, the two and a half ton truck veered out of control — the Czech driver slumped over the steering wheel. Its front end plunged over the shoulder of the road and into a six foot-wide drainage ditch.

Gasoline sprayed out of the breached tank, simultaneous with the head-on collision of the truck with the far side of the ditch. An explosion followed and the truck was engulfed in flames.

Two vehicles on the opposite side of the road contained heavily armed fighters of the Czech Red Guards. A second explosion was set off when the flames reached the gas tank itself. The Red Guards contingent, satisfied that no one could have survived the conflagration, drove speedily away.

Lugash Magyaar, crouched low, had lifted the canopy and jumped off the side of the truck the instant it had plunged into the ditch. Still in the air, he had tucked his body into a parachutist's roll away from the truck.

The explosion catapulted him into the trees beyond. There he lay unconscious, with a broken left wrist, separated right shoulder and several broken ribs, one of which punctured a lung. His face and bare hands were a mass of scratches, bloody cuts, welts, and bruises. A huge bump had formed on his forehead where his head had struck the ground. The force of his fall had been somewhat diminished by the crash of his body into a low lying tree branch, which had cut through his shirt sleeve and left a long laceration on his right arm. Metal shrapnel from the explosion had lodged in the flesh of his legs, side, and back. But all those years as a pole-vaulter had taught Magyaar how to fall. That — plus his superb physical conditioning — had saved his life and prevented even more serious injury.

Magyaar slowly came to, perhaps roused by the throbbing pain in his shoulder and chest. He lay conscious but unable to move for at least fifteen minutes, as his body fought nausea, disorientation, dizziness and a searing pain that seemed to spare none of his naked nerve endings.

He knew from past experience that he had a concussion. That, more than anything, was what was immobilizing him. But he had to get the message from Carlton to the G.M. *Everything* was riding on it. He heard himself speaking aloud, "Vienna...have to...the Coach."

All the disciplines of a lifetime were slowly galvanizing to combat the pain and vertigo — the physical challenges of the world-class athlete, combating the Reds in Budapest under Imry Nagy, the lessons learned from Horst, and the new responsibilities so brilliantly articulated by the young "Coach."

The broken left wrist and separated right shoulder made the act of rising from the ground the most pain-filled feat of a lifetime. After finally making it to his feet, he leaned against the tree whose branch he had hit on the way down. He vomited, then gathered himself and began moving his feet.

He wasn't actually walking. It was more like directionless motion, staggering and swaying. He fell again. Excruciating pain pierced his shoulder like the point of a lance. Somehow he rose, stumbled forward and stayed upright.

Magyaar didn't remember staggering out onto the road and waving his left arm at several passing vehicles before a commercial trailer truck stopped to pick him up. Nor did he remember how his separated shoulder had wound up in a sling, his broken wrist and ribs heavily taped and his wounds bandaged after being treated with hydrogen peroxide and iodine.

Maybe it was a good Samaritan — a doctor or nurse perhaps fleeing Czechoslovakia just as he was. He probably blacked out multiple times before finally regaining consciousness and awareness, while laying on a cot in the Vienna safehouse.

Magyaar knew he had to contact the Coach immediately. It was now 0300 hours on August 21, 1968. Unable because of his condition to operate the telex machine, he would have to risk a phone call.

Two serious looking men sat near him on hard folding chairs. Their dark suit coats hung on the backs of the chairs. They wore shoulder holsters over white dress shirts, their collar buttons open and their ties askew.

"I am a foreign agent of the 409th Special Investigations Detachment in Munich, and I must get through to my control," said Magyaar fiercely. "It is a matter of life and death."

"We know who you are," calmly replied one of the two men, in a flat Midwestern cadence. "Munich is waiting for your call."

A telephone sat on a bridge table in front of the cot. The man who had spoken rose and dialed a number. He then handed the receiver to Magyaar and, with his companion, walked out of the room, shutting the door behind them.

Prague

Uri Putyagin had been carrying around the explosive information imparted to him by the KGB in East Berlin for several months now. He had been waiting for exactly the right time to schedule a meet with Fred, so that he could pass it on to his friend. But his government had crossed him up by invading Czechoslovakia without warning and, inexplicably, following two successive weeks of complete calm in Prague. Of course, in retrospect he understood why the invasion did not necessarily have to take place at a time of heightened tensions. The U.S.S.R. had decided to move, irrespective of all such concerns.

Magyaar had succeeded Horst Berkenfeld (Agent 14332) as the cut-out between himself and Fred, and undoubtedly there would be at least one other cut-out between Magyaar and Fred as well. To his intermediary, Magyaar, Uri was known as 'Carlton.' Both of them referred to Fred by the code-name, 'the G.M.'

It had now been ten hours since he had left a coded message for Magyaar at the predesignated Prague dead-drop, that an immediate meeting with the G.M. was of the highest urgency. Still no word.

Fred and Uri had decided long ago that — if they had to meet — Uri would go to Prague under the guise of official Warsaw Pact business. There the underground would take him to the remote airstrip carved out of the dense forest, 30 miles southwest of the city. At the designated hour — 0500 — a CIA (BOSS) twin engine Cessna (designed with the lowest engine noise possible) would dim its lights and land at the strip where Uri would be waiting.   It would fly him to an equally remote airstrip, northwest of Munich, where the two men would meet in a van driven by Tonelli. The back of the van had been designed as a small but well-lighted and insulated meeting room containing a lavatory, refrigerator and coffee maker. Its walls were reinforced by steel.

Uri looked at his watch. It was now 0400 hours. He could wait for word no longer and would have to take it on faith that the Cessna would get to the airstrip by the predetermined time. Uri called for his driver to pick him up.

A chill, caused not by the Prague pre-dawn temperature, but rather by the precariousness of his situation, coursed through Uri's body as he stood at the edge of the airstrip. But the Cessna taxied down the short runway at exactly 0500 hours.

"I should never doubt my people," Uri said to himself as the door to the plane swung open.

About six hours earlier, Olney, who always sat facing the entrance to Oscar's while Blake sat across from him in their favorite booth, had one eye on the entrance and one on Sock-It Toomey, who as usual sat at the far end of the bar.

The first sergeant was drunker than usual on this particular night — falling down drunk. His stability on the bar stool was tenuous at best, and Olney expected to see him slide to the floor at any minute. Oscar also had an apprehensive eye on Toomey.

Blake, on the other hand seemed oblivious to Toomey, just as he was to O'Malley, Penchak, and Tonelli as they walked through the front door and approached their booth, with an M.P. following. Blake had started another one of his soliloquies about the 409th and Group and was now really warming to his topic as the Glen Livet began to take hold.

Olney wondered what the hell their visitors were doing here. He had seen Tonelli and Mattatussu in Oscar's more than once, but never had he seen O'Malley or Penchak here. The scuttlebutt around the unit was that Penchak did not drink at all, and O'Malley only on special occasions. And why was an M.P. tagging along?

Were they here to pick up Toomey, maybe on orders from the CO who was said to be fed up with his drunkenness? But oddly enough, they didn't seem to even notice Toomey.

Something wasn't right... The somber expressions on the faces of his colleagues from the 409th were a harbinger of trouble. And the M.P. looked tense, with one hand on his holstered .45. Olney sensed that the four men, all of whom could handle almost any kind of trouble, were tonight bringing trouble along with them.

The group stopped next to their booth with two men blocking each side. Now he could see that Toomey had noticed their presence and seemed uncomfortable and troubled by their arrival. Maybe they were here for Toomey after all. If so, there could be big trouble because Toomey had gotten up from his stool and was walking steadily and in a straight line towards them.

"What the fuck!" whispered Olney. "He can't be drunk or he wouldn't be able to walk like that. What's going on? Could it be me they're after? Okay, I grabbed some gold bullion off a convoy at the Brandenburg Gate once. But that was eight years ago and all the spooks — BOSS, MI-5, the Italians and so on, were helping themselves too. The stuff belonged to Hostile, and they deserved to have some of it lifted and..."

O'Malley spoke. "Captain, by order and warrant of the Provost Marshal, Homer Winn, and the Judge Advocate General of United States Army, Europe, dated August 19, 1968, you, Mitchell Blake, also known as 'Michael Bonner,' also known as 'Morgan,' are under arrest. Here's the warrant and our credentials issued by the Provost."

O'Malley laid them on the table in front of Blake. "The charges are high treason against the Government of the United States, murder, and attempted murder."

Olney was so shocked as to be temporarily speechless.

Tonelli was the next to speak. "Captain Blake, please extend both wrists in front of you."

Blake sat impassively without moving a hair, as if being told the score of a World Series game he didn't really care about.

But now Olney found his voice: "You guys must be nuts! You can't be serious! Who's behind this circus? I'll bet it's LeBron, the brown-nosing bastard. I never trusted that sneaky son of a bitch."

"Warrant officer, please lower your voice and stay in your seat," said the M.P.

"I will not," shouted Olney "I want to speak to Reitenhauser. Get him over here."

The M.P. ignored him. Now the two other M.P.'s had entered the room from the rear and were standing tensely near the bar. "Captain Blake, please extend your wrists."

"Don't do it Mitch," said Olney.

With that, the other two M.P.s quickly covered the distance from the bar, joining the group. They were a corporal and a master sergeant.

The sergeant addressed Olney. "Chief, if you don't calm down and stop interfering, we'll have to slap the cuffs on you too."

Toomey, whom Reitenhauser had placed at the bar just in case something like this happened, got ready to weigh in. He was cold sober and had done a great job of acting in playing the part of a drunk.

Of course, he had a perfect subject to study in preparation for the role: himself. But Toomey was now going to AA meetings, and hadn't touched a drink since the night Tallifierro was attacked.

On this night he thought things had gone too far, and so he spoke quietly and directly to Olney. "Look, son, I can understand why you're upset. But, you have to let these police officers do their job. They have a warrant and you can't interfere. Come on Warren, back-off. If there's been a mistake it can be straightened out later."

With that said, Olney sat back and had nothing more to add — at least for the time being.

Blake extended his wrists, was handcuffed and escorted out of Oscar's by the M.P.s.

Penchak and Tonelli rode with the M.P.s, who transported Blake to the main U.S. Army Stockade in Munich.

Toomey and O'Malley returned to the unit in the Mercedes.

Olney despondently walked down the street and away from Oscar's and away from one of the most baffling and depressing nights of his life.

O'Malley and Toomey went directly to the CO's office and briefed him on what had transpired at Oscar's. Before commenting, the colonel filled them in on the raid of Blake's house. This particular night had been chosen because they knew that Blake's wife and daughter were away, visiting the wife's parents in Bonn.

Rhymes had not had any trouble picking the lock to the back door. The search team had firm orders not to disturb anything in the house unless absolutely necessary for the removal of relevant photographs, tapes, film, letters, cards, documents, journals, and diaries. A treasure trove of inculpatory records was found in a false ceiling of the basement.

More shocking was the telex report the CO had received a half-hour earlier from Group, reporting the incursion of Warsaw Pact forces over the border into Czechoslovakia in great strength.

O'Malley sat back in his chair, stunned by the news. "It's been quite a night, sir."

"Yes and I hope none of you had any plans for the evening, because you can expect to pull an all-nighter. Sergeant Toomey, please relieve Davis as duty officer. Then, contact all military personnel and tell them to get in here ASAP. We're back on full alert again. And, call Penchak and Tonelli in the M.P. radio car. As soon as Blake is booked, I want them to join Mattatussu and Tallifierro at the safehouse."

The colonel had no sooner finished his instructions when Gerda's voice came over the intercom. "Sir, I am sorry to interrupt but I have two men calling from Vienna on the line from the Five-O-Deuce. They say that they have one of our men who has been badly injured."

"Can our man get on the phone, Gerda?"

"No, sir. They say he is unconscious, but he keeps repeating the same name over and over again."

"What name?"

"Carlton. He keeps saying 'see Carlton.'"

Fred would allow only Tonelli to accompany him to the rendezvous point about twenty miles northwest of Munich. While Tonelli drove the van, Fred sat in the rear compartment, to be alone with his thoughts.

Of course, he wondered what it was that was so urgent that it triggered only the third face-to-face meeting between him and Uri since he left him in that small Vienna pastry shop so many years ago. But, he would know soon enough. For the present, he would put this quiet solitary time to use preparing himself for the meeting. For that he needed no notes or documents.

The most pressing thing was to make sure he fully comprehended the Morgan/Blake affair in all its aspects, so he could explain it to Uri. Together, they could weigh its consequences, especially those which might have an impact on whatever it was that Uri was about to tell him.

After Tallifierro had come up with the clear link between the Red Guards in Regensburg and Barnstable, Fred had ordered an intensive search for every letter, memo, and cable Barnstable had sent or received during his tenure at the 409th. Collectively, these documents showed that Barnstable had been deeply suspicious of Blake. He had been hot on Blake's trail when he'd been abruptly transferred to the States.

It was more than likely that the apparent original file lifted from Barnstable's office was taken by Blake, although it was too early to determine whether its contents were among those papers seized from Blake's home.

Barnstable's fatal error, which had ultimately cost him his life, was in not sharing the results of his private investigation with anyone else. Instead, when he got to Holabird he began pulling his notes together and drafting a report.

The notes found in his Baltimore apartment were cryptic. The report was only in its early stages, and did not identify Blake by name. But when matched up with the data that Barnstable had left behind in Munich, it firmly established his pursuit of Blake and the direction of his investigation. Penchak's tail of Blake had corroborated Tallifierro's conclusion that the guilty party (operating under the pseudonym of Morgan) had been obtaining Swiss francs at various banks in Zurich, and using them to pay his operatives.

That's where the story got interesting. It was now clear that there were several Hostile operatives who used the sobriquet of 'Morgan.' Why they did so was not yet clear; but Group — which was now hunting down the *other* Morgans — had no shortage of possible theories. Reitenhauser's own theory was that it was used as a form of intimidation and control. A message was being sent to those with whom the particular Morgan had dealings that he was "Red Guard" and therefore, able to mete out terrible retribution. Psychologically, it created a power imbalance between agent handler and confederates, which made it easier for him to manipulate them.

Another thing that was crystal clear was that Blake's traitorous and murderous acts were not about ideology or emotional attachment. Nothing in his long history in the intelligence game revealed the slightest proclivity towards Marxist thought. He was not a communist, or even a socialist. For that matter, he wasn't that much of a fan of democracy either.

Apparently, for Blake it was strictly about the money. His marriage to a debutante with its attendant life-style among the rich and influential — hobnobbing with the elite of the diplomatic corps on the continent and in England — carried a huge price tag. Of course, Blake could have tested his wife's love by saying no to the excesses of her social world; or perhaps simply tamped them down a bit. But the sad fact was that he was just as much a captive of the elaborate and intriguing embassy-based social network as she was. And as fond as he was of his socialite spouse, he was more in love with the milieu which surrounded her; and now him.

Blake lacked the talent to earn the kind of money he needed by legal means. Area intelligence provided him with the pool of operatives from which to draw for his illicit activities. His basic occupation was that of a salesman. His product was information. His suppliers were the weak, the desperate, and the addicted. Their collective addictions were varied and numerous. But one thing they all had in common was that they were expensive: illegal drugs, prescription pain-killers, alcohol, sex, gambling, power, status, access, fame, glory, and money for money's sake.

Blake's greatest boon to his successful criminal enterprise was a booming market. Little by little, the Soviet Union was falling behind the United States and the other NATO powers in the Cold War. Economically they could never become a serious competitor to the U.S.; and now that was impacting the race for international supremacy. The U.S. was starting to pull away in the arms race with superior numbers in ICBM missiles, nuclear submarines, planes, bases, trading partners, and allies. In the race to the moon, the U.S. was also far ahead of the Soviet Union. The Warsaw Pact defense network, thinking it had to find a simpler way to get an edge on NATO, had developed an obsessive and insatiable hunger for its enemy's secrets. Thus, Blake had a thriving market for his wares; and his intelligence gathering work gave him the contacts for learning *who* was in the market and *what* they were looking for.

As to his methodology, Blake had just one predominant talent — that of human exploitation and manipulation. Rarely astute when it came to perceiving a person's strengths, he had an uncanny knack for sizing up an individual's character flaws and discrepancies, almost instantly upon their meeting.

His psychological control over Olney was almost total. From the beginning he had intuited that Olney was a social cripple. By treating him to a taste of a glittering life that Olney would never have had otherwise, he made Olney feel accepted — even if he only tagged along with Blake as his aide and body guard. He thereby won Olney's undying fealty. He knew, however, that Olney was also a patriot and Blake was ever vigilant in keeping Olney in the dark about his nefarious activities. The off-duty side of Olney's character lived vicariously through Blake.

Blake's two natures were polar opposites. They were really two different persons occupying the same body, rather than two separate sides of one nature.

Thus, when one Blake was present and the other dormant, no play-acting was necessary. When he was Morgan he was *only* Morgan, and when he was Blake, he was *only* Blake.

Was he bipolar? A schizoid personality? A mid-twentieth century Jekyll and Hyde? Maybe yes to all of those things, but one fact that all psychiatrists would agree upon was that Blake/Morgan was a total sociopath. In place of a conscience was a perfect ruthlessness.

Ultimately, however, one of Blake's inherent traits was his downfall. Unable to fully apprehend the strengths of mind and will of Doug Booker, he had badly underestimated the man. It never occurred to Blake that Booker was both smarter and more relentless than he. When he saw that Booker was on his trail, he decided to eliminate him slowly by arsenic poisoning, rather than immediately in the manner of Barnstable and Belson.

This gave Booker the time to assemble enough evidence on Blake to spur Reitenhauser into action.

Fred had not yet figured out exactly how Blake was able to administer the arsenic to Booker on such a regular basis. He strongly suspected that the meetings of the unit's leadership group at Oscar's had much to do with it.

The solving of that mystery would have to wait. Right now a single flash light was guiding the van across a clearing to a totally darkened airplane sitting on a crude runway. Fred sensed that the meeting soon to occur between two old friends and allies would be portentous — perhaps even for the ultimate outcome of the war between the forces of freedom and the forces of tyranny.

Chapter Thirteen

Feint & Thrust

Major Ivan Petrovich had sworn loudly every time the column reached a major intersection, only to be stymied by more blackened road signs. It seemed that the only signs the Czech bastards hadn't sabotaged were the ones pointing towards Moscow. It was 2:00 a.m. and he could tell by the sharp increase in the number of service stations, restaurants, and stores that somehow they had managed to make it to the outskirts of Prague.

Patrols and forward observers were now reporting back with frequency that not a single Czech tank, patrol, weapon or uniform had been encountered anywhere up to the perimeters of the city. From every outward appearance, Dubček and Svoboda, the two top Czech leaders, had not mobilized the Czech Army and would offer no organized resistance.

But all along the approach to Prague, crude barriers had been placed on the roads by the civilian Resistance, costing the Soviets and their allies valuable time, as infantry patrols had to be deployed repeatedly to clear the obstructions and make the roads passable. And as the infantry performed these thankless tasks, they were pelted with sticks, rocks, and eggs thrown by unseen assailants hidden under the cover of darkness.

Patrols ordered out to subdue the assailants rarely found anyone. But after the invaders entered Prague, the groups of resisters grew larger and better armed, with Molotov cocktails, clubs, sticks of dynamite, and some World War II vintage rifles.

Now the infantry was engaging these guerilla-type defenders in actual skirmishes and scattered pitched battles. The crudely-armed and thinly-manned groups of Czech fighters were taking casualties, but at the same time were causing chaos all along the route. Petrovich, however, had been ordered not to turn the tanks on civilian resisters unless the column was in danger of taking serious casualties or sustaining damage to the tanks.

Jan Palach, the Czech firebrand, led the largest and best organized group of resisters — keeping the Soviet tanks and foot soldiers under constant harassment from the time they entered the city, all the way to the capital center, their ultimate destination. Groups of young Czechoslovaks would lay down in front of the tanks. When Russian troops moved in to physically remove them, other Czechs at strategic positions would pelt the troops with various hard objects.

The troops were ordered to return fire. Illa Kadish, one of the female student organizers, took a Soviet bullet in the right arm and screamed out in pain, frustration and rage. But she wrapped a kerchief around her wound, cursed her enemies, and continued to rally the militant students to fight on.

For two and a half hours the confrontations continued unabated. Individual Russian soldiers were bleeding from cuts to the head and face, and some could only limp forward. Those who fell were sometimes kicked by the Czech defenders, but the Warsaw Pact forces had sustained no known fatalities.

All along the route to the government center and Dubcëk's official headquarters, the screams, curses, cries, and revilements by the Czechoslovaks pierced the night air — punctuated by the sounds of gun shots everywhere.

A low moan of pain mixed with sadness seemed to rise from the bowels of the city, gathering volume as it reached out to entrap invaders and resisters alike in a surreal dance of rage and death. The frustration and anger of the invading troops was genuine but situational; while that of the Czech civilians was an intrinsic part of their beings — an all-consuming force of hatred and implacability. They wailed in outrage and grief.

By the time the smoke cleared and the invasion came to a halt with the arrest of Alexander Dubcëk in the early morning hours of August 21, 1968, a total of 175,000 to 500,000 troops were said to have attacked Czechoslovakia. Approximately 500 Czechoslovaks had been wounded and 108 killed.

As Petrovich's lead tank approached the government buildings, his anger and annoyance had been replaced by a mixture of horror over the civilian casualties, and admiration for their courage and tenacity. Petrovich shook his head in dismay as bleeding and battered citizens were being loaded into ambulances everywhere he looked. The single thought which penetrated his consciousness was the newly born realization that the hunger for freedom and human dignity cannot be snuffed out by tanks and guns. This truth did not bode well for the future of the Soviet empire.

Fred and Uri sat in the rear compartment of the van sipping black coffee. Though they had embraced upon meeting, Uri immediately made it clear that there was no time for small talk. Placing a map of Czechoslovakia, Austria, and Germany on the small table between them, he gave Fred the bare details of the Soviet-Warsaw Pact invasion currently in progress, code-named 'Operation Danube.'

With pencil in hand he drew two straight lines — one from the Western border of the Ukraine to Prague, and a second line extending from Prague to the West German border near Weiden in der Oberpfalz, on the German side and Cheb on the Czech side.

Fred needed no further explanation. A flash of grim recognition immediately seized his attention. In only a second he knew why, as Tallifierro had reported, a heavy concentration of Red Guards existed in the Regensburg region. They had been placed there to pave the way for the Soviet invasion of West Germany!

Simultaneously, Fred realized that the invasion of Czechoslovakia was cover for the more important objective — the invasion and occupation of the Federal Republic of Germany. He should have realized it sooner. Perhaps if Booker had not been so ill, he would have figured it out before now.

Immediately upon reading the expression on Fred's face, Uri knew that Fred understood. He wouldn't have to spell out a lot of unnecessary details. Instead, he was able to go right to the heart of the matter.

"The source of my information was the KGB Bureau Chief in East Berlin," Uri said. "It was part of my briefing as Regional Defense Minister; though frankly, my duties are mainly administrative rather than operational. All strategy, plans, and operations come straight from the Kremlin. As far as the planned invasion is concerned, only 50,000 troops are to enter Prague."

Uri tapped the map with his forefinger. "The Soviets had advance word that Dubcĕk would not call out his army to defend against the invasion. That was wise on his part. The Czechoslovaks could not hope to win, and resistance would have caused the greatest slaughter. Dubcĕk and Svoboda themselves would have been standing in front of a firing squad by morning's first light. His acquiescence has allowed the main body of the Warsaw Pact Forces to remain on the southwestern part of the city's outer regions where, even as we speak, they are either forming up or beginning a lightning thrust on this straight line to the West German border south of Cheb."

"They have planned this operation for well over a year," Uri said. "Since the Czech revolution presented them with the opportunity to kill two birds with one stone. They eliminate the irksome Czech liberation movement, while surreptitiously placing themselves in an ideal geographic and logistical position to overrun West Germany before NATO's forces even know what hit them. The plan is near perfect. It combines the elements of surprise and strategic positioning. First they feint toward Prague, and then thrust towards Germany."

Without responding, Fred picked up the secure phone he had never before had to use. He quickly dialed the number he had long ago committed to memory.

On the third ring, General Stansfield picked up. Fred rapidly related what Uri had just told him. Stansfield asked no questions. He ordered Fred to stay by the phone and await his return call.

For the time being, until he received his orders from the general, the crisis was out of Fred's hands, but not out of his head. He and Uri sat silently just staring at each other for a couple of minutes. The almost mystical power that each possessed of intuiting what the other was thinking had not abandoned either of them over the passage of years.

"I need to bring Teacher in," said Fred. 'Teacher' was Magyaar's cover name.

"I'll dispatch Coach to pick him up tomorrow. He's in danger in Vienna — even at the safehouse. I'll send my Samoan along as muscle, just in case. And, I hope to send a team to the Czech border to join with the Regensburg C.I. Detachment in neutralizing the Red Guards now preparing the way in the border regions for the impending invasion."

Fred exhaled heavily "I'll try to convince General Stansfield to approve the plan and send some demolition and sabotage people to join my team as well. We need to disrupt communications by jamming their transmissions, taking out as many of their telegraph and radio transmission stations as possible, and sending out bogus messages for them to intercept. We also need to intercept and break their encoded messages. I already have one of the best interpreters of coded messages sitting in a safehouse twenty miles from here. But, this is a new ball game now and I can't do any of that stuff without Stansfield's go-ahead."

The phone rang and Fred picked it up to receive the general's orders.

NATO Headquarters in Belgium had considered Fred's information to be of such moment, that it had ordered Stansfield to proceed to Weiden in der Oberpfalz[*] immediately, where he would personally conduct and coordinate all pre-invasion reconnaissance and intelligence operations.

A battalion of airborne rangers would soon be in the air from Mannheim Air Force Base to assist the counter-intelligence types in liquidating as many of the Red Guards as possible. Reitenhauser was to join Stansfield in Weiden with his own people. Fred then briefly outlined his ideas to his commander and the general approved them all.

---

* A West German town located near the Czech-German border.

He next called LeBron and ordered him to make sure Mattatussu was still at the safehouse, and to round up Penchak, Olney, Smith, and Rhymes and "see that they haul ass over there too."

"And Art," continued the CO, "I want everybody armed. Tell them to wear field operation civvies and bring a change of socks and underwear. Lieutenant Ryan and Sergeant Berger will wait behind in the Ops Support section for further orders. O'Malley will be in charge at the Detachment till he hears otherwise. Scones will stay on duty in the telex room until relieved. Tell him that if he wanders away, I'll have him brought up on charges. Everybody else is to go about their regular business. And have O'Malley issue weapons to Ryan and Berger also. That's it for now. I'll meet you at the safehouse as soon as I can get over there."

Fred and Uri again fell silent, each in his own way trying to absorb the magnitude of what was happening.

Finally Uri spoke, almost whimsically. "Do you remember, Frederick, the second time we had dinner at Allemagne in Berlin to celebrate the convictions in the Nuremberg trials — late 1946? By the time we finished dessert and started working on our after-dinner brandy, we were in high spirits from the alcohol and relief that the grueling 'ordeal was over.'"

"You suggested in one of your rare fanciful moments that we invent a game for spooks to be called 'Deception.' To give it a bit more allure, and in deference to where we were dining, I suggested it be named 'Allemagne Deception.' There were to be two teams. One team would plan a military campaign against a particular objective, such as Normandy in June 1944, and would also have an alternate objective, like Pas de Calais, which would be a phony, diversionary target. The attacking team would attempt to deceive the defending team into accepting the primary target as the true objective of the operation. It would write the name of the real objective on a piece of paper numbered 1 and the diversionary objective on a piece of paper numbered 2; and they would be folded and placed in the middle of the table. The opposing team would be counter-intelligence agents who would interrogate the invaders in an attempt to discover the true site of the intended invasion. The invading team would, by their answers, seek to convince the interrogators that the fake target was the real one. The counter-team would be allowed twenty questions before offering its conclusion as to the true objective. The pieces of paper would then be opened to see which team had prevailed in that round. The winner of 3 out of 5 rounds would win the game. To add a little intrigue, any member of the invading team could also answer the questions in a way suggestive of false objectives, in addition to the one written on the second folded piece of paper."

"I do remember," replied Fred, enjoying the brief respite Uri had provided from their monumental concerns of the moment.   "I also remember that you and I played a couple of practice rounds as the brandy really kicked in, but that you declared me disqualified when I wrote "Lichtenstein" on the first piece of paper as the target of my invading army."

"True," said Uri. "I pointed out that the target country had to have an army, which Lichtenstein did not. Otherwise, why would you need a diversion against a nation which wouldn't or couldn't defend itself anyway?"

The Russian smiled sadly. "I hope to get to play a full game of Allemagne Deception with you one of these days, my friend. But it will have to be another time. Right now, I need to get back to Prague before I am missed. That is, if my absence has not already been noticed."

Fred Reitenhauser nodded gravely. "Go with God, my friend. You are..." He paused, and began again. "You are a great man."

Uri responded with a Mona Lisa sort of smile. He gave Fred a farewell handshake, opened the door of the van, and was gone.

Tallifierro sat in an armchair in the living room of the safehouse reading Barbara Tuchman's '*The Guns of August*.' He had now been sequestered in these dull, agonizingly quiet surroundings for three and a half weeks. True, he had been able to catch up on some of his history reading in the house's amply supplied library. He also realized that he had been in real danger, and was grateful to the CO for doing his best to protect him.

But a painful loneliness had crept into him about five days after his arrival at the safehouse, and had grown worse each day since. His longing to see Kate or at least talk to her on the telephone was overwhelming. He had been allowed to write unsigned letters to her, which were delivered by an M.P. to her apartment. First however, the letters were censored by Tonelli or Mattatussu, to make sure they contained no names and nothing which would provide the slightest hint as to his location.

Kate had no way of responding because the M.P. was not permitted to accept any return letters, notes, or cards from her.

Tom's bodyguards, Tonelli, Mattatussu, and Penchak, who each worked an eight hour shift, were no company either. Tonelli and Mattatussu did nothing all day but look out the window and occasionally watch German television. Penchak didn't like television, but enjoyed small talk even less. When he wasn't wandering through the old house and looking out its many windows for signs of Hostile's presence, he silently read Czech novels.

Tom did keep track of the dates and when he awoke shortly after dawn on the morning of August 21st, the place was already abuzz with activity. He heard the familiar voices of Káz and Osi downstairs, but now there were others as well. The atmosphere in the house had changed from one of dull tedium to tightly-strung anticipation, beginning with Osi's arrival the night before. The voices from downstairs carried none of the usual light-hearted sounds of comradely banter.

Something big was going on, thought Tom, as he threw on his Levis and moccasins and headed down the sturdy oak staircase.

In the kitchen stood Káz, Osi, Art LeBron, Anders Smith, Warren Olney, and Mal Rhymes, all drinking coffee and speaking in business-like tones.

"Good morning, sir," said Tom to LeBron.

"Good morning sergeant, but from now on and until I tell you otherwise, we are all strictly on a first-name basis."

Tom noted the dark, ready-for-action clothing of all those present, and the contours of holsters on more than one ankle. A wave of excitement coursed through his veins.

LeBron wasted no time in giving Tom a bare-bones briefing. "Tom we're going operational, and that includes you too. The Warsaw Pact Forces invaded Czechoslovakia last night, and we believe the invasion is still in progress. Captain Mitchell Blake has been arrested for treason and is in U.S. custody. The colonel and Mario will arrive shortly. Whether hungry or not, we'll all have breakfast. I don't know when we'll get another opportunity to eat."

As LeBron spoke, Osi began scrambling two dozen eggs and multiple strips of bacon on the kitchen stove.

"Tom, go upstairs and finish getting dressed," LeBron said. "Get your weapon too."

As Tom sat on his bed and pulled on a pair of hiking shoes, his shock was so great that he had no recollection of leaving the kitchen and climbing the stairs to his room.

The CO and Tonelli arrived about fifteen minutes later and all nine men sat down to breakfast around the large, though strictly functional, dining room table.

Reitenhauser had received an updated reconnaissance report from Group and briefed the men on the latest developments from Czechoslovakia.

"So far, our reconnaissance planes report no major troops movements away from the massive concentration of Warsaw Pact forces near southwestern Prague. But East German planes have been spotted directly over the route from Prague to Cheb. Soviet radio transmissions along the entire route and near the Czech-West German border are about ten times their usual volume. Also, Group's agents in Prague report that the Warsaw Pact forces are moving into formation with the lead tank columns pointed west toward Cheb. Army C. I. in Regensburg reports so many Red Guards personnel moving toward the border regions near Cheb that one would think they're headed there for a convention. Finally, Signal Corps has picked up a massive amount of static along the border in the Czech province of Zapadocesky through which the suspected enemy attack route runs. They call this 'white noise' and Signal Corps' transmission analysts are now trying to interpret it."

"All of this seems to corroborate what our sources told us earlier this morning," the CO said. "An invasion of West Germany by Warsaw Pact Forces will occur within the next 24 to 48 hours, near the West German town of Weiden in der Oberpfalz."

Stunned silence mixed with a few soft imprecations greeted the CO's announcement.

After allowing his own words to sink in, the CO continued. "Prague is said to now be under Soviet control, and Secretary Dubček has been arrested and flown to Moscow. We do not know whether or not he is still alive.

"A small bus, borrowed from the Provost Marshal — the kind usually used to transport prisoners — will pick us up at 0730. Our destination will be Weiden. Tom you will sit next to me at the rear of the bus. As I am sure Art has already told you, no last names until we return from our mission.

The colonel looked at his assembled team. "One more thing… Our top man in Prague, the Teacher, is out of Czechoslovakia. I am trying to have him picked up today and brought to us within 24 hours. He was injured in a clash with the Red Guards, during which one of our other agents was killed. I shouldn't have to tell you men but I will anyway. Watch yourselves out there, and don't take unnecessary chances."

Austria - The Orient Express - 21 August, 1968, 0900 Hours

"Mattatussu was supposed to be sitting next to you on this trip," said Lonnie Ryan to Ben Berger. "But I think the colonel decided that he needed Mattatussu's muscle on a more dangerous mission. Instead, all you got was me."

"Don't sell yourself short," replied Ben. "If the CO thought you weren't up to it, he could always have sent O'Malley and left you in charge of the Detachment."

"True enough," conceded Lonnie.

"The CO knows what he's doing. He sent you to find 14332, and then put you in charge in Vienna of the new recruitment operation. Now *this*. He trusts you with critical missions."

Reinvigorated by Ben's positive words, Lonnie spoke about their current mission for the first time. "The CO expects us to somehow paste and glue together a man suffering from multiple untreated injuries, and transport him by some unspecified means from Vienna to Weiden, through what very well may be a war zone by the time we get there."

"That sounds about right," replied the over-droll Berger.

"So what's the problem?" deadpanned Lonnie.

After a momentary silence, both men broke into spontaneous laughter.

Vienna 21 August, 11:30 Hours

As Lonnie and Ben were admitted to the safehouse after first exchanging the predetermined bona fides with their Five-O-Deuce greeter in the entrance hallway, they were met by a strong medicinal smell mixed with some anonymous disinfectant.

In the parlor Magyaar sat on a straight-back chair wearing briefs only, being attended to by a middle-age bearded man in a brown suit with a stethoscope around his neck and blood pressure equipment on his lap.

"Good morning Coach," said Magyaar in a gravelly voice. "What's the score of the game?"

"No score yet, Teach. It's only the first inning. Do you feel well enough to suit up for the game?"

"Damn right!" Magyaar said. "Oh by the way, this is Dr. Leo Strauss, a renowned Vienna physician."

"Nice to meet you doctor. This is my colleague, Larry Rawlins," said Ben. Larry Rawlins was another of Lonnie's cover names.

After an exchange of greetings all around Lonnie asked, "How's the patient doing, Dr. Strauss?"

"He has a concussion — not too severe, but not mild either. He also has broken ribs, a fractured wrist and a dislocated shoulder. More troubling is his punctured lung. I've taped him together pretty well and fitted him with a sling. The lacerations and contusions have been treated. Right now I'm giving him a shot of Penicillin and I'll leave a supply of pain pills and an antibiotic as well. I took a few stitches in his wounded arm. In general, I need x-rays,; and the man needs to be in a hospital for a few days at the very least, and then bed-rest for a couple of weeks after that. Under no circumstances is he well enough for overland travel."

Turning to the 502nd agent hovering over the group in the background, Lonnie asked if there was a room where he and Ben could speak in private. The stolid G-man pointed in the direction of a small office.

Once inside, Lonnie noticed there was no phone, a fact which sparked an awareness that had been quietly seeking his attention.

The CO's substitution of him for Osi Mattatussu on this mission was not primarily because the colonel needed Osi's muscle elsewhere. It stemmed from the exigencies of their mission. Ben was right. The CO had purposely chosen him for his decision-making ability and judgment. Why? Because the colonel knew that effective communication between the parallel missions to Weiden and Vienna might be impossible, or possible but too risky. He had better face it. He and Ben were on their own.

The CO was interested only in the result — getting Magyaar to Weiden. How it was to be accomplished had been left in their hands because he trusted them. And this was no humanitarian rescue. The CO had strong operational reasons for extracting Magyaar and bringing him right to the location where World War III might be about to start. But Lonnie knew he had to get Magyaar there alive, and keep him alive once there.

"Ben we need a medevac chopper to pick us up and fly the three of us to Weiden. There we need to be met right at the landing site by an ambulance, a medical team, and an armed security detail."

Ben taxed his memory, trying to recall from his many agent recruitment and operations meetings in Vienna and surroundings, where a chopper could safely land without attracting attention and without the rigmarole of getting clearances. After about a minute he had it.

"There's a landing pad on the roof of the U.S. Embassy, only six blocks from here. But, we need a non-descript ambulance to pick us up and somehow we have to convince the doctor to fly with us to Weiden."

"Okay, here it is," said Lonnie. "We have no time to go through the various national and international bureaucratic channels to get this done. We need to accomplish the mission quickly by violating a whole bunch of international protocols and aviation restrictions. This has to be an entirely covert operation and there is only one outfit that can pull it off — CIA." Now Lonnie suddenly knew why the only pre-mission assistance the CO had provided was a last name and a Vienna phone number.

Lonnie and Ben moved fast. The former told the 502nd man that he needed a secure phone and privacy. He did not intend it as just a request;

and one minute later he was behind a closed door dialing the number of BOSS.

Ben pulled Dr. Strauss aside and gently but firmly informed the physician that they expected him to accompany his patient to Germany with them by helicopter. He would not need anything other than his doctor's bag, and need not worry about his lack of a passport.

The doctor was reluctant, but Ben said they were taking his patient anyway and his presence was necessary not only for the well-being of the injured man, but also to possibly save the lives of millions. Ben, who could sell air conditioners in Antarctica, seemed to make a serious impression on the physician.

But it didn't really matter. Dr. Leo Strauss of Vienna's renowned College of Physicians and Surgeons was going for a helicopter ride — willingly or not. So was the J. Edgar Hoover look-alike standing silently to the side. They needed all the help they could get to move and protect Magyaar and the doctor.

The 502nd man had no inkling as to his new assignment, and Ben decided to let Lonnie break the news. After all, it was Lonnie who had been vested with authority by 7th Army Command.

Colonel Reitenhauser would have left no doubt in his advance word to the safehouse as to who was in charge. General Stansfield would have been equally firm in his communiqués establishing Reitenhauser's operational authority.

Within a half hour a Vienna City Hospital ambulance pulled up in front of the house, and two burly men dressed only in grey coveralls hopped out of the rear doors. The 502nd man let them in and they quickly placed Magyaar on a gurney after connecting him to an IV and portable oxygen tank.

The injured man and his four fellow passengers were transported to the U.S. Embassy, up a private elevator to the roof, and onto a waiting ambulance chopper for their trip to Weiden in der Oberpfalz.

Weiden in der Oberpfalz, West Germany, 21 August, 1500 hours

Colonel Fred Reitenhauser accompanied by Lieutenant Anders Smith stood at the edge of the landing area as the Huey helicopter, refitted as a flying ambulance, landed safely at a U.S. Air Force heliport on the outskirts of Weiden.

First to disembark from the craft was Lieutenant Lonnie Ryan, followed by Sergeant Ben Berger and the 502nd man, who were carrying the injured Magyaar on a stretcher.

Magyaar was awake though groggy from the pain medication. The last man to climb down from the chopper was the portly, middle-aged, Dr. Leo Strauss.

Quick introductions were made and the colonel was pleased to see that the bearded Austrian had an excellent command of English. Everyone wore civilian clothes and the colonel was introduced to the doctor and Magyaar simply as 'G.M.' Magyaar was 'Lou' and Smith was 'Andy.' Ryan and Berger used their cover first names. Save for Dr. Strauss, surnames were nowhere to be heard. The 502nd agent was just plain-old 'Pete.'

The colonel gave 'Pete' permission to return to Vienna on the departing helicopter. The rest of the men clambered into an oversized truck-model ambulance — more like an emergency room on wheels — containing a bed for Magyaar.

As tough as he was, Magyaar was relieved to be off the aircraft and on to a comfortable bed. Before the CO signaled the driver to take off, Dr. Strauss injected Magyaar with a shot of Penicillin followed by a shot of Demerol. He also set him up on a saline IV.

"I can't thank you enough, Dr. Strauss, for agreeing to accompany your patient."

"Well, G.M., let's be honest... Did I really have a choice?"

The colonel noticed the combination of mirth and kindness in the Austrian's eyes and laughed appreciatively in response. He liked the man already, and felt he owed him some explanation.

"Doctor, I will share with you that both your country and the Federal Republic of Germany are in danger of invasion. I don't know how you wound up as the treating physician for our man here, and I don't want to know. We're just grateful and happy that you did. I'll try to get you back to Vienna just as soon as I can — probably before evening. Your patient's health is vital to our shared cause. We are headed for a small U.S. military hospital in Weiden in der Oberpfalz, and as soon as you get Lou situated and stabilized in a private room there, you'll be free to go. We'll arrange good transportation for you back to Vienna."

"That's not really necessary," the doctor said. "I have nothing more pressing to do, and will be happy to attend to Lou until he begins recovering. Right now, I need to keep an eye (as you Americans say) on his lungs and head injury. I also need to run a number of tests and take some x-rays to check for internal injuries."

The trip from the landing pad to the hospital took forty minutes, much longer than the CO had anticipated. Government vehicles, including U.S.

Army jeeps and trucks, never seen before in Weiden, were now everywhere — blocking intersections, causing traffic jams and far outstripping the capacity of local traffic control. A sense of frenzied urgency was in the air.

At the emergency room entrance, Reitenhauser turned to Strauss and somewhat apologetically informed him that Andy would accompany him to Lou's room, which was standing ready.

An M.P. would meet them at the door and take them directly there, without signing-in or any other red tape. But Lou would stay with the G.M. and his team in the ambulance for about a half hour, and then be brought up under guard. The driver was a well-trained paramedic, in case of an emergency.

Dr. Strauss was not particularly happy about this arrangement, but for some reason, he trusted these peculiar Americans with no last names. He followed Smith without protest.

"Sorry Lou," said the colonel, "but we need to ask you some questions. Since about mid-morning U.S. Army Special Ops has had a full-scale operation up and running here. I have seven of my men working right now as part of a special task force composed of elements from CIA, U.S. Military Intelligence, West German Intelligence, U.S. Special Forces, and Army Rangers. Our latest reconnaissance information is that a Warsaw Pact invasion force, including 1,000 tanks, has just disembarked from Prague, headed towards the West German border.

"I'm confident that NATO will be deploying its defensive forces as quickly as possible," the colonel said. "But under cover of the invasion of Czechoslovakia, the enemy has gained the element of surprise. Prague is about 200 miles from the border, so the invasion force will not reach here until sometime late tomorrow.

"The Task Force's mission is to intercept and analyze enemy communications, establish a recon network along the border, capture and interrogate as many Red Guards and other covert operatives as possible. We will use whatever info we extract from them to assist the Rangers and Special Forces in conducting sabotage and other disruptive activities against the vanguard of the invasion force. By doing all these things quickly and efficiently, NATO Command and its man on the scene right now, General Stansfield, hope to compensate for the Warsaw Pact's clear advantages in speed and preparedness."

The CO continued. "Four of my best-trained and most experienced black ops men are at or near the border as we speak, and three more analysts are at General Stansfield's headquarters, hard at work on enemy intercepts."

This was the first that Lonnie and Ben had heard of the fact that so many of their colleagues were on the scene.

"I'm ready whenever you are, G.M.," said Magyaar in a weak voice.

The colonel nodded. "Good. Let's get started... Have you ever met or spoken to a man calling himself Morgan?"

"Which Morgan?" Magyaar asked. "There must be a half-dozen spooks in Austria calling themselves Morgan."

"So we've heard," the colonel said. "How about an American using that name?"

"No."

"In your work for Horst and then us, have you dealt with any Russians other than Carlton?"

"No," Magyaar said

"How about Americans other than your regular two-man team of handlers plus the two man launch team from Munich?"

"No," Magyaar said again. "Not until today."

He paused, and then corrected himself. "Wait... Just one — the polygraph operator."

Both Lonnie and Ben were puzzled by the CO's line of questioning. What difference could any of this make right now, on the eve of invasion and war? But unlike Lonnie, Ben's natural instincts as an undercover man were sending him some kind of a vague alert. He found himself shifting uncomfortably in his seat. Those same instincts told him that something was gnawing at the colonel as well.

"How many times did you meet the polygraph operator?"

"Once."

The colonel nodded. "When was that?"

"When he put Étan and I on the box, before our trip to Czechoslovakia."

"I see," the colonel said. "Were there any questions that he asked you during your polygraph exam that you found out of the ordinary?"

Magyaar did not respond. Now his head was beginning to nod and he as having trouble keeping his eyes open. The shot of Demerol, combined with his general weakness, were taking their toll.

"Lou," said the colonel in a loud voice, "Wake up! These questions are critical."

Lonnie and Ben exchanged glances. Neither man knew what the colonel was driving at.

Magyaar's eyelids fluttered. "I'm sorry," he said. "What was the question again?"

Fred repeated the question.

"Out of the ordinary? I have to think back," Magyaar said.

Lonnie reached over and patted Magyaar's face with a wet washcloth. It seemed to help.

"Yes," Magyaar said slowly. "The polygraph operator asked me if I knew of anyone from behind the iron curtain working for Western intelligence."

"Did you?"

"I had heard rumors," Magyaar said.

The colonel's voice took on an edge of tension. "*What* had you heard?"

"Just that a high Soviet official had been turned by some western spy agency."

"How did you answer the polygraph operator's question?"

"I said 'No'."

"You said you heard rumors. From whom?"

"I don't know," Magyaar said. "From a lot of sources. It was common knowledge within Horst's network."

"Think hard, Lou," the colonel said. "Who *specifically* did you discuss these rumors with?"

A pause, Magyaar's breathing was now labored. His voice was clearly becoming weaker. He motioned to Lonnie to wet his face again. His coloring was a deathly white, and his eyes were slits.

"I can only remember Étan for sure."

"Étan Gaborski?"

"Yes."

"Had he heard the same rumors?"

"Yes."

"And the polygraph operator examined him the same day as you?"

"Yes," Magyaar said quietly. "Because he was going with me to Prague."

"Do you know if he was asked the same question?"

"No."

"If he *had* been asked the question, how do you think he would have answered?"

"I don't know," Magyaar said. "All I can tell you was that Étan was incapable of telling a lie. That's why he was only useful for security."

Ben still didn't know where this was headed, but O'Malley's admonition of well over a year ago had become an insistent and discomfiting mantra in his brain... "*In the intelligence game, things are seldom what they appear to be.*"

Fred Reitenhauser was silent for a full minute — seemingly lost in thought.

Finally he spoke. "Okay Lou, we're going to take you up to your hospital room now. What you have told us is of immeasurable importance."

He might have saved his breath because Lugash Magyaar had plunged into a deep, healing slumber.

August 21st Weiden, West Germany, 1600 hours

General Stansfield's headquarters in Weiden in der Oberpfalz were in one of the smaller castles built in the late 1800s by Mad Ludwig of Bavaria. In recent years, it had been refurbished and converted into a modernized high-end resort for top German government officials and politically-connected industrialists. But now it had been commandeered by Bonn and NATO, and handed over to the special task force headed up by General Stansfield, with Colonel Reitenhauser as his Chief Deputy.

Immediately upon his return to headquarters from the hospital, the colonel called together his brain trust — LeBron, Rhymes, Ryan, Tallifierro, and Berger. Lieutenant Smith was sent to join the other four members of the black ops team near the border. They were Tonelli, Mattatussu, Olney, and Penchak. Smith who held the highest rank among the five, was now designated by the colonel as black ops team leader.

The colonel had been provided with an office in a penthouse suite with a breathtaking view of a long and sweeping manicured lawn, surrounded by spectacular flower gardens running downhill on a gentle slope for easily a quarter of a mile before coming to a graceful stop before a lush, green woods.

All along its length, the lawn was dotted with fountains, reflecting pools, ponds, and miniature waterfalls. The irony of planning for war in such a peaceful place was not lost on the colonel, but he had no time to dwell on such incongruities.

He was satisfied completely with his black ops team. It was a team composed of all-stars only. But the loss of Booker — now out of his coma but extremely weak — as top man in his brain trust, was incalculable. However, he still had two exceptional analysts in LeBron and Tallifierro, one rare operational talent and intuitive thinker in Berger, a man of sound judgment in Rhymes, and an officer of discipline and organization in Ryan. It would have to do.

It was a team with gravitas, of which it would need every ounce to work through the intellectual conundrums he was about to spring on them over the next couple of hours.

The six men sat gathered at a large round table in front of a panoramic window. The colonel called to have sandwiches, fruit, soft drinks and coffee sent up from the mess. Then he started.

"Gentlemen, the fact that we are here in Weiden planning against an invasion we expect to come across the border about 26 or 27 hours from now does *not* mean we have made any final assumptions or conclusions. I want you to challenge every point and ask any question which comes to mind. Doug Booker can't be with us, but his spirit is in this room. I also want his skepticism and relentless intellectual curiosity to be alive here through us. Each of us needs to challenge, doubt, question, and probe as he would. For the next couple of hours, there will be no military rank at this table. Look at it as if it were a college graduate seminar, but one where a failing grade could mean a major defeat for the free world."

His men nodded, and he continued. "I will start the discussion by outlining why we believe the Warsaw Pact Forces are in the process of launching a massive invasion of West Germany to take place about twenty miles from here."

The CO then gave a succinct summary of what he learned from a 'mole' embedded deep within the Soviet system; and that he could personally attest to the man's reliability. He described the strong corroborating evidence of the diversionary feint of the main Warsaw Pact force towards Prague and then its pivot and thrust towards the Czech-German border. He reported the heavy enemy radio traffic all the way from Prague to Cheb, Regensburg and Hof and the spike in white noise as well. He cited the reported vast numbers of tanks and troops headed towards West Germany and the concentration of enemy bomber practice runs over the border regions. Finally, he told how our black ops people had already interrogated many Red Guards' operatives who fully confirmed that the invasion was coming right at them.

Oddly, thought Tom Tallifierro, the CO also recapped his interview of Magyaar, who he referred to as the 'Teacher.' To Tom what the Teacher had to say seemed an extraneous non sequitur.

Reitenhauser's instincts, however, told him that Gaborski had named Uri to Belson, and that this fact was significant.

"All right gentlemen, comments, questions?" The CO's tone left no doubt that this was an order, not a request.

As XO, LeBron led it off. "Fred, what information do you have as to when NATO's defensive forces are going to get here?"

"None. I think the general has chosen not to share that information with me because he wants us to have no distractions from our sole mission

— to develop effective intelligence on the apparent invasion; to provide analysis, and to formulate counter-strategies, including black ops."

Tom suddenly felt an enormous burden resting on his shoulders. With Booker down, he had become the 409th's Chief Intelligence Analyst. Well, so be it. This *was* what he had trained for.

He asked his first question: "Colonel, how do we know for sure the size of the invasion force?"

"We don't. It's an extrapolation from Group's top analysts — a projection from air reconnaissance — still shots and film, taken together with reports from our agents near the enemy's main encampment."

"Group's top analysts?" murmured LeBron. "God knows, *they're* never wrong."

His comment evoked laughter around the table and broke the tension.

Tom asked a follow-up question. "Doesn't the invasion of Czechoslovakia and the ousting of its popular leaders seem like an awful lot of trouble to go to if that's not the main mission?"

He didn't wait for an answer. "If the Soviets are *really* planning to take on NATO, why would they risk pissing off millions of Czechoslovaks just before they make their big move? If they're planning to go head-to-head with the West, they should be working for maximum unity among the Soviet bloc nations. It doesn't make sense to stir up a massive internal resistance movement at the very moment when they need solidarity the *most*."

"I can't argue with that," said Rhymes.

"Yeah, but maybe that's the point," offered Lonnie. "The improbability of what they're doing may have been by design. We would never expect them to do something so outlandish. Maybe that gives them the advantage of surprise."

"Like MacArthur planning the Inchon invasion," observed LeBron. "He sold it to the Pentagon brass by pointing out that Inchon was such an impossible place for an amphibious landing that the North Koreans would think that no sane commander would ever land there. 'This will give me the element of complete surprise,' said MacArthur, 'and I will use it to crush them'."

"And he *did* crush them," said Ben. "And the Warsaw Pact *did* catch us by surprise. So, if that was their plan, it certainly worked."

At that moment the phone rang and the CO answered it. The frown on his face slowly dissolved, replaced by a smile. The caller did all the talking except for the CO's "Thank you, general," right before he hung up.

"Good news," said Reitenhauser. "At my request, General Stansfield has ordered the XO of Stuttgart Station to relieve Ted O'Malley as acting

CO of the 409th. Ted is on his way here. He should be joining us in about half an hour."

A few enthusiastic hand rap sequences on the table, and 'here-here's' followed the announcement. O'Malley's knowledge and experience would be welcome additions to their discussions.

There would be no hiatus, however, awaiting his arrival and the CO picked up the thread of the dialogue right away.

"Group's cryptographers are hard at work trying to decipher intercepted messages. I have repeatedly been reassured by the general that the internal security disaster of a year ago has been completely resolved. The department has had almost a complete turn-over in personnel; and has installed tough new procedures for oversight."

"That sounds fine," ventured Ryan. "But are their people any *good*?"

"I don't know," replied Reitenhauser candidly.

Mal Rhymes cleared his throat. "Speaking of being any good, what do we know about our agents who are reporting on the troop and tank movements towards the border?"

"They number about a half-dozen," said LeBron. "They were already in place when I took over the Czech section. Most of them were recruited by Káz, one or two of them by Doug. We have been evaluating them on an ongoing basis, and they all have passed muster. Does this mean that none of them could have been turned or turned and doubled? Of course not. Any agent can be turned by the right set of inducements."

"Enigma," murmured Rhymes, almost inaudibly.

The colonel looked across the table. "What did you say, Mal?"

"Just thinking out loud, sir," Mal said.

The colonel motioned for him to continue.

"I was thinking about the German espionage agents in England during WW II, and how British Intelligence caught every one of them, and turned them to work against the Third Reich. The Polish Cipher Bureau had cracked the codes from Germany's Enigma encryption/decryption machine before the war. The Poles turned the cipher keys over to the British just before Great Britain and France declared war on Germany, after the invasion of Poland in 1939. As a result, the British had the advantage of being able to decipher encrypted German messages regarding planned operations. The turned Nazi agents added valuable confirmation of the legitimacy of the British decryptions. Those same German double agents also helped deceive the Wehrmacht into believing the allied invasion on D-Day would take place at Pas de Calais, rather than Normandy, by verifying that Patton's bogus 1st Army of rubber tanks and wooden artillery poised to invade Calais from England, was real, as opposed to the fake it actually was."

The others stared at Rhymes — once again amazed by his incredible command of both the major events and minutiae of history. His near total recall was a special talent — particularly useful for an intelligence operative.

Ben chewed on the relevant piece of history just offered by his partner of the "Rhymesberger" tandem, looking for a way to make further use of Mal's photographic memory. Something was gnawing at Ben about the CO's interview of Magyaar. With Ben, unlike Tom who was a master of cognition, it was the feel of things, his intuitive grasp of the often-hidden meaning of gestures and words, which fueled his engine.

"Mal, remember when we told the Teacher and Étan that we had to put them on the box? What was their reaction?"

It took Rhymes only a second to respond: "Teacher gave it a typical 'what a load of bullshit,' but that was Teacher. He actually accepted it without any problem. But Étan wanted to know *who* the operator was going to be. When I used Belson's unofficial cover name, 'Torquemada,' I noticed a look of skepticism on Étan's face."

"Yeah," Ben said. "I noticed that too. But I don't remember if he said anything."

"You were busy checking out Teacher for signs of his reaction," Rhymes said. "But Étan *did* say something. It was almost a whisper…"

"What did he say?" asked Lonnie.

Rhymes rubbed the back of his neck and frowned slightly. "He said, 'who's going to put Torquemada on the box?' Then later he said, 'You Americans are polygraph-happy. Doesn't it ever occur to you that it's a dangerous thing to put a spy in a situation where he has to tell the truth?' And then Teacher added, 'Yeah especially if he knows some of your biggest secrets.' The four of us had a laugh over that."

"I remember that part," said Ben. "At the time, I figured Teacher was just joking, as usual. Maybe he *wasn't.*"

That thought was interrupted by the phone again. It was the duty officer informing them that O'Malley was on his way up.

O'Malley was soon greeted with the usual combination of warm welcomes and gentle ribbings. So much had happened, it was hard to believe that it had only been about fourteen hours since most of them had last been together with him.

*   *   *

Weiden in der Oberpfalz, West Germany, 21 August, 1645 hours

After O'Malley grabbed a quick sandwich and provided a briefing on things back at the 409th, the discussion continued where it had left off.

LeBron picked it up. "Okay, so suppose we all put ourselves in Belson's shoes. Étan has probably caught him by surprise by revealing the existence and possibly the identity of our mole. Knowing Belson, what does he do with the information?"

"Tries to sell it," said O'Malley.

"Right," responded the CO "But, the information is of lesser value, without knowing exactly who the mole is working for."

"So he has two options," said Tom. "Number one, he tries to find out himself. Or number two, he goes to someone who is best-positioned to learn exactly who the mole works for."

"Let me add one fact to that," said Ben. "Both the Teacher and Étan knew the cover name of one of our key people on the other side. *Carlton*."

"So what would Belson's next step have been?" asked Lonnie.

A momentary silence seized the group.

The CO looked at each man and asked, "How would Doug Booker have answered that?"

"That's easy," O'Malley said. "Booker would have reminded us about Ockham's Razor."

The junior members of the group were clearly puzzled by that cryptic answer.

O'Malley continued: "The medieval logician, Ockham, held that the solution to a mystery or puzzle is almost *always* the one requiring the fewest new assumptions of fact. Doug is a strong adherent of Ockham's theory."

"Well, I roomed with Belson for over a year," said Rhymes. "And he would have been too lazy and impatient to make any real effort at trying to learn anything more about the mole on his own."

"Begging your pardon, sir," said Tom. "I *have* to ask... Was the mole an operative of our unit?"

The CO hesitated before answering, just long enough to emphasize that what he was about to say was an unusual admission. *"Yes."*

Tom looked toward the CO. "Then, colonel, I think it is most likely that Belson went to Captain Blake with the information."

No one disagreed with Tom's conclusion.

"Okay," said O'Malley "But where are we going with this? What difference does it make *who* sold out our man to whom?"

"It may make no difference Ted," said the CO. "But I think we should keep connecting the dots, and see where they lead. We now have identified very possible links from Étan, to Belson, to Blake And then to the Soviets, because we know that Blake would try to get as much money as he could for the information; and the Soviets would offer the highest price."

Tom's thought process had already passed that point and was now at the headquarters of KGB in East Berlin. "Colonel, do we know the time line from Belson's death to the mole's meeting with the KGB chief?"

"Yes, that meeting took place about two weeks after Belson was murdered."

The conclusion was self-evident. The KGB and the Soviet hierarchy had *known* that the mole was an American spy when the KGB had approached him. It might just as well have been printed on the wall, in large block letters.

The CO knew it was now up to him to lead the dialogue forward. "I will reveal to you that Carlton and the mole were the same person. When the Teacher went to Prague, he became Carlton's go-between with us. So, that leads to the question of what the Soviets were most likely to have done upon learning Carlton was an enemy spy?"

The CO posed the question to O'Malley, by far the most knowledgeable in the room concerning how the Soviet intelligence system operated.

"Well, we know they didn't exercise two of their options," O'Malley said "They didn't shoot him immediately, and they didn't milk the situation for propaganda by staging a show trial, and *then* shoot him. And that tells us they had a more important use for Carlton."

The CO nodded for him to continue.

"It could be that they went for a *third* option," O'Malley said. "If Carlton's cover was blown, the KGB could have used him to plant false information with us. If that's the case, the whole thing about using a diversionary invasion of Czechoslovakia as cover for the real invasion of West Germany is false. It's the KGB feeding us misinformation through Carlton."

LeBron immediately pounced. "I don't get it. Are you saying that the Soviets duped us into believing their main goal was to squash the Czech insurrection, and then fooled us a *second* time into believing their true objective was the invasion of West Germany? What would be the point of that?"

O'Malley shook his head. "No, Art. What I'm saying is, if we conclude that KGB knew that Carlton was our agent, then we have to question everything they said and did afterwards, including the possibility that there *is* no invasion planned for West Germany, and the suppression of the Czech liberation movement was their main goal after all."

"Ted, you still haven't answered my question. Why would they do that?"

O'Malley shrugged. "I don't *know* why. There's no sure-fire method for divining their intentions. We can use Ockham's Razor or Ockham's Pen-Knife for all I care. It's still not going to penetrate the dark pool of the Soviet mind — sometimes just plain unknowable. What we need are more facts, not assumptions. But as long as we're playing the assumptions game, let me ask you a question. If the Soviet Union actually intended to attack us in West Germany, *why* would they tell our agent? They obviously *knew* he would warn us. What possible reason would they have for revealing their true plans to a known traitor?"

O'Malley's question hung over the table for what seemed an eternity of silence.

Finally, Reitenhauser spoke: "I agree with Ted that we need more facts."

Before LeBron or anyone else in the room could comment, the phone rang again. The CO picked up the receiver and after a second or two said, "This is he."

The often sphinx-like demeanor of the CO defied a reading of his thoughts but one could see in his eyes as he listened for several minutes that he was not being given good news.

"Thank you," said Reitenhauser. He replaced the phone in its cradle.

"Gentlemen, our four-man black ops team has been engaged in a firefight on the other side of the border with what is believed to have been an enemy reconnaissance patrol. One of our men is down. That's all we know at this time."

Chapter Fourteen

The Final Deception

The late afternoon sun was warming on his face as he squinted into it. The clouds reminded him of slightly misshapen pillows, floating serenely on an azure blue sea. The thing he loved about the Bavarian clime was that even in the middle of summer it never got too hot, high 70s to low 80s were the norm.

He was moving. He couldn't remember why. Had he again fallen asleep on one of the rafts on the Isar after too many steins of Spatenbrau? That would explain the uneven up and down motion of his ride. Wait... Oh yeah... He'd been shot.

The slightly bumpy ride was caused by his being carried on a stretcher. The morphine was doing its job. He lapsed in and out of consciousness and felt little pain. Nine years in special ops and his first time shot. Ah, screw it! They told him during special ops training at Langley that if the Cold War turned hot, his chances of taking a hit were just as good as those of a Second Looie leading an infantry charge up Pork Chop Hill.

This was his life, the one he had chosen, and he wouldn't have traded it for any other. He'd take nine years of intrigue, adventure, service to his country and camaraderie, over 40 years of playing golf and going to an office, any day.

His one regret was not having been able to marry and have a child. But there was still time for that. That is, unless this was it. If he didn't make it, thought Mario, he would definitely miss Osi and the colonel and a couple of his CIA buddies; and his parents too. But, maybe they'd all hook up again in the sweet hereafter. Who knew?

Weiden in der Oberpfalz, August 21, 1715 hours

"This is Colonel Reitenhauser, Deputy Chief of Operations in Weiden. Captain, why is it taking so long to get us troop movement reports? I called for them a half hour ago."

"Sorry colonel, but aerial reconnaissance has run into a low cloud cover along the entire Czech-West German border and as far north as Gorzow on the Polish-East German border." The officer providing this discouraging report to Reitenhauser was Captain Peter Durlewanger, Group's liaison to the 232nd Air Force Reconnaissance Detachment, headquartered in Hamburg.

"But the good news, sir, is that we have received some fresh ground reconnaissance data and electronic intercepts revealing that the Prague to Bavaria invasion force is moving at a snail's pace."

"You know captain, what you just said tells me we have a problem. Since when have you received clearance to refer to the troop concentration in Czechoslovakia as an 'invasion force?' I could almost forgive it, if you were infantry. But that kind of sloppiness in an intelligence officer is inexcusable."

"I am very sorry, sir."

"All right, captain. I'm going to give you an opportunity to redeem yourself. You are to put all else aside and spend the next half hour moving hell and high water to get me cumulative and integrated enemy troop movement reports for the border regions from the Baltic Sea to the Austria-Bulgaria border. And I will accept no excuses about cloud covers and all that nonsense. We are on the brink of *war*, captain. Start acting like it."

"Yes, sir."

"Fine, I'll expect your call no later than 1750. Oh, and Captain Durlewanger, don't try to complain to General Stansfield. Number one, you'll never get through to him; and number two, even if you did, he would only tell you he has placed me in charge of operational details." The colonel hung up the phone.

During the brief pause in their deliberations, while the CO was trying to get information over the phone, the brain trust was mostly silent, some of them studying the map of the two Germanys and surrounding countries, laying on the table. Others were doodling on pads, lost in thought. LeBron was studying the interrogation reports garnered from the captured Red Guards.

After laying down the phone, the CO stared out over the magnificent lawn gently easing its way to the edge of the Bavarian Forest. Reitenhauser was not religious in a formal sense, though a non-denominational Christian of sorts. The 23rd Psalm had always been his favorite prayer. He recited it silently now in a supplication for clarity of thought.

"Allemagne Deception." He silently mouthed the words. This helped him to formulate a question in his head, transcending immediate tactical decisions. "If I were Brezhnev, what would I do?"

He gazed at the map. "Art, find anything interesting in those interrogation reports?"

"I'm not sure. Here's a report from a guy our boys captured near the border, and one from an operative grabbed by C.I. in Regensburg. They are pretty much representative of the whole bunch. Both captives were pressed as to the where and when of the East Bloc invasion. One guy said, 'All along the way from the Austrian border in the South to Cheb in the North — a 350 km front.'

"The one our guys grabbed said, 'along the Czech-West German border — a 350 km. front.'"

That got Tom's attention and he looked up from his notes and asked LeBron if he would read the answers to similar questions in a couple of other reports.

"Okay, here's one that says, 'the invasion force will be massive, a thousand tanks, two hundred fifty thousand troops, fifteen divisions spread over a 350 km front.' Here's another, 'We will smash NATO. They won't know what hit them; we'll establish a 350 km front.'"

Tom asked LeBron what the remaining four reports had to say, if anything, about the width of the Warsaw Pact's front. All but two of them used the identical words, "a 350 km front;" yet only three of the eight who were interrogated were specifically asked about the size of the front.

"What does it tell you?" asked O'Malley. "Six out of eight interrogated prisoners used the exact same wording… A 350 km front."

"They were all prepped to give the same canned response," said LeBron.

"Correct," announced O'Malley gently.

The CO had been listening carefully, occasionally looking down at the map, and all the while hearing Uri's noiseless refrain… "Allemagne Deception… Allemagne Deception…"

The colonel broke his silence. "Everyone look at the map and concentrate on the area and distance from the Czech-Austrian border to Cheb. Then tell me what, if anything, jumps out at you."

It took the former infantryman, Ted O'Malley, a mere two or three seconds to respond. "How are the Commie forces going to get across the Danube once they move into Bavaria? The river runs the length of more than half of their so-called front, all the way to Regensburg."

"And even if they could make a crossing," said LeBron, "by the time they moved their divisions across to the opposite bank, NATO would have mobilized its major forces in Munich, Nuremburg, Frankfurt, and Stuttgart. They would have had plenty of time to move in and crush the Warsaw Pact divisions as they attempted to make the crossing."

"All right," said Reitenhauser, "Let's put Ted's question on the table again for discussion. If the Soviet Union intended to attack us in West Germany, why would they tell our agent who they knew would warn us?"

Tom was the first to answer. "Because the Soviets' entire Operation Danube is a compound deception — at least a double deception, possibly a triple. The priority objective was *not* Czechoslovakia, although it was an important secondary one. It also probably wasn't to stage an invasion of West Germany across the Czech border. That no longer makes a lot of sense. But, I agree with Art that they would never have gone to all this trouble unless it was a diversion — in this case a double diversion at least — designed to deceive us as to their real and immediate objective."

"All of the stuff they did," added Mal Rhymes, "the heavy traffic in messages, the white noise, the canned, phony disclosures by their captured agents, the creation of a large but bogus invasion force near Prague, their reconnaissance patrols near the Czech border, the step-up in Red Guards' activity, the fly-over operations etc., had all been done by the Allies in WW II before and even during D-Day, in an attempt to convince the Germans that the real invasion would come at Pas de Calais. It had worked and it had kept on working. Even after the invasion of Normandy, Rommel still would not commit all his Panzer divisions to crushing the Allied invasion of Normandy, believing that the main invasion might still come at Calais."

"True enough," said LeBron, "but that just raises another question. Knowing that the U.S. had the benefit of what we had done before in WW II, might the amateurish and transparent effort they are now making in Czechoslovakia have been designed like the Trojan Horse, to lull us into complacency, all the while positioning themselves to invade across the Czech border after all?"

"That's possible," said Lonnie Ryan.

Ben also nodded his head in assent.

But O'Malley wasn't buying any of it. "Their effort hasn't been all that amateurish and transparent. They fooled us, Stansfield, and NATO Command for close to 24 hours — enough of a diversion to give them valuable time to advance towards their real military objective — whatever that is."

Something in O'Malley's words caused the CO to rivet his attention on the map. Almost simultaneously he had the phone off the hook and was calling Captain Durlewanger.

"Captain? Reitenhauser again. You're on speaker phone, so keep your voice up. Any progress?"

"Yes, sir. I was about to call you. Still no troop concentrations anywhere along the Polish or Czech borders, but West German Intelligence in Bonn has advised us of heavier than usual troop concentrations and movements in East Germany around Berlin, Leipzig and Dresden."

"Holy Shit," said O'Malley.

"It gets worse," Durlewanger's voice said over the phone. "They've known about this for three days, but didn't share it with us because it had been discounted as mere war games and practice maneuvers."

"All right, Captain Durlewanger. Good work and just stay near the phone," replied the colonel.

Reitenhauser then called General Stansfield and filled him in on both what they had learned and what they had surmised. The general listened calmly and did not interrupt until the CO had gotten everything out.

His one comment concerned the failure of the West Germans to share the information they had on the Warsaw Pact troops in East Germany. "That explains why we detected no enemy troops at or near the borders. The probable main Warsaw Pact Force was already well into East Germany at least two days before their other forces crossed into Czechoslovakia. Assembling vast numbers of troops present no particular challenge to the Warsaw Pact nations. The Soviet Union has a million troops in the Ukraine alone. Right now I want to get some U-2s up over East Germany. Fred, I'll get back to you. Keep your team intact. I am ordering all our black ops units to stand down until further word from me. Incidentally, your man code-name, 'Philly South,' was shot in the abdominal region but the report I get is that he's in critical but stable condition in the same hospital as the Teacher. He's a tough kid and the doctors give him a better than 50-50 chance of pulling through. The Teacher has developed a lung infection and is running a pretty high temperature. They have him on antibiotics. Someone will keep you apprised." With that, the general hung up.

Fred passed the news on to the others, extremely grateful that a general would take the time in the midst of a crisis to care about his men. The others around the table however, saw it as a sign of the deep respect of a Commanding General for his second in command.

The CO decided to take their discussion in a different direction. "I think we have a pretty good handle on the Soviets' first and second deceptions. Unless there's another shocker hidden in there somewhere, which I doubt because the logistics of a triple deception would be too complicated for them to manage, they intend to invade West Germany from East Germany at three locations. I think the U-2 flights will confirm this. Let's call their armies Columns A, B, and C. Column-A, located near Berlin will strike across the border, sweep through the North Rhine-Westphalia region and capture Bonn, the capital. Column-B, near Leipzig, will cross the border further south and then move southwest to seize Frankfurt. Column-C, from the vicinity near Dresden will cross the border north of Hof moving in a westerly direction. I expect it to then sharply pivot to the south through the State of Hessen to hit Heidelberg and Stuttgart. Then, I believe Columns B and C will converge and combine to make a concerted attack on Munich. This makes the most sense from a strategic standpoint. Their strategy, however, is contingent on the success of Deception Number 2."

"If NATO took the bait," he said, "it would have moved its main forces towards the Czech border, rendering them totally out of position to offer any meaningful resistance. It's a classic bait and switch. Their main tools for pulling it off were the invasion of Czechoslovakia and their learning from Blake that Carlton was a U.S. spy. They then drew the inference that we did not know that Carlton was blown. We would, therefore, take the bait carried by Carlton, indicating a massive invasion along the Czech-West German border, hook, line and sinker. Carlton hasn't been doubled. They knew that for Carlton to be most effective as a bait salesman, he couldn't *know* that he had been blown. They know their guy as well as I do — *almost* as well. They certainly know that the man needs to be committed to whatever cause he espouses, in order to be convincing. I met personally with Carlton about 12 hours ago and I can tell you that in my estimation — and I have been his case officer for over 15 years — he absolutely believes that the invasion will be across the Czech border."

The CO's soliloquy had left his team temporarily speechless and more than a little awe-struck.

"Wow," said LeBron. "You've hit us with some powerful stuff. I need some time to digest it."

"That's two of us," commented O'Malley.

"Fine," the colonel said. "But don't take too long. Time is becoming a major factor. We need to come up with a counter-deception good enough to persuade the Soviet Union to call off the invasion."

The CO was again interrupted by the ring of the phone. The colonel listened intently to what General Stansfield was telling him, after first getting permission to put him on speaker phone so they could all hear the news first-hand.

The report was short and succinct. Aerial photographs from U-2 flights confirmed three large Warsaw Pact forces moving towards the West German border. At the pace they were moving, their vanguard elements were projected to hit the border in roughly nine hours, or 0400 on August 22nd. Colonel Reitenhauser was to immediately begin work on a counter-deception plan to be submitted by no later than 1945 hours. It was now 1845. Group was also preparing its own plans to be comprised by several different scenarios.

Weiden in der Oberpfalz U.S. Military Hospital 1915 hours

Mattatussu, Olney, Smith, and Penchak sat in the Critical Care Unit waiting room. Mattatussu and Smith smoked cigarettes while Olney and Penchak sat motionlessly — all of them awaiting news on Tonelli's condition.

The waiting room door opened abruptly and two serious looking men in American-cut suits entered. "Warrant Officer Olney, we have orders from General Stansfield to return you to headquarters," said one of them. As they spoke they flashed their Army CID credentials.

A veteran of many similar encounters, Olney immediately and without speaking followed them out of the room. Twenty minutes later at 1935 he sat at the round table with the CO and other team members.

"Provided Group approves," said the colonel, "this is the plan: Warren, you've made many surreptitious entries into East Berlin. How you have gotten over, through or past the Wall, I have no idea. But now you are being asked to do it one more time. Your mission may be necessary to prevent World War III. Captain O'Malley will accompany you as far as Checkpoint Charlie, but then you are on your own. Once on the other side, you are to contact your boys, 13799 and 13993, meet with them and have them disseminate the word throughout the East German Intelligence Network and KGB Area Intelligence, of the deployment of massive U.S. and other NATO member airborne and infantry Divisions in Munich, Frankfurt, Nuremburg, Stuttgart, Bonn, Hamburg, Antwerp, and Amsterdam, supported by full deployment of fighter planes and bombers, all pointed in the direction of the East German border and already beginning their advance. Then, you will contact Carlton by phone. He should be at his East Berlin office. Give him the standard coded message that tells him to go to the dead-drop. You will get there first and leave an encoded message which will direct Carlton to tell the East Berlin KGB Chief, the opposite of what you will relay through 13799 and 13993. Specifically, Carlton will be instructed to report to the KGB Chief regarding massive NATO deployments, except his message will have them headed towards the Czech border instead of East Germany. The idea is that they will believe your guys as they always have in the past, but will disbelieve Carlton. They will disbelieve Carlton because they know he is a U.S. agent, and also think we are unaware that he has been blown. They will therefore, view whatever he communicates to them as a deception by us. We hope that Carlton's story, which in their eyes will be unworthy of belief, will, in effect, confirm the word spread by your two agents that NATO believes the real invasion will come across the East German border and is moving in full force to counter it. In fact, the main NATO force had already moved considerably East towards the Czech border."

The U.N. Agrotech Commission had as its avowed purpose the international exchange and sharing of the latest technological advances in agriculture. Its representative for the two Germanys, Hans Brevoort, a native of Amsterdam, was regularly granted one day visitor permits or visas by the East German authorities at several of the nine check points in order to cross over into East Berlin.

With the loss of so many scientists and technologists through emigration to the West, the East German Government was always looking for ways to improve industry and agriculture. Brevoort never had trouble getting a one day visa to cross, which could be granted right at a check point for good cause. Of course, payment of the usual bribe of 1,000 marks ($250.00 in American dollars) at the crossing point didn't hurt. And Hans Brevoort was really not a United Nations representative. He was actually Warren Olney, a U.S. Army Intelligence Officer.

East Berlin, August 21st, 2330 hours

The light CIA plane had landed on an airstrip at the United States Army Garrison in West Berlin at 2245. Olney and O'Malley alighted from the aircraft, were whisked away in an automobile and deposited in the center of West Berlin's commercial district. From there they took a taxi which dropped O'Malley off at Checkpoint Charlie. The cab continued on and took Olney (aka Brevoort) to one of the two diplomatic checkpoints.

Once on the other side, his meeting with his two agents took ten minutes; his phone call to Carlton and follow-up trip to the dead-drop another half hour; and at 2330 he was walking swiftly on an unlighted street lined by equally darkened warehouses and loading docks, in the direction of the diplomatic checkpoint.

Olney had been aware of the footsteps of two men behind him for the last three blocks. But now the footsteps seemed closer. Olney quickened his pace. The lights of the checkpoint could now be seen but even if he made it there before his pursuers caught up with him, he would be grabbed at the checkpoint while the East German border guards were examining his

Visa. And in another 250 feet or so, the dark street would empty out onto a busy and well-lighted boulevard. Once there, Olney would lose the cover of darkness.

"Halten si," one of his followers yelled.

Olney slowed but did not stop. The pursuers were now no more than 50 feet behind him. It was decision time. If caught, he would have no way of letting the colonel know he had fulfilled his mission and set the wheels of the counter-deception in motion.

Olney stopped and turned slightly to his right showing the two KGB men his profile. He withdrew a cigarette and lighter from his camel hair coat. He put the cigarette in his mouth and lighted it. The click of Olney's lighter was the last thing the two pursuers got to hear in this life. A bullet hit each of them in the middle of his forehead before the sound of the two shots fired from Olney's Walther PPK pistol could reach them.

Weiden in der Oberpfalz, August 21st, Midnight

Fred Reitenhauser felt a heightened tension — more intense than any he had experienced since first receiving word of the invasion of Czechoslovakia. He had no guarantee that the two-pronged ruse he was attempting to foist upon the Soviets would work. But it was the last best chance that NATO had of avoiding war.

Although he didn't show it outwardly, his anxiety level was rising by the second. He should have heard from O'Malley and Olney by now. NATO Commanding General, Tugwell Saylor, was waiting for word from General Stansfield as to whether he should unleash his forces towards the East German border. Once the tanks started rolling and the planes were in the air, it would be difficult to call them back. NATO Command would wait until 0015 hours, no later.

Fred thought of Gerda for the first time since all this started. How would she fare if she fell into the hands of the East Germans — a German working for an American spy agency? This horrible thought caused a stirring in him he found unfamiliar. He couldn't quite identify it but knew it made him uncomfortable — a discomfort caused by a blend of longing and fear.

He felt almost an irresistible urge to call her, but he must not. He had to keep his mind fixed on the problem at hand. Work the problem. If something happened to Olney, he may have to send O'Malley into East Berlin — at least to make sure contact was made with Uri. He had already worked out the plan in his head but needed to re-test it carefully, to assess and reassess, to probe for flaws. Everything might depend on it.

He wasn't particularly worried about Olney being broken under torture. If he had been captured, by the time the East Germans or KGB were able to break him, the Warsaw Pact invasion would have either taken place or been cancelled; and the issue would be moot. But he had to know the fate of the mission. It was now 0015 hours and still no call. Even if O'Malley called right now, it would still be close. Then the phone rang and it *was* O'Malley.

"Mission accomplished."

"Copy that," said the CO and hung up. It took another precious 4 minutes to reach General Stansfield. Five minutes left to H Hour.

"General, it's Fred. Mission accomplished."

"Thanks Fred. Gotta go."

Five minutes passed. The phone rang. It was Stansfield: "Okay Fred, we are standing down until 0400, to see if we made the sale."

Reitenhauser sighed, sat back and lit his pipe. Then he called O'Malley and Olney at the Checkpoint Charlie station. "Get out of there ASAP, and get back here."

"Roger that," said O'Malley.

A mere third of the NATO force would be immediately available to confront the Warsaw Pact divisions. The rest were already out of position well along the way to the Czech border as a result of the Soviets' Deception Number 2.

The initial 22 hours or so during which Deception Number 2 had worked, had given the Warsaw Pact Forces a tremendous advantage. Whether the force NATO could muster to meet them somewhere southwest of the East German border would be able to hold them long enough to give the other two thirds of NATO's available armies time to join them, was simply unknowable at this time.

Somehow the Soviets had to be convinced that Western Intelligence had discovered the deception and would confront the Warsaw Pact Armies — now getting close to the East-West German border — in full force. Whether Reitenhauser's counter-deception would do the trick should be known in a few hours.

Fred had no doubt that NATO Command was already planning its next moves in the event that the counter-deception did not work. Should the Warsaw Pact's Forces mount a blitzkrieg through West Germany, the United States could not sit idly by. The integrity of NATO and America's entire national defense policy depended on a free and independent West Germany. The use of nuclear weapons against the Eastern Bloc would undoubtedly be part of the discussions and on the table. The consequences of a decision to use our nuclear missiles were too terrible to imagine.

Even now, U.S. Polaris submarines armed with nuclear warheads were probably moving into strategic positions. And he could only imagine what was going on in the White House. How much did the President know? Surely he had been informed that Operation Danube was a cover for the invasion of West Germany. But had he been advised of the delicate feints and counter-feints now in progress? Had the White House or State Department attempted to make contact directly with Chairman Brezhnev, and if so, how might that affect the counter-deception?

Would a diplomatic solution be reached which would make all these games unnecessary? Or would the United States make a preemptive strike upon the Soviet Union or one of its satellites? Reitenhauser knew he could not, or for that matter, *should* not try to answer such questions. They were far beyond the scope of his narrow mission, which now was solely to await word from the general, to carry out any new orders and to get his men back from Berlin.

He placed a call to BOSS. Still no word on O'Malley and Olney. Next he called the hospital. Tonelli was stable but Magyaar had taken a turn for the worse. The infection was raging through his body and the doctors had just started a more aggressive regime of medications. The prognosis was guarded.

That conversation was followed up by his phone call to Munich to inquire after Booker's condition. Good news — he was gradually getting stronger and more alert.

Tom Tallifierro sat at the table and worried. Was Kate about to become one of those innocent foreign non-combatants trapped in a war zone, as happened to so many thousands during World War II when Hitler gobbled up countries like so many Whitman Chocolates? Right now, she was at her desk, hard at work just like the rest of the personnel back at the 409th.

Tom knew about the plan in place to evacuate the unit's military personnel and their dependents. The military people would be evacuated to Switzerland, their dependents to London. But what of Kate who was neither a soldier nor a dependent? He should have anticipated this and married her — that is, if she would have had him. As things stood, she was in danger of getting lost in the shuffle.

Ben had been studying Tom closely for the past several minutes. Ever the astute reader of people, especially his friend since childhood, Ben had a pretty good idea what was troubling Tom. He slowly and as unobtrusively as possible stood up, got his friend a cup of coffee and took the seat next to him.

He turned towards Tom and spoke to him in a low voice: "Hey old Buddy. The CO will do everything in his power to safeguard every single soldier and civilian of the 409th."

Realizing that Ben had once again read his mind, Tom chuckled softly. "Thanks pal. That does help a bit."

Lonnie Ryan, on the other hand, was happy that Megan had not yet agreed to marry him and was safe back in Boston.

All of Tom's private thoughts were interrupted as Mattatussu, Smith, and Penchak entered the room amidst warm greetings from the others present. LeBron quickly briefed them on the current situation, including the involvement of O'Malley and Olney.

The new arrivals had eaten no food since breakfast at the safehouse the previous morning. They were famished and immediately helped themselves to fruit, sandwiches, and black coffee. While the men ate and chatted with the others, Reitenhauser had another concern persistently gnawing at him.

If the balloon went up and the Warsaw Pact forces moved towards Munich without being effectively checked by NATO's bifurcated army, the acting officer in charge at the 409th would undoubtedly be called back to Stuttgart, leaving First Sergeant Toomey in charge. Fred had gambled on Toomey's continued sobriety when he pulled O'Malley out of Munich and brought him to Weiden. Actually, it was really not that difficult a decision. The best interests of the United States demanded that O'Malley join them. This always takes precedence over the welfare of any one person or group of people.

Toomey seemed a changed man — chastened and restored to sobriety. He regularly attended AA meetings. But, could the crisis and new responsibilities of leadership cause him to backslide? Fred didn't think so, but he still was concerned. The lives of thirty-eight people back at the 409th, plus another twenty or so dependents were at stake. And those lives might depend upon the fragile sobriety of one man.

The phone shattered his troubled reverie. It was the duty officer. O'Malley and Olney were on their way up.

Weiden in der Oberpfalz, 0300 hours

BOSS had issued a joint intelligence agency alert, a composite of NSA, CIA and M1-5 individual reports. The Warsaw Pact Forces, comprised half a million troops from four nations plus an estimated 2,500 tanks were forming up in three different regions along the East-West border. An invasion was imminent.

Munich, 0300 hours. 409th Special Investigations Detachment

The temporary officer in charge had been ordered back to Stuttgart immediately. Kate was working almost non-stop translating Czech-language intelligence intercepts into English, and trying to keep her mind off Tom. All she knew was that he was away on assignment. She assumed — although was far from certain — that since all the officers plus Tom, Ben, and Mal were gone, they were all together.

But for all she knew Tom could have been captured, injured, or killed. Neither she nor any of the 409th personnel without a need to know, were even aware of Booker's illness. And to them, Tonelli and Mattatussu were just distant memories.

They heard Penchak was in rehab somewhere and Blake was rumored to have been arrested on some unknown charge. Even these rumors, floating around the Max Shop emanated from the local M.P. unit, not the 409th.

Gerda had been temporarily assigned to Toomey as of 0245 hours. She was concerned about Fred, but not worried. They had spoken on the phone only fifteen minutes earlier.

Toomey delegated to Gerda the full responsibility and authority for the civilian evacuation. Evacuation plans had been in place for some time and regular drills had been conducted. Each civilian employee had been assigned a locker in which he or she was permitted to keep one small suitcase only. In addition, the unit had provided each of them with an emergency kit containing first aid items, a day's supply of K rations, a flashlight, and a bottle of water. The kit and suitcase were stored in each person's locker and it was a condition of their employment to keep them in a state of readiness at all times.

Female employees were also permitted to carry a standard size pocketbook. Once an order to evacuate was issued, Gerda would assemble the civilians in the large conference room, take attendance, accompany them to their lockers and then to the motor pool where they would be picked up by a bus and transported to Munich International Airport for their flight to London. No individual was allowed to carry more than $100.00 or its equivalent in foreign currencies on his or her person. In London, they would stay in a hotel at full government expense, including meals and lodging, until more permanent arrangements could be made.

The military personnel had their own locker room with separate male and female changing rooms. Each soldier was responsible for keeping in his or her locker, a clean and pressed uniform, a complete emergency kit, canteen and gas mask.   No weapons were allowed.   A diplomatic evacuation agreement with Switzerland would be strictly enforced.

The signed protocol called for evacuation of non-combat personnel only by Swissair flight from Munich Airport to Berne. As a neutral nation, Switzerland would allow no weapons to be brought into the country.

Upon landing in Berne, Swiss security agents would board the plane and fully inspect both the plane and occupants for weapons. If any were found, the diplomatic agreement permitted them to deny the Americans the right to de-plane and the Swissair pilots would be instructed to fly them back to Germany.

At 0315 hours on August 22, 1968, Gerda led the civilians and Toomey led the military personnel through final pre-evacuation inspections and drills.

Pete Toomey had waited all his life to be placed in a position of such authority, and he wasn't about to screw it up. He deeply regretted the way he had allowed himself to unravel over the past couple of years. But a great man, Colonel Frederick Reitenhauser, had not only given him a second chance but had helped him to rehabilitate. He felt nothing but gratitude for that, and was determined to prove himself worthy of the CO's confidence.

As he walked from one soldier's locker to the next, he personally inspected each one's emergency kit to be sure it had all the required items, and carefully examined each gas mask to make sure it was functioning.

Finally, he had each male soldier lay out the contents of his duffel bag on the bench in front of the locker to make sure it contained a change of uniform, socks, underwear, toiletries and nothing else. Gerda performed the same function with the two female soldiers.

Satisfied, Toomey gave the troops final evacuation instructions. He reminded them that if they had to evacuate, that would be their mission — one just as important as any other. They were to carry it out with the same discipline, dedication to duty, and esprit de corps as they would any other job assigned to them. As area intelligence personnel, they knew secrets which made them vulnerable. It was vitally important that none of them fall into enemy hands. But if the worst happened, under no circumstances were they to give more than name, rank and serial number. Finally, Toomey inspected the lockers to make sure each soldier had his or her dog tags.

Then at 0345 he gave the troops an 'as you were' and returned calmly to his office, where Gerda was waiting with a cup of black coffee. He had not had even a drop of alcohol in several weeks.

Weiden in der Oberpfalz, August 22nd, 0345 hours

As the self-imposed deadline of 0400 for NATO to begin its forward thrust towards the German East-West border approached, Colonel Reitenhauser received a phone call from Captain Durlewanger, with an updated military report. The Warsaw Pact forces had now moved major artillery and rocket launchers onto high ground in positions at multiple locations along the West German border.

According to Durlewanger, NATO Command, which had established a field headquarters in Frankfurt, now expected an artillery barrage to soften up various American and British airfields and heavy weapons installations within artillery range of the Warsaw Pact guns.

Accordingly, NATO forces had received an order from Commanding General Tugwell Saylor at 0330 to mobilize in advance of the previous H Hour of 0400.

NATO ground forces were now on the move and airborne forces based in West Germany, England, Belgium, and Italy were in the air. Equally ominous was the fact that the United States Strategic Air Command had been ordered by Washington to send three of its long-range bombers towards Europe from the continental United States. All signs pointed to a dramatic military showdown between the Western bloc and Eastern bloc nations within hours.

At 0400, General Stansfield called and ordered the colonel to have his entire team stand down and retire to quarters on the floor below to get some sleep. They had all been awake for over forty straight hours. With the exception of the CO and LeBron, the group gratefully complied with the order and left the conference room. The two top officers planned to follow within minutes after first securing the room.

As they piled files, maps, photos, and documents into a steel filing cabinet, Fred and Art chatted briefly about what might come next. If the Communist Bloc forces overran the U.S. and other NATO members' armies, they and their other team members would undoubtedly be evacuated to Switzerland to join up with the other personnel of the 409th. If, on the other hand, a protracted battle ensued, they probably would stay to perform whatever duties they were given by Higher.

One thing was certain. They could not be captured by Hostile. Unless immediately evacuated, each man might be given a little black pill to be taken in the event of capture. But the CO and XO were far too exhausted to speculate about that. They locked the cabinet and the door to the room, and walked down one flight of stairs to their sleeping quarters.

Both men went straight to their bunks, climbed in without bothering to undress, and fell asleep instantly.

Weiden in der Oberpfalz, August 22, 0530 hours

An Army Signal Corps radio transmission station located on top of Weiden's highest hill was unprepared for the dramatic spike in messages suddenly flooding the station. It was almost more than the two Specialists Second Class on duty could handle. All of the voice communiqués were coming from U.S. and British observation posts along the East German border and from Air Force spotter planes.

To accommodate the traffic, one of the G.I.s handled the radio while the other copied the messages down in shorthand and then began transmitting them to headquarters a mile away. The messages were varied but taken together as a whole, their clear content related that Warsaw Pact tanks were turning around — heading East. Artillery and Rocket Launchers were disappearing from their elevated positions, and heavy troop movements were reported, but none of them had been seen crossing into West Germany.

Now, the most recent messages were unanimous in reporting that some Warsaw Pact Forces were in formation while others had broken formation and were marching in large numbers in an easterly direction, away from their border encampments. In the Headquarters' Communications Center, similar messages were flooding in, not only from radio transmission stations but also via telex. A runner was dispatched by the 1st Lieutenant in charge of the Communications Center to awaken General Stansfield.

This being accomplished, the general then sent a runner to Colonel Reitenhauser ordering him and his team to report immediately to their posts in the penthouse conference room. It was now 0615.

Weiden in der Oberpfalz August 22nd, 0630 hours

The eleven special ops team members from the 409th breakfasted on K rations and black coffee. Suddenly, a voice laden with drama came booming out of the intercom speaker on the wall. "Attention all personnel. General Stansfield has directed me to read the following message. 'Beginning some time between 0500 and 0515 this morning, Warsaw Pact Forces at the border between East Germany and West Germany commenced an orderly retreat, moving away from the border in an easterly direction. As of 0615 hours, all enemy forces in East Germany appear to be in full retreat towards the Polish border. In addition, a sizeable separate force concentrated southwest of Prague, Czechoslovakia, has also turned around and is headed northeast towards the Russian border. The crisis appears to be over. We will continue to track the apparent retreat of the hostile Eastern Bloc armies and advise each unit individually. Stand by for further orders.'"

A boisterous cheer broke out throughout the entire building, loud enough to be heard several blocks away.

It was over.

Chapter Fifteen

Aftermath

Although it would never be known for certain what had caused the Soviets to back down, General Stansfield harbored no doubts in his mind. He fully credited Colonel Reitenhauser and his team with having turned the tide through the planning and execution of its counter-deception. Of course, the details of the final deception could only be divulged to one or two of Stansfield's top aides and to General Saylor's G-2. But a month after the event, General Stansfield and his aides appeared in Munich to conduct a secret award ceremony during which each participant at Weiden received a special presidential citation for "distinguished and exemplary service to his country." No other details were contained in the citation. To these men of the 409th, it was the proudest day of their lives.

No public mention was ever made by the Soviet Union or its satellites of the aborted invasion. The activity in East Germany was simply reported as 'war games.' The forces concentrated southwest of Prague were referred to in all official statements as a 'reserve force.'

After numerous secret deliberations among the NATO nations, it was decided that the public mention of the details of the crisis would "run the unacceptable risk of causing panic and unrest in the countries most endangered by the thwarted Eastern Bloc action." It was, therefore, to be kept secret. Publicly, the NATO Military actions taken in West Germany were described as "preventive measures to deter any possible incursion by Warsaw Pact Forces from Czechoslovakia into West Germany."

For the top secret official history and record of the counter-deception, Colonel Reitenhauser was accorded the privilege by Group of naming the operation. He named it 'The Allemagne Deception.' Allemagne, the restaurant and café from whence its name derived, had been closed for nearly a decade and was now an exclusive club for high ranking diplomats and their wives in West Berlin.

Uri Putyagin, codename 'Carlton,' suffered no obvious retribution for his part in the operation, or for being a Western Bloc agent. Group's best explanation for this was that the Soviet Union did not wish to suffer the embarrassment of acknowledging that such a high Communist Party official, who was widely portrayed as a Russian war hero, was in reality an American spy. Uri was quietly transferred back to Moscow where he was given a position at the Lenin University as Professor of World Economics. His position was largely ceremonial, although he did teach one seminar class. Of course, Uri had great reason to fear for his life, but had become fatalistic about that and tried to spend as much time as possible with his family. Naturally, he was kept under constant KGB surveillance.

Cognizant of the danger Uri was in, Fred Reitenhauser began lobbying Group, NATO Headquarters, the CIA and the State Department to help Uri defect to the West. But after the State Department made some sub-rosa inquiries, they reported back that Uri had rebuffed their overtures. He did not wish to defect. He would rather die than leave his family.

Because of the admirable way they had handled the crisis, the Army rumor mill was working overtime concerning the futures of General Stansfield and Colonel Reitenhauser. The general was being mentioned for the soon-to-be-open post of Deputy Commander of NATO, with the colonel succeeding him as commanding officer of Group. But their appointments apparently never got past the rumor stage.

There were, however, some promotions as a result of Operation Allemagne. Warren Olney received a direct commission as a captain and was appointed as Chief of the German desk at the 409th. He was not permitted however, to assume his new post until he successfully completed a Dale Carnegie course at the University of Maryland in Munich on 'How to Win Friends and Influence People.'

Lonnie Ryan was promoted to the rank of captain. Anders Smith decided that the spook game was not to his liking, and transferred to the Army Rangers. He was sent back to North Carolina to undergo Ranger training, after which he was named to head up a company of Airborne recruits.

Ted O'Malley's temporary commission was made permanent. He was promoted to major and continued on as Operations Officer of the 409th.

Art LeBron refused a permanent commission, reverted to civilian status, was promoted to GS-14 and continued as Chief of the Czech section. His new Deputy Chief was Sergeant Mal Rhymes.

Mario Tonelli recovered fully from his wound and was reunited with Osi Mattatussu in Spookdom, where they happily resumed doing whatever it was that they did.

Doug Booker continued to make progress towards recovery but it was slow going. He was sent to a U.S. Armed Forces convalescence center near Barcelona, Spain, where he was reported to be spending long sunny afternoons on the veranda reading '*An Uncertain Trumpet*' and '*The Confessions of Nat Turner*'. This was hardly, however, the sum total of his reading. Theretofore an agnostic, he now read St. Augustine; theologians Cardinal Newman and Teihard de Jardin; and the philosopher, Kierkegaard, as part of his preliminary reading for his forthcoming conversion to Roman Catholicism.

Lugash Magyaar's recovery was still uncertain. His lungs had been severely damaged by a combination of his injuries and subsequent infection. He had been sent on the U.S. Government's dime to an expensive rehabilitation center in the South of France. There he underwent rigorous physical and inhalation therapy under the skilled supervision of some of France's finest nurses and physical therapists. His stay there was said to be indefinite.

In return for re-enlisting for another three years, Káz Penchak was granted a special sixty days leave to return to the small village in Czechoslovakia where his family had been so brutalized during the Stalinist coup of 1948. He needed to walk the same streets, eat the same food, drink from the same wells, sit in the same church and get to know his surviving cousins who still lived there.

He had told Higher that if he could not make this long-overdue connection, he would never be able to know real peace. If not granted the time off, he would leave the military and go as a civilian. His leave request was granted with only token resistance.

Former Captain Mitchell Blake was convicted of treason, murder, attempted murder, and violation of the Official Secrets Act after a Court Martial held in Frankfurt. He was sentenced to life imprisonment without parole at the Federal Correctional Institution at Leavenworth, Kansas. Only his long military service and his wife's family's political connections saved him from the gallows.

In prison, he established a gambling syndicate composed of both inmates and guards. Known as 'Morgan Enterprises,' the syndicate took book mainly on professional football and college basketball games. Blake was stabbed to death in the shower in 1986, when his syndicate failed to pay $100,000.00 in winnings on a basketball game to a capo regime of the Lucchese crime family. By then Blake was running the syndicate like a Ponzi scheme, with the bets placed by the latest customers used to pay the earlier winners. The reason he gave for refusing to pay the winnings to the capo was that they resulted from a dishonest bet, alleging that the crime family fixed the score through point shaving.

Blake apparently was unaware that there is no honor among thieves.

Lonnie Ryan received a 'Dear John' letter from Megan in February of 1969. She had met a Boston Brahmin stock broker from Beacon Hill in an upscale tavern across the street from the Boston Commons. His parents disapproved of their upper-class, Harvard educated son's relationship with an Irish Catholic from Southie, but mesmerized by her great beauty and charm, the Brahmin broker had vowed to marry her anyway.

Despite his heartbreak, Lonnie still managed to make the most of his four years in Munich, earning a bachelor's degree in sociology from the University of Maryland evening division.

With strong recommendations from the colonel and Art LeBron, Lonnie was accepted into the FBI Intelligence Division, upon resigning his commission in 1970. In 1982 he was named as Agent in Charge of the FBI's Richmond, Virginia office. By then he was happily married and had three small children.

In April of 1969 Fred and Gerda stunned everyone by announcing their engagement. They were married in the military chapel in Munich that June. Gerda was assigned to the new position of executive secretary and administrative assistant to the Operations Officer, Major Ted O'Malley. In 1971 she gave birth to a baby boy, named by his proud parents, Uri Frederick Reitenhauser. He was usually called by his middle name, Fred.

Ben Berger liked the Army and especially the Intelligence Corps. Well in advance of his scheduled 1969 discharge date, he applied for Officer Candidate School. He was immediately accepted and left Munich after the CO's wedding in June of 1969, for Georgia, where his OCS class started at Fort Gordon on July 1st.

Melissa accepted a position with the Domestic Peace Corps in a poverty-stricken mountain region of Georgia and she and Ben got to see each other most weekends during his six months at OCS. He then did a year-long tour in Vietnam following his being commissioned as a second lieutenant. There he served in Saigon at General Creighton Abrams' Headquarters, as a Staff Officer in the G-2 Section.

Ben got back to Munich in 1971. By then, he was a first lieutenant. Colonel Reitenhauser was happy to see him and promptly named him as Chief of the Ops Support Section. A year later he was promoted to captain and named Deputy Operations Officer of the Unit. O'Malley was delighted.

Melissa accompanied Ben to Munich but after a few months of just spending time with Ben and enjoying Bavaria and the Alps, she received an offer from the International Red Cross to serve as Deputy Chief Administrator of its office in Salzburg, Austria. She and Ben were once again weekend lovers. There were those who commented negatively on their vagabond existence, but it was the early 70s and the relationship suited them just fine.   They were able to combine their personal relationship with work they loved, travel and adventure. Neither one of them was giving any serious thought to marriage at that point in their lives. But the directionless underachiever, the Ben Berger of the mid-sixties, was only a distant memory.

Tom Tallifierro continued to serve as the lead intelligence analyst for the unit after Operation Allemagne; but was sent by the CO to Spain three times to confer with Booker to get his take on some particularly thorny problems. The loss of Uri as a resource had left a gaping hole in the unit's capacity to obtain high level intelligence on major developments in advance of their occurrence. Tom had spent countless hours vetting agent reports on top level Eastern Bloc officials who might be pitched to assume the role of an agent in place behind the iron curtain. The unrest and resentment throughout the Soviet Republics over the invasion of Czechoslovakia was creating fertile ground for recruiting new agents. From a list of a hundred, Tom had narrowed the group of potential candidates down to ten. His trip to Barcelona in January of 1969 was for the purpose of reviewing the short list with Doug Booker and getting his rare brand of insight.

Perhaps as a reward for the extraordinary work Tom had done on the Morgan crisis and Operation Allemagne, the CO allowed him four days leave in Barcelona following the meeting with Booker. Kate took some vacation time and since Tom was not traveling under cover, Kate was permitted to accompany him on the trip. After their return from Spain, Tom and Kate announced that they were engaged to be married. This came as no real surprise to anyone.

Tom was anxious to get back to his academic career and on his discharge date in July of 1969, he and Kate flew to Washington, D.C. With Ben as Best Man and Melissa as Maid of Honor, Tom and Kate were married on September 15, 1969 at the historic Episcopal Church in Falls Church, Virginia where George Washington had once served as an alderman.

Tom returned to his teaching duties at Georgetown. Using his contacts in academia, he was able to help Kate land a position at American University as an instructor of Eastern European languages.

Four years after his discharge from the Army, Tom became a full Professor of History at Georgetown University.

Tom Tallifierro, Ben Berger and Lonnie Ryan were in many ways typical of the citizen soldiers who have always been essential to the defense of their country. They served quietly and without fanfare during an era in which military service was undervalued by their fellow citizens. They brought their unique talents to the jobs at hand and made exceptional contributions to the defense of America during the Cold War. They garnered no public medals, received no veterans' benefits, and had no homecoming parades in their honor.

When operational in Germany and Austria, they were always in harm's way. But they didn't even have the pleasure of telling war stories later on, because they were forbidden from talking about their military adventures for the rest of their lives. Each of them was able to relax that stringent restriction one time.

In 1981, Ben, Lonnie and Tom met for a three-man reunion at the Gettysburg Hotel in Gettysburg, Pennsylvania. At a table in the small bar of the historic hotel, they reminisced among themselves, without using any names — real or cover — into the wee hours of the morning. The experience was a type of catharsis for each of them — an outpouring of hidden and repressed fears, tales of adventure, patriotic fervor and nostalgic admiration, mixed with bemusement for the amazing men and women for whom and with whom they served.

All three men would experience many high points of exhilaration, achievement and personal enrichment in their lives, but none would match the intensity of those days in Munich, Vienna and Weiden in der Oberpfalz.

Epilogue

The invasion of Czechoslovakia was the last instance in which the Soviet Union was able to force its will on a neighboring country. The U.S.S.R.'s costly and humiliating war in Afghanistan ended in defeat after Afghanistan was able to secure modern weapons from the U.S.

Although Alexander Dubcëk was arrested and transported to Moscow on the morning of August 21, 1968, the rumors of his impending execution turned out to be false. After entering into an agreement with the Soviet leadership to accept the rollback of most of the reforms of the 'Prague Spring,' Dubcëk was returned to Prague where he resumed his post as First Secretary of the Czechoslovakian Communist Party. He was deposed from that post in March of 1969 and with him went the rest of his liberation reforms. Soviet leader Leonid I. Brezhnev had successfully enforced the Brezhnev Doctrine mandating the elimination of any Soviet Republic government seeking to undermine socialism by adopting capitalistic policies.

After 1968, however, the slow decline of the Union of Soviet Socialists Republic began. Appalled by the repressive measures used by the Soviet Union in Czechoslovakia, Rumania and Albania eventually withdrew from the Warsaw Pact.

Student revolutionary, Jan Palach, immolated himself during the winter of 1969 in Prague — a dramatic protest to the methods the Soviet Union had employed in putting down the Czech liberation movement. His action further undermined the authority of the Soviets.

In the 1970s, Lech Walesa co-founded *Solidarity*, the Soviet Bloc's first independent trade union. Though persecuted by the Polish communist government and arrested several times, Walesa was instrumental in August of 1980 in leading the negotiations which led to the progressive Gdansk Agreement between striking workers and the Polish government. For his efforts towards democratization in Poland, Walesa won the Nobel Peace Prize. His efforts led to parliamentary elections in June of 1989, a Solidarity-led government and his election in 1990 as President of Poland.

In the summer of 1969, the U.S. handed the Soviet Union a major psychological defeat by becoming the first nation to land a man on the moon.

The age of mutually assured destruction, driven by ICBM missiles, shaped the remaining years of the Cold War. However, in 1983, U.S. President, Ronald Reagan, instituted the Strategic Defense Initiative, referred to in the Press as "Star Wars," a program to use ground and space-based systems to protect the United States from attack by strategic nuclear ballistic missiles. Though the system took heavy criticism for being unrealistic and even unscientific, it did have the result of forcing the Soviet Union to expend enormous sums of money in the development of technology to counter SDI, further weakening its already tenuous economy.

In the 1980s under Mikhail Gorbachev, the Soviet Union greatly moderated its hard-line stance against the United States by embarking upon a policy of détente, or peaceful co-existence. Détente manifested itself in mutual trade agreements, arms reductions accords and cultural exchanges, through programs such as "Perestroika" and "Glasnost."

The die, however, had been cast and the slow but inexorable decline of the Soviet Union continued. The economic successes of the United States, the European Union and Japan fed the burning desire of the Soviet Republics and other Eastern Bloc countries to adopt some of the methods of capitalism, and to achieve democratic reforms. The Soviet Union had become too economically weak to stem the tide. Massive German unrest, both East and West, over the Berlin Wall led to its opening in November of 1989. Demolition of the wall was completed by the summer of 1990.

The Soviet Union, besieged by revolutionary movements in almost all of its republics, officially dissolved the Union of Soviet Socialist Republics on December 9, 1991. The Cold War was over.

OTHER BOOKS BY DONALD J. FARINACCI

When One Stood Alone

The story of United States District Court Judge, John J. Sirica's courageous battle to defeat the criminal conspiracy led by President Richard M. Nixon, to cover-up his administration's secret and illegal program which came to be known as "Watergate."

ISBN: 978-1438977829

Last Full Measure of Devotion

There were no marching bands welcoming home returning troops from Vietnam, no ticker-tape parades for its heroes and no celebrations in Time Square. Instead, returning Vets were confronted with indifference, silent disapproval, criticism, hostility and even contempt. This book calls upon us to revisit a remarkable generation of military heroes and, at long last, accord them the recognition withheld from them for almost four decades.

ISBN: 978-1434318572

Truman and MacArthur
Adversaries for a Common Cause

A chronicle of events which occurred during a brief but momentous period in American history, involving two extraordinary men, President Harry S. Truman and General of the Army Douglas MacArthur. The story tells of their interaction during a time of grave national crisis, how they veered badly off course and ultimately collided head-on. It was a collision which both altered the course of history and irreparably changed their personal destinies.

ISBN: 978-0557409020

www.ingramcontent.com/pod-product-compliance
Lightning Source LLC
Chambersburg PA
CBHW050027180626
46810CB00002B/607